Masters
of Souls

MASTERS OF SOULS

Cover designed by Vista Townsend. Contributors who own
copyright to some images are Andrey Kiselev, Manina, Potowizard,
Timurd, and William Langeveld. Used with permission. Map
designed by Vista Townsend.

Print Edition 2017 ISBN 978-0-9906168-8-7

First Edition

Printed in the United States of America

Salt Legacy

Masters of Souls

Vista Townsend

Books By Vista Townsend

Science Fiction
Age of Quintessence series

Synthetic Genesis
Shadow Legacy
Vortex Crucible

Fantasy
Salt Legacy series

Masters of Souls

Historical Fiction

Jagged Road To Sainthood

Dedication

To Yahweh, who has brought me through many quests in life.
Thanks for an awesome journey.
I look forward to meeting you face-to-face.

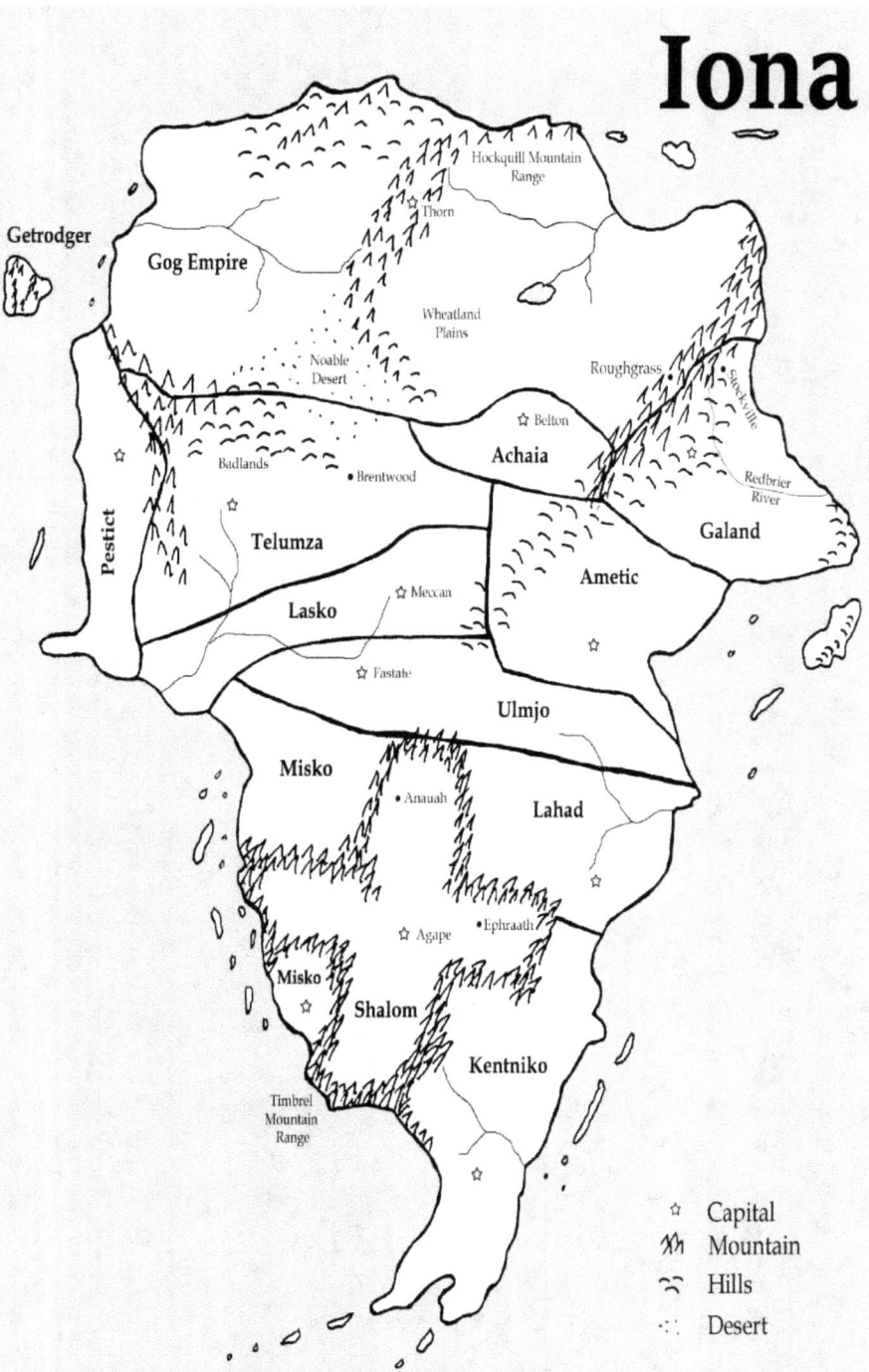

Part I

"For our struggle is not against flesh and blood, but against the rulers, against the authorities, against the powers of this dark world and against the spiritual forces of evil in the heavenly realms."

~Ephesians 6:12

Prologue

In the beginning the planet Tanlep was beautiful and peaceful, but corruption came into it. Darkness consumed the hearts of mankind, eating away at humanity's soul. Yahweh, the creator of Tanlep, desired to save the human race from the miasmatic evil of Beelzebub. He spoke, commanding massive mountains to rise from the fertile plains on the largest continent on the planet. A peaceful country was formed, protected from evil by the surrounding mountains. Numerous caves ran through the mountains, guarded by immortal Mal'ak, creations of Yahweh. Only those who bore the mark of the deity on their souls were allowed entrance into the serene kingdom. Located in the center of the nation, an immense city raised its lofty towers towards the heavens, too sacred for mortals to enter.

Enraged by the deity's monument on Tanlep, Beelzebub sent his minions throughout the planet, ravaging all Yahweh had created. One thing obsessed its dark mind, the prophecy that said, "When none living bares the mark of Yahweh outside Shalom, the mountains will crumble."

Millenniums passed. Zuzumza, God of War and secret ruler of the Empire of Gog, was nearing the completion of its ghastly goal.

Chapter One

Thick forests shed the last of their leaves, covering mountains and valleys with their debris. Birds sang their ancient songs while deer munched on what growth they could find this late in the season. Through the wilderness labyrinth, rode a woman on a gray gelding. Dressed in leather armor with long black hair pinned closely to her scalp, the young woman scrutinized the trees and thickets ahead, looking for an ambush. Her alert brown eyes missed nothing. In her saddlebag near her sword was a note containing orders from General Tryphena for the Twelfth Regiment. She had no need to read the paper to know what it said. She had spent the last two days delivering the same message to other regiments—the ones not yet wiped out.

Ducking under a low tree limb, Junia's thoughts wandered to her lover. Handsome and intelligent, Major Urbane Herron was General Tryphena's top aid. Where was he at this moment? Most likely trying to fulfill another foolish command from the general. A curse escaped from her lips against General Tryphena. The arrogant man had the gall to tell the Emperor of Gog that Galand would fall in six weeks. Six weeks! And that due date ended today. He would face his moment of reckoning when he stood in front of Emperor Erastus and tried to explain why, after burning the capital of Galand, he could not hold his troops together to capture the fleeing king. Junia grinned as she imaged Tryphena nervously blaming the mountainous wilderness for his failure. The Emperor was not known for mercy. She knew firsthand.

Junia reined her horse to a halt and studied the ground, observing tracks of infantry and supply wagons. Some place ahead marched the Twelfth Regiment. How much further? She was tired of being a messenger, but she was needed. Too many had disappeared in this wilderness. Normally she worked closely with Urbane, keeping behind the scenes—the perfect position to know everything happening in the army.

She raised her reins to signal her mount to continue but suddenly froze with hands in air. Something was not right. No birds sung. An unnatural stillness had settled across the forest. Remembering the Eighth Regiment had been completely

3

wiped out when caught in a box canyon, Junia turned her horse off the path and directed it up the steep hillside. Breath ragged, the creature almost stumbled twice. When the mountain became too steep, Junia climbed barehanded up a huge outcropping of boulders that raised its bare tops above the surrounding forest.

Panting from her excursions, Junia scanned the valley. About a mile ahead, the Twelfth Regiment traveled in a long, thin line through the thick forest. Further ahead the two mountains closed in, creating a narrow valley bordered by sheer cliffs. Junia's heart skipped a beat as her eyes caught the sun's reflection gleaming off what seemed to be bare rocks, but she knew better—it was sunlight hitting metal. Heart pounding, Junia half climbed, half fell to the forest floor and hurried her horse down the mountainside at a dangerous pace. Once the valley floor was reached, she spurred the animal to its fastest speed. Junia ignored the animal's rasping pants and demanded more speed. Time seem to stop, the path stretching into infinity. Finally, she spotted straggling troops but continued onward until she found an officer.

She reined up in front of the captain. "Sir, you must stop the regiment at once!"

The officer eyed the female coldly, "Under whose orders?"

"Mine! There's a trap ahead where the valley narrows." The captain stared at her, doubtful. *Prejudiced boars*, she cursed silently. "I saw the glint of sun on armor when I went up the ridge."

A subordinate came over to converse with the first man. Finally, the captain asked Junia, "What are General Tryphena's orders?"

She pulled the note from her saddlebag and gave it to him. Having delivered several others, she quoted it from memory without waiting until he finished reading it. "Continue forward. Eradicate any guerrillas you meet. All regiments are to assemble at Redbrier River tomorrow where he plans to trap the Galand King."

The captain turned to his lieutenant, "We must get through this valley. Going back will cost too much time."

The subordinate replied, "I suggest, sir, that we send a small band ahead to draw out the enemy. Once they're flushed out, we'll send in the rest of the troops."

"It won't work," broke in Junia, "They have a good perch, and at this moment see your entire regiment. They'll wait until most of your forces enter."

"Then what's your idea for getting through this valley?" Captain Rahad snapped.

"Two strike forces quietly sneak over the two mountain ridges and come in behind the guerillas while the main regiment pretends to set up camp near the draw. At the strike forces' signals, the rest charge up the mountains' sides. The Galanders will be so busy with the main force that they'll make easy pickings for the strike forces to hit from behind."

After a few minutes debate, the officers decided to go along with her plan. The lieutenant volunteered to lead one strike force, Junia the other. The captain turned her down immediately, but Junia persisted, declaring she was as highly trained as any under his command and it was her idea in the first place—she omitted the tiny detail that she had never been in actual combat before.

With the sun threatening to soon disappear behind the horizon, Junia led a dozen specially chosen men through the rocky forests. Nerves tight, Junia scanned the thick foliage for scouts. Hearing a commotion to her left, she whirled with sword out, only to see one of her soldiers, Rex, pulling his bloody blade out of a Galander. With a nod, Junia signaled the team to continue the advancement. Slowly they made their way over the zenith of the mountain and followed the ridge until they judged the gorge had been passed. Creeping upward, the squad hid in the boulders making up the backbone of the rocky ridge. They did not have long to wait before the other strike team signaled.

Slowly they skulked down the steep slope, grabbing tree limbs for balance. Suddenly a man appeared in front of Junia as she prepared to drop to a ledge several feet below her perch. He was as surprised as Junia at the encounter. Everything seemed to move in slow motion. With a sinking feeling, Junia realized that in order to pull her weapon out she would have to let go of her tree branch, but that would cause her to lose her balance and tumble uncontrollable down the mountain. With a grin, the Galander raised his dagger to throw. Involuntarily Junia shut her eyes, wincing as she heard a knife whoosh through the air and hit solid flesh. Feeling no pain, she opened her eyes in surprise and watched the guerilla drop to his knees with a soft moan. Rex appeared beside her.

"That's two you owe me, commander. Going for a third?" he added as he jumped down beside the dead soldier to recover his dagger.

Anger flashed across Junia's face, but she kept it in check. "Thanks, but it won't be necessary." She brushed pass him, feeling like a clumsy child. Cautiously she proceeded, determined not be caught unaware again.

In the foliage it was difficult for her to keep track of the members of her squad, but every so often a thump or muffled cry could be detected as they made quick work of stray Galanders. Eventually, they reached the main force stretched out along the edge of the cliff. Junia motioned for her team to spread out among the boulders. Below her most of the enemy soldiers were relaxed, some cooking, napping, or conversing. Several hunched at the sheer edge of the cliff, carefully observing the regiment making camp far below in the valley.

Now that she was on the edge of her first long-awaited battle, Junia felt fear. Not afraid-of-the-monster childhood fear, but gut wrenching, terrorizing fear. This was no glorious fantasy. It was reality where she could die—turned into a bloated corpse for birds to feed on. At that moment everything inside Junia rebelled, and she wanted to run away, fast. Her sweaty hand gripped the pommel of her sword, the engraved metal image of Gog's god warming under her touch. Zuzumza. If anyone could help her, it would be the god of her people, the god her family had sworn allegiance to.

Silently she prayed, *Zuzumza, if you bring me through this, I will serve you forever. I will dedicate my life to destroying your enemies.* The words were barely finished before rage engulfed her. Painful memories of events that led her to this time and place resurfaced, added fuel to her fire of hatred.

Chapter Two

Bitter memories stirred through her mind—young Junia watching secretly from a doorway as her beautiful mother put on make-up in front of a gold-framed mirror. Any minute Junia's blundering nurse might find the wayfarer, but the child cared little. She loved the thrill of outwitting her guardian who she saw more often than her own mother.

Queen Ruby was humming to herself for parties always put the young queen into a jovial mood. Hidden, the child observed the queen's preparations in awe. Realizing she was being watched, the exquisite woman turned with a smile and beckoned her young daughter to sit beside her. On a whim, the queen ordered her maidservant to style the princess's hair. Junia sat quietly as the maid twisted her long black hair into braids. Unsatisfied, the queen brushed the servant away and styled Junia's hair into the latest fashion, piling it high and fastening it with a fancy pin. As a final touch, she added make-up. The young princess savored the attention from her mother, wishing it would never end. When Junia finally saw herself in the mirror, she laughed joyfully for now she was a miniature version of her gorgeous mother. It was the happiest moment in Junia's young life—a feeling she would not know again for many years.

In a foul mood Emperor Erastus entered the room. His military uniform hid the fact that his once muscular body was slowly turning obese, yet he still was deadly with a sword—or without one. Ignoring his daughter, he gruffly muttered to Ruby, "Why must you always take so long to get ready? The ball has already started, and our entrance will be so late that…"

"Tsk. Tsk. We are the masters of everybody's eyes no matter what time we arrive," the queen absently replied. "What do you think of your daughter?"

Straightening her shoulders as she had been taught, Junia met her father's eyes proudly. The king glanced at his young daughter. "She's fine. Now let's go before I lose my patience."

"As if you had any."

As the couple left in royal pageantry, the young mother paused to say goodnight to her only child before exiting. It was the last time Junia saw her mother alive. Two nights later, the queen was put to death to make room for Emperor Erastus's newest love interest who he had met at the ball.

Junia never forgot the night she lost her mother, no matter how much she would later try. For some time in the wee hours of the morning, she had lain in bed listening to sounds of people moving up and down the hallway. When her nurse creaked opened the bedroom door, the child feigned sleep.

"Junia? Dear Junia, are you asleep?"

There was something in the servant's voice that bothered the child. She pretended to wake slowly, stretching her arms and yawning until she realized tears glistened on the old woman's face in the moonlight. Goosebumps formed on the princess's arms. Taking on the authoritative voice she used with common servants, the child commanded, "What is wrong with you? Why do you dare wake me so early? I might just report you to my mother."

With pity in her eyes, the nurse sat on the edge of the bed. "Your mother, child, is dead."

Junia sat up. "You lie! I shall have you whipped in front of the whole court."

"You poor, poor child." More tears slid down the nurse's cheeks.

"You…you shouldn't make up such jokes." Terror edged the princess's voice. Jumping out of bed, Junia dashed through the corridors to her mother's chambers. She continued to call her mother's name, but only silence answered. The child raised her voice higher, screaming frantically. A door to the king's bedchamber opened, and a lady clad in nightclothes emerged. Junia watched the scene unfold as if outside her body. Emperor Erastus came to the doorway, muttered that it was only his daughter, and placed an arm around the woman's waist, drawing her back into the bedroom. The child's lips quivered as she fled from the sight.

Blindly Junia dashed along a hallway. Rounding a corner, she bumped into her oldest half-brother, also dressed in nightclothes.

"Look where you are going, crybaby," teased the Crown Prince. "You are waking up the entire palace."

Used to his torments, Junia pleaded. "Tell me where my mother is. Tell me!"

"Who cares? Go back to sleep, or I'll just have Dad put you in the dungeon," the tall boy threatened, caring nothing for the daughter of the woman who had replaced his own mother.

"Leave her alone, Phlegon," commanded another child, his young face full of indignity. "Have you forgotten our mother so quickly?" Though shorter than his elder brother, Rufus was not intimated by the arrogate Crown Prince.

"My mother? Have you seen my mother?" Junia was desperate, grasping for any hope.

8

The brown-hair boy looked at her with pity. "She's with my mom now."

The young princess's body began to shake and tears ran down her face. Though she knew he spoke the truth, she did not want to accept it. Feeling grief anew for his own mother, the boy also began to cry. Prince Phlegon shook his head at the weeping siblings and slammed his bedroom door in disgust. The two crying children held each other tightly in the empty, dark hallway.

The months following were bleak and dark. The monarch quickly remarried, the new queen ignoring her stepchildren. For toys and clothing the children lacked nothing. The servants were ordered to obey the children's every whim. But in the loneness of night, it was a small horse necklace, a gift from her beloved brother, which Junia clutched for comfort as she cried herself to sleep. The day after her mother's death, Rufus had snuck away from the palace and searched the stores and booths at Market Square until he found the perfect gift his one bronze coin could buy. Junia would hold the wooden figure tightly, dreaming she was galloping bareback with the wind blowing through her hair—the destination did not matter—as long as she was heading away from the black-stoned palace.

As time flowed pass, more children were born. Emperor Erastus grew bored, and his wife divorced him due to adultery. Other marriages, affairs, and children followed—no concern to the Emperor. His focus was war—not family. The large, aggressive country had become stagnated over the last century, and the ruler was determined to build his nation into a vast empire. From palace balconies Junia would watch the capitol city's citizens celebrating each military victory, fireworks brightening the night sky, yet Junia's life remained dark. Her only light was Rufus, yet even he was taken away from her.

Concerned for the posterity of his kingdom, Emperor Erastus scrupulously trained Phlegon and Rufus in politics and warfare. Eventually both sons led armies into battle and won renown across the empire. The bright-eyed boy Junia remembered came back a man. The day he arrived at Blackwall Palace filled Junia with joy, but it was hours before she could wrestle him away from the throng surrounding him. As they walked through the Royal Garden, the teenager eagerly listened to Rufus's stories, clinging to every detail of battle.

"I wish I had been there. I would have killed every prisoner—no mercy."

Rufus rebutted his sister. "You are sounding like our father. I prefer mercy. Those prisoners had families to go back home to."

"I'm not my father! All good citizens of Gog know that our enemies are to be destroyed no matter the case—in honor of Zuzumza."

"Yes, for the glory of Zuzumza," replied Rufus dully as he led Junia to a stone bench. Pain pierced Rufus's heart as he observed his sister's blooming beauty and youthful eagerness. The horrors of war had changed him, but he did not know how to make her understand. "I see you no longer wear the horse I gave you."

The princess glanced at the ruby hanging from a silver chain that graced her neck. "Oh, I stopped wearing it when Lina Rahaham said it did not match a dress I was wearing. It is so good to have you back. You will never know how much I have missed you. Everything has been such a bore without you. Gossiping and creating the latest styles are the highlights of my *lovely* palace life. Most teens dress like me, but Lina had the nerve to wear a veil identical to the Grand Witch. And the gentlemen wear . . ."

"Junia, that is no way to talk about the Queen. You should respect her." Junia rolled her eyes and made such a comical face that Rufus found himself laughing in spite of himself. Becoming serious again, the prince realized Junia needed a decent role model to spend time with. "How about I teach you some fencing moves with the sword?"

"Really? Really! That would be splendid!"

"It takes discipline to become a good warrior. Being female, you won't have the strength to last long in a battle."

Fire flashed in the teenager's eyes. "I can handle anything you dish out to me, and I will prove a woman can be as deadly as a man. Someday I'll join the army and come back a hero like you."

"Not as long as you believe war is glorious. You wouldn't make it one day, *Princess*." He emphasized the last word, reminding his sister of the position she had been born into.

Thus began Junia's training. What started as a whim began by her brother became an obsession for Junia. The first lessons went terribly with the princess quickly losing her temper. The lessons would have stopped there except Junia overhead Lina call her training "foolish notions of a spoiled brat." With renewed vigor Junia attacked her lessons. The more her peers talked about her, the harder Junia trained. But no matter how skillful Junia became, her father never glanced her way, and Crown Prince Phlegon publicly declared her a fool. Despite her dreams for fame, Junia continued to play the role of arrogant princess, concerned with gossip and vanity—until the fateful night of the ball celebrating Achoziez's Ascension.

Dancers twirled to fast-paced music. Wearing costumes imitating Zuzumza and his army, the dancers acted out Gogian legends. The enormous palace ballroom and its numerous balconies were crowded with nobles enjoying the yearly celebration. The crowd cheered then hushed as drum beats filled the darkened room, and actors performed amazing acrobats, each attempting to outdo the last. Finally, the performers departed from the room as lights brightened. Jubilant music filled the huge chamber causing the crowd to surge forward and begin their own dancing.

Laughing gaily, Junia let her body move freely, her ravishing blue dress swirling around her legs, feet moving in unison with her partner. Envious looks directed towards the princess from highborn ladies fed Junia's ego. As the music ebbed, Junia drifted innocently over to Lina and chatted a little too friendly with her rival's fiancé. Completely oblivious to the glare from Lina, Lord Richmon talked freely. When a new song began, it was the princess who danced with the young nobleman. Angrily Lina snatched her beau away as soon as the music ended.

Smiling, Junia strolled to the edge of the dance floor and leaned against a marble pillar, relishing the offense. Being the first among her peers to become engaged, Lina enjoyed showing off her rich lord. Lina's sudden enhanced position created jealousy in Junia who thrived on being the center of attention, and she used every opportunity to remind Lina which one of them was of royal blood.

As Junia watched dancing couples, her ears picked up a conversation behind her. Without turning her head, she strained to hear.

"She's just finery and pomp—worthless in the real world. I would never let my son marry her. Her own handmaids say she's a spoiled brat." Junia listen carefully for a name, eager for new gossip.

Another voice spoke. "What I heard is that she trains like a common soldier. Can you believe that? I heard Prince Phlegon say so himself." Realizing she was the topic of the conversation, Junia's body involuntarily stiffened.

"Personally, I believe all the royal offspring are a waste besides the Crown Prince and perhaps one backup. All they ever do is spend our tax money on their selfish whims and then throw their finery in our faces, like tonight. All that jewelry and fancy clothes. Back home, I could feed my entire village for a year with what Princess Junia is wearing."

Angrily, Junia peered around the column, annoyed at seeing two middle-aged maids conversing on their break. *How dare they insult me! I am a princess—they are nothing.* Blood boiling in anger, Junia turned down an invitation to dance with a handsome noble then pushed her way through the crowd, searching for the offenders who had disappeared. Suddenly she stopped cold. What was she going to do? Complain to dear daddy that maids were talking about her and should be thrown into the dungeon? Did she expect he would smile warmly and obey her wishes? No, he would brush her request aside without a thought.

The maids were right. All her finery meant dirt. She was a princess—but without power. Used to being loathed by servants, peers, and family, Junia had created a wall of arrogance that protected her from being overwhelmed by the pain of rejection.

For the first time she was forced to look at the image others saw her as. A palace decoration that served no formal purpose. If she died tomorrow, only Rufus would feel something resembling sadness.

Pushing her way to a second level balcony that opened to the outside, Junia felt tears well up. No, she would not show weakness by crying. She fled down board stairs to the palace gardens. In the cool night air, her mind cleared. *The truth is that the entire world is against me except Rufus. I envy his freedom of being a man, the exploits of war, the attention he gets from our father. The gods cursed my birth by creating me female. My only talent is beauty. No—I can use a sword.*

An idea weaved its way into her mind, but she rejected it as farfetched. It came again, pulsing with excitement, demanding attention. She could walk away from it all—her life, her empty title, her hated father. Hands clenched into fists, Junia turned towards the palace. She would prove to her father and the world who she really was.

Acting before reason could stop her, Junia quickly went to her room and packed a few belongings into a backpack. It took nearly half an hour searching through her large wardrobe before she located several changes of clothing that might be worn by commoners. In the midst of the citywide celebration, nobody noticed the cloaked seventeen year old walking through the streets. By dawn, she had reached the southern gate of Thorn.

It was some time before she could get a ride, for in the morning, traders and farmers headed into the city to sell their commodities, not out. When a wagon finally stopped, Junia used such an authoritative voice that the driver rode off laughing. With the next opportunity, she remembered to keep her place, ask, not demand. The rough-looking driver, suffering from a hangover from last night's fun, gave her a ride to his village. There she found a ride in a cart full of cackling chickens. Later she jarred back and forth between six dirty children and a pig in a creaky wagon to the next town.

Despite her precautions, the princess made many mistakes, especially with her language. She quickly discovered that average people used slang, and the upper-class dialect she spoke gave her away quicker than fancy clothing would. Whenever she noticed somebody staring curiously at her, Junia was quick to find another ride.

By the time the princess fell asleep in a smelly barn that night, Junia was so fed up with being a commoner that she would have returned to the palace if she had the energy to do so. But as the sun rose in the morning, so did her determination. She set her face towards the direction of Fort Belton, the military base Rufus had trained at, considered the best in the Empire.

It took Junia two weeks to reach the fort—two weeks of harsh reality. Coarse males leered at her, wagons splashed her with mud, and pickpockets stole most of her money. The only thing that kept her going was the burning hatred smoldering in her heart against her father. Over and over in her mind, she played an image of Emperor Erastus forced to honor her in front of everyone for an incredible victory she would win.

Fantasies vanished when she finally entered the large gray fort. The soldier at the registration desk laughed when Junia asked to sign up. "A skinny little scamp like you? Try the nurse's building down the street."

Heart pounding, Junia retorted, "I am going to be a soldier, and one day I will be your superior officer."

The private laughed harder. "The only thing women are good for is warming the bed of a real soldier before he heads into battle."

Junia leaned across the table, voice stern, eyes challenging. "Put my name down on the women's enrollment. It's Julie Blackwall."

"You won't last a week."

"Watch and see."

Life in the military began like a harsh nightmare and only became worse. In the small, dingy barrack set aside for females, Junia felt out of place. Many of the women were rough looking and muscular, though some had beauty. All had harsh, unfriendly mouths. Several women quickly made it known that they were the top-notch of the group. The princess kept aloof, though her temper almost got her into a fight several times.

By the end of week two, the company's number had dropped by one-third. Each night, Junia went to bed exhausted, every muscle aching. Never had training with Rufus been anything like this. At the palace she only practiced several hours a day when the mood hit her. Now there was non-stop weapons training, exercises, and drills. The princess was no longer in control of her life. Sergeant Urbane Herron dictated every minute of hers.

The man was cold and distant, making Junia wonder if Urbane was tougher on them because they were females or simply because he hated his job. Rumors stated that he had been a distinguished officer on the battlefront but had stood up to a superior officer once too many times and been sent to Fort Belton as a punishment. His muscular, striking form drew the attention of many in the women's platoon who tried to win his favor, but he ignored them.

Junia kept her focus on training, avoiding the flirtations of her peers. While others socialized during breaks, she practiced by herself. In grueling drills, she converted her hatred into energy. The harder she was pushed, the stronger her determination shone. It did not go unnoticed by her superior. For a month, Urbane observed her, demanding much from her in the drills. She met every challenge. The searing fire that burned inside her attracted him like a moth to a flame.

One night he placed her on sentry duty in an isolated guardhouse. Two hours into her shift, he dropped by, pretending it was a routine checkup. He praised her performance. Junia returned his compliments and casually brushed her fingers against his hand. He caught her arm and gently pulled her to him. She smiled playfully but lightly shoved him away. The teasing and flirting continued for a while, ending with Junia giving away the last of her innocence. The next day it was with great difficulty that Junia stayed focused on her drills. She was tempted to boast to her peers how she had won his favor while they had failed, but she instinctively knew he would dislike such bragging. Three nights later, she was again assigned guard duty, and the sergeant visited again. It became a regular event for the remaining of basic training.

As graduation neared, excitement filled the fort as privates congratulated each other. Most of the male recruits had made it through the harsh training, but only a third of the Women's Platoon had succeeded. To many officers, female soldiers were considered a crude joke.

Two nights before the ceremony, Junia was again assigned night duty, and Urbane made his expected visit. With smooth words he told Junia that she had been a great private and he wished her well in the future.

"So you're breaking up me, just like that?"

Urbane tilted his head and gave her a charming smile. "We both have our separate lives to live. I've recommended you for private first class and suggested you would make one fine corporal. Be happy. You're getting what you wanted out of this."

You can't dump a princess! Junia's mind screamed, but she held her anger in check. "Thanks, Lieutenant. I hope you enjoy your own promotion to the battle front." *And die the first day.*

Urbane bent to give Junia one final kiss, but she pulled back from him. With a goodbye and a nod of his head, he vanished into the darkness beyond the doorway, leaving Junia feeling empty.

The ceremony went smoothly. From the stands, families and friends cheered as hundreds of graduates in battle armor marched across the grassy field. They stopped in perfect unity before a large wooden platform. After several minor officers spoke, General Nereus was introduced. The commander gave a rousing patriotic speech that ended with the whole audience bursting into cries of "Gog! Zuzumza!" As the cheering reached its zenith, Junia found herself scanning the crowd, looking for Rufus. She would have given her new gleaming sword to see his smiling face or hear his voice giving out advice that she rarely heeded. She wondered if her father would have been proud or pretend not to notice the new corporal sharing his same brown eyes leading the Woman's Platoon. Did he even know she was missing from the palace? Angrily she focused back on General Nereus and lifted her voice louder.

As the audience rushed from their seats to meet the new soldiers, loneliness consumed Junia. Lovers embraced and children laughed. No one greeted the princess. Several times she caught glimpses of Urbane, smiling and patting comrades' backs. He never looked her way once. This should have been her moment of glory; instead, a bitter hollowness rang through her heart. Born of royal blood, she was now a trained killer. She wanted to possess the world, but her own soul did not seem to belong to her. Why did happiness always elude her? As she glanced around at her merry comrades, she again spotted Urbane joking with a friend. *Never again*, she vowed to herself, *will I let a man use me.*

Several days later, the graduates were given their new assignments. A dozen women were sent to join the Women's Platoon stationed in the small border town of Roughgrass, a city that lived up to its name. Filled with boisterous soldiers stagnant with boredom, nights were routinely wild. It did not take Junia long to realize that her platoon's main purpose was to serve as entertainment for the men. Most of the women did not seem to mind. Every day was a battle for Junia as she attempted to keep her platoon on a disciplined schedule. Most were older than Junia and resented her authority. Many days Sergeant Sagina, suffering from a hangover, would stagger out of her bunk and override Junia's orders in front of the other women. The male soldiers made Junia's life the most miserable. They were constantly flirting with the women and making vulgar gestures that the grinning women returned.

At night, she lay in her hard bed wondering why she had gone through all the rigid training for such an appalling life. What happened to her glorious dreams of honor and heroism? Had she really once been a princess dressed in the finest clothes with servants to obey her every whim? A bittersweet memory played across her mind of Rufus and her practicing in the lush Royal Garden. The child who thought she was grown-up exclaiming, "Someday I'll join the army and come back a hero like you." The wise brother saying, "Not as long as you believe war is glorious. You wouldn't make it one day, princess."

Her heart's desire was to have just one person on her side. There was no greater hell than a human standing against the world alone. Urbane's handsome face flashed through her mind. Angrily she pushed the memory away. From the first minute he had showed up in the guardhouse, she knew he had been using her just as she was using him, yet part of her still craved him. Why? Neither cared about the other.

"Urbane, is there anything inside of you? Can you feel love? Can I?" she whispered into the unanswering darkness.

~~~~~~~~~

With a sigh Urbane tossed a file onto the wooden table. *Another day as the general's secretary*, thought Urbane in disgust. When General Tryphena had handpicked him, Urbane thought he would be leading troops into battle; instead, he handled paperwork. True, he was learning how to coordinate various regiments and supplies, gaining needed knowledge of the overall problems of war management. Still, he preferred to have a sword in his hand.

The day General Tryphena selected him, Urbane had been standing at attention with several other lieutenants.

Leaning close to Urbane's face, the hardened commander had said, "I see a lot of potential in you, Lieutenant Junior. You just might turn out to be a major someday. But before that time comes, I will demand your best and then some. Do you think you can handle that?"

Standing with shoulders stiff, Urbane had barked, "Yes, sir!"

The past weeks had been challenging, even intriguing, but it was still an office job. He missed the uncertainty of battle, the blood and sweat, living from day to day. You made no plans for the future because the next day might be your last. Now he helped plan for the future of the entire country, and unconsciously it was changing him.

"You're looking down a bit today. Hangover?" asked Troy, sitting across the wooden table from Urbane. The other lieutenant was tall and lanky, more interested in socializing than paperwork.

"No, just pondering the nation's problems."

"Ha. You take things too seriously. Responsibility falls on General Tryphena. If we lose a battle, Tryphena takes the blame. If we win, we all look good and wear new medals. We lieutenants don't have a thing to worry about. When's the last time you had a woman?"

When I was with Julie, Urbane's mind responded. Not caring to discuss his personal life, Urbane tossed a file in front of Troy. "Now's the time to worry about national problems. General Tryphena is coming."

Both men stood rigidly at attention as their commander enter the small room. "At ease," barked the general. Even in a relaxed mood as he was today, Tryphena always spoke with dominating authority. "Things are looking up. My report to Emperor Erastus said that Galand will fall within six weeks."

Urban glanced uneasily towards Troy. Both officers had privately discussed that Tryphena was pushing the war too fast. Knowing he would get no support from bootlicking Troy, Urbane said, "Sir, with winter coming, that goal may be unreachable."

The general dismissed the idea. "Nonsense. Our troops were born in this weather. Snow will not affect their performance."

"But horses pulling heavy supply wagons over mountain passes may. It will be difficult keeping the troops fed."

The general stroked his beard. "You're right. It's a difficult job getting the supplies to troops in this savage mountain region." He faced his young officer. "That'll be your job."

Caught off guard, a "What?" escape Urbane's mouth.

"I'm giving you the official title of Captain of Supplies. It's your duty to fix problems before they occur. Gog's glory rests on conquering Galand and eliminating its Tnias parasites. Do you think you can handle this?"

Urbane stood tall as he met the general's eyes. "Yes, sir."

"Good. I will give you extra manpower to handle the problem. Lieutenant Troy, get him the files he needs." As Troy scrabbled to comply, General Tryphena left.

"By the gods, you just had to go and open you big mouth," complained Troy.

"I got a promotion out of the deal."

"At what cost? Now when Beard Face can't meet his promise to the Emperor, you will be his fall guy. That's going to look nice on your credentials."

"Galand will fall in six weeks." The words came out with steel determination but only met Troy's laughter.

"Yeah. You and what army?"

"Zuzumza will not let his country be disgraced. Any country which lets Tnias run around freely will be crushed."

"I can't believe you're that idealistic. What matters is today. Hey, look here!" Troy tossed a file in front of the new captain. Urbane glanced over the list of troops until he spotted the words beside Troy's fingertip. "We could send for a Woman's Platoon. That will create some excitement around here. There's one stationed at Roughgrass and could be here in two day."

Julie. Her image popped uninvited into Urbane's mind, and his body ached for her. "No. They can't handle moving winter supplies."

"We don't need them for labor."

"No." Urbane stepped away, ending the discussion.

"Of course, O Great Captain of Supplies. Whatever you say."

Troy kept aloof the rest of the day, resentment a barrier between the two friends, but that was not what bothered Urbane. He could not shake the image of Julie from his mind, her fiery determination overcoming every barrier that stood in her way. She was the one person in the entire army who seemed as dedicated and serious as he was. It would be nice to have something to look forward to besides the end of his short military career.

At the end of the day—to Troy's delight—he signed the form ordering the Women's Platoon to Stockville. As Urbane walked towards his bunker after work, he pondered about Julie. She was a dedicated soldier with a good head on her shoulders. If she had been born a man, she would have climbed high in power. He could picture her standing up to General Tryphena, telling the commander that he was making a mistake. At that moment Urbane knew what he wanted most—comradeship. In this harsh world everybody was out for himself. But what if two people shared the same goals by helping each other? Was such a relationship even possible? He could either look like a fool in front of the other officers by attempting it or get used to loneliness being his lifetime comrade—however long that may be.

~~~~~~~~~

Tired soldiers slowly munched on their bland lunches. Many of the whispering women tossed angry glares towards Junia who ignored them. With the sergeant still in bed with a hangover, Junia had awaked the platoon, only to discover two guys hiding under the bedcovers and bottles strewn everywhere. Her temper was uncontrollable, creating a miserable day for the women who were forced to dig drainage ditches and split firewood, jobs ordinarily reserved for men. She had hoped that in moving closer to the battlefront, the women would take their job more seriously. She had been wrong.

When they had arrived at their new post a week ago, she had hoped the Women's Platoon would finally be taken seriously. Instead, many of the women were soon flirting with male soldiers and hanging out at the local tavern whenever they had a free moment. The only highlight for Junia was that Urbane was here. She had spotted him when they first marched into the town. Her heartbeat had quickened as he inspected the new soldiers, but he had said nothing to her. As her platoon headed towards their new barracks, her eyes met his. Briefly she saw an intense expression in his eyes, but the look quickly vanished. Since then, she had only spotted him at a distance across crowed streets.

As the princess ate her tasteless breakfast, images of Urbane danced through her mind. She swatted them away like unwanted bugs. Slowly she became aware that

18

the platoon had quieted. Turning around, she spotted scowling Sergeant Sagina heading towards the table.

Reaching her corporal, the sergeant barked, "What is the meaning of having my ladies dig ditches?"

Junia stood at attention, straining to keep her voice level. "They had an unauthorized party which included men staying overnight, sir."

Sagina leaned close, and Junia grimace at the woman's foul breath. "Have I not said that it is every woman's duty to serve Gog?"

"Yes, sir."

"And doesn't this include fulfilling men's needs?"

Junia heard snickering behind her. "It was an unauthorized party."

"Did I ever say the ladies couldn't enjoy themselves?"

"No, sir."

"Then under what authority do you punish them?"

"Under mine. They lack disciple and will always be slaves to man." Her temper was beginning to take over.

"Women's place is under men."

"How can you say that?"

"I've had enough of your insubordination. I'm going to apply for your demotion."

The weakened dam inside Junia finally broke, and her hand reached for her sword.

With a sly smile, Sagina said, "Go ahead. Draw. Attacking a superior officer is punishable by death."

At that moment Urbane walked up. Seeing the tension between the two officers, he asked, "Sergeant, is there a problem here?"

"Yes, sir. I'm recommending this soldier for a demotion for insubordination to a superior officer."

Calmly the captain glanced at Junia. The crowded cafeteria quieted as curious people paused to watch the confrontation. "That's strange. I was just about to promote her as my personal aid. Corporal, are you guilty of what she says?"

"If you count disagreeing with her on the role that female soldiers have in our army as insubordination, then, yes, sir."

"And what are the opinions you disagreed upon?"

"She believes females soldiers' responsibility is to serve male soldiers. I disagree by believing it is our purpose to serve Gog by behaving as true warriors."

Urbane struggled to keep a serious face. "I have to say I agree with you, Corporal Blackwall. Sergeant Sagina, you will have no more problems because Blackwall will be serving as one of my personal aids."

Sagina's mouth opened, but she wisely held her tongue. Her second attempt to speak kept to the acceptable phrase of "Yes, sir."

Turning towards Junia, Urbane ordered, "Follow me, *Lieutenant* Blackwall."

"It will be an honor, sir." Junia could hear surprised whispers from the table behind her. Following her new commanding officer, a smile spread across the princess's lips.

Urbane led his new lieutenant to the officers' table and indicated an empty chair beside his. As she sat down, her breath caught as she realized General Tryphena was eating directly across from Urbane. "General, I would like you to meet my new lieutenant, chosen for her dedication and skills."

The princess gave a brief smile, though her stomach felt like lead. Did he recognize her from palace parties? The commander's eyebrows rose, and a questioning look pass over his face. "I'm a little surprised you chose a woman, but I can see her beauty is an added bonus. As long as the supplies make it through, I'm satisfied, Captain Herron."

Junia let go of the breath she had been holding. *He doesn't recognize me.* "General, you will find I'm well qualified and have a few surprises of my own. In Zuzumza's name we will win this war." The princess felt intoxicated by the thrill of the challenge awaiting her—finally the opportunity to prove herself to the world.

General Tryphena gave a brief nod before continuing his meal.

The day passed like a dream. Urbane kept both Troy and her busy arranging for the next shipment of supplies. Junia took special joy in delivering the order for the Women's Platoon to pack wagons in the snow. Throughout the day, Urbane stayed focused—most of the time. Every so often Junia caught him watching her, and he received a warm smile in return. After dinner Urbane took her for a walk. Snow crunched under their feet as they passed barracks housing soldiers. Conversation stayed light until Junia asked where she would be sleeping.

"In my quarters, unless you have an objection," he said.

At first Junia did not answer as the conversation with Sagina played through her mind. If she stayed with Urbane, she would be doing exactly what she had protested against during lunch, yet through Urbane she had power. She could seek revenge against enemies and go up in prestige as Urbane did—or fall with him. For the first time in her young life, she would have to put somebody else's interests first in order to provide a better future for herself. It was a new concept—one she was ready for.

With an enticing smile, she wrapped an arm around Urbane's waist. "I would love to move in with you."

Urbane took her hand and led her through the darkness.

~~~~~~~~~

Debating, spurring, and finally using her womanly ways that Troy could not compete against, Julie convinced Urbane into introducing some of her plans to General Tryphena. Always at such times Troy sat in tense silence, waiting, sure that all three of them would be hanged the next day. But Zuzumza's blessing seemed to shine on the determined couple and crazy plans succeeded—not with just supplies but other military operations. Urbane soon found himself becoming one of the general's favorites. During heavy battles, promotions became too common due to death of officers, so it was no surprise to anyone when the Gogian army finally made its way through the snowy mountains to siege the capitol city of Galand that Urbane wore the strips of a major.

The day the city burned, Junia sat regal as a queen on her horse beside Urbane, listening to the various reports carried by runners. He was a rock of calmness in the mist of chaos: soldiers rushing pass, citizens screaming, the air filled with the smell of smoke and blood. Enviousness pricked her as she observed the respect officers gave Urbane, yet they ignored her. Still she was satisfied with the power she wielded, gloating in her dreams of glory. Her attention was yanked from her fantasies when twenty chained prisoners were plodded forward by tyrannizing guards.

The brawny leader of the guards stepped forward. "Major Herron, these prisoners refused to swear allegiance to Zuzumza." He spat the words out like a curse.

It was Gogian tradition for lower ranking captured soldiers to be sent to work camps and slowly released after national control had been firmly established by the new ruling government; however, all high-ranking officers were executed in order to crush the fighting spirit of the conquered people. Neither, though, were considered as dangerous as the heretical Tnias, followers of the false god Yahweh. Top priority of every invasion was to eradicate all Tnias from the conquered regions.

With a stern, yet slightly bored expression, Urbane addressed the prisoners. "You have one last chance. Do you pledge your loyalty to Zuzumza, God of War?"

For a moment the captives stood silently, their ragged breaths forming white clouds in the cold air. Junia noticed that most were not clothed in soldiers' outfits; instead, they worked in common professions such as bakers and blacksmiths.

Wrinkling her nose in contempt, she thought, *Disgusting Tnias—you can never tell who they are.*

The shabbiest dressed prisoner lifted his head high and proclaimed, "There is only One True God, Yahweh!" The man knew he had just uttered his death sentence. Without a warning the guard stepped forward with a knife and sliced the Tnias's throat. The injured man dropped to his knees, life's vital fluid staining the snow red.

"So lies the fate of all Yahweh's mistresses!" cursed the fervent guard, fresh blood blemishing his leather armor. Hoots and jeers filled the air from the growing crowd of soldiers enthralled with blood lust.

Stomach sickening, Junia jerked her head from the sight. She had seen many wounded and dead over the last few weeks, but never anyone killed before her eyes. It had happen so fast. One second a strong man stood defiant before his accusers. The next moment he was a dying, gagging wretch. Out of the corner of her eyes, Junia spotted Urbane observing her closely. Shame and anger flushed through her body. How could she show repugnance like a naïve, pampered maiden in front of everybody? Forcing her face forward, she attempted to keep a stony expression during the other ghastly executions—only wincing twice. Her brother's voice echoed through her mind, *They are someone's son, someone's lover.*

With the crowd's attention focused on the bloody show, Urbane drew his horse nearer Junia. "Are you okay, Julie?"

"I'm fine!" she shot back harsher than she meant. "It's just my first time seeing an execution. It won't bother me again."

She kicked her heels into the flank of her horse and galloped away, not seeing the concern which crossed Urbane's face.

Chapter Three

The memories faded as Junia focused on her enemies walking and conversing just yards below her on the mountainside. As her prayer to Zuzumza ended, she envisioned her cold father smiling as he watched her mother die, his lustful eyes sweeping across the execution scene, focusing on a beautiful woman in the crowd who would be his next wife. She heard her brother's mocking laughs polluting the air as she wept in despair at the queen's death. A wild fierceness filled Junia, and she gripped her sword in raw eagerness for the ensuring battle.

From the valley floor came a tremendous roar as men suddenly surged from the Gogian camp. Many directed arrows against the cliffs while others attempted to climb. With the Galand's forces focused on their visible enemies, the strike teams rushed forward, stabbing men in the back. Junia struck an archer with all her might, feeling the sharp edge of her weapon slice through flesh and strike bone in his neck. The man cried out in agony and turned to draw his dagger, but his body refused to obey. Downward he fell in a pool of blood. The innocent child still inside Junia rebelled at the sight, but she brushed her conscience away as a nearby soldier realized her presence and raised his weapon. Predator-like, the princess killed without thought, her demonic hatred sending her into a blind frenzy. A heavy-body man rose up in front of her, and for a split second, Junia thought she was looking at her father. She stuck him down as easily, never realizing that the gold crown the man wore on his head was not an illusion.

The last sight the sun had before it slipped behind the horizon was of the Twelfth Regiment army cheering in victory. As soldiers rounded up prisoners and plundered the spoils, Rex approached his captain. In his hands was a gold crown splotched with dry blood.

The commander studied the crown for a moment before speaking. "So you've killed the Galand king, soldier. Emperor Erastus ordered him taken alive." His voice did not carry a sharp reprimand. If his troops had just defeated the main branch of Galand's remaining forces, then he would be considered a hero. Taking the king's head back would ensure medals and a promotion. He licked his lips in greed.

"No, sir. It wasn't me," said Rex who felt it was his duty to tell the truth. "Blackwall did it. Stuck him down as if he was nothing more than a sapling."

Caption Rahad's eyes opened wide in surprise. "The female lieutenant?"

"Yes, sir. The female."

~~~~~~~~~

From its birthplace in the jagged mountains, winding and twisting through the craggy hills, the Redbrier River roared its defiance to the world, but once it reached the fertile plains of Galand, it became a gentle stream, oblivious to the political struggles on its shores. On the southern bank gathered the remaining forces of Galand, milling around, worried about the late arrival of their king. On the northern bank rested the exhausted troops of Gog.

General Tryphena marched back and forth in front of his tent, lashing out at anyone near at hand. He wanted to attempt a frontal attack but too many of his regiments were still missing. "This is the last day. I will accept nothing less than King Hozild's surrender today." The commander slammed his fist into the palm of his other hand. "Nothing less!"

While other officers sought tasks to keep themselves busy and out of their chief's sight, Urbane dared to speak. "Sir, the troops are exhausted. They have traveled for days on pure adrenaline with no rest. If we wait a day or two, it will give the missing units time to find their way out of the mountain maze. Our troops will be refreshed, and we could cross the river at night on…"

"Unacceptable! I promised Emperor Erastus that today Galand would belong to him. Today! Not tomorrow or next week. Tell the officers that we cross in two hours."

Shocked, Urbane protested, "If we attempt a river crossing in broad daylight we will be sitting birds for their archers."

The general gave his major a stern glare. "Do you dare oppose your commanding officer?"

"No, sir. I was just offering another point of view for your consideration."

"My mind is made up, Major Herron. Now start spreading the word."

"Yes, sir." Urbane answered with sinking dread. Many men would die today— good men—because of a general's obsession. The major vowed to himself that when he became a general, he would always put his men first and never a personal agenda. If he lived through this day, he could at least look forward to seeing Tryphena explaining to the Emperor why his highly trained army who had routed the capitol were defeated by a few frayed, leftover troops.

A messenger rushed up to his chief. "General Tryphena, the Twelfth Regiment has just arrived."

"How many causalities did they take? What news do they have of Galandian movements?"

"I don't know, sir."

"Well, I suggest you find out!" barked the general. The messenger scrambled to comply.

As Urbane watched the messenger vanish among milling troops, he wondered about Julie. He had not seen her since she had been sent to the Twelfth Regiment. Had she delivered the message or disappeared like too many others? Though he had to prepare the troops for the river crossing, he found tasks that kept him within sight of the general's tent. Finally, he spotted several officers making their way through the bustling camp, but his eyes only focused on Julie who walked behind them.

Captain Rahad stood rigidly in front of his commander-in-chief. "General Tryphena, the Twelfth Regiment reporting in. We encountered a trap, but due to a warning from Lieutenant Blackwall," he gave a nod towards Julie, "we were prepared. We sent in two strike forces, one lead by Lieutenant Asal, and the other by Lieutenant Blackwall. With the main forces attacking from the front and the strike teams from behind, we completely wiped out the guerillas. And we bear you this gift." With a nod, he signaled Rex who reached into a sack he carried and pulled out a lifeless head wearing a glistening gold crown.

Gasps from bystanders filled the air as the lieutenant bore the ghastly trophy to the general. Tryphena's mouth opened wide in astonishment then spread into a wide grin. Taking the head, he asked, "Who do I honor for this trophy?"

Relieved that the general was not angered because the king was dead, Rahad said, "Sir, it was Lieutenant Blackwall who struck him down in the heat of battle."

Dozens of surprised eyes turned towards the young woman, many seeing her for the first time. Junia stood at attention, but her eyes roved over the crowd, searching for Urbane. Realizing that she was expected to speak, the princess said the first thing that came to her mind. "I didn't realize who he was at the time because he was dressed like a commoner."

The general burst into deep laughter. "A common man? A common man. The ultimate insult for this pompous fool." Chortling he held the head high and yelled, "So shall be the fate of all Zuzumza's enemies."

Nearby soldiers shouted in triumph. The victory chant was picked up by neighbors and carried onward from regiment to regiment, gaining in volume until it become a deafening roar to the Galandian soldiers on the other river bank who looked at each other in confusion and fear.

Back slaps and congratulations were poured on Junia, but it was Urbane she searched for in the jubilant crowd. Finally their eyes met, and a slow smile spread across her face. She pushed her way to him. He wrapped his arms around her, silently mouthing, "Good job, Lieutenant." Junia knew most men would be filled with jealousy if their mate achieved higher recognition than themselves. Urbane was not like other men. Oblivious to the deafen roar around them, the couple locked in a passionate kiss. •

~~~~~~~~~

Galand's army surrendered. With no king and no successor for the throne, the heart of the nation was lost. General Tryphena sent messengers to Emperor Erastus announcing the victory. Then he presided over standard post-war procedures that included plundering the land, creating POW camps, taxing the people, and claiming the best animals and crops for the Red Army—with a large bonus for himself. All Galanders in leadership positions were rounded up and sent to concentration camps. Then the Red Army performed its deadliest function that had led to its sinister name—the eradication of all Tnias.

No one was safe from the searches. Women, men, children, the elderly, and handicapped were slaughtered. Soldiers went house to house, set up roadblocks, and grabbed people off the streets. All were asked the same basic question, "Who do you worship?" Most were quick to say Zuzumza or a local deity's name, leading to their immediate release. Because of a religious belief, Tnias only pledged their allegiance to Yahweh. The lucky ones were immediately put to death. Others were dragged through the streets, put on display in marketplaces, kicked, beating, and spit on. Some were severely tortured. Eventually all shared the same fate—death. The countryside was marred by mass graves and bloated corpses. The great Gogian Empire was formed upon the bedrock of terror and blood spilt in holy wars.

Thousands of refugees flooded the roads heading south. Some traveled in wagons filled near the breaking point with belongings. Others had only the clothes on their backs. While many fled from religious persecution, others just wanted safe homes and peaceful lives. All were desperate to escape the coming reign of Gogian dictatorship.

Junia took little notice of the plight of Galand's citizens for she was too busy having the time of her life. The soldiers considered her a hero—and an equal. Repeatedly she was forced to tell her story of victory, each retelling becoming more embellished than the last. Whenever she stepped into a tavern, soldiers competed to buy her drinks, boasting of their own battle heroics. The princess basked in the attention, drinking it as if she had been marooned in a desert and their attention was life-giving water. Always by her side was reserved Urbane, quickly letting others know who her lover was.

Due to a blizzard, it took nearly three weeks for Emperor Erastus's representatives to finally arrive. General Tryphena welcomed the half-dozen officials cheerfully, inviting them into the mansion he claimed for his headquarters. Soon they were sitting in the warm living room, toasting Gog's victory.

Gray-haired General Nereus, battled scarred from his long life of service, lifted his glass into the air. "Now a toast to my old friend who finally has his name in the history books." He winked at General Tryphena as a dozen officers raised their own glasses.

Both Urbane and Rahad enjoyed the privilege to be included in the jovial gathering. Neither could get over the fact that they were in the same room with two famous war heroes: General Nereus and Prince Rufus. Urbane kept his excitement hidden, but Rahad's nervous voice betrayed the captain whenever he spoke.

"So," said General Tryphena, sitting his wine down, "Who has been chosen as the first governor of the new Galand province?"

"That's still under debate." General Nereus glanced at the prince before continuing. "Emperor Erastus offered the territory to his second heir, but it seems that Prince Rufus has other plans."

Rufus gave a polite, apologetic smile. "I don't want to be tied down yet."

"Want to sow your royal oats, I see," laughed Tryphena. He wondered if Nereus was the monarch's second choice but dared not ask. He had worked hard conquering this country and wanted the pleasure of reaping its resources himself. Deciding it was time to change the subject to hide his motives, Tryphena said, "I would like to introduce you to two of my upcoming stars, Major Herron and Captain Rahad. Herron kept the troops feed and in line while Rahad led the fateful charge that netted us King Hozild."

Nods and congratulations were given. "Tell us about your great battle," said the prince as he sat his half-empty glass down. "I love a great tall tale."

"I'll try to keep it as truthful as possible," said Rahad before launching into a long, elaborate version of the victory.

Throughout the meeting, aids quietly came in and out, reporting to various officers. As everyone laughed at an exaggerated point in the story, Rufus's eyes suddenly froze on a woman whispering to Urbane. He stared, attempting to get a clear view of her face but she turned towards the exit with her back to him. He could have sworn it was his sister. His eyes did not leave the young woman as she walked across the room and vanished through a door. Urbane's body became rigid as he caught the prince's reaction to Junia. The story was drawing towards its conclusion when the woman reentered the room.

Rahad ended his story with, "Oh, and speaking of the demon, here's the hero of the hour, Lieutenant Blackwall."

Every eye focused on the perfectly formed female who smiled at the officers. Then their attention was pulled to the prince standing with mouth wide-open. "Junia? Junia!"

The young woman looked at him blankly for a moment then joy filled her face. "Rufus! I can't believe you're here. I didn't recognize you with that beard." Junia raced to her brother who embraced her in a bear hug. Everyone was too busy attempting to figure out why the prince was given such a warm reception to her to notice the dark cloud passing over Urbane's face. He had no difficulty keeping men attracted to Junia at bay when they spotted the major stripes on his uniform, but Urbane knew he could not compete with a highborn prince.

The two joyful siblings talked at the same time, leaving their audience in the dark.

"I thought maybe you had been kidnapped or killed."

"Me? Who would want to kidnap me?"

"About two-thirds of the palace. I should have expected you would do something like this."

The princess laughed. "I had to prove I was more than a palace decoration." She stepped back from her brother and raised her arms. "Well, I did!"

"I see. Father will pin the Medal of Zuzumza on you himself."

"Prince Rufus," broke in General Nereus, "This reunion is a pleasure to watch, but we wouldn't mind an introduction to the young lady."

Putting an arm around Junia's shoulder, the prince said, "You don't recognize my sister, Princess Junia?"

Smiling, the aged commander stood up. "Pardon my memory, Princess. It's been some years since I last saw you. You've grown up quite well—quiet well indeed."

Several men voiced their agreement, while it took a few moments for other to recover from the shock. A few in their minds examined every conversation they had spoken with the princess, wondering if she had somehow been offended and might later seek revenge. Junia noticed Urbane sitting silent and grim faced. Was he angry she had kept her identity secret or feared she would drop him like a tattered hat for someone more refined? Other than Rufus, he was the only person who had ever supported her. Plus he was in favor with General Tryphena, had a strong head on his shoulder, and was an excellent bed companion.

The princess walked over to Urbane. Taking his hand, she whispered, "Remember as one goes up, so does the other." He smiled, squeezing her hand. She led him to the prince. "Brother, I like you to meet Major Herron, my lover."

Smiling Rufus shook the young officer's hand. "With the recommendation I've heard about you today, you might find yourself a general someday."

Urbane gave a polite nod, relieved that he would not have to compete with the prince for Junia. "My life is to serve Gog and Zuzumza."

With fragile peace established for a time, the couple traveled back with Prince Rufus to Blackwall Palace. Proudly the princess stood in full battle array in the Great Hall of Kings in front of hundreds of guests as her father bestowed on her the Medallion of Zuzumza and a dagger with the royal insignia. The newly honored princess whispered the right words to Prince Rufus who recommended Urbane for the exalted position of Captain of the Royal Guards. Once again Princess Junia dazzled across the dance floor in scrupulous apparel, gemstones ablaze in the bright lights. Always by her side was Captain Herron arrayed in ceremonial black with royal gold embroidery. Many an eye glanced their way, some out of envy, some from fear, and others with hatred.

A whirlwind of activity, Junia kept herself in the social spotlight. She drank flattery from nobles and plotted swift revenge of those who scorned her. Sometimes she used Urbane's position as leverage for ruining her enemies' reputations by having them arrested on real or false charges.

There was only one thing that the princess dreaded—the ominous loneliness late at night when sleep eluded her and uninvited thoughts of her failures paraded across her mind. Her father with his cold eyes, smiling in public at his oldest daughter, completely ignoring her in private. Crown Prince Phlegon did not even attempt to disguise the scorn he felt for his half-sister. Anytime they met in public, he would recount a joke with her as the butt of it. She smoldered in hatred as people laughed around her, but his birthright protected him from her plots—for now. Junia kept smiling, pretending that darkness was not eating her soul, separating her from the happiness she craved.

Chapter Four

Roses climbed up arch scaffolds, creating fragrant living roofs over the bricked path that wound through the enormous royal garden. Rare plants and beautiful flowering flora grew beside the brick path a small group of nobles strolled along. Junia left Urbane's side to walk nearer Lord Richmon as he continued the humorous tale of his family's adventurous journey to Blackwall Palace.

"Then the ranger looked at me, all covered in mud, and said, 'Next I'll expect you'll be telling me you are the Crowned Prince himself.' With my most pompous air of nobility I could muster, I looked the ranger straight in the eyes and said, 'No, but I will be seeing him in two days unless you arrest me. Then I'll be sending him a letter saying I was detained by a ranger—what's your name—for poaching.'"

Laughing, Junia leaned close and put a hand on the lord's arm. "I would have loved seeing his face when you said that. Did he let you go immediately?"

The noble loved an attentive audience. "Oh, no! He thought I was a drunken bandit." As Lord Richmon launched into more details, he forgot about everyone around him—including his wife. Smiling encouraging, the princess wrapped her own arm around the young noble's outstretched arm and guided him towards the most attractive areas of the gardens. Junia's childhood nemesis, Lady Lina Richmon, casually chatted with Prince Rufus, but her eyes followed the departing couple locked in deep conversation.

Rufus attempted to keep the conversation going. Inwardly he felt like an angry father, seething at Junia's rude behavior. For the last hour he had vainly watched tension building in both Urbane and Lady Richmon. They kept to protocol, chatting lighthearted, pretending all was well while painful betrayal hunted their eyes. Rufus was becoming quite tired of it all.

The prince offered his arm to Lady Richmon who graciously accepted it. Urbane politely bowed and dismissed himself, offering the excuse that he had a meeting with his head guards, but Rufus caught the captain's cold glaze directed towards the trees his lover had disappeared behind. Rufus led Lady Richmon along the branching paths, finally finding the missing couple in a small clearing where the late sun, sinking behind the palace, cast the long shadow of the Claw over the humans.

Junia stood close to the young lord, one hand on his shoulder, the other pointing towards the lofty tower. "According to legend, our country was once tiny and oppressed from all sides. The people cried out to the gods for help, but they were too insignificant to be noticed by busy deities. King Achoneiz wanted to help his people so he visited all the temples, sacrificing to every god, but he was not important enough to attract their attention. One night as he lay in his house, a beautiful woman sent by Zuzumza visited him in a dream. She said the Ultimate God had heard the prayers from the people of Gog, but the god could not come to earth and help them unless he had a home. King Achoneiz woke up and ordered for Blackwall Palace to be built with the central tower to be raised higher than the others. Once it was finished, the growing town had a celebration in honor of Zuzumza. At the height of the dancing, King Achoneiz climbed to the top of the tower, and Zuzumza met him there face to face. The god promised the king that his descendants would rule all the kingdoms of the continent if only the king would serve the Ultimate One. So Achoneiz declared Zuzumza the national god and himself the first Emperor of Gog."

The lord gazed intently at the tallest of Blackwall's lofty towers. The edifice not only rose a third length higher than any other towers, but was uniquely designed with a narrow column topped by a huge black mass shaped like a gigantic thorn or claw. The narrow front of the claw formed a balcony and the curve claw's body rose high, tapering back over the balcony to create an elegant roof. The whole structure was made from a rare black stone that seemed to collect the light around it, creating a black void in the sky even on the brightest of days. The inhabits of the city pretended there was nothing unusual about the structure the city was named after, but subconsciously they avoided looking in the direction of the mystical tower as they went about their everyday lives in its shadow.

In awe, Lord Richmon said, "I've heard many dark tales of the Claw, but never believed them till now." Junia leaned her head against his shoulder.

Silence filled the clearing for a moment until Prince Rufus cleared his throat. "Lord Richmon, your wife is feeling tired. I believe she needs a rest before dinner."

"Oh, certainty. Come, dear." The young lord took his wife's hand. "Princess Junia was showing me some of the Emperor's prized plants."

"Yes, I could see she was showing you something—pleasant."

Catching the sharpness in his wife's voice, the naïve man looked at his wife in confusion. "Would you like some aoyatoes or bluetips in our garden? I'm sure the Emperor wouldn't mind giving a few…."

"No!" Lady Richmon glanced icily towards Junia. "I prefer leaving my garden untouched. Come, husband."

31

With a polite smile, Junia said her good-byes. "Lord Richmon, I look forward to hearing the end of your story at dinner."

"It would be my pleasure, Princess Junia." Lady Richmon jerked his arm, turning him towards the palace.

Rufus studied the polite smile on his sister's lips that spread into a malicious sneer when the couple disappeared behind foliage. "You have not seen her in many months. Why are you torturing her now?"

"Because she always bragged she would marry a rich husband and I would be left in the shadows to rot an old woman. I just wanted to show her what kind of man she married."

"Your behavior was inexcusable today. What about Urbane? How does he like being discarded on your revenge trips?"

"I was perfectly polite. I think she made a fine choice for a husband. He's rich and witless. A fine, handsome fool for a husband is easy to mold."

Rufus would not be distracted from his point. "What about Urbane? Do you even care about his feelings?"

"He knows I was just playing around."

Rufus's eyes narrowed, revealing his anger towards his sister.

"Hey, do not judge me. I can do anything I want to."

"Yes, you can. But have you ever thought that what you do hurts others?"

A mischievous grin spread across the princess's lips. "That's why I do it."

Disgusted, her brother turned away, taking a few steps to gather his thoughts. His eyes focused on a delicate flowering bush. When he spoke, his voice was gentle as its petals. "Junia, you are my sister, and I care about you fiercely. Ever since your mother died, I have tried to protect you, shelter you from all the darkness in this world, but I have failed. It tears me apart inside to see what you have become."

"What is that supposed to mean?" sneered Junia. "What have I become?"

The prince faced her with sadness in his eyes. "Another Erastus, with all the ambition and lust for power. You don't care who you destroy—just like our father."

"I am not my father! Do not ever say that again!"

"The worst part is, if you had been born male you would already be plotting how to assassinate Phlegon and me so you could be the next monarch."

"Do not be silly. I would never kill you."

Rufus shook his head sadly. "I see the same rot which controls our father poisoning you, Phlegon, this entire nation. And I am helpless to stop it." For a moment he studied his opened hand then closed it into a fist. "I want to believe there is more to life than petty jealousies, revenge, wars, and religious purges." Dropping his hands, he looked towards the horizon. "There has to be."

The princess looked at her brother as if seeing him for the first time. "I'm starting to believe the latest rumors I heard about you. Are you in love with some poor peasant girl?"

Rufus looked her straight in the eyes but kept his voice neutral. "I am."

Junia sputtered, "It cannot be true. I had the servant who told me fired, believing I was defending your honor. She said you kissed a peddler in downtown Market Square, in front of over a thousand shoppers and traders."

"Even if a million had seen the kiss I would not care. Henna was overwhelmed by the birthday present I gave her so I naturally kissed her—for the first time."

Horrified, the princess spat out, "You're a fool!" then turned to leave.

"And you're a bigger one." Junia whirled to face him. "I chose someone who is not spoiled by political corruption. You are throwing away the one man who can keep up with your temperament."

"I'm not throwing him away! We are doing perfectly fine. I give him prestige. He gives me power in a man's world."

"For how long? Will he put up with your flirtations forever or seek a sympathetic heart in a kinder woman?"

"He will never leave me. I'm a princess."

"With no heart. What a man needs is love, not a woman whose only asset is her body."

Junia lost control of her temper. "How dare you say such things about me! My tour in the army proved I am a great warrior, dedicated and intelligent. I was presented the Medal of Zuzumza, marking me a hero."

Rufus looked at his sister with pity, the look piercing her soul deeper than words ever could. "You might have all that, but you do not have what counts most—love."

Junia felt betrayed by the one person she had trusted her whole life. "It does not exist. Not in you and especially not in our dear father. But, of course, I guess your little peasant girl does have it."

"Henna may only wear plain clothing, but her beauty outshines the fanciest aristocrat. Every day she walks an hour from her village to the city to sell homemade wares because her father is an invalid and her mother has nine kids to tend. She goes through exhaustion and beyond for her family every single day and asks nothing for herself. Her blood runs with truer nobility than any noble I have ever met."

Junia refused to hear more. "I hope you enjoy your marriage with the serf. I am sure our father, during dinner engagements, would love discussing with his lords how you gave up the chance to rule a providence for the opportunity to court a low-born peddler. Everybody across the Empire will be discussing it for years to come." The princess stormed off before he could say another word.

High above the spiraling city of Thorn, Junia leaned against the ancient stone sill of the window seat in her room. For a while she absently watched the tiny moving people and carriages far below as her temper slowly dissipated. People going through their careless lives—and would never amount to anything. In her jewelry box nested the Medallion of Zuzumza beside expensive gold and silver accessories. She was a princess and an accomplished soldier. The power she had craved all her life was hers now. So why did her brother's words haunt her?

You are just like our father. The same father who had her beloved mother killed. Never would she forgive or forget what he did. Never. She had nothing in common with him. Rufus was right about one thing—if she had been born male she would find a way to assassinate her father and oldest brother for their cruelty to her, yet despite her anger she could never harm Rufus. Neither did she understand him. *Why would he prefer his peasant girl above power? Above me?*

"He's a fool," she muttered aloud.

And you're a bigger one, came the memory of her brother's voice. *You are throwing away the one man who can keep up with your temperament.*

Surely Urbane would never leave her. She was his open door to prestige, to power. He was only in the social spotlight because of her. Her betraying mind whispered, *Who is the one that actually wants glamour?* She brushed the idea away. Urbane was nothing without her.

She walked over to her vanity and searched for a hairbrush. Absently, she opened a drawer and spotted a sketchbook and pencils. As a child she had enjoyed drawing until at the age of eleven when she had shown the book to Lina who had laughed at several of her drawings. Junia never drew again. *Why have I not thrown this away?* It was useless to her, part of a childhood best forgotten.

From her open jewel box glittered various medals and ribbons she had won. She had always been competitive, even in childhood. Her fingers traced an image of an ice-skater engraved on a small golden medal. At thirteen she had won this at the annual Winter Sports, though the next year she had only placed second, bested by Lina. As soon as the award ceremony was over, she had thrown the silver medal in the snow and walked away in disgust, never skating again. At least the agility she had developed as a skater had served her well as a swordsman. She picked up the heavy Medallion of Zuzumza. *Lina, I have something that you will never do better than me. Perhaps I could challenge you to a fencing match and accidently kill you.* The idea brought a smile to her lips.

The chamber door opened to admit her lover who turned to the closet without greeting her. Sweetly Junia smiled, "What? No hello kiss?"

Urbane continued flipping through various clothing. "You can always kiss Lord Richmon."

Junia forced light laughter into her voice. "Urbane, you know I was only jesting. I was trying to get under his wife's skin. We are old enemies."

"On the battle field you kill your enemies, not flirt with their spouses."

"You are being silly."

Urbane changed into his work uniform while ignoring her.

"Are you going to dinner tonight?"

He headed for the door.

"Where are you going?"

"What concern is it of yours? Remember you have Lord Richmon to seduce and a marriage to ruin." The heavy door slammed behind him like a steel hunting trap ending the life of the creature trapped in its grip.

Junia just stared at the door. "He's just being silly and will get over it soon."

Why then did fear knot her stomach? A voice whispered through her mind, *There are richer and more powerful fish in the ocean than Urbane.* Yet the thought of life without him left a void inside her. Urbane and Rufus were the only two in the world who were on her side, and she was losing both. Then she would truly be alone.

Seated on the wide windowsill, Junia studied the darkening sky. It seemed a reflection of her own moody soul crushed by the weight of living in a world where love did not exist. Yet her brother had found the allusive emotion in a dirt-poor peasant. How? What was love supposed to look or feel like? The memory of the last time she saw her parents together flashed through her mind. Love had never been an ingredient of their marriage. Had love ever been a part of her relationship with Urbane?

Tears fell on the princess's hand. Angry at her own weakness, Junia quickly brushed them away. In the army, she kept loneliness at bay by focusing on her training and bossing subordinates. The answer for her problems now was to find a new project to put all her energy into—one where Urbane and her would be partners again. Leaning out the window where the last light escaped from the vanishing sun, Junia shouted to the world. "Love does not exist! It never has!"

The words cling to night breezes, whirling against the impermeable castle stone, rising until reaching the ears of a dark, scaly creature hiding in the shadows covering the Claw's balcony. As the harsh words faded, a lustful smile spread across its toothy snout. In the huge, symmetrical chamber behind the fiend, a key turned in the only lock. The creature whirled with a speed that belied its bulk. The gold inlaid door creaked open, admitting two finely dressed nobles. The older, heavyset man moved with boldness, but the lean youth treaded as if on broken glass.

"Welcome, Emperor Erastus and Crown Prince Phlegon," boomed a deep voice, echoing through the lofty chamber.

The prince jumped and vainly examined empty shadows, seeking the speaker. Erastus walked towards a raised dais in the center of the ornamental room and dropped to his knees before it. "Master, my son is of age to finally meet the power behind Gog's glory." The Emperor beckoned his nervous son forward and indicated for him to bow—a new experience for the proud prince.

On his knees, the prince studied the dais, completely bare except for six burning ceremonial torches, yet he knew the chamber was inhabited for he could feel a presence piercing his thoughts, scrutinizing his unprotected secrets and fears. The prince's instinct was to bolt from the room or grab a sword in defense. How could one attack a foe that was invisible? Phlegon swallowed, determined to go through with the initiation, to gain the dark power that his fearless father possessed.

"It is an honor to, uh, meet you," he said to empty air.

"I am here and everywhere," echoed the deep voice. The wall behind the dais seemed to simmer, and light from the torches on the far side of the dais became dimmer, as if a cloud had pass in front of the sun. Phlegon rubbed his eyes to clear his vision, but a dark mist continued to form on the platform. Darker and denser it became, absorbing light around it but reflecting none back. Then the black cloud solidified, forming leathery wings, clawed limbs, a gaping maw, and eyes that could peer into souls. The distorted face smiled at the gawking prince.

"The Ultimate One, I...I presume?" sputtered Phlegon, overwhelmed by the sudden hideousness.

"You presume wrongly. My master is Beelzebub, a name rarely spoken by mortals." Folding its wings, the dark creature studied the human kneeling before it, but Phlegon was unable to return the gaze. "I am Zuzumza, God of War. I am the power of the Gogian Empire, the source of its victories, the provider of its prosperity. I will rule this entire continent one day. Time is irrelevant. You are here to answer only one question. Will you serve me or should I name another as future Emperor?"

Heart racing, the Crown Prince answered, "From infancy I have craved the power only you can give. I was born to rule Gog and am ready to fulfill my destiny."

"I require more than just your desire to rule. To be my Hand, you must give me your soul. Then I will give you wealth, power, and glory beyond your greatest fantasies." The last instinctive fears inside Phlegon were extinguished as an invisible wave of power suddenly surged around the youth, erotic visions danced before the youth's eyes.

Ecstatic from the sensations, Phlegon stood up and walked up the broad steps of the dais towards the waiting god. "My soul I freely give to you, great Zuzumza. Take me."

An insatiable hunger spread across the creature's face as its head bent downward until prince and god were eye-to-eye. For a brief moment a part of Phlegon's mind rebelled, and he could see himself from a distance—scrawny youth inches away from unnatural fiend. But the prince's desire for power vanquished his fear, and he stared into his new master's eyes. The black eyes become mystical pools filling his vision, his mind. Suddenly he found himself high above Blackwall Palace, looking down on the sprawling capital city. Then the landscape began rapidly flashing pass him—rugged Hockquill Mountain Range, vast farmlands of Wheatend, scorching Noable Desert. The hills, swamps, and rivers became a blur as Zuzumza revealed what the continent once had been like and could yet be.

All this I give you to rule in my Master's name, whispered the god into the Crown Prince's mind.

A dark mass appeared on the horizon. At first it was just a thin line, but as the prince drew closer, he realized with a shock that it was an immense mountain range surpassing in size and ruggedness of any he had laid eyes on before. He felt Zuzumza's loathing for what lay beyond the rocky barrier—he also realized this was the one place the god had no power to visit. They flew onward until Phlegon could make out individual trees and crags. Suddenly the human found himself plunging towards the ground at a rapid speed. Instinctively the youth threw up his hands to protect his face, expecting a painful impact. There was only silence. Uncovering his eyes, Phlegon found himself falling in a dismal abyss, varied rock layers flashing past him. A steam of molten rock spewed from a fissure, and the human screamed as he passed through it—but there was no pain.

The prince found himself in the bowels of the Great Abyss—in the past his lips had used its name for a curse. Never would he do so again. Below Phlegon was an ocean of bright lava, broken here and there by jagged islands of varies sizes. Everywhere flew beasts from out of the darkest of nightmares—hideous distorted apparitions of spikes, claws, teeth, multiple pairs of limbs and eyes. Half an hour before, the prince would have been appalled, but intense power surged through him, dissolving all fear. He laughed in ecstasy to behold a sight few mortals had dared to glimpse. Onward his body flew towards a craggy island the size of a small continent. He zoomed lower towards the churning molten ocean, randomly spewing huge, fiery geysers hundreds of feet upward. Human heads and arms reached upward from the boiling sea, screams escaping from misshapen mouths. Phlegon was detached from their plight—until he recognized several faces. His feeling of pity only lasted a moment, for he was detracted by a blackened mountain formed into a fortress with numerous large openings. The nightmarish flying creatures were more concentrated here.

The Crown Prince glided through the largest entrance into an enormous chamber. Half a dozen powerful gods similar to Zuzumza and numerous smaller apparitions occupied the rocky room formed from cooled lava. From the wall itself protruded a massive throne on which sat an immortal being that could only be mighty Beelzebub. Phlegon's feet touched the floor several yards from the gigantic, stone throne embedded with diamonds and blood-red rubies. Beelzebub fixed his intense glaze on the prince, making the human tremble. Then the god turned towards a small, monkey-like fiend perched on an armrest of the throne. The creature lurched itself into the air and flew straight towards Phlegon. It did not turn aside when it reached the mortal, but flew inside the prince, into the seat of his soul. A change came over the Crown Prince's eyes—they became hard and cold like his father's, the last traces of humanity erased.

Coming out of the trance, Phlegon saw Zuzumza's distorted reptilian face only inches away from his own. He felt no repugnance; instead, comradeship filled him as if recognizing one of his own brethren.

"Arise," boomed Zuzumza with an ominous smile. "It is time for Telumza to fall and you to lead the attack."

Phlegon's face mirrored the god's grin. "And Tnias to destroy."

Emperor Erastus had remained quiet, watching intently the attention his son received from their master. Finally, he asked. "How come you have not asked me to lead a campaign in the last decade?"

Eyes of hate pierced through the monarch's soul. "Because you have lost your dedication to me. Now you are satisfied with a full table and ravishing harlots. Enjoy your gluttony in what time you have left. I now have a servant after my own heart who will crush my enemies."

Erastus opened his mouth to say more but shut it again. Jealousy against his own son consumed him.

Chapter Five

Mid-summer Gog declared war on Telumza. Gogians buzzed in surprise since only two seasons had passed since the victory over Galand. Phlegon had several motives for not waiting: Telumza might be caught by surprise, crops could be raided or destroyed leaving the Telumzans with little food for winter, but secretly the Crown Prince was impatient, eager to seize the destiny promised him. It would be his first time to lead a full-scale military operation, and many privately questioned his abilities. Though he had won medals in battle before, rumors always circulated that he had taken credit for subordinates' successes. On the other hand, Prince Rufus had a strong reputation for integrity and clear judgment. Many soldiers were disappointed he had declined to fight this time. Phlegon knew the people favored his brother, and it added fuel to the fire that already burned inside him. He vowed to become the greatest ruler Gog had ever known.

Missing the thrill of battle, Urbane asked for a transfer into his old position of major and Junia came along as one of his lieutenants. Away from the vanities of palace life, the couple's relationship flourished. Once again they worked side by side with one goal—victory for Gog. Neither was content to sit on the sidelines directing troops as Phlegon did. Though Junia had little combat experience when the war started, she soon earned a fierce reputation. With death so near each day, many soldiers held to strong superstitions. When they saw the fiery-eyed princess rushing into the heat of battle—men falling to her right and left but herself always escaping with only superficial injuries—it was whispered that Zuzumza himself fought beside her. Junia's reputation spread, and soon she was leading her own troops into the heaviest battles. Gogian soldiers competed with each other to win a position in the princess's cavalry unit. Junia heeded some of Rufus's advice—her eyes did not stray from Urbane. During the glimpses Urbane could gleam of his lover in the midst of battle, his eyes would shine with pride.

Overlooking the battles from a high position on hills or knolls, Phlegon was upset though Gog was gaining more territory with each battle. His sister and Urbane were becoming too popular with the troops. Hatred ate through his soul as his eyes caught what was invisible to others—beside Junia in every battle fought two demons, one on each side of her. In the heat of battle, far too many enemies near the princess accidentally lost their balance, for a split second exposing vital areas of their bodies. Arrows aimed directly for her missed their mark, and sword thrusts bounced harmlessly off her mail or shield. She was the first to shout Zuzumza's name in victories chants, the first to call on him when the tide turned. Gogian soldiers admired her dedication and fiery spirit. The Crown Prince was not pleased at all.

King Hermes of Telumza knew war was inevitable and had spent years building up his military. The two armies met among the desolate hills of Noable Desert. After several bitter weeks, the Telumzans were forced to fall back, but the determined soldiers used the rugged Badlands to their advantage. Deep natural gullies cut randomly across dry plains, making excellent trenches. The jagged hills and cliffs impeded the Gogian cavalry.

Leading an infantry charge on the right flank of the main attack, Urbane's company scrambled down the steep wall of a gully, hand-to-hand fighting furious. Under cover of dark, Junia had lead the Royal Cavalry, as her squadron was now called, two miles further down the gully where their horses could descend safely. When dawn's first light broke across the sky, Junia signaled the advancement, hoping the timing was right. Their horses thundered through the narrow, pebble-strewn valley. When war cries grew close, the Royal Cavalry pulled out their own weapons and charged into the midst of frenzy battle.

Both Telumzans and Gogians dashed towards the cliff walls to avoid flying hooves. The princess's war stallion crushed a slow moving Telumzan, and her sword struck down several others. The Royal Cavalry left a bloody wake behind it, leaving the Gogian infantry to finish off the dazed enemy. For a brief moment, Junia spotted Urbane, and she saluted him with her bloody sword as the horses pressed onward through the rocky canyon. The valley twisted randomly, occasionally splitting into false ends or joining larger gorges. Junia attempted to keep the cavalry together, constantly moving, for their strength lay in a quick surprise. Mounted soldiers made easy targets for archers positioned high above on the rocky edges of the canyons.

Suddenly Junia reined her horse to a stop. Before her the valley floor rose up steeply, creating a dead end. Before she could give the signal to turn around, a rain of deadly arrows filled the air. Several riders went down immediately, and Junia's horse scream in pain as an arrow pieced its flank. Quickly the Royal Cavalry fled the way it came. Junia tried to regain the front of her unit, but her injured horse lagged behind. With no leader to follow, the riders soon became separated in the chaos of battle. The princess cursed in frustration but was soon too busy fighting for her life to be concerned for her squadron.

Her horse sidestepped to dodge a blow, while Junia aimed for a soldier on her left. Suddenly her mount screamed in terror as a blade sliced through his back leg, hamstringing the magnificent stallion. Junia attempted to jump free from the saddle as the horse fell, but her left leg hung in the stirrups, pinning her under the injured beast. Immediately the man Junia had been combating raised his sword, aiming for her head. Though dazed, Junia instinctively pulled out a dagger from her belt and threw it straight into the leather-clad soldier's chest. Coldly she watched her defeated enemy drop to the ground then she focused on her immediate problem—getting free of the horse. High on adrenaline, Junia's mind registered no pain. She pushed with all her strength against the stallion, but her leg did not budge.

Noticing the horse's head raised, she kicked with all her might, yelling, "Get up, you lazy beast! Get up!"

The wounded animal struggled to regain its footing but fell back down. Those precious seconds were enough for Junia to pull her leg free.

After dragging herself several feet from the threshing animal, she checked hurriedly for broken bones. There was some tenderness, but she did not sense a break. Climbing to her feet, Junia realized the sounds of fighting were moving further away. Eager to rejoin the battle, Junia needed to quickly find Gogian troops and demand a new horse. After recovering her sword and dagger, Junia attempted to climb the ravine's side, but the loose sand skidded her back to the bottom, sending a jolt of pain through her left leg. She had to settle for walking along the dry streambed, ignoring the dead and dying soldiers she passed. Her injured leg began throbbing, but the princess pressed onward.

There was a shout from overhead. Suddenly two soldiers half scrambled, half fell down the cliff face. The Gogian man was quicker to recover his feet. Sword in hand, he stabbed downward but the Telumzan rolled out of the way. Intent on the combat, Junia was slow to recognize the sounds of horses galloping behind her. She turned expecting to see members of her own squadron, but to her horror she realized they were four Telumzans. And they were far too close.

For the first time Junia felt real fear. She had killed too many others in the same fashion not to know she now looked upon the face of her own death. The princess jumped out of the path of the first two horses, just like the third rider predicted. He was ready for her. Though Junia attempted to dodge, his mace slammed into her side, snapping bones. A tormented scream tore from the princess's throat as she fell limp to the ground, her sword thrown several yards away. The horseman turned his mount around and studied the fallen woman. Realizing she was still alive, he dismounted with a lustful gaze in his eyes. He kneeled down and roughly removed her helmet. Her eyes were open, but she was too dazed to move. He bent his head downward to kiss her.

"Wait!" shouted a voice with authority. The horseman glanced around him, seeking the speaker. The Telumzan Junia had earlier seen fall from the ravine wall marched forward. Fresh blood stained his sword from his victory over his Gogian opponent who had also fallen from the cliff above. "I'll take care of her."

For a moment the horseman looked as if he would challenge the contender, but something in his rival's eyes convinced him differently. The horseman laughed. "You won't get much fun out of her. Her god will soon claim her soul." With that the man leaped on his horse, racing after his comrades.

"Not if my god has anything to do with it," mumbled the remaining Telumzan. For a long moment, he looked up towards the edge of the gorge. Junia remained perfectly still except for her right hand slowly slipping her dagger from her belt and hiding it by her side. Still the man looked upward. Junia's vision blurred as she struggled to keep conscious, agonizing pain throbbing through her body. Finally, the man came closer. Junia braced herself, waiting until the right moment for the kill. He squatted beside her and touched her side. The Gogian could not control the scream that escaped her lips.

"Sorry," said the Telumzan in a calm, gentle voice. "I was checking to see how bad you're hurt. I think some of your ribs are broken." Silently Junia studied her enemy. He was young, probably still in his teens, dressed in cracked leather armor—obviously not a noble. He turned his attention to the medical pack around his waist. Instantly Junia plunged her weapon towards his unprotected side.

The blade missed.

Impossible, Junia's mind screamed. Despite her crippled state, her aim had been true, yet the weapon was buried in sand up to its hilt an inch from the man.

Glancing at the dagger, the youth said, "I would advise you not to kill me until we're both out of this dry river bed. You can't get out of here alone in your shape." He gave a hard jerk to free the blade from the packed sand and tossed it across the gorge. Then he dressed her wounds. The pain grew worse causing Junia to fade in and out of consciousness.

"Can you walk?" Junia blinked her eyes, unable to comprehend his words. "Can you stand up?"

"I...I think so." Carefully he helped Junia to her feet. As soon as weight was put on her left foot, pain shot through the leg. Junia groaned and would have fallen if the stranger had not been holding on to her. "I think my left leg is fractured."

"Let's sit you back down then. Hopefully Sunshine is still hanging around up above."

"Sunshine?"

"Yes, that's the name of my horse. First time I saw her, she was standing in a sunbeam suckling her mother. I knew immediately she and I were going to be great companions." Scrabbling up the steep wall, he yelled back, "I'll be back shortly."

For a moment all was quiet until a neigh broke the stillness—presumably Sunshine greeting her master—and the gentle answer of the stranger, his muffled voice filled with affection. The prattle of hooves fading in the distance. Silence reigned across the gorge again. For a few moments all Junia concentrated on was raw pain from her injuries. By shear will she forced her mind to focus on the new problem—she was a prisoner of war. Gogian policy was to kill all enemy officers, but she had no clue what regulations the Telumzan government followed. For a moment she considered escape—but that was futile. The most she could accomplish was to painfully crawl across the rocky ground until the soldier returned and scooped her up like a baby. She could always go after her dagger, but she was unsure where he had tossed it. Her sword had also disappeared.

For a moment she clenched her teeth as dizziness washed over her. Afraid she might lose consciousness before finishing her task, Junia ripped off her officer stripes and other identification, scooping loose sand and small pebbles on top of them. Blurring in and out of reality, Junia never knew if it took minutes or hours before the stranger found a place to descend with his horse into the ravine. Vaguely she remembered stabbing pain as she was lifted onto the animal but recalled little else for many hours.

~~~~~~~~~~

Grimly Urbane stared at the dead war stallion. It was no different from hundreds of other dead beasts—except it had been Junia's horse. Her mounts had been killed out from under her several times before in battle, but always she had quickly bounded back into the fray. In their tent last night, he missed her presence, but the major had presumed she was just busy with another new scheme. At least that was what he told himself. It was not until she was absent from the combined breakfast and officer's meeting that he admitted that something had gone terribly wrong. Urbane asked various comrades when they had last seen his lieutenant. A few remembered seeing Junia the day before thundering pass on her stallion during the battle, but no one had observed her later that day. With a sinking feeling of dread, the major took a small squad to search yesterday's battlefield—fortunately the front had moved a mile southwest.

Now with the sun nearly straight overhead, Urbane stood near his lover's dead horse. In war, death was a routine reality, yet they had both beheld its face many times and lived to tell the tale. Urbane, hardened from countless battles, had even started to believe that the gods protected Junia, but that fantasy was now shattered. Glancing around the ravine, the major noticed a soldier approaching with a thin metal object in his hand. Urbane recognized it immediately.

"I found this dagger, sir, around the next curve in the bend. There is still no sign of the princess's body." The major fixed his subordinate with an angry glare. "Uh, I mean we have not discovered her whereabouts yet."

Urbane gently rubbed his thumb over the royal insignia craved in the dagger's hilt. For a long moment, he studied the blade soiled with a mixture of dried blood and caked sand. Did the blood belong to her or an enemy? "Keep looking. I want every inch of this maze of ditches searched and the plains above. Get as many men from camp as possible."

"Sir, we're in the middle of a war. We can't afford…"

A dangerous look crossed the major's face.

"Yes, sir. I'll get two more squads."

Urbane watched the subordinate dash away. *Where are you Junia? I will not accept death as the answer to your disappearance. I cannot. You are too stubborn to die so easily.* White-knuckled he grasped the blade, squeezing until the soft flesh of his palm was sliced with its sharp edge.

Chapter Six

Sensing her rider was injured, the bay plodded slowly across the grassy plains, carefully choosing the smoothest route. The sun threatened to sink behind the hills of the badlands far to the west before the woman awoke. The man leading Sunshine paused to unfasten a canteen from the saddle then handed it to the injured Gogian.

Revived from the water, Junia surveyed her surroundings. In the distance a shepherd hurried his flock of sheep across rolling hills. Wincing from pain, Junia said, "Where are you taking me?"

"To a village I heard was somewhere this direction. By the way, my name is Matthan Denett."

"Mine's Julie Stuler. Why a village and not your camp?"

The youth paused for a moment before answering. "Because Telumzan POW camps were not created with women in mind. What almost happen to you back in that ravine would happen over and over again—if you don't die from your injuries first."

"How thoughtful of you. Won't you be missed by your captain while you're guarding me?"

Matthan repacked the canteen before answering. "You're not my prisoner. I'm finding someone to care for you then report back to my regiment. When you have regained your health, you can do whatever you like."

The princess laughed at the rescuer's naïveté. "Weeks from now I may be the one who puts a sword through your heart."

"That may be so but not today." Matthan pulled Sunshine's reins and the obedient animal started forward.

The stranger bewildered Junia. "By not turning me over, you betray your own country."

"I answer to a higher power than King Hermes." That was when the princess began to suspect she owed her life to her most loathed enemy—a Tnias.

Following the same direction as the shepherd and his flock, the travelers soon reached a dirt road leading into the small town of Brentwood. As Sunshine and the soldiers plodded down the main street, curious faces glanced towards Junia's armor, quickly identifying her as Gogian. Seeking aid, Matthan tried to make eye contact

45

with passing individuals, but the townspeople averted their faces. Reaching the edge of town, Matthan paused and glanced around, uncertain. Junia found herself staring at a shrine on the far side of the road. Simply designed, the structure was created from rough-hewed rocks. It was large enough for over a hundred to gather inside and had several decorative flowering bushes along its sides. Hatred raged through Junia, flashbacks burning in her mind of dozens of sanctuaries of Yahweh she had helped to incinerate.

Matthan missed the Gogian's dark expression for his head was tilted towards the sky, eyes closed. For a long time his body did not move, but a peaceful expression crossed his face. When he finally opened his eyes, the first sight that greeted him was a bouncy teenager exiting the shrine, an empty basket in hand.

"Excuse me," said Matthan. The young woman turned in his direction. "I'm looking for a place to keep a wounded soldier."

Smiling, the maiden drew near. "Wow! You're one of our guys, right?"

"Yes, but I have an injured soldier here who is not." The teenager came within a foot of the horse and studied Junia carefully. Their eyes met and Junia shuddered from a sudden inner coldness. Dealing with one Tnias at a time was bad enough.

"My mother may be able to help," replied the maiden. "She's kind of a midwife, doctor, and vet all rolled into one. There are no real doctors out here because Brentwood is considered too far from civilized life."

As the teenager led them through the village, she chatted non-stop, revealing much about her family. Danielle Brick was the oldest of four siblings. She had been visiting the sanctuary to deliver a fresh fruit pie her mother Rose had baked as a gift to the ecclesiastic's family. Her father had fought many years ago in a war against Achaia, lost one leg due to poor medical treatment, and was now a fine carpenter. Finally, she halted in front of a small wooden house with several flowerbeds in front and a large garden in the back.

"This is my home." While Matthan helped Junia dismount, Danielle dashed onto the porch yelling, "Mother, we have guests. One is injured."

A stern, dark-haired woman in her mid-thirties emerged from the house, wiping flour-covered hands on her apron. "Who's hurt now?"

Matthan smiled respectfully while propping up Junia. "I'm a soldier of the Telumzan army, madam, and this woman is a Gogian wounded in battle."

Frowning, the midwife studied the enemy of her people. Though uneasy about the situation, Rose said, "Bring her in."

Junia was laid on a bed in a small room and quickly lost consciousness from searing pain when the bandages were removed. Rose grimaced as she viewed the raw mass of open wounds created when the mace's spikes had struck Junia's side.

At first Danielle hovered nearby to retrieve varies supplies, but with supper needing to be cooked, she gave up the aide position to her eleven-year-old brother Ben.

As a splint was being made for her leg, Junia awoke. Though groggy, she menacing said, "Why are you trying to keep me alive?"

"Because Yahweh commands us to love our enemies." Busy wrapping gauze around the injured leg, Rose glanced towards her son. "Ben, I need cutting shears from the kitchen." The boy hurried to obey.

"That's the stupidest advice I have heard from a god yet."

"That commandment is keeping you alive, so I wouldn't complain too much if I were you."

"You serve a pathetic excuse of a god. Tells you to aid the very ones killing you while he frolics with the other gods in the Third Firmament. I think he's getting the better deal."

Rose forced calmness she did not feel into her voice. "Yahweh doesn't live in the Third Sky or whatever you call the home of you mythical gods. Tnias believe there is only One True God and he created all things in the beginning." As Rose wrapped the leg, she talked out of habit to calm patients. "All other gods are either human fabrications or Yahweh's own creations which turned evil. Yahweh loved the people he created but was sadden that many fell into the same darkness that consumed Beelzebub and his followers. So he came to Tanlep and lived among humans, sharing their pains and sorrows, helping as needed. Then certain leaders became jealous because the common people loved him, so they put him to death."

"Mortals killed a god? Does not sound like much a god to me. Ow!" Junia clenched her teeth in pain.

"Sorry," the midwife apologized. "He descended into the bowels of the Great Abyss, fought against Beelzebub. Yahweh won then created Shalom, Land of Peace, where no evil may enter."

"Until all the Tnias are killed and the Timbrel Mountains collapse. I know that part of the story. Ouch! In the name of Zuzumza, do you enjoy torturing me?"

"Relax. I'm almost finished." Rose kept her voice even, but her heart pounded in anger. How dare the heathen soldier use sacrilegious oaths in her own house. "Sleep for now. I'll bring you supper when it's done."

It was a relief to emerge into the inviting atmosphere of the family room. Danielle was setting the table for a late supper and chatting with Matthan as if they were old friends. On the floor near the Telumzan soldier sat nine-year-old Watt, thoroughly absorbed in a story the stranger was telling. Nearby stood Ben with scissors in hand, equally engrossed.

As the bedroom door shut behind Rose, all eyes in the room turned towards her. "The Gogian has a fractured leg, several cracked ribs, and a severely battered side. With the trek here, it's a miracle her lung wasn't pierced from a bone fragment. But her worst ailment is her black soul."

"I agree," said the newcomer.

"Matthan's been a Tnias almost his whole life," spoke Danielle. "He heard Yahweh tell him to help her."

Walking towards the washbasin Rose asked, "But why her? With hundreds of soldiers dying on the battlefield today, why help her?"

Matthan shrugged his shoulders. "I don't know. It's just that when I saw that soldier about to…kill her, an inner voice told me to save her."

Danielle nodded her head. "Yahweh must have a special plan for her. Maybe while her body heals, we can help her soul to heal."

Keeping her face away from the youngsters, Rose pretended to be busy with last minute supper preparations. Out of the corner of her eye, she watched lighthearted Danielle, so full of life and good intentions, naïve to the horrors that lurked beyond quiet Brentwood. Rose was not about to let the amoral stranger sleeping in the guest room destroy the happiness of her family. Turning around, the mother asked, "Where's your father?"

Ben answered, "He's on the front porch carving the horse for Lunen."

Outside Rose paused to watch her youngest daughter give various tools to her father as he needed them. Petals was like any typical five year old, loving to mimic older siblings and parents. Sitting on a bench he had made several years back, Jon carefully brought alive the details of the animal's mane. Rose admired her husband as he put life into dry wood. Before the Achaian war they had planned to be farmers, as both their families were. All their plans had been laid out—the dream house they would build down the road from Jon's parents' ranch, the animals and crops they would raise, children dashing everywhere. But their dreams were shattered when Jon came back from war only a shadow of the man he once had been. For nearly a year he withdrew from even his closest friends, but Rose stayed beside him. Her medical skills developed as she attended the stomp that had once been her husband's knee. Despite Jon's angry altitude, ecclesiastic Simeon visited regularly and eventually Jon discovered peace through Yahweh.

Spotting her mother, Petals said, "Mommy, the horse is almost finished! Daddy says the stranger is staying. Can I see her?"

"No!" Both mother and daughter were startled by the sharp edge in Rose's voice. More gently, she commanded, "Go in and help your sister set the table." Cheerfully Petals complied.

"So what's bothering you? The wounded soldier?" Jon could read his wife like a book.

Rose sighed and settled on the bench beside her husband, rubbing her hand across the large wooden animal. Soon it would be a rocking horse for farmer Lunen's son. "It's shaping up real fine." She was quiet for a while. "I think we need to find another place for the Gogian to stay."

"That won't be easy since you're the only one within miles experienced enough to care for her. Why do you want to move her?"

"I don't want her around our kids. She used such blasphemous language. And the hatred in her eyes—there is no telling what crimes she has committed. I don't want our kids subjected to that."

Gently Jon brushed his hand across Rose's chin. "Our children are stronger than you think. Are we not commanded to help strangers? If we turn the injured Gogian out of our home who would take her in? We can't just leave her to die on the streets. That would be blood on our hands."

His wife looked towards the empty road in front of their house. "She's not just a Gogian but part of the Red Army."

Silence built between the couple, both thinking about Rose's sister. A decade ago Zara and her family moved to Achaia to build a sanctuary of Yahweh. Six years later Gog invaded the country, and Rose never saw her sister again. Rose spent weeks volunteering in refugee camps before discovering someone who could tell her what happened to Zara's family. In the middle of the night the family had been dragged out of their home, forced to watch the shrine burned to the ground, then the children were murdered in front of their parents. Lastly the couple was killed. Over the last few years, Rose sometimes suffered nightmares of the scene, watching her nieces and nephews murdered, herself helpless to save them—sometimes in the dream it was her own children who died.

"Rose, Matthan seems a dedicated man with a good heart. He believes Yahweh wanted this woman's life spared. He was directed to this house after he prayed for guidance. If Yahweh has given her to us to help, how can we refuse?"

Unable to answer, Rose held her tongue. Danielle's voice broke the silence. "Time to eat! Come and get it!" Standing up, Rose handed Jon his walking cane. As they walked into the house, Jon used the cane for balance as his wooden peg leg tapped against the floor.

The late supper was jovial with Matthan jesting with the children and swapping tall tales with Jon. The children roared with laughter, Danielle the merriest of all. After the meal, the family moved to the living room where the newcomer shared his own stories of faith on the battlefront. Rose noticed her oldest daughter's eyes shining brightly as the teen clung to every word. Only a year or two younger than Matthan, Danielle was of marriageable age but had shown no interest in anyone—until now. Jon pulled out his guitar, and soon the house was filled with music and dancing. He started out with fast-paced folk tunes, later changing to slower worship songs. Rose peacefully watched her family, the bloody war seeming a continent away.

The next morning the family waved their sad good-byes to Matthan as he headed back towards his regiment. Though he had only stayed one night, he seemed part of their family. Petals studied Danielle's mournful face. "Daddy, is Matthan going to die?" the child asked somberly.

"He's in Yahweh's hands, sweetie. We don't know what will happen, but we must always trust Yahweh. He loves us very much and knows what's best for us."

The child pondered his answer. "Every night I will ask Yahweh to protect him."

"Yes, do that. And I will too."

As the words faded Petals was once again a child, dashing off to play with her brothers. Envious, Rose watched, wishing her fears could vanish so easily.

~~~~~~~~~

The two boys dashed by Jon, eager to explore the dusty aisles of the general store. Leaning on his cane, the carpenter hobbled to the counter where two men were in a deep discussion about plows. Both men nodded to Jon.

"I think I'll order that new design. If it's half as good as the company claims, I could plant at least ten more acres next spring—if it arrives when promised," spoke Bentic. Though rough-looking from a life of hard work, the farmer, who was a childhood friend of Jon, retained a good sense of humor.

From behind the counter, the storeowner responded, "I would offer a guarantee, but with the war, delays are inevitable. And the price of the plow has doubled since the government started demanding almost all iron ore for weapons." Ozias was short and stocky—and the richest man in Brentwood. His wealth had earned him the position of town mayor.

Normally even-tempered, Bentic slammed his fist against the wooden counter top. "I knew I should have bought it last year, but with the baby sick I thought..." The farmer's voice faded as he studied his fist. "Well, it doesn't matter. Looks like I won't be getting that plow this year either. Curse this damnable war." For a moment the other two men remained silent. Jon understood his friend's frustration. He knew Bentic's desperate struggle to keep his large family fed and clothed. Located in the foothills of the badlands, the farmer's land was rocky. A better plow meant greater acreage, more crops to sell, and food for his children to eat.

Ozias broke the silence. "Well, if you do change your mind, put your order in quickly before all the plows in stock are gone." The mayor turned towards the carpenter. "Jon, rumor says you have a Gogian soldier in your house."

"That's right," responded Jon cautiously. "One of our soldiers found her wounded and brought her to my house to be nursed back to health."

"And then you're turning her over to our government?" inquired Ozias.

"No. We're helping her out of kindness as Yahweh asks us to do."

Both listeners were shocked. Ozias said, "This is war—not an exercise for your religious beliefs."

"Yahweh's word says whatever you do to a stranger, you do to him."

"She's the enemy!"

"She's a human with a lost soul."

Bentic was calmer. "Jon, I respect your intentions, but think about what you are doing. If she is allowed to just walk away from here, she may come back with a raiding party and burn this whole village to the ground."

"I know that. But if we could change one—just one Gogian, then there might actually be hope for this chaotic world we live in."

The farmer reluctantly nodded. "My prayers will be with your family. You're going to need them. Never would I put my family through what you're doing."

As Jon waved goodbye to his friend, the carpenter silently said his own prayers for his family. Behind the counter Ozias darkly watched the one-legged man limp out of the store.

~~~~~~~~~

Waking hours were torturous to Junia. To shift her weight meant a battle against intense pain—even breathing hurt. But sleep brought no relief. She was haunted by nightmares often depicting battle scenes where her body would not obey, leaving her helpless as a baby as enemies attacked. Sometimes Junia's real body would attempt to dodge an imagery blow, and she would awake from the movement in throbbing agony. Questions constantly played across her mind. Was Urbane alive or had he been struck down in battle? Would he still be searching for her? Frustration built inside the princess. The war was passing her by while she lay helpless day after day tended by her loathed enemy. Anger built like a volcano, exploding against anyone who dared to enter the tiny sick room that had become her prison. Rose was careful to protect her family from being exposed to the stranger, but sometimes she was called away on emergencies. Then it was up to Danielle to care for Junia.

On one of the last warm days in autumn, Danielle entered the room carrying a tray of food, carefully shutting the door behind her. "Hello. I hope you like potato soup because that's what I brought you. I've baked an apple pie but it is still cooling."

Junia watched as Danielle sat the tray on a table then pushed back the curtains covering the window.

"It's so beautiful outside today."

"Why are you so damn cheerful?"

Danielle shrugged her shoulders. "I guess it's a gift from Yahweh."

"Would you not have preferred wealth or power? Your father is a feeble cripple. Why does your mother keep him around?"

With angelic patience the teen answered, "Because she loves him. We all do. My mother nursed my dad back to heath when he lost his leg in the Achaian war, and now he's a carpenter making beautiful things."

"Which will become ashes when the Red Army burns down this town."

Danielle changed the subject. "Is your father still alive?"

"Unfortunately, yes. Would you like to join me in a dance on his grave when he finally croaks? It should be quite fun."

The teenager looked away, shocked by the disrespect. She moved the table and tray closer to the bed before speaking again. "I'm sorry your life's been so bad."

Kindness enraged the princess more. "And I'm sorry your dad's still alive, but we can fix that problem, you know. It's not hard at all. I've killed many, and the best part is deciding how to do it. With your dad I suggest…"

Danielle turned and walked out of the room without a word. From the couch Petals glanced worriedly at her sister's dark expression, but the teen continued onward until she was alone in the kitchen. Inside she trembled, appalled by the evil she saw in the soldier.

Yahweh, help me. It's so hard to see the good in her. I don't know what to say to show her that you care about her. For a few minutes Danielle, with eyes closed, rested her arms on the back of a wooden chair. Peace slowly stilled her fear. *Thank you, I understand. She can't understand love unless she first feels it. Help my family and me to give that love to her.*

~~~~~~~~~

Far too soon the weather turned cool, and farmers worked dawn to dust gathering their last crops before snow fell. The cuts and bruises on Junia's side healed but her broken bones were slower to mend. On the first warm afternoon in over a week, Jon and Danielle carried their patient outside, sitting her in a rocking chair. Rose was not pleased with the arrangement. She found various odd jobs in the yard requiring her attention, not letting the Gogian out of her sight for a moment. The younger kids played while Jon craved on the porch. Danielle left to visit a friend.

Junia rocked quietly, pretending not to care that she was outside for the first time in two weeks. Inwardly she savored the fragrance of late blooming flowers, the gentle breeze ruffling her hair. It was strange that the finest gardens on the entire continent were outside her window in Thorn, yet she had scarcely noticed them. Now she was grateful for a few late blooming orangebells. Still, she felt no peace for the interaction between Jon and his children troubled her. For hours at a time, Ben diligently worked on his own carvings, Jon gently coaxing, Ben stubbornly keeping at it until he got the problem right. Junia kept her head turned from the intimate interaction between father and son. They possessed a bond she and her father never had, and the scene stirred up bitter memories.

Petals dashed onto the porch with a handful of wildflowers that she held out to Jon. He hugged her then placed the flowers in a vase on a shelf holding various finished cravings. A few minutes later Petals was back with more flowers—this time as a gift for Junia.

"I tried to find brown ones to match your eyes, but all the brown ones I saw were dead. But the blue ones would look nice in your black hair." The child sweetly prattled on.

Surprised, Junia slowly twirled the flowers in her hand, remembering the last time she had received a gift with no strings attached—the wooden horse necklace Rufus had given her as an attempt to cheer her up over the loss of her mother. "Um, thanks. They're lovely flowers."

A beautiful smile danced across the child's face. She pulled up a stool and chatted about everything from a boy's missing tooth to the cute puppies down the street. The princess listened awkwardly, unsure how to react. All the insults she had been so quick to use on adults were useless to her now; instead, she was drawn by the innocence of the child. Had she once been like Petals? Seeing the world as a large playground, full of curiosity and happiness, eager to please others? Realizing her own childhood had ended too quickly in grief, Junia felt pity for herself. After her mother's death she had never tasted the simple joy of being alive again.

"Petals!" shouted Rose, desiring to find an excuse to send her daughter away from Junia. "Will you run these flowers to Widow Tubbs?" The child sprung up, eager to comply.

As the princess watched the five-year-old dash across the street, golden hair waving in the gentle breeze, an image of another child entered Junia's mind—a kid screaming in terror, running pass the bodies of her dead family, a Gogian soldier chasing, sword crashing down on the blond curls of the scared child. Junia shook her head, pushing back the dark memory. Never had she considered killing Tnias as wrong, but now she wondered why innocent children were slaughtered. They were moldable and could be taught to serve Zuzumza.

Jon's cheerful voice pulled Junia from her dark thoughts. "Petals looks just like her mom when Rose was that age. Those were the days. At the age of seven, I asked her to marry me."

Curious, Junia looked in his direction. "What did she say?"

The one-legged man laughed. "She ate the candy ring I gave her then said, 'Not if you are the last boy on Tanlep.' How things have changed. Now she's the mother of our four children." Warmth sparkled in his eyes.

Junia turned her attention away toward the flowerbed. If her father had been like Jon, she would have grown up a totally different woman.

An elderly couple, which had been walking down the street, entered the yard through the gate. "Good to see you, Simeon," greeted Jon.

The lady stopped to talk with Rose, but the tall man came onto the porch and leaned against a railing. "Good to see you, too." Simeon turned to Junia. "And this must be Julie. I've heard a lot about you and been eager to make your acquaintance."

Junia stiffen, uncomfortable with his friendliness

"Simeon presides over our sanctuary in town," explained Jon.

"There are no sanctuaries in Gog," said Junia.

"I know," responded the ecclesiastic. "I was born in Gog. Spent my youth hunting and fishing in Loken Forest." He noticed the sudden interest that flashed through the woman's eyes. "It is a beautiful, wild country with large sections still unspoiled by civilization, but its long history is built upon blood. Have you noticed the nobles' hunger for power at the expense of the common folk?"

An ironic smile crossed Junia's lips, but she kept silent.

Jon cut into the discussion. "Simeon is the only person I've ever met who has seen the city of Agape."

Surprised at the bold statement, the princess studied the elderly man reclining comfortably against the porch railing. Junia had grown up hearing stories about the impossible city. Agape supposedly was the home of Yahweh, an immense gold city hundreds of square miles across with lofty towers so high that they pierced the clouds. The wildest tales claimed it glowed brighter than the sun in broad daylight. At elite Gogian parties, nobles mocked the city, using it as an illustration of the ridiculous beliefs of Tnias. Now a gray-haired man claimed to have seen the myth with his own eyes.

Keeping her voice casual, Junia asked, "So what did this great city look like?"

The old man's face lit up. "Beauty beyond description. Night or day its brightness can be observed from anywhere in the nation of Shalom. And Yahweh's presence can be felt everywhere—such peace. Infinite love." Eagerness and longing filled Simeon's eyes. "If you saw the city just once, your life would never be the same again."

Some hidden part of Junia craved to see the same vision Simeon possessed. Instead, she forced mocking laughter into her voice. "The next thing you'll be telling me is that beings of light fly from this city."

"Yes, they do," the Tnias replied seriously.

"So why didn't you enter this city of your dreams?"

"Because it wasn't time yet. Yahweh had work for me to do. He is pleased for his people to live in Shalom for a time, but he sends many to the lands beyond the Timbrel Mountains to tell others about what they have experienced."

"Your god is cruel to wave this city of destiny in your face then send you away."

"On the contrary, Yahweh is love. He always has our best interests at heart."

"By giving you a ton of rules to control you—don't sleep around, be nice to those who curse you, don't deny him at the expense of your own life. You are weak slaves to this god. In Gog we are the masters, doing as we please."

"Are you happy?"

Junia was taken aback by the question. "Of course."

"In the stillness of the night, do you know peace?"

Patience at an end, the princess wished she could physical walk away from the conversation. "Zuzumza is more powerful than Yahweh."

"If that is so, why can't Zuzumza enter Shalom?"

"He will—the day the last Tnias lies in his own pool of blood."

Chapter Seven

Nightmares tore through Junia's mind that night. Burning buildings surrounded her, turning the night sky a haunting orange. Looking down, Junia observed that she was equipped in full leather armor, her right hand tightly gripping her sword. Screaming people raced pass in panic, pursued by Gogian soldiers. The princess had lived through such scenes many times before.

"Lieutenant, we await your orders," barked a voice from behind.

Junia turned and saw a line of shabby prisoners in chains. Moving with authority, the lieutenant marched up to the first Tnias. Two guards held the captive tightly as Junia ran her sharp blade across his throat. Even as he fell, gasping, she stoically moved to the next prisoner, repeating her actions. Down the line she went until only one Tnias cowered before her. The princess raised her weapon, only to hesitate as her eyes met those of a blond-haired child. The girl's frightened eyes begged for help. Suddenly the child's face wavered, and Junia took a step back in shock, realizing she now looked on the face of Petals. The five year old's eyes pleaded for mercy.

"Kill the Tnias," commanded a soldier standing beside Junia.

Automatically the lieutenant raised her weapon, but again the child's face shimmered, her hair darkening. Horrified Junia's hand froze in mid-air—the child's face was her own.

"Kill her!" shouted the soldier.

"I...I can't."

"Do it!"

"No! She's me." Junia lowered her sword.

The soldier roughly pushed his commander aside, drawing his own weapon. Junia lunged for him and found herself falling, falling endlessly. At first there was only foreboding darkness. Then faces of the dead—some she had watch die and others she had killed with her own hands—flashed around the princess. Eyes from conquered soldiers glared in hatred at their victor. Others screamed or laughed silently. Flesh melted from faces, skulls zooming towards her with their mouths open in hideous laughs. Junia screamed, throwing up a hand to protect her face.

Looking downward Junia realized the bottom of the abyss consisted of molten lava boiling angrily. In panic she attempted to swim upward in the air, but nothing could stop the downward plunge. Her nostrils were attacked by the foul odor of sulfur. Heat singed her body. Yet the distance to the fiery lake did not change. Mocking faces grew thicker around the frantic woman, and bony fingers pointed in accusation. Through the crowd of hatred, a man appeared with a face that literally glowed with gentle love. He held out a hand beckoning Junia to him. Looking into his eyes, the princess forgot the faces, forgot all the evil she had committed, forgot the pain and hatred she felt towards her family. For one moment her soul found indescribable peace. Then the ghastly faces swooped closer, blocking her view of the shiny man. The boiling lava became too close. Hideous demons flew upward, grinning hungrily.

Screaming Junia bolted upright in bed, body covered in sweat. Her mending ribs sent stabbing pain through her side. The door flew opened as Rose hastily entered. Seeing the wild look of terror in the invalid's eyes, the midwife's motherly instinct took over. She sat on the edge of the bed and put an arm around Junia.

"Shh….shh. It was only a nightmare. All's well now, honey."

Junia shook Rose's arm off. "I don't need your pity! I've killed a hundred Tnias and will kill a thousand more. Go save someone who still has a soul."

The midwife stood up, uncertain what to do. "You have a soul, and Yahweh loves you."

"I don't need your cushy answers."

"No, who you need is Yahweh."

"Yeah, I need him like a noose around my neck."

"You're already trapped. The only way to freedom is through him."

A sneer darkened the princess's face. "I hate Yahweh. I hate you. I hate my family. My father, mother, and siblings. Does that make you happy?"

Angrily Rose opened her mouth, but closed it before she said something she would regret later. She walked out of the room without a backward glance, leaving Junia to sulk in her misery.

~~~~~~~~~

Chill wind rattled window shutters. Thick clouds blocked the sun's warming rays. Utter loneliness suffocated Junia as she lay trapped in the tiny bedroom that had been her prison for three weeks. Though her body was on the mend, Junia's soul knew no peace. She had far too many hours to do nothing but ponder life—an occupation she had long avoided by emerging herself in revenge plots and war strategies. Living with a close, caring family forced the princess to ponder what was lacking in her own life. She attempted to divert her tormented thoughts by planning her escape from Brentwood. Before the first snow fell, she would simply sneak out the front door at night, steal a horse, and make her way back to the Red Army's camp—not that the Bricks would care if she left.

Danielle dashed into the room. "Guess what, Julie! You would never believe it! Matthan wrote us. See, it's right here." The happy teenager waved a wrinkled letter in the air, and plopped down on the bed before Junia could react. "He says Yahweh is keeping him safe in the midst of battles. He sees miracles every day."

"And deaths," cut in the invalid.

Ignoring Junia's pessimism, Danielle continued, "He was able to guide several soldiers in giving their souls to Yahweh. And look right here," the teen excitedly pointed at the letter. "He writes, 'If I die tomorrow, I know the cost of my life is worth the treasure of these souls.' Have you ever met a man with such dedication?"

"Yes, my father to Zuzumza."

"Oh, Julie," Danielle reprimanded. "I wish I possessed the faith Matthan does."

Junia laughed. "What's this? You serve the same god he does. Is that not the same faith?"

The teenager puzzled over the statement for a moment. "I guess you're right. Thanks, Julie. Sometimes you have insight I can't see."

The Gogian's mouth opened in astonishment at the turn of events. "Thank me? I don't understand you at all. Every curse I say you turn into a damn compliment."

"It's because I care about you. I want you to know I'm your friend. Whenever you need someone to talk with, I'll listen—no matter what it's about."

"Even about guys?" A dangerous gleam flickered in Junia's eyes.

"Sure."

"Aright. I'll give you some tips about how to please Matthan."

"Please Matthan?"

"You want to make him yours, don't you?"

"I…uh…never really thought about it."

Junia was a cat playing with her prey. "Come on, the way you talk about him all the time? 'Oh, Matthan. Have you ever met such a man?' It's written all over your face that you want him."

Embarrassed that her heart could so easily be read, Danielle turned red-faced but held her tongue.

"If you want him, you have to know how to please a man. For starters, you need to show some flesh. Guys like that—it's what turns them on."

Hastily Danielle stood up and headed towards the door. "I have to cook supper."

Junia pretended her feelings were hurt. "You said I was your friend, and we could talk about anything."

Pausing at the door, Danielle glanced back. "I am your friend. I will be here when you need me, but I can see now is not that time."

As the teenager left the room, a malice grin spread across the Gogian's lips.

~~~~~~~~~

Rose wearily walked through town towards her house. The birth she had just aided had been a difficult one. The child was premature, not ready to face the harsh world. It was doubtful the child would live through the night. The infant's plight added to Rose's own feelings of hopelessness. The whole world was in chaos, and she worked hard to keep her home a safe haven, protecting her family from darkness. Then the Gogian came. The spiteful words Julie had spoken last night ate at Rose.

Passing the sanctuary, Rose entered on a whim. Hearing a visitor, Simeon cheerfully called a greeting from his tiny office. The midwife settled into a wooden chair across from the elderly man. For a few minutes they chatted about how the weather would affect local farmers. As Rose slowly relaxed, she spoke about her day.

Simeon listened then said, "I'll visit the Renkins later today. We must not give up hope. Tell me, Rose, how is your visitor doing?"

If it had been anyone else, Rose would have shrugged the question off with, "Everything's fine." But this was Simeon. Near tears, Rose described the events of last night. "I can't take it anymore. She keeps pushing and probing. Never in all my life have I met someone so venomous. Her poison is worse than a viper's."

"As a teen, I believed the same as Julie. There are two things Gogians are taught from birth: obedience to the Emperor and loyalty to the gods. Since we Tnias claim their gods are false, they see Tnias as traitors and heretics belonging to a caste lower than animals."

The midwife was not reassured. "I can't cope with her hatred. She should not be in my house."

"How does the rest of your family feel?"

"Jon is extremely patient. Danielle sees Julie as her mission in life. I keep Petals, Ben, and Watt away from her. They don't know what evil is."

Simeon leaned back in his wooden chair. *Yahweh, give me wisdom,* he prayed. "Rose, do you believe Yahweh has the power to change people?"

Rose looked out the window for a minute before answering. "I know the answer I'm supposed to say is 'Yes,' but it's easier to say the words than believe them." She looked back towards the gray-haired man. "Every time I look into Julie's cold eyes, I see my sister. I hear the screams of my nieces and nephews as they are slaughtered again and again in front of me. Last night Julie boasted of how many Tnias she has killed then claimed she would take more lives. How am I supposed to love a monster like that?"

"There are no easy answers. I wish I knew the perfect words which would suddenly wipe away all your grief." Simeon opened a worn leather-bound book. In Gog it was a death sentence to possess the Word of Yahweh. "We are told, Rose, to forgive seventy times seven. Not over a lifetime but each day."

"She kills Tnias!"

"She is misled, raised in a land of darkness. She may be just as lost and frighten as you and I once were. This is her first glimpse of real love, and she doesn't know how to handle it."

"Even if she was a Tnias, I don't know if I could forgive her."

"Not in your human heart. You must draw from a higher power."

"I pray to Yahweh numerous times a day."

"But do you ask him for help to forgive and love Julie?"

Rose looked again towards the window. "No, I guess I haven't." A bitter smile crossed her lips. "When my sister died, I asked Yahweh to send fire from the sky to destroy Gog. Instead, he sent a Gogian to my house. It's much easier to hate than to love."

"Would you like to talk with Yahweh now about how you feel?"

With trembling lips, Rose nodded her head. With heads bowed, Simeon clasped both her hands in his wrinkled ones. The midwife's lips moved silently, murmuring words that seem to hang heavily in the air. Finally she realized that her words would never fly to Yahweh if she was not honest. Looking deep inside herself, Rose realized hidden anger burned in her heart against her god. *Yahweh, why did you not rescue my sister's family? Why?*

A peaceful presence filled the room and a memory stirred in her mind of Petals asking her father if Matthan would die. He answered, *He's in Yahweh hands, sweetie. We don't know what will happen, but we must always trust him. He loves us so very much and knows what's best.* Letting go of the anger that had poisoned her heart for many years, Rose felt a new peace fill her soul. Tears ran down her cheeks.

~~~~~~~~~~

With her body healing, Junia restlessly hobbled about the house, to the delight of the three younger children. Though Rose kept a close lookout, she did not interfere as the children directed dozens of questions towards the battered soldier. At first, the Gogian responded with short answers, but their innocent curiosity weaved through her tough outer core. Soon she was entertaining them with humorous stories. In return they talked eagerly about the coming Festival of Peace—the biggest celebration of the year. With the entire town at the square, the princess realized the festival would be the perfect day to leave—or escape, depending on how one looked at it.

Many visitors came to the Bricks house, but almost all of them ignored the Gogian—or pretended to. Out of the corner of their eyes, the villagers were always watching, never trusting. Feeling the same way, Junia avoided the townspeople at all cost. Simeon and his wife Sarah were the only ones who purposely sought her out, visiting at least twice a week. Though the princess always responded tartly to their questions, she secretly found the conversations intriguing.

On warmer days, the Gogian sometimes sat on the porch and watched Jon carve. Perhaps it was the peace of the outdoors that drew her or curiosity about the one-legged man.

One day the carpenter turned to her, holding out a finished carving. "Do you remember what this piece of wood looked like before I started carving it?"

"Yeah, it was a dirty, gnarly stump. I wondered why you didn't burn it in the hearth."

"When I looked at it, I didn't see the outside, I saw its heart and its potential." Jon smiled, waving his free hand at the carving. "Now look what it has become." The magnificent piece consisted of a flying eagle, wings outspread with small mountains at the base creating the illusion of distance. The odd grain patterns enhanced the many curves of the piece, making it worthy of a king's mantel.

"Our lives are similar to this piece of wood. People see the outside—repulsive and misshapen—but the master carver sees the heart. He cuts away the debris. Sometimes the cuts are deep and painful, but when the master carver is finished, a masterpiece is created which can bring joy into other's lives."

Junia was quiet, knowing he was referring to her.

He handed the piece to her. "Here. It's yours now."

Junia's mouth opened in surprise. Jon had spent days craving the figure, and the profit it would fetch at the market was needed for his family. "I can't take it."

"Too late. I already carved your name on the back."

The Gogian rubbed her fingers alone the smooth curves of the eagle, remembering how ugly the wood had originally looked. Was it possible that she could be transformed as it had been? At elite parties she had dressed in ravishing outfits, but clothing could not hide the ugliness lurking inside her. She had everything: power, prestige, wealth, and a handsome lover. Yet something was missing. The Bricks' house was not made from marble nor had gold statues and rich tapestries decorating the walls, but they had love—and it made their family richer than the Emperor himself.

~~~~~~~~~

Junia stared out of a frosty windowpane, staring at the newly fallen snow. Last night's storm had left three new inches. Children played, throwing snowballs and chasing each other. Youths helped with preparations for the coming Festival of Peace, talking eagerly of who they hoped to dance with. Townspeople strolled down the snowy streets carrying packages of gifts and food. Everyone seemed happy, but Junia knew it was an illusion. Despite the anticipation for the celebration, a shadow lingered over Brentwood. Behind smiles crept fear—the latest disheartening news from the battlefront warned that the Gogians were pushing further into Telumzans' ancient homeland.

The princess had planned to escape tonight while most of the townsfolk would be at the square, but the hidden sun hindered her plans. With the snow not melting, an angry owner—or a posse—could easily track the horse she would need to steal. With the trip delayed yet again, frustration built inside Junia. She should be back on the frontlines, preparing for the latest battle, not here in the den of her enemies pretending to be a commoner. What was Urbane doing right now? Searching for her? No, probably arguing with General Tryphena about battle tactics. The image of her handsome, calm lover standing up to arrogant, boastful Tryphena brought a smile to Junia's lips.

"Oh, I wish you would come, Julie." Danielle studied herself in a full length mirror which reflected a slim teen dressed in a lacy white dress and chestnut hair pulled tightly into a bun. "You will have so much fun. There's more food than a king could eat, and the dancing is divine…"

"I have not healed enough for dancing."

"There's still good food, and people you've never met."

"And I do not want to meet them."

Unsatisfied with her hair, Danielle loosened several locks to create a braid. "Julie, tonight is a celebration of peace, held for centuries in honor of Yahweh's promise. Three millennium ago he created Shalom, promising one day to restore peace to the entire world." Seeing Junia's scowl, Danielle changed tactics. "We have tremendous fun, but it's also a time for reflection."

"A party for philosophers. How boring. I have attended far better celebrations." Danielle faced the Gogian. "How do I look?"

"Like you are in desperate need of a fashion designer. I know several excellent ones in Thorn—it would only cost your entire family's earnings for a year."

Danielle ignored the rudeness. "You can wear one of my dresses if you wish. We are about the same size."

"Your archaic dresses are not up to my standards."

"Well, if you change your mind, the celebration will last beyond midnight." Danielle headed out of the room to help her younger siblings get ready.

Junia was relieved when the front door of the house closed behind the Brick family. Finally she was alone. But still trapped. Perhaps she should risk the snowy night trek. As she crossed the bedroom, her aching side sent a painful reminder that she had not fully healed. A trip across the icy badlands would be dangerous enough if she was fully healed. Alone and injured, while being tracked by an angry posse through territory she barely knew was suicidal. *You must wait,* she told herself. *Be patient.*

With the entire family out of the house, silence reigned though the empty rooms. At first, the Gogian princess enjoyed the stillness until images of Urbane swirled through her mind, leaving her heart pounding in longing for just his voice whispering her name in the quietness of the night. Frustrated, Junia roamed through the still rooms. She attempted to carve with Jon's tools which had been brought inside due to the weather, but after only a few strokes of a chisel, she gave up. Two hours later, her restlessness finally drove her to don a fur jacket and head outdoors.

Following merry sounds of laughter and music, the Gogian soon arrived at the town square. Brightly colored lanterns illumined tables loaded with tasty dishes. Dancers twirled in time with festive music. Jon preformed with a ragtag band playing simple, upbeat folk music. Rose and Danielle spun energetically around the square with various partners. The younger Brick children munched on treats while attempting to win prizes from various booths. Junia hovered in the shadows of a stone building, but she found no solitude as several couples walked past, jesting merrily.

Suddenly someone slammed into the Gogian from behind. Junia held tightly to the stone wall to keep her balance. The accidental assailant was Watt, caught up in a friendly game of tag. Soon Petals and Ben dashed up, excited their adult friend had finally arrived at the celebration. Tired from the walk, Junia sat on a bench while the boys raced to the tables, seeking their favorite foods to serve their guest. Seated beside the Gogian, Petals chatted non-stop. Jon spotted Junia across the crowd and gave her a friendly wave. Most townspeople ignored the Gogian, but a few nodded in passing. Junia relaxed, reluctantly admitted to herself that she was enjoying the festival. The music lowered in tempo, and Junia noticed the people had stopped dancing. Hands full of goodies, Ben and Watt made their way through the crowd.

"It's time for the serious part," said Petals. "Watt, it's not nice to eat half the cake you get for someone else."

The boy grinned, revealing green icing stuck to his teeth. "I…uh…it's my wages for getting the food."

His older brother jabbed Watt in the side then handed Junia a heavy plate of food.

Junia laughed, finding it difficult keeping a callous attitude around the children. "Thanks, Ben. And thanks for the thought, Watt." As Junia ate, the boys settled on the packed snow by her feet. Musicians played a popular hymnal, and most of the townspeople began to sing along. Junia whispered to Petals, "Is everybody in town a Tnias?"

"No, Mommy says the Festival of Peace is traditional so everyone celebrates it, no matter what they believe. Who would want to miss out on the fun?"

"Oh." She scanned the singers, realizing many Tnias could be picked out of the crowd by their serene faces. Seeing her enemies so blissful sent a strange shiver down the princess's spine. New songs were chosen, each more sacred than the last. Their meanings were incomprehensible to the Gogian, yet her soul trembled. It seemed as if the night sky was a two-way mirror through which Yahweh watched the crowd, knowing who sang from the heart—and who pretended. Coldness swept through Junia, yet no wind blew.

As the last notes faded, Simeon stepped onto the raised platform the band had played on.

"He's going to preach now," whispered Petals.

Junia looked for an escape route, but Petals was leaning against her and the boys crowded her feet. Glancing around, she noticed many townspeople were still eating and drinking, taking little notice of the gray-haired ecclesiastic on stage. Others gathered near the platform, giving the old man their full attention.

Simeon opened his leather-bound book and read in a deep voice, "Can an ax claim to be greater than the person who wields it? Is a saw more important than the person who uses it? A club doesn't lift up a man; a man lifts up a club." Simeon paused to look over his neighbors. "On this night of celebration for peace, many fellow Telumzans—including some of your sons—are fighting to keep peace in our beloved nation."

The ecclesiastic reached behind the lectern, pulling out a broad sword. Watt and Ben gasped in awe as light reflected off its gleaming surface. They were not the only ones, for the raised weapon grabbed the attention of even the jolliest drunk.

"Some of you have carried weapons similar to this sword into battle, striking your enemy down before you. And several of you bare scars from others' blades. A sword symbolizes much in our lives. A sword is power—to kill, to protect. It is freedom from our oppressors. Yet can a sword claim to be greater than the person who wields it? Can this blade perceive between friend and foe?"

To Junia, frailty seemed to disappear from the old man, and he was a mighty Tnias warrior raising the sword high, challenging all within hearing. Challenging her.

"My friends, each of us are this sword. We can protect the ones we love or cut down the people around us—both physically and verbally. I ask you, who is the power behind you? Who is the master who wields you?"

Simeon scanned the crowd, looking each individual in the eyes. Glancing downward, Junia took several bites of food. When she looked in the cleric's direction again, he was looking straight at her. Chill bumps ran down her arms. It was not the eyes of a man looking at her, but a powerful presence looking through the old man into her very soul, exposing every dark deed she had committed. Nothing was hidden. Junia's instincts demanded flight. Gently she extracted herself from Petals and slipped around the boys. The children looked at her curiously.

"You leaving?" asked Watt.

"Don't go," Petals pleaded. "We dance again soon."

Junia gave a brief apologetic smile. "I'll see you later." Then she fled into the night to escape the supernatural presence lurking in the square. Ben understood more than his younger siblings. Quietly he sought out Danielle in the crowd.

The moon peered through thin clouds, illuminating a snow-covered prairie, occasionally broken by large clumps of trees. The lonely hoot of an owl echoed through the darkness. The night's stillness was only broken by one other sound— the rasping gasps of Junia, stooped over, attempting to catch her breath. Fleeing from the disturbing presence at the festival, the princess had ran until her body, still weak from its long affliction, began complaining by sending shooting pains through her side. Still the Gogian ran, feet crunching on snow. There was no destination, but there was a pursuer—her past. Lungs searing, Junia's flight was stopped as she bent double, gasping for air. The princess dropped to her knees in a snowdrift, her heart rate slowly returning to normal.

She must return to the Red Army, quickly. There, the vulnerability and helplessness of the past weeks would be forgotten. Once again she would be invincible Princess Junia leading her Royal Calvary into the thick of battle. Soldiers would admire her, obeying her every order without question. Noblewomen would stew in jealousy at her beauty at royal parties.

And she would lead a false, hollow life. Before living with the Bricks, she had believed that power was life itself. She had it all—prestige, wealth, honor, a handsome lover—yet she had never felt love. Now a ray of light pierced her darkened world and she fled from it.

As her breathing slowed down, Junia's mind cleared. The logical steps to follow was to return to the Brick's house, find the pack she had hidden for a fast getaway, steal a horse, and ride night and day until safely behind Gogian lines, trusting Zuzumza to protect her. Life would go on as it had before. She would fight against Telumzan soldiers until their nation fell.

Her mind whispered, *What will you do when the new providence is cleansed?* Could she kill another Tnias child in cold blood? The haunting nightmares she had been suffering lately had forced the princess to confront the conscience she had pretended did not exist, finally leading her to admit that killing innocent children was wrong. If she was ordered to destroy Brentwood, could she slaughter without remorse those who had smiled at her in the streets? Could she kill the Brick family? Junia shook her head to clear the probing thoughts, telling herself the situation would never have to be faced, but deep inside she knew that when the Telumzan government fell, so ended the life of every Tnias in Brentwood including Petals, Ben, and Watt. She could keep busy elsewhere in the fallen country, pretending their deaths had nothing to do with the cause Junia fought for, but she could never escape the images of their dead bodies or the guilt. There was no need for her to be present to know exactly how the scene would play out—she had been a participant enough times already.

Looking up at the dim moon barely visible through the clouds, the princess wondered how the Bricks could believe in a god of love and peace in the cruel world she knew too well. How could they dance in a festival of peace while soldiers fought within their country's borders? For the first time in her young life, Junia craved to know a life of peace, where death could not claim those you loved, where children grew up with mothers who hugged them, fathers gently coaxed them through life's problems, and brothers never turned against siblings. The princess yearned for the simple joy a child possessed before the world slowly steals it away, but the past can never be reversed or bitter betrayals erased.

"Yahweh, if you're so powerful, show me this land of peace where everyone is happy. Show me this unadulterated love you are supposed to possess. Can you wipe away the memories of those faces I have killed?" She laughed bitterly into the night sky. "I dare you to change me—to turn me into a Tnias! If you want me, well, here I am. Can a mere god handle the burning passion of human hatred?"

For a few minutes, Junia studied her surroundings. Nothing had changed. An owl hooted from a nearby grove, and the moon remained shadowed. Far away, festive music drifted across the cold snow, so faint it seemed a ghostly melody from a forgotten memory. Feeling foolish, the Gogian wished the sky would split open or the earth shake violently with the god's anger at her challenge—anything to prove Yahweh was real. Why would he even bother answering a dare from his enemy? A simple lightning bolt would quickly end her. If the god was all-powerful, why had he not just sent a massive earthquake to destroy Gog and save his precious Tnias? A real god would annihilate his enemies.

Yahweh could not be real. Maybe Zuzumza was a myth also. Bitter loneliness overwhelmed Junia. If there were no gods then humans were responsible for all evil. Mankind created the pains of the world, and there was no redemption from the poison. No hope, no reason for life except personal glory—a path Junia had pursued her entire empty life.

Feeling like a sinking ship in the midst of a hurricane, Junia addressed the sky in a whisper. "Yahweh, please be real. I want to believe that the love Danielle and Jon claim exist really does. There has to be more to life than what I know. All that I have believed is false, but I have nothing left to cling to."

Across the snow, a white-clad woman approached, darkness creating the illusion of Junia's dead mother. The princess grasped in shock, heart quickening, only to realize when the figure drew nearer that it was Danielle.

"Julie, are you okay? I went to the house looking for you and got worried when there was no one there."

"I'm fine," the Gogian answered roughly, attempting to hide the conflict in her soul.

For a moment Danielle studied the kneeling figure, unsure what to do. Repelled by the Gogian's anger, she almost turned away, but she obeyed an inner voice prompting her forward. Danielle bent down beside her enemy, putting an arm around Junia's shoulder. The simple token of friendship was the last chip which broke through the stone wall guarding Junia's heart, causing tears to flow down her cheeks. At first it was only an occasional rill, but as each gate imprisoning Junia's buried pains opened, the stream became a river of cleansing tears. The princess cried for the mother taken from her too soon, the father who could not love, Rufus who she had disappointed, Urbane who had been pushed away too many times, the innocent people she had killed. She cried bitterly from disappointments life had fed her.

Gently Danielle said, "Julie, Yahweh loves you."

Tear-streaked Junia looked up. "How can he love me after what I have done? I've killed his people."

"He knew you before you were formed in your mother's womb. He never stopped loving you. He wants you to come to him now."

"How can mere humans come to a god?"

"By talking to him. He hears you right now."

Junia looked away. "He will not listen to me. I have done too much."

Tears welled up in Danielle's eyes. "We all have fallen short of Yahweh's glory, but he forgives us when we mess up. All you have to do is ask."

"Ask. Just ask?" Doubtful, the Gogian looked into the teen's eyes, so full of faith and love. With a shock the princess realized Yahweh had answered one of her challenges—he was showing her incomprehensible love, deep and boundless—through Danielle. Instead of splitting the firmaments open in rage at a human's dare, he had sent love in the form of a teenager. Junia prayed then. At first she did not know what to say, but as the words came, so did peace. An invisible river of power flowed through her body, cleansing the darkness that had consumed her for a lifetime.

For a long time the two young women remained bent in the snow, both crying. Finally, they stood, limbs numb from the cold, but the discomfort went unnoticed in their happiness. From the outside the Gogian looked the same, but now her once cold eyes shone with warmth.

Looking at Danielle, the princess said, "My name is Julie, now and forever more."

Part II

"I consider that our present sufferings are not worth comparing with the glory that will be revealed in us."

~Romans 8:18

Chapter Eight

History would record the winter as one of the harshest in Telumza. Brutal blizzards swept southward from the frigid north, snowdrifts sometimes massing over five feet. Though many died from the harsh weather, the storms did create a false peace between the warring nations, forcing both armies to concentrate only on their own survival. Yet the weather was barely noticed in Brentwood for the transformation of Julie sent ripples of deep emotions through the inhabitants. Rumors circulated that the healed Gogian claimed conversion to escape arrest. If Rose and Jon had not been highly respected, Julie would have found herself in a POW camp weeks ago.

The first day the Gogian walked into the sanctuary, many glared angrily at her. Simeon preached about forgiveness that day, and a few people warmly greeted the new Tnias as they left the building. It was more than Julie expected. Though the princess now publicly served a new god, she spoke little of her past, but its weight rested heavily on her shoulders every time someone mentioned another cruel act of the Gogian Empire.

Still it was the happiest season of the young woman's life. Like all the princess's projects over the years, once the Gogian had set her course, she embraced it with a passion. Endlessly she grilled the Bricks and Simeon with questions about Yahweh, determined to understand concepts even Simeon could not explain. Eagerly Julie helped Danielle and Rose. For the first time in her life, the princess cleaned, learn to cook, mended clothes, and did other various household chores, executing roles only servants performed in Blackwall Palace. She aided Rose with tending the injured, her heart swelling with pride the first time she aided a birth, seeing the tiny infant taking its first breath. Instead of viewing people as objects to be manipulated by her whims, Julie learned to serve the needs of others, and in doing so, gained joy that thawed the coldest parts of her heart. The villagers were diligent in observing Julie's behavior, and by spring thaw many believed her conversion genuine.

As streams overflowed their banks from melt water, war returned to the land, chaotic violence claiming more lives than the harsh winter. In quiet moments, Julie wondered about Urbane, praying for his protection in battle. With new understanding, the princess realized their relationship had been built on passion, love a ghostly thread that never tied them together. As Julie learned to open her heart to the people around her, so grew her feelings for the only man she had ever kissed. She wanted to share her new faith and insight with him, but seeing him was near impossible. They now served separate masters, their worlds far removed from each other. To return to Gog meant a death sentence for the princess unless she renounced her new god.

Feet sinking into slush, Danielle and Julie made their way towards the wooden post office located in the center of town, the teen a spring of raw eagerness. Since the war began, the porch in front of the tiny mailroom had become the focal point for the town where villagers and farmers freely shared war information gleamed from letters of friends and family. News of deaths, victories, and defeats traveled quickly by word of mouth across the region.

"Danielle, you don't have to walk quite so fast. If there is a letter, it will still be there an hour from now," Julie said.

Pretending to be unconcerned, the teen kept her voice flat. "His letters usually come every five to seven days, so probably there's one today."

"The floods may have stopped the mail."

Ignoring the comment, Danielle hurried up the steps, unable to keep her eagerness hid. Julie smiled in amusement. Over the last few months, she had enjoyed watching the teen's crush develop. Danielle attempted to keep her feelings secret, but the signs were obvious to everyone. Entering the room, Danielle paused to greet Widow Tubbs. Every day the feeble woman slowly made her way to the office, hoping for a letter from her only son who, like his deceased father, was a soldier.

"Good to see you too, honey," the elderly woman answered with a thin smile. "There's no mail today."

Disappointment spread across the teen's face. "Are you sure?"

"Yes, I'm quite sure. Thank your mother for the medicine. I'm feeling more myself today."

"The floods must have slowed the carriers. Come on, Julie. School's about out. If we're fast enough we can walk the kids home."

The Gogian followed Danielle outside where Bentic held up a hand to grab their attention. "Julie, maybe you're the one who can solve our heated debate between Lunen, Jenik, and myself." The other two rugged farmers glared at the intrusion, but Bentic continued, "Having been on the front yourself, who do you believe will win the war?"

Julie pressed her lips firmly together, wishing the question could be avoided. "Gog has a powerful, highly trained army under the command of Prince Phlegon and General Nereus. Telumza's forces won against Achaia two decades ago, so many commanders have experience. The war could go either way."

"But who do you think will win?" Jenik pressed for a more precise answer.

In her heart, Julie wanted Telumza to defeat the Empire, but truth did not belong in the world of wishes. Meeting Jenik's stare, she replied, "Gog will. They have superior numbers and more experience. Both Achaia and Galand fell to the Red Army in the last three years." Julie noticed Danielle's face turn gloomy thinking about Matthan.

The men nodded thoughtfully then Lunen asked, "When do you think the fighting will resume?"

"If I know Prince Phlegon, the first attack occurred a week before the sun melted the last snowfall."

Jenik challenged, "No one would fight in three feet of snow."

"Phlegon cares nothing about the comfort of his soldiers—only winning." The princess realized her fist was clenched in hatred for her brother. Quickly she excused herself from the conversation.

For a few minutes Danielle walked in silence beside her, but the teenager finally voiced her inter-thoughts. "Yahweh won't let Telumza fall."

"Why do you think that?"

"Because we're on his side."

"Is your king and other national leaders Tnias?"

"Uh, King Hermes doesn't claim to serve Yahweh, but neither does he oppose the many Tnias leaders on his council. And all Tnias in our nation are praying for victory."

"So were the citizens of Achaia and Galand."

"Julie, you must have faith. Yahweh will protect us."

The Gogian studied a distant building for a moment, images flashing through her head of Tnias she had watched die. Some had called out to their god even as steel blades pierced their hearts. Why had Yahweh not spared them? There was much Julie did not understand yet. "Danielle, I'm trying to help you be realistic. Zuzumza's power is real and Tnias die. I've seen it with my own eyes." *And done it with my own hands.* "You have to be prepared."

Danielle looked away, troubled. She held Matthan in awe because he was not afraid to die for his god, sharing his faith in the middle of war. Danielle, with youthful zeal, had proclaimed in the past she would proudly suffer for Yahweh, but the words were untested. Never had the dark reality been a possibility—until now. "I…I will do what Yahweh ask of me."

"Even unto death?"

"Yes, if it comes to that." The teen struggled to regain her normal cheerfulness. "It won't be so bad, I guess, because as soon as you die your soul goes to the beautiful city of Agape."

Since they were nearing the school, Julie dropped the subject, silently praying the issue would never need to be faced. Petals gleefully hugged her sister, bubbling with news. Ben and Watt chatted happily, planning a fishing trip with their father.

~~~~~~~~~

Telumzan soldiers carefully made their way along a curvy road towards a village. A command given further up the line brought the company to a halt for a few minutes. Horses stomped impatiently, and men scanned the hills for danger. With sinking dread, Matthan realized what he had taken for a strange, reedy pond in the distance was actually a mass open grave—and the road led right beside it. As the unit continued forward, soldiers stared at the decaying bodies of fathers, mothers, and children. More than one man uttered curses against the Gogian Empire.

Soon they arrived at a recently occupied village. Wary people peeked from behind closed windows at the passing soldiers. Realizing it was their own army, the villagers came out of their homes, cheering, children clinging to parents despite the jubilee. When Matthan looked into the faces of those he passed, he saw fear haunting their eyes. The war had turned the once prosperous village into only a shadowy shell of its former days. Scattered throughout the shabby buildings were reminders of the recent occupation of the Red Army: overturned wagons, an unburied corpse hanging from a noose, the Gogian flag still flying high in the plaza.

Soldiers stood at attention as their commander barked out commands. "Our orders are to evacuate everyone who wishes to leave. We don't have much time before the front shifts again, so get busy."

Quickly the men scattered through the streets, moving in twos. Matthan paired with Manasse, an awkward teen who over the last months had become a close friend and a recent Tnias convert. Many townspeople asked questions that the young men had no answers for.

One elderly man grabbed Manasse, begging, "Please, have you seen my daughter and her children? I was digging ditches for the Gogians—when I got back, my family was gone."

Manasse tried to gently pull away from the man's frantic grasps. "No. I haven't seen anybody."

The old man would not give up. "They were taken away several days ago with many others. Please, I can't leave till I know they're safe."

The young soldier glanced towards his partner for help. With a silent prayer and heavy heart, Matthan tenderly gasped the man's callous hands. "Sir, I'm sorry to say this, but they may have been killed. There is a mass grave in a valley about a mile down the road."

The bent, wrinkled man stepped back, shaking his head. "They're not dead! Maybe they're hoeing a field or digging ditches. I just have to find them, that's all."

"Sir, that could be true. But now is the time to leave the village before the Red Army comes again."

The elderly man stared blankly ahead, a tear running down his cheek. "They're not coming back are they?"

Manasse cut in, "Sir, they will attack again."

"I meant my grandchildren. May Yahweh hold their precious souls close to him." The feeble man's body shook as sobs poured from his broken heart. Awkwardly Manasse watched Matthan wrap his arms around the weeping man, holding him for a long moment.

The villagers quickly packed what they could carry and the soldiers escorted them southward. Though it took longer, the captain found a trail that did not pass the open grave on the march southward. The moon was high overhead before the tired travelers reached the safety of the large Telumzan war camp. The next day Matthan's unit continued to aid refugees. Diligently he worked beside comrades digging latrines, washing dishes, and sorting supplies, never viewing the most repugnant job beneath him for he knew many were watching him, wanting to believe the warmth of his personality really did reflect the love of Yahweh in the midst of a bloody war.

Mid-afternoon another platoon arrived in camp with a dozen thin survivors from a desolated village. As Matthan served them soup in the open-air cafeteria, a paper-thin woman with clumped, dirty hair gasped his hand. "Matthan? Are you him?"

The young soldier peered at the woman who appeared old. "Yes, I am, madam. Who are you?"

"You don't recognize me? You use to sit behind me in that one room schoolhouse, sometimes pulling my hair. I would get so mad at you."

Matthan's eyes opened wide in astonishment. "Loreena? I can't believe it's you." Once she had been the prettiest girl in town. Like many boys, he had a crush on her, but shyness kept him from speaking to her. He had resorted to boyishly pulling her hair, gaining only a lump when she hit him with a book.

Sadness filled her eyes. "Come, I must tell you grievous news."

As Matthan followed her to a table, he realized several in the group were from his hometown. Once seated, the survivors attacked their food ravenously. It was not until the plain meal was finished that Loreena and other old friends talked about their experiences, recounting destruction and death.

With eyes still living the horror, Loreena spoke words that shattered Matthan's complacent shell. "Your family is dead. All of them." Matthan just stared at the woman who was old before her time, not comprehending her words. "Your parents were brave to the end, refusing to honor Zuzumza."

"My sisters. What about my sisters and little Joey?"

"Joey died with the others. Only two of your sisters escaped with me, but they were killed as we attempted to cross the front at night." Her voice cracked. "I'm sorry. They died saving my life. I should be the one lying face down in a ditch."

Unable to hold back the flood of tears, Loreena's frail body shook. A once young man sitting beside the weeping woman held her tightly, offering what little comfort he had. Numbly Matthan watched the couple in front of him, realizing they were married. Excusing himself, Matthan walked pass crowded tables, keeping his eyes focused on the open horizon. Observing his friend's dark expression, Manasse hurried out of the food line, calling Matthan's name, but the stricken soldier only glanced back once then continued onward, passing the corralled horses. Sunshine neighing a greeting, but her master, refusing the comfort of his four-legged friend, disappeared into the forest.

Out of sight of people, Matthan broke into a fast-pace run, wishing to escape the words he had just heard. Always as he fought in the bloody war, watching friends die, he held tightly to childhood memories of his peaceful hometown, dreams of the reunion with his family, plans to one day start his own. It was not supposed to happen like this. He had chosen to fight in this war in order to protect his family. Onward his feet carried him, eating the miles. Coming to a split in the path, he chose the rugged one, climbing up a steep hill, breath ragged.

Finally exhausted, he dropped to the ground, screaming into the empty air. "Why, Yahweh? Why my family? Why have you forsaken us?" The tears came, but there was no one to offer comfort.

It was not until after nightfall that Matthan returned to camp. He quietly entered the sleeping tent and lay on his cot. Manasse peered through the darkness at him.

"Are you okay? Some of us have been worried."

"Yeah, I'm fine."

"I talked with Loreena. I'm very sorry about your family." For a moment the only sounds were crickets. "You got a letter today from the Bricks—in fact several, since the mail hasn't ran in a long time. I think that Danielle really likes you."

For a long time Matthan just stared blankly at the canvas ceiling, wishing sleep would dull the hollow emptiness. Finally, he lit a lantern, keeping the wick low, and opened the letters, sorting them by dates. Detached, he began to read.

Dearest Matthan,

A miracle has happen! Julie now serves Yahweh! I'm still amazed myself, but you should see my mother. She didn't believe Gogians could be redeemed. Boy, was she ever wrong! Julie has done such an about-face that you would never guess she was the same person. And it would never have happened if you had not listened to Yahweh but went with human instinct. You were very brave to help your enemy, and now she is our sister. Yahweh is far more powerful than us mere humans could ever imagine!

Lovingly yours,
Danielle

Matthan read the letter three times in disbelief, but as he scanned the other letters, he realized Julie's conversion was real. Depression vanished in the soldier's soul, replaced by joy raining down like a needed storm on a hot summer day. For a while he clutched the letters, silently praising Yahweh, warm tears flowing down his cheeks.

"Matthan, are you alright?" came Manasse's voice in the darkness.

"Yes, friend, very much so. Yahweh decided to take my family to paradise but has given me a new sister."

Chapter Nine

Danielle put down her knitting and glanced out the window for the twelfth time today. Just the usual met her eyes: blooming flowers, blue sky, children playing, neighbors casually strolling down the street—nothing to explain the ominous feeling in her soul.

"Can you show me how to move the needles again before I lose patience and throw this wool mess into the fire?" a frustrated Gogian asked.

"Sure." The teen moved closer to Julie to help with the knitting, pausing to glance out the window again.

"What is it with you and that window today?"

"I don't know," sighed Danielle. "How about we take a break and check the mail?"

"Good. I think you just saved me from accidentally strangling myself with this thread."

Singing birds and fragrant smells stilled Danielle's apprehension as they walked through the bright spring day towards the mailroom. Before heading into the building, the ladies greeted Widow Tubbs who held an official looking brown envelope.

"Anything today, Maragent?" Danielle asked the postmistress.

"No, Danielle," replied the middle-aged woman, worriedly peering through the open door, watching Widow Tubbs opening her large envelope at the edge of the street.

Disappointment spread across the teen's face, but no one noticed. Trembling, Widow Tubbs stared at the letter and slowly sunk to the ground. Julie and Maragent bolted out of the door, quickly followed by Danielle.

Seeing their concern faces, the old woman spoke brokenly, "It's my son—he's dead. I feared this day would come. I've prayed every day that he would not die like his father. They were so much alike. Both wanted to serve their country—and now I've lost the two men I love the most." Her wrinkled fingers crumpled up the paper she clutched. "Now I'm truly alone."

"No, you're not," insisted Danielle. "We're here for you—Maragent, Julie, and myself."

The others voiced their agreement. The frail woman stared silently at the monstrous letter her fingers clasped.

Placing tender hands over callous ones, the teenager continued, "My parents would love for you to stay with us as long as you like."

Grief too great for words, the elderly woman tightly hugged the teen. Maragent went indoors to get a glass of water for the widow. Julie watched awkwardly, grateful for Danielle's gift for comforting others. The Gogian suddenly caught a glimpse of a military uniform, and instinctively she whirred, hand reaching for a nonexistent sword. Heart pounding, Julie studied a disorganized military band of Telumzan soldiers walking down the main street, one leading a horse.

"Uh…Danielle, look behind you."

Turning around, the teenager stared in astonishment. With a cry of excitement, she dashed down the street and hugged a tired soldier. "Matthan! You're back! It's so good to see you again." Joy beamed across her face. Refusing to be ignored, Sunshine nudged Danielle.

A smile bloomed across Matthan's face like flowers after a desert rain. His comrades silently watched the homecoming. Julie noticed their grim faces, haunted eyes, bandaged wounds, and shabby clothes—not a victorious war party returning home. Two thin, crippled men rode on Sunshine. The uniforms drew the attention of passing townspeople, several stopping, hoping to hear news of the war.

"Such a reception warms a man's heart on the coldest of winter days." Matthan said to beaming Danielle. To Julie he was more formal. "I heard you and I serve the same god now."

"I have come to the conclusion that love is far richer than hate."

"Wait till Mother and Father see you," Danielle rattled on cheerfully. "Ben and Watt won't be able to contain themselves. Petals claimed you would be visiting soon." Suddenly she remembered the widow and paused to introduce Matthan.

The gray-haired lady smiled, "Yes, I've heard much about you from Danielle."

The maiden looked away, blushing with embarrassment.

Knowing his comrades were tired, Matthan asked, "My fellow travelers and I have come a long distance and were wondering if there are places for us to sleep in town?"

"Oh, certainly," chirped Danielle. "Several can stay at our house."

"My house has plenty of room," the widow added in a soft voice. "Cory would have wanted me to help. My son had a big heart." Several bystanders volunteered their homes, providing a refuge for every exhausted soldier.

When Jon looked up from his carving to see two uniform men and a horse walking with Danielle and Julie, he heartily called out a greeting. "It's a welcome sight to see you, son, but I didn't expect your visit so soon." Like Julie, he sensed ill news.

The tired soldiers glanced at each other uncomfortably then Matthan said, "We lost the war, sir. King Hermes surrendered and the remaining troops were ordered to return to their homes."

Danielle's mouth dropped open, speechless. Grim faced, Jon nodded. "You boys put up a good fight. I'm honored to have you stay in my house."

There was more dark news the disconsolate soldier needed to share. "My family was killed by the Red Army a few months ago. I only recently found out."

"Oh, I'm so sorry, Matthan." Danielle's face paled.

Jon said, "It heavies my heart to hear that. I want you to feel free to consider our house your home."

"Thank you, sir."

"Call me Jon. Now you two come on in, and we'll get you some food."

The children excitedly clamored around the soldiers, eager for stories. Manasse immediately felt at home, remembering his own younger siblings. Sunshine was picketed in the back yard. Danielle and Julie prepared supper—that is Danielle spent most of her time chatting with Matthan, occasionally dashing into the kitchen to save Julie from creating another disaster. When a tired Rose arrived from delivering a breached calf, she discovered a house filled with warmth and laughter—and the smell of burnt pot roast. After supper, Jon pulled out his guitar. Merrily Danielle pulled Matthan up, luring him into a dance. Determined not to be left out of the fun, young Petals grabbed Manasse's hand. He did not disappoint the child. Both couples swirled around the modest dance floor, joined by Watt and Julie.

For a moment the approaching darkness was forgotten.

Hours slipped by. Burning logs in the hearth turned into smoldering embers. Yawning children were carried to bed. Slipping outside, Matthan leaned on the porch railing, studying the stars. Quietly Julie joined him.

For a moment both listened to the sounds of the night. Finally Matthan spoke, "What the Bricks are doing for Manasse and myself is very generous. We both needed some laughter in our lives."

"They seem to have a habit of taken in strangers." Hands gripping railing, Julie studied the dark yard and street. "I want to hear the worst. What happened with the Red Army?"

It was the Telumzan's turn to peer into the night. Darkness covered bushes and flowers, all things beautiful. "I can't even begin to describe what it was like. Day after day we gave ground, dying like animals. They kept pushing us throughout the winter. A small advance here, another village there. When the snow began to melt, they were prepared while we were struggling to just keep ourselves fed and clothed." His voice rang hollow in the moonless night. "They attacked at night. We couldn't take the onslaught. There was confusion and fire everywhere. Our supply wagons and tents were ablaze. Hard-core warriors panicked and many good men died that night. Yahweh seemed to have turned his back on us. The next day King Hermes surrendered."

Julie offered what comfort she had. "I know what it is like. I see the scenes of death when I am asleep. They haunt my waking day. The horror does fade with time," she attempted a stab at humor, "with good people to dance and laugh with."

Matthan teased back. "And create smoking volcanoes on the stove." The light mood faded in the shadowy darkness. "I saw a village ravaged by the Red Army. They rounded up all the Tnias, taking them out of town then killed them." His voice became harsh. "There were children, Julie, children laid naked and dead in the streets. Gogians are monsters, inhuman beasts."

Sharply Julie looked away, hands tightening on the railing.

Realizing what he had uttered, Matthan attempted to apologize. "I'm sorry, Julie."

"It's true. I was one."

"But now you're not."

Changing the subject, she looked him dead in the eyes. "They will come here."

"I know." The dark night swallowed his weary voice.

~~~~~~~~~

As Manasse and other downtrodden soldiers returned to their homes, fear rippled through Telumza. Prince Phlegon sent messengers throughout the new province, proclaiming the new laws Gog would enforce. To calm the rising flood of panic, Mayor Ozias called for a meeting in the only building large enough to hold all whose lives depended upon Brentwood. Farmers, shepherds, and skilled craftsmen crowded into the rough stone Sanctuary of Yahweh beside clerks, laundresses, and soldiers. Still more came, sitting in the aisles and lining the walls. With great pomp Ozias read the Declaration of Gog then explained its meaning.

"Life will go on as it has before. You will plant your crops, sell your products, and raise your families—just with slightly higher taxes."

"And no more Festivals of Peace." Postmistress Maragent yelled out her disapproval.

"I won't let my hard grown crops go down the gullets of Gogian swine!" shouted hot-tempered Jenik. Many voiced their agreement.

Raising his hands, the mayor demanded silence. "Emperor Erastus is now our ruler. The quicker we obey the new laws, the easier it will go for all of us."

"Then we'll show them our fighting spirit!" yelled Lunic, a sheepherder. "In every town we can rise up against the vultures, fighting them tooth and nail."

"Make them bleed for every step they take in our country," said the blacksmith.

"Gentlemen, let us keep order." Ozias waited until the talking subsided. "We must face facts. Our army is defeated, our leaders now imprisoned. King Hermes himself asks us to obey our new monarch. We can do nothing less than comply with his last command."

"What about us?" demanded a weary woman. "Gog slaughters Tnias."

"Let us separate truth from rumors. Emperor Erastus desires stability and resources from our land. If Tnias are really killed, a major portion of the work force would be eliminated. What would be the purpose of that?"

Townspeople angrily murmured to each other in disbelief, remembering the horrifying stories told from refugees and read in letters from relatives. Clenching his fists, Matthan glanced at Julie sharply. Both were shocked by Mayor Ozias ignorant boasts. Thinking of her sister, Rose closed her eyes, one hand tightly holding Jon's.

Above the growing din, Ozias shouted, "Life will go on as it always has."

"Not if you're a Tnias!" Shouts filled the room. The mayor attempted to quiet the crowd, but his efforts only added fuel to the burning frustration of people tired of living the past months under the threat of Gog's invasion—and now their worst fears had been realized. Patience wearing paper-thin, Ozias motioned for Simeon to come forward to address religious concerns.

The old man stepped forward, slightly stooped with age, standing quietly in front of the talkative crowd. Respecting the ecclesiastic, the crowd hushed. Simeon's firm voice filled the chamber. "I have lived in Brentwood for nearly thirty years. I have performed the rituals for your births, I united you in marriage, and I resided over your kinsmen's funerals. I view each of you as a brother or sister in my large family. It is true that we face difficult times now, friends, but we are called to do no less than what Tnias have done for centuries for our beloved Yahweh. We study the lives of our heroes, praying to have their same faith and dedication. Well, the time has come—not the way many wished, and it is frightening. Many will die for proclaiming Yahweh as the One True God, but never will he forsake us, in life or death."

For a long moment there was complete silence, then a bearded shepherd yelled, "I didn't become a Tnias to die a martyr."

Simeon looked towards the speaker. "Death comes for all of us sooner or later. The question is who will your soul belong to when that time comes?"

Voices rang through the air. "We can hide until they're gone." "They only close down the sanctuaries." "What about my children?"

Bentic stood up among his large family, his wife sitting close, holding their youngest child. "We can all unite and refuse to tell who are Tnias and who are not. They would not wipe out the entire town." Many agreed with the farmer.

Matthan gripped the pew in front of him, knuckles white. Julie's vision filled with images of dead and dying Tnias betrayed by neighbors and former friends. Was Matthan and her the only two who truly understood what the town faced? Petals clung to Rose, the young child viewing her mother as a rock in an ocean tossed storm. Ben and Watt listened wide-eyed, glancing often towards their father for reassurance. Seated on the left of Matthan, Danielle had not stopped silently praying since entering the building.

As Simeon attempted to calm fears, a weaver stood up, his voice booming out, "I love my family, and I'm not going to watch them die. If I have to live under the name of Yahweh, Zuzumza, or Beltzer, it's all the same to me. I'll claim any god as long as my family is safe."

A richly dressed woman stood up from among her family. "Yahweh is a forgiving god. We can tell the soldiers sent here that we serve Zuzumza, and when they leave, we'll continue worshipping our god."

Other voices rose in agreement. "Who cares about Yahweh, Zuzumza, Beltzer, and the host of others…What counts is our lives, not the gods… If they exist, let them war it out in the firmaments."

The words spoken in fear pierced Simeon's heart, cutting him deeply. He viewed the people as sheep and himself the shepherd. How many of his flock would die spiritually in the near future by losing their faith and how many would be slaughtered who held onto their beliefs? Only Sarah, his wife sitting on the front row, understood his feelings. Holding up his hands for silence, the elderly man spoke. "Yahweh is a forgiving god, but he is also a jealous god. His holy word says, 'Love Yahweh with all your heart, soul, and body. Put no other gods before me.' To deny him is direct disobedience against him."

Crysta, a recently widowed young mother, shakily stood, holding her tiny infant. "He can't ask us to die! I have a child to look after. I won't let myself be killed for a god's name." Tearfully the mother looked at her babe cradled in her arms. "My baby deserves a chance to live, even if it's under the Gogian government."

Moved by the young mother's plea, the crowd became silent, but Matthan could not. Every eye focused on the soldier as he rose. "I have fought on many battlefields and know the dangers of conflict. There is a war going on in this building tonight, and it's not about land. It's here." He thumped his chest. "Our souls. To deny

Yahweh is to deny the very essence of who you are and what he has given you. Material wealth, your lands, and houses will all pass away. You can't take it with you when you die. That may be fifty years from now—or tomorrow, but the decision you make tonight will mark the difference if you will live in Agape or burn with Beelzebub in the Great Abyss. As for me, I chose to die for my god."

As Matthan sat down, Danielle gently squeezed his arm, showing her approval for his speech. Julie felt words dancing off her own tongue, but she studied her shoes instead. Conversations started buzzing again.

"There has to be other alternatives," said a worried woman.

"Yes, you can flee to Lasko, a refugee with no land or food," shouted Jenik.

Looking across the room, Simeon eyes rested on the Brick family. "Julie, I feel Yahweh has something he wants you to say."

Shocked, the foreigner looked up. How did he know? Simeon beckoned her forward to the front of the crowded room. Swallowing in apprehension, the princess looked upon the faces of rugged farmers, shopkeepers, new widows, and innocent children—all with uncertainty in their eyes.

With a slight tremble in her voice, she opened up her heart. "When I first came here, I hated the very word Yahweh, but then I began noticing the difference between my god and the one many of you serve. Yahweh is the God of Love, and for the first time in my life I understand what that really means. Because of you, I changed. At the Festival of Peace, I saw most of you dancing and worshipping this god. Many of you come into this building several times a week, boldly proclaiming you're a Tnias. It's easy to serve your god when it's socially accepted. It's the hardships which reveal how deep your faith really is."

For a moment she paused, silently hearing haunting voices of the dying. "I know what you will face when the Red Army comes because I was part of it. I can't forget that, no matter how hard I try. I hear your words. 'They wouldn't bother with our small town.' 'We're too far away.' 'The stories are too horrible to be true.' You can keep living as if nothing has happen or worry until your gray—the results will be the same. The Red Army will come. First they will stop people in the streets, asking, 'Who do you serve?' They will go door to door, pulling people out of their homes. The building you are in right now will soon be only ashes. Statues of Zuzumza will be placed in businesses, and you will not be able to buy or sell unless in the name of a deity."

Someone called out, "What can we do? Even if I die, I want my children to have a chance."

Jenik stood again. "I live near the forest, and I think it's possible for Tnias to hide there when the heathen swine are in town."

Grief washed over Julie. She knew many in the room would be dead within a few months and the rest living through an endless nightmare. "That might work until one of the spies placed or bought in each town turns in the location of your hideout. Neighbor will turn against neighbor, brother against brother."

As the crowd began discussing the meaning of Julie's words, Rose stood, holding her husband's hand. Everyone turned towards the trusted midwife. "I will not watch my family be killed neither will I deny Yahweh. Jon and I are taking our family to Shalom. Anyone who would like to join us is welcome."

~~~~~~~~~

Over the next few days, turmoil rippled through Brentwood. Households were divided, spouses arguing over the decision to leave homes, land, and businesses, walking away from the sources that provided for their families, becoming refugees who might starve the next winter. It was not very appealing. Neither was being slaughter like cattle. Some preferred to believe the Red Army would never come to peaceful Brentwood. Others, holding no allegiance to Yahweh, felt immune to the sting of the military.

As Bentic stacked bags of seed grain on his wagon, he conversed with Jon. "I think the Gogian Empire has greater problems to handle than a handful of Tnias in a tiny hamlet."

"It's Gogian's creed to eradicate all Tnias." It bothered the carpenter that his lifelong friend was so causally throwing away his family's freedom.

"Look, Jon, wood carvers can work anywhere, but I'm a farmer. Everything I have is tied up in the land. If I leave, I lose everything and my family starves."

"We travel on faith, Bentic, and trust Yahweh to provide for our needs."

"I believe in Yahweh the same as you. He gave me two hands and a head to use. With that my farm has prospered."

"What's more important, security or your family's souls?"

The farmer paused in his stacking, troubled. "I'll think about what you've said and talk it over with my wife."

Jon nodded. "Think fast. We leave in two days, early morning."

~~~~~~~~~

With a basket under one arm, Danielle walked along the main road beside Julie and Matthan. She chatted excitedly about the coming trip. Secretly she already deeply missed the only home she had known, but there was no time to mourn. The younger siblings viewed the trip as an exciting adventure, and Danielle was determined to keep a cheerful face to encourage them.

Arriving at Widow Tubb's house, Danielle bounced onto the porch, knocking loudly. Smiling, the elderly lady shuffled to the door and inviting the youths in.

The maiden held out a large basket. "My mom and I baked you a pie and rye bread. Plus some of her special soup."

"Thank you, darling. Give Rose my appreciation."

As everyone settled into cushioned chairs, Matthan asked, "Are you going to Shalom with us?"

The widow smiled, but grief lingered in her eyes. "When I was your age I would have jumped at the chance to glimpse Yahweh's city, but I'm old and feeble. Just walking to the general store wears me out."

Danielle broke in, "You can ride in our wagon. There'll be plenty of room."

"No, honey, I can't handle the trip, even riding."

Sadness overwhelmed the teenager. "But you'll be killed if you stay here."

"Danielle, death will claim me if I stay or go." The widow's voice contained both warmth and sadness. With a tear running down her smooth cheek, Danielle walked across the room and embraced the elderly lady, "There, there. No need to cry for me, honey. I'll see you again inside Yahweh's City. Most likely I will beat you there."

~~~~~~~~~~

On the third morning after the town meeting, the Brick family drove into the town square in a wagon, its roof consisting of a wooden frame covered with stretched hides, pulled by two stout draft horses purchased after selling their home for half its value to the mayor's son. What belongings that could not be sold had been given away, with each member only allowed to pack a few personal items. Petals held tightly to her only doll, tears streaming down her face, wishing for one last goodbye to her best friend she would never see again. Danielle attempted to comfort her young sister while Rose tried to focus the boys' youthful energy into useful tasks. Sitting in the driver's seat, Jon conversed with Matthan who was riding on Sunshine. Julie leaned against the tailgate, scanning the empty streets, apprehension building in the pit of her stomach.

Pounding hooves and jingling harnesses announced another wagon approaching. The driver brought his horses to a halt and called out a greeting. "Morning, Jon. Looks like a good day to be a gypsy."

The one-legged carpenter laughed goodheartedly. "Good to see you, Bentic and Vasia." Children poked their heads out from behind hides of both wagons and called out cheerful greetings.

The rugged farmer smiled. "Thought I might as well come, since Vasia didn't take warmly to hiding out in the woods while the vultures ransacked our home."

Other families arrived in wagons and carts. Several single men only had their horses and the clothes on their backs. Joy spread across the Bricks' faces as they recognized friends including Jenik and his family. In Simeon and Sarah's wagon rode Maragent the postmistress and Crysta with her new born infant.

As the numbers grew, Julie's spirit darkened. Getting one family across the border should not be too difficult, but nine families plus an assortment of others? Impossible.

"Isn't this exciting!" Danielle beamed.

"Sure, if you like traveling with a huge 'Arrest me' sign on the side of your wagon," said Julie.

Hope for the future stirred in Matthan for the first time in weeks. Until this moment, he believed only death brought release from the onslaught of Gogian's corruption, but if Tnias could flee from a conquered land, rebuilding their lives in a free country, then hope was possible. After greeting the new arrivals, Matthan directed Sunshine to halt beside the Brick's wagon.

"Yahweh's blessings are on this journey."

Jon smiled, adding his own prayer. "His will be done." Slapping the reins, he signaled the beginning of the long trek.

Chapter Ten

The caravan made good progress during the first days, despite several pauses to rest animals and fix broken wheels. Merry tunes were carried from wagon to wagon, children laughed, and adults joked. Chickens squawked from cages while several cows and sheep plodded beside their masters. Two goats, family pets, followed behind Bentic's wagon. Dogs dashed this way and that, enjoying the adventure. Quick to forget the past, children created games, holding competitions between wagons, but sadness lingered in many adults' eyes who mourned homes and friends left behind.

The wagons headed south towards the Lasko border by first following a dirt path that soon joined a well-traveled road. At night food was cooked over campfires. After supper Jon and other musicians played popular tunes. Every night and before the caravan moved in the mornings, Simeon held devotions and prayer. Faith shined on faces gathered, the people drawing strength from Yahweh's promises recorded in the worn book the ecclesiastic held.

On the third night as a song's last chords vanished into the air, Ben asked his father, "How long are we going to be traveling like this?"

Across the warm fire Jon smiled, studying his eldest son whose body had begun to grow like a weed. "Why? Are you enjoying the trip?"

A smile beamed across the twelve-year-old's face. "I'm having more fun than I can ever remember. All my friends are close by."

"No school!" said Watt, to the amusement of the adults.

"Oh, no. I'm going to teach you everything I know," said Danielle. The boy's face fell, creating more laughter from those around the campfire.

Jon answered Ben's question. "We're hoping to reach Lasko's border in a few weeks, then our wagon train will split as families head in several directions. We plan to reach Lahad by late summer."

Confused, Petals asked, "I thought we're going to Shalom to see Yahweh's beautiful city?"

Her father answered, "We hope to, darling, but permission must be granted before anyone can travel through the Timbrel Mountains. We will ask for it in

Lahad. Remember, it's one of only two countries left on the continent which is governed by Tnias."

"Oh," said the six year old. "Does that mean it's a good country?"

Laughing, Rose scooped up her youngest daughter, sitting the child in her lap. "Yes, honey, we'll be safe in Lahad."

Silently Julie slipped from the friendly atmosphere to check on the horses. As her hand drifted over Sunshine's flank, a memory of her father resurfaced. Gloating over the Achaian victory, he pranced in front of his gold throne, goblet held high, claiming one day to give the head of the last Tnias king to Zuzumza on a silver platter. The princess quickly pushed the memory away, wishing to never think about her father again. Lifting one of Sunshine's hooves, she checked for pebbles in the dim light. Sensing someone approaching in the darkness, she turned, spotting Matthan. Sunshine neighed a friendly greeting to her master who rubbed her forehead.

"You're very good with horses," remarked Matthan.

"I've been around them my whole life." Julie continued to examine hooves while Matthan watched. Bothered by his presence, she finally said. "Is there a reason you're standing there?"

"I've been wondering what's been on your mind."

"Who said I'm concerned about anything?"

"You're checking for stones in the dark."

Straightening, Julie dropped the leg then uncomfortably stared into the night. "It's everybody here. They all have this faith that Yahweh's going to protect them, and they're going to merrily march over the border as if they own it, expecting to live happily ever after." She looked directly at Matthan. "We both know life doesn't work that way. The borders will be guarded with soldiers searching for Tnias."

Matthan studied Julie. The Gogian had changed much over the last few months, but there was still pain buried deep inside her soul. Sometimes the darkness seemed only a step away from swallowing her, extinguishing her tender faith. Praying for wisdom, he asked her. "When morning comes each day, do you expect to see the sun rising beyond the horizon?"

"Sure, unless it's cloudy."

"Do you know what makes the sun rise each day?"

Uncertain where he was taking this argument, Julie shrugged her shoulders. "Every culture has a different answer. My favorite legend as a child was that two gods who were blood brothers fought over the most beautiful woman on Tanlep. Forever they are doomed to chase each other across the sky, one as the sun, the other the moon. Another says that Yahweh is the sun and Zuzumza the moon, and one day the moon will catch the sun. On that day the Timbrel Mountains will crumble."

"The words of Yahweh give us a different story. The sun and moon are not gods but creations of Yahweh, declaring his sovereignty to all of Tanlep."

Julie became impatient. "What do these stories have to do with our problems now?"

"If a god can create huge monuments in the sky to announce to the world his power, can he not handle our problems?"

"Creating stars is one thing, but saving lives is another."

"Julie, he saved yours, both physically and spiritually. Can he not keep protecting us?"

"Zuzumza is just as real. His powers are tremendous."

"Yes, but the Evil One is just a creation of Yahweh who rebelled against his maker. He is not a god, and his powers are limited."

"Hello? Where are you?" Danielle's cheerful voice broke through the night. "There you two are. Bentic is telling one of his epic tall tales again." The two soldiers greeted Danielle—Matthan smiling, Julie haunted by doubts. "Come on, you're missing the fun." Danielle grabbed Matthan's hand, pulling him toward the warm campfires. Julie slowly followed.

The young couple sat on the crowded ground near Bentic. The jovial farmer had already launched into his long, humorous fairy tale about a six-legged sheep with silver wool. Julie remained in the shadows of the wagons, watching the couple holding hands, loneliness overwhelming her. Where was Urbane now? Sipping wine with generals or supervising the elimination of Tnias from a city? Like with the memories of her father, Julie pushed thoughts of Urbane into the archives of her mind. Their lives were separate now.

"Julie, there you are." Simeon emerged between two wagons. "I've been looking for you. Come, I have something to show you." Politely, Julie followed the elderly man pass several carts until they arrived at his wagon. There he pulled out something long and cloth bound. "I've been planning to give you this since the beginning of the trip but never had the chance."

Julie watched the ecclesiastic unwrap the gift, wondering if it was some type of cane. She was perplexed to see it was a sword and scabbard. Why would a clergyman carry a weapon? Then again, he did have one when giving that speech at the festival.

Pulling the gleaming blade out of its sheath, he said, "This weapon is known as the Sword of Justice. All military graduates from Salt Academy in Shalom receive one. I have carried this weapon for over forty years, but I'm old now. I knew at the last Festival of Peace that I wielded it for the final time. Now it's yours."

Wrinkled hands held out the long sword. Julie hesitated, feeling unworthy of the gift. "I do not understand. Why me?"

"Because you are a warrior of light in need of a strong weapon," he answered. "Take it."

Gingerly her right hand wrapped around the golden hilt. The smooth double-edged blade seemed alive as reflected light from the campfire danced across its polished surface. The hilt contained an insignia of a burning flame.

"It seems to be a weapon of fire," the Gogian said. "The sword is light for its size."

"Yes," agreed Simeon, pleased to see the awe on Julie's face. "It's created from a rare alloy found only inside Shalom and smelted in hot furnaces using methods unknown beyond the Timbrel Mountains, resulting in a lightweight blade that will never rust. Only extreme conditions causes it to chip or break."

Confidence kindled inside the young soldier as she held a weapon for the first time since the crippling accident. "I'm truly honored by this gift. How can I repay you?"

"By using it only to protect Yahweh's people."

~~~~~~~~~~

As the caravan drew closer to the border, more refugees crowded the roads, fleeing like rats before a flood. They came from all walks of life. Like the emigrants of Brentwood, some ran from religious persecution, others fled for political reasons. All were terrified of life under the Gogian government. Rose's heart broke as they passed small carts pulled by ragged peasants, tired parents trailed by barefoot children, people traveling with only the clothes on their backs. Several times Rose ordered the caravan to stop as she offered rides to the worst cases. Every night the caravan grew as more wagons joined with the Brentwood emigrants, swelling the numbers to over a hundred and fifty.

Excitement mounted the night it was announced that the border was only ten miles away. Festive music and dancing broke out across the camp, but Julie felt foreboding. The next day started out cloudy. By midday, rain fell heavy, lightening flashing across the sky. Lost in thought, it took Julie by surprise when suddenly she realized the steady thundering she was hearing was the pounding of hundreds of hooves. Jon pulled the wagon off the road, others following suite. Curious children attempted to peek out, but fearful parents sharply reprimanded them. Julie's heart pounded as she peeked through the animal hides of the wagon she rode in. Mounted soldiers dashed pass, all wearing red and black armor. The Gogian Army.

Rose and Danielle's faces turned ashen, and Petals began to cry. Julie drew her sword while Ben and Watt sat still as rocks. An older couple traveling with them hugged each other in fear. The horses continued to march pass on the muddy road. Apprehension filled Julie. There were too many soldiers, far too many.

"Do…do you think they will stop?" Danielle's voice trembled.

"It's an entire regiment heading for the border where they will occupy a fort or town, closing the route for all travelers. From that base they will spread out, searching for Tnias." Julie spoke matter-of-factly, refusing to give in to the terror lurking inside her. "We have to get off this road."

Still the Red Army rushed pass. When the rumbling finally subsided, Julie moved to the front of the wagon to talk with Jon and Matthan. Worried, Bentic, Jenik, and others walked over. A new plan was hurriedly settled on, and the men returned to their wagons. At the next village, the caravan turned onto a less traveled road heading east, winding through thick forests, barely wide enough for one wagon. The rain turned into a drizzle, but the sky remained cloudy.

An hour before sundown, the wagons stopped and camp set up. Matthan, Julie, and several young men scouted the woods south of the camp. They did not return at nightfall. In camp, Tnias put on cheerful faces for each other, but apprehension built steadily. The border was only a couple of miles away, yet death lurked closer. Simeon led a worship service, focusing on faith. The people clung to every word, prayers lifting high into the night sky. Danielle kept busy shepherding younger siblings, her cheerful attitude drew other frightened children who clung to the teenager. Rose attended the sick while Jon and a few others played music to calm people.

Campfires turned to embers. The refugees slept except for the posted watch. Out of the darkness emerged the scouts, tired and wet. The leaders of the caravan were aroused, and a quick meeting held. Julie had been correct on the regiment's purpose. They had occupied a town on the border and already were beginning to search nearby settlements.

"We must cross now, tonight." Matthan announced. "We can walk through the forest, avoiding patrols." The other scouts backed up his opinion.

"The wagons won't make it through the forest," said Bentic.

"Then we leave everything except what can be carried or pack on animals," replied Julie.

Jenik said, "It's dark and raining. We can't make a trip through the forest at night. We'll lose each other in the darkness. Children and animals will wander off." Others voiced their concerns.

Julie's temper rose. Why were they so short sighted? "There is no other way to cross. The roads are blocked and if you wait until daylight, patrols will discover the caravan. Believe me, this whole region will be covered with soldiers tomorrow. It is now or never."

The men glanced at each other uneasily, weighing the dangers. To leave behind the wagons meant losing their last connection with civilization.

Finally Jon said, "I haven't come this far to stop now."

Others reluctantly agreed. Simeon led a brief prayer before the meeting broke up. Each man woke up his reluctant family and neighbors then began the preparations. After leaving so much behind, it was difficult for many people to separate themselves from the last of their precious belongs. By the time the Tnias were ready to move out, the rain had begun to fall again, furiously.

Lightening ripped across the sky, revealing only for brief seconds the labyrinth of wet foliage. Swift wind gave life to the trees, creating illusions of assailants hiding, waiting to pounce. Between the rumbling thunder was the swish of hundreds of feet, cries of young children, and an occasional neigh or moo, yet talking was almost non-existent. Apprehension smothered the refugees like a blanket. The procession moved slowly. Their only sources of light came from lanterns kept dim from low wicks. Parents held tightly to children in the darkness.

Scouts lead the way, occasionally pausing to orientate themselves. Matthan, guiding a very packed Sunshine, aided at the front. Julie stayed close to the Brick family near the rear of the caravan. The rainy night seemed to stretch into eternity, yet the heavy-laden Tnias continued onward. Several elderly began praying in quiet whispers. Others joined, creating the illusion in the darkness of holy chants rising from invisible ghosts, sending goosebumps down Julie's arms.

Suddenly she came to an abrupt halt, realizing the person directly in front of her had stopped. Blinded by the night, someone ran into her from behind, Julie instantly half pulled her sword out its sheath before gaining self-control. Waiting impatiently, people readjusted packs and checked on family members. Watt and Petals complained they were hungry. Rose nervously shushed them. Ben and Danielle patted their fidgety horses. Finally the party moved forward again. Thunder resounded louder, becoming a constant roar. Danielle stumbled but regained her footing. Behind her, Julie's foot hit a rise in the ground, almost causing her to fall. Stepping up, she realized they were crossing a rough, narrow road cut through the forest. She wondered if it marked the boundary between the two countries.

Lightning struck a tree somewhere nearby, and screams escaped from frightened mouths. Julie felt exposed on the open road. It was a relief when the trees closed around her again. The thundering increased, growing deafening. People still crossing the road began running, frantically yelling. With a shock, Julie realized the thunder was actually horses. A night patrol had stumbled upon the refugees.

The procession panicked. Among the chaos, Gogian soldiers directed their mounts into the thick underbrush. Finding their progress hindered, most soldiers jumped off their horses, drew weapons, and attacked the nearest moving shadows. Though refugees further up the line had no clue what was happening, their comrades' screams put them to flight. In the chaotic rush, it was difficult for families to stay together. Rose ran, tightly holding onto Watt and Petals. As a horse galloped through the underbrush, Rose tripped over a fallen limb, and Watt's hand slipped from her clasp. Before the mother could stand, the child had disappeared in the confusion. Fanatically Rose called her son's name, and Jon picked up the call.

Julie heard a child crying and veered left, discovering a toddler standing still, bawling in fear. Behind the small child, a soldier with sword raised emerged from the bushes. There was a ringing of steel as the princess's weapon blocked his swing. Breaking apart, Julie dodged another strike, sending her own blade deep into her antagonist's stomach. His eyes bulged in shock as he slowly sank to his knees. Julie turned to grab the toddler, only to feel red-heated pain shoot through her head as another soldier brought the hilt of his weapon crashing against her skull. All became blackness.

~~~~~~~~~

When panicked people and horses began rushing past Matthan, he guessed what had occurred and turned back to help. In the confusion he was knocked to the ground twice. The second time, a flash of lightening revealed an iron blade slicing through the air, aiming for his neck. Matthan rolled, sword striking the ground only an inch away from the Telumzan's neck. As the soldier swung again, Matthan brought his own weapon up, and the Gogian impaled himself.

Rising from the muddy ground, the Tnias continued forward, spotting a woman being mauled by two soldiers. Immediately he rushed forward, taking down one before the enemy had a chance to realize there was danger. The second man released the woman, who dashed off, then attacked Matthan. The blades clanked together, the Gogian's bulky weight pushing the Tnias backwards. Suddenly Matthan slipped on the muddy ground. Before he could recover, a cold blade pushed against his unprotected throat.

"Freeze, scum, or I will gut you now."

~~~~~~~~~

Pain. A throbbing headache raked through Julie's head. Slowly she forced her eyes open. Bright, unfocused light made the Gogian close her eyes for a moment. Looking again, she saw through the tree limbs above her blue sky broken by clouds.

"I think she's awake. Julie?"

Recognizing Danielle's voice, the Gogian forced herself into a sitting position, wincing from pain. Glancing around, she wished unconsciousness would claim her again. Scattered in a loose circle on the narrow road huddled seventeen captured refugees, muddy and miserable, many with bruises. Five guards stood watch, weapons drawn, two others tending horses—none recognized the princess. Nearby Jon comforted trembling Watt. Bearing several purple welts, Matthan grimly studied their captors. Danielle hovered over Julie.

"Mom, Petals, and Ben are not here. We think they got away."

Matthan scooted closer, whispering, "There's no officers with the guards. They're young and inexperienced. If you and I each attack a guard, we might buy enough time for the others to escape."

Julie nodded. Both understood it was a suicidal plan—two unarmed prisoners against seven guards—but it was better than waiting patiently until they were all executed. As they calculated which soldiers to jump, Danielle's face turned white, terrified that her friends were about to die. She protested, but Matthan gently reminded her it was better for a few to die than all the captives. Casually Julie and Matthan moved to separate edges of the circle, preparing to spring. Muscles tense, Julie waited for her partner's signal.

From the woods emerged five more soldiers, one wearing lieutenant stripes. The guards immediately straightened, paying full attention to their prisoners. Julie cursed under her breath, their only chance for escape lost. Four new captives were thrown into the circle. One was Simeon, holding a bloody rag against his head. Another was a small, crying child lost from her parents. Danielle beckoned the frightened child to her, and the sobbing toddler buried her dirty head into the teenager's bosom.

The officer conversed with several soldiers for a few minutes then walked to the edge of the circle. Scanning the ragged prisoners, he pointed to Bentic. "Stand," he commanded in a firm voice.

Nervously the tattered farmer rose, a young son clinging to his waist.

"Who do you obey?"

"I obey the king of the land. That would be Emperor Erastus now," Bentic answered carefully.

"That is not what I meant." Anger laced the lieutenant's voice. "Which god do you worship?"

The farmer held the Gogian's fierce gaze for a moment, then glanced down at his young son, holding him trustfully. The next words he said would condemn either the youngster's life or soul. Looking directly into the commander's eyes, Bentic replied, "I proudly serve Yahweh. There is no other god."

The nearest guard stepped forward, pulling out a knife, but the lieutenant held up a hand. "Wait. It would make quite an impression if we brought in so many Tnias." A lustful gleam filled the officer's eyes as he fantasized receiving a new promotion for bagging twenty-two fanatics. "We'll take them to Fiennes."

Every step along the five mile trip was torturous. Many refugees were already wounded. Their bodies ached. Senses were dulled from lack of sleep and hunger, but the darkest shadow was the gut-wrenching knowledge that each step brought them closer to death. Several felt prepared for what lay ahead and attempted to encourage the others. One woman cried hysterically. Simeon moved to her side and placed a comforting arm around her shoulders. Jon prayed continuously that the Tnias would have the strength to endure. Danielle and Matthan took turns carrying the parentless toddler.

Of all the captives, Julie carried the heaviest burden. Only she had witnessed Tnias massacres. Only she had coldly killed defenseless victims. Only she had watched detached as their blood soaked the ground. Only she. Perhaps Yahweh's justice was for her to die the way she had killed so many others. *It is only fitting*, the princess told herself. Yet there was a part of Julie's spirit that screamed in defiance. If only she had her weapon! The Sword of Justice would gleam in the blood of those she would send to the Great Abyss. But the mounted guards remained vigilant, preventing any escapes or attacks.

The sun was nearing the horizon when they finally reached the border town of Fiennes. Originally it had started as a fort built on a hill between the conjunction of a large stream and river. Over time, a bustling city had grown up around the fort since the last war with the neighboring country of Lasko. Soldiers marched the captives through the crowded main street. Most townspeople quickly glanced in other directions, ignoring the prisoners, but some yelled and threw stones. Exhausted, several captives fell down, only to be kicked by guards until they rose again. At last the possession entered the stone fort, coming to a halt in a courtyard surrounded by high walls and stout structures.

The lieutenant marched into the nearest building to report. More soldiers gathered, jeering, looking for entertainment. A few minutes later, the strutting lieutenant and several officers exited the building. Heart pounding, Julie pulled her cape's hood over her head then ducking behind Matthan. The prisoners waited tensely, several whispering prayers.

The commanding officer commended the gloating soldier in front of his peers. "Well done, Lieutenant Boute. You have performed a great service for your country. It will not be forgotten." Studying the ragged captives, the major spoke loudly. "Let it not be said that Gog is without mercy. Any prisoner wishing to claim Zuzumza as his god may sup with my men tonight."

Quietness settled across the courtyard, captives taut. A couple in their early thirties hesitantly walked forward. Julie recognized them as refugees who joined the caravan about a week ago.

"Who is your god?" asked the major.

"Zuzumza," answered the couple together, the woman clasping her husband's arm.

With a wave of his hand, the officer called a soldier to escort the couple to the cafeteria. "Is there anyone else who wishes for a long life?" Slowly he walked among the Tnias, finally stopping in front of Danielle, holding the crying child. "Your daughter could grow into a woman."

The teen's faced paled, but she replied without hesitating, "I prefer to die with my Tnias family than serve a demon."

"Very well." The major signaled. Three soldiers stepped forward. The child was taken from Danielle as two soldiers grabbed the teenager's arms. The third raised a knife to her throat. Danielle trembled but did not cry out. Anguished, Matthan tried to reach her but guards held him back. Somewhere a woman began weeping. Jon covered Watt's eyes.

Watching indifferently, the major scanned the prisoners. Suddenly his face registered shock as he stared at a person behind enraged Matthan. Eyes still focused on the hooded woman, the commanding officer raised his hand, stopping the proceedings. "For such a large group of Tnias, it would be a waste for just us to enjoy their deaths. To instill the respect of the Telumzans, there will be a public execution tomorrow at noon which the whole town will watch." Cheers and hoots arose from the rowdy soldiers.

Turning to the honored officer, he said, "Lieutenant Boute, these prisoners are under your care until noon tomorrow. Lock them in the dungeon."

Standing at attention, the officer barked, "Yes, sir, Major Herron."

As the captives were lead away, Urbane stared at the disappearing figure of the woman he knew as his lover Princess Junia.

Chapter Eleven

The terror of the night with panicked refugee and monstrous soldiers did not end at daylight. The bright sun, peeking through clouds, brought little warmth to Rose, huddled under a tree with her younger daughter. Singing birds and humming insects could not remove the fact that they were alone, lost in a hostile forest, not even knowing what country they were in. Lost—the word sent silvers of terror through the woman. Lost was something that happen to kids, not midwives. Worse than being alone was the mounting fear that she would never see her family again. *Yahweh, please keep them safe*, she desperately prayed.

She studied her mud-clad daughter, brushing her hands through the child's matted curls. Petals slowly stirred, looking around in a daze. "Where's Daddy? And Danielle?"

Forcing fear out of her voice, the mother soothed, "We'll find them, honey. They just got separated from us in the darkness. We're going to look for them now."

Heading south, Rose scanned the forested hills for any signs of people, but there were only trees. They climbed up the next hill, only to see more empty woodlands. At every apex, Rose told herself they would discover friends—only to be disappointed each time. The sun climbed steadily across the sky, reaching midday. Anxiety steadily built inside Rose, blooming into barely contained panic.

As they paused to drink from a small stream in a valley, Petals cried out, "Mommy, I see somebody."

"Hush, we don't know who they are." Rose glanced nervously around, seeing nothing.

"It's two women!" Suddenly the child began running up the steep hillside.

"Petals, come back here, now!"

The youngster refused to wait. "It's Sarah, Mommy. Come on!"

Clambering after her daughter, Rose spotted her child hugging Simeon's wife. The tattered elderly woman heartily embraced the midwife. Smiling shyly, Crysta stood nearby holding her infant.

Sarah said, "We just finished asking Yahweh to send us friends when suddenly your daughter appears from nowhere. A much appreciated miracle."

Rose smiled flatly, wondering why Yahweh did not suddenly materialize the rest of her family. She was tired of this wilderness. She wanted the comfort of Jon's strong arms around her, telling her everything would be fine.

Eyes shining with faith, Petals said, "Can we pray again? I want to see my brothers and Sunshine."

The older woman dropped to her knees, eyelevel with the child. "There is no such thing as praying too much." Rose vainly attempted to stop the elderly woman, afraid Petals' hope would fly, only to be crushed. Shifting her baby's position, Crysta knelt beside Sarah. Feeling awkward, Rose kneeled on the fallen leaves too.

Voice harsh with age, Sarah talked to her god as if he stood in front of the tired women. "Yahweh, we thank you for answering our plea for comradeship. Now we ask for your help again. We are lost and missing our families. Give us the guidance to find them. Thank you for your help."

As they stood, Petals scanned the hills. "We'll find them soon." She skipped up the hillside.

The women followed, Sarah and Crysta chatted as if the trek was nothing more than an adventurous outing in the woods. Rose remained silent, desperately desiring to believe help would be found soon yet mentally preparing for the worst. Reaching the crest, Petal saw nothing new. Face momentarily downcast, she quickly scampered downhill, determined to find her missing family.

The women had almost reached the valley floor when the sound of pounded hooves reached their ears. Rose screamed, dashing after her daughter. Petals froze, staring at a dozen horses charging towards her. The mother grabbed her child, mind reeling in fear, knowing it was too late to flee. The herd split, dashing pass the humans, then slowed. Several people waved from the backs of their mounts.

"Going my way, ladies?" called out the familiar voice of Jenik.

"Mom! Petals!" a lanky boy jumped down from his mount, jubilantly hugging his missing family.

"Ben, I thought I would never see you again." Tears ran down Rose's face in relief.

"I never let go of Midnight's reins. I kept up with Jenik's family. And we found Sunshine and Prance."

The farmer added more to the story. "Just before dawn, I had Ben climb a tree looking for lights of farmers who might be preparing for morning chores. Ben led us straight to a farmhouse where most of my family is staying now. We're still missing my second youngest daughter." Jenik quickly pushed away the grief which showed on his face. Best to keep busy. "The farmer helped us organize a search for others still lost in the woods. Since my mare is well liked by the other horses, I've picked up many of the missing beasts."

"They still have on their packs," said Ben, now more man than boy.

Sunshine nuzzled delighted Petals, while Sarah and Crysta talked with the rescuers. Awe filled Rose as she realized Yahweh had answered her young daughter's heartfelt prayer. Part of her family was still missing, but for the first time, the midwife believed Yahweh could protect them.

~~~~~~~~~

The tired prisoners, divided by sex into two large cells, collapsed on rough, wooden benches or the dirty floor. For lunch they were only given a bucket of warm water and moldy bread. With her eyes, Julie inspected the windowless stone prison that consisted of a large chamber divided by strong iron bars into six cells. The few lanterns cast deep shadows. Guards bunched together, talking, occasionally strolling pass to jeer at captives.

Frightened children huddled against haggard adults. Some Tnias were thankful to still be alive. Others thought only about death awaiting them tomorrow. Danielle sat in a corner, pale and lifeless, trembling inside. The parentless toddler nestled in her lap, but the teenager held the child without really seeing her. Julie sat on the cold stone floor beside her friend, lost in her own problems.

One withdrawn woman huddled miserably on a bench muttering, "My husband catches cold so easily. He doesn't have his scarf. I need to give him his scarf." Several nearby women glanced uneasily at her.

Scratched and bruised, postmistress Maragent sat beside the dazed woman and placed a comforting arm over her shoulder. "Your husband's not here. He's safe so you don't need to worry."

"He gets sick so easily. I must find his scarf." The woman continued mumbling to herself, blind to the world around her.

Julie watched, detached, trying to remain lost in the emotional void which kept her sane when soldiers around her died in the midst of war. She would not let fear overwhelm her—though it was very close to doing so. Had Urbane recognized her? That must be the reason he delayed the executions. Could she face her former lover without breaking the commandments of Yahweh? Memories of Urbane danced through the princess's mind, filling her with longing. His caresses against her soft skin, his fingers running through her long hair. *Yahweh, I can't face him. Kill me before my soul is lost to you.*

Whimpers from the toddler slowly aroused Danielle. Glancing around, the teen spotted her father in the cell directly across. Watt's arms were tightly wrapped around Jon. But it was Matthan who held her gaze. Concern filled his face, but he remained silent least the guards' attention focus on Danielle. There was no need for words to convey his emotions for his eyes spoke volumes. Danielle knew now and forever that he loved her.

Brushing damp hair away from the child's face, Danielle spoke softly. "I want to tell you a story."

"Story?" sputtered the child.

"It's about a beautiful city and a kind god who wanted to stop all the evil in the world." As the teenager launched into a long, embellished story of Yahweh's creation of Shalom, the fascinated toddler stopped crying. The prison cell became quiet as others listen to the tale all knew but needed desperately to hear again. Curious children scooted across the stone floor to be closer. Adults' faces relaxed and kids forgot for a moment where they were.

Pulled from her own dark thoughts, Julie listened, the City of Yahweh becoming vivid in her mind. Her soul ached for serenity, the absence of pain and horrifying memories. She was tired of fighting the darkness that oppressed her soul, tired of beholding death as it claimed both friends and foes. *Tomorrow*, she promised herself, *you will walk on its shiny streets and know peace.*

"And then he died?" asked a dirty five-year-old.

"Yes, that's when they killed him." Danielle answered.

Across the room, a boy said, "Why? He didn't do nothing wrong."

"You're right. He was innocent, but administrators in power became jealous because the people loved and wanted to follow him."

"That's not fair! The good guys are supposed to win."

Danielle smiled sadly. "The good guys did win. You see, when Yahweh died, he descended into the Great Abyss, fought Beelzebub, won, then created a land where evil cannot exist. When those who serve him die, they go to live in his dazzling city of Agape."

The toddler in Danielle's lap asked, "Can me?"

"Yes, if you serve Yahweh."

"I do," shouted the boy.

"Yeah, me too," came other cries.

"Me ready to die," spoke the toddler. "I pick flowers with Yahweh to give Mommy when she comes." Danielle hugged the child.

Tears ran down the cheeks of several adults. Someone began singing a praise tune that was quickly picked up by others. Voices joined in harmony, declaring their faith. Fears vanished as a sweet presence filled the dank prison. The woman beside Maragent blinked several times as if waking from a daze then added her voice to the song. Yielding to the invisible presence, Julie sung also as peace filled her soul.

As the dank chamber became alive with a supernatural presence, the guards became uneasy, sensing something they could not understand. They countered with violence. Opening the men's cell, two guards pulled out the nearest prisoner—Simeon.

"You filthy Tnias, I'll give you something to sing about." The guard slammed his fist into the elderly man's stomach. Groaning, Simeon doubled over. The second soldier smashed his elbow against the captive's head, knocking the old ecclesiastic to the floor. They kicked him repeatedly.

Enraged, Julie jumped against the bars, yelling, "Pick on someone your age, putrid vermin dogs."

One guard smiled lustfully at her. "All in good time, beautiful. I will enjoy breaking your spirit then you neck." He found a broom, and walked back towards the aged man to finish him off, while Julie called him every insulting name she knew—which was a long list.

"Enough!" barked a voice, demanding instant obedience.

Surprised, the guards snapped to attention. "Uh, Major Herron, we were just putting the parasites in their place."

Urbane studied the soldiers who shuffled uneasily under his gaze. "I have announced the execution of twenty Tnias tomorrow. Twenty. The crowd expects to see that amount, and I will not disappoint them. If I lack any, I will find replacements. Soldiers who disobey orders will do just fine."

The guard holding the broom answered, "I...uh...the man will be alive tomorrow."

"For your sake, I hope so." As the soldiers dragged Simeon back into his cell, the handsome major studied the female prisoners. Women avoided his gaze. Julie, keeping eyes downcast with hood shadowing her face, walked back to Danielle. But it was too late. Urbane had observed her aggressive display only moments ago.

"The spirited one with black hair will do nicely. Bring her to my chambers—untouched." Urbane turned and left the prison.

The two reprimanded guards opened the cell door and pulled Julie out. The princess walked between her escorts without a struggle.

"No!" screamed Danielle, rushing to the bars. "Yahweh, help her!"

"Julie," called out Matthan. "Yahweh doesn't give us more than we can endure."

The Gogian held her friends' eyes until the iron door to the prison banged shut, cutting her off from her friends.

Silence settled over the prison. Danielle tightly gripped the cold bars, eyes closed, tears running down cheeks. She never guessed following Yahweh might lead to rape. Loss of home and possessions she could handle. Even death. But not this. Not torture or rape. Yahweh could not ask this of them.

"Danielle, look at me," whispered Matthan, between passing guards. Looking across the corridor, the trembling teenager met his gaze. "Yahweh has not deserted us." In the soldier's eyes, the scared teen found faith and determination.

Jon's voice broke through the stillness. "At the town meeting, Julie said it's easy to obey our god when it's socially accepted. It's the hardships which reveals how deep our faith is."

Surrounded by several attending his wounds, Simeon lifted his cracked voice in song. Though faint, the defiant words cut through the tense atmosphere. Others joined in, filling the prison again with hope.

~~~~~~~~~~

Heart pounding, Julie stood outside the door leading to Urbane's room. It took every fiber of her being not to snatch a sword from an unwary guard, defeat her escorts, and flee—alone. It would be suicidal to attempt to free the Tnias trapped in the well-defended prison. The moment slipped pass. The guards pulled Julie into the modestly furnished room then hurried away.

An inviting fire crackled in the hearth. A bed with tall oak posts took up a fourth of the room. Relaxed, Urbane was seated in a padded chair, feet propped on a large desk. Seeing her handsome former lover reclined in a position she had observed many times, tender feelings swirled through Julie.

Arms folded behind his head, the major's deep voice pierced the silence of the warm room. "So the great Gogian princess has returned. Is this another one of your elaborate plots to win renown?"

An idea forming, the Tnias wrapped emotions and memories of Junia tightly around her like a garment, face liven with haughty arrogance, voice dripping with sarcasm. "I was doing quite well until your excellent night patrol blundered the crossing."

Straightening in his chair, Urbane asked, "What is this great plan of yours that forces you to wait until a knife is pressed to your pretty throat before revealing your identity?"

Flaring in anger, the princess answered, "I wouldn't have to wait till the last second if you kept your garrison slightly less defended and a guard sleeping near the cell with a key sticking out of his pocket. But no, you have to do things the hard way, running everything efficiently."

Laughing, the major stood and leaned against his desk. "What is this brilliant scheme that requires you to travel with your enemy?"

"That's oblivious. I wanted to infiltrate their underground network, discover their weaknesses, and then use it against them."

Looking serious, despite a twinkle in his eye, Urbane said, "It might be possible to arrange your escape."

"Not just me. Everybody—down to the smallest child."

"Everyone?" Genuine shock crossed his face.

"They are planning to cross the Timbrel Mountains. Traveling with them, I would be the first Gogian to penetrate the enemy's homeland."

"Impossible. Only Tnias can enter Shalom."

Cruel laugher frosted the princess's voice. "I'm surprised by you, Urbane, believing old myths. They tell it to keep weak-minded fools out to protect this god of theirs."

"Junia, you're as arrogant as ever." He moved forward, still talking, until inches away. "If slipping into Shalom was that easy, we would have done it centuries ago. What did you expect to accomplish there, cut off from all military aid?"

Pretending not to notice how close Urbane stood, Julie answered, "Their god was killed by mortals long ago but came back alive. If he died once, he can be killed again."

"Your ambitions are to be praised." Urban wrapped a muscular arm around her slender waist as he spoke, "but your plan would have failed." Julie opened her mouth in protest, and Urbane firmly pressed his lips against hers, his arm pulling her body close.

Heart racing, Julie pushed against Urbane's chest, breaking away. She spat out, "Don't dare tell me what I can and cannot do! I am a princess, remember. I know what I am doing. By worshipping with them and taking their vows, they believe I am a Tnias."

"No. I've lost you once. I'm not about to let you get killed on another foolish quest." He paced the room, frustrated. "When you disappeared, I had men searching for days across the battlefields. I refused to believe you were dead. Every moment I expected you to boldly march into camp holding the head of the Telumzan king, heedless of my worries."

His voice softened, revealing a tender side Julie had never seen before. "When days stretched into weeks, then months, I told myself you must have been captured, abiding the perfect time to escape. When the snows melted, I said, 'Junia will come'—but you didn't. Now that you're finally here, all you desire is another glorious adventure to net you more fame."

Seeing his agony lowered Julie's defenses. "I...I thought you would have found another woman to replace me."

Urbane stroked his lover's chin. "With your passion and talents?" Genuine warmth flowed through his voice. "Junia, the gods only made one of you."

Julie closed her eyes, turbulent feelings storming through her. As Junia, she had used him as a stepping-stone, abused his feelings, mocking his affection, but never opening herself to real intimacy. Living with the Bricks had taught her what love should be—accepting, trusting, enduring all wrongs without counting those wrongs. All those feelings and more rushed through her, warm and pleasant.

"I love you, Urbane," the true Julie answered.

"I've never stopped loving you, no matter how difficult you make it." Bending his head down, Urbane gently kissed her.

Julie embraced the kiss, both lingering. Urbane pressed firmer, arms encircling. For a moment Julie only thought of the warmth of his body, ignoring warnings from her conscience. An image of imprisoned Tnias, tattered and miserably, flashed through her mind.

Julie pulled away. "I need...supposed to get back to the prisoners."

"Why?" asked her lover, perplexed by the sudden change.

"They will know if I slip in any of the vows I was forced to take."

"Junia, they know what's going on in this room, only they think it's forced." Urbane attempted to laugh, but it came out hollow.

Emotions combating, Julie walked halfway to the door. Desire raged through her body, but her mind screamed it was immoral. But if she could save the prisoners by sleeping with Urbane, was it wrong? It would only be for one night. Simeon had said that Yahweh was a forgiving god. She recalled Matthan's face when leaving the dungeon, full of faith and determination, *Yahweh doesn't give us more than we can endure.* Deep inside, Julie knew her friends would choose death rather than see her break one of Yahweh's sacred laws created to protect his people.

Walking up to the princess, Urbane rested his chin on her shoulder, arms circling her waist. *Yahweh, I can't handle this,* Julie prayed. *You have to help me.* The officer kissed her neck then nibbled her ear. For only a moment she relished the sensations then pulled away.

"I...I can't, Urbane. I must go back."

"Into a smelly dungeon instead of a warm bed?" When Julie refused to answer, the major became concerned. "What is wrong with you, Princess?" With one hand, he forced her face to look directly at him. For a long moment he searched her eyes, looking for the woman he knew—and not finding her.

"You're one of them." He spoke slowly, yearning to find something to counteract his judgment.

Julie almost spoke, but words felled her. The major took her silence as admittance. Violently, Urbane shoved Julie away as if her very touch defiled him. Off balanced, Julie hit the floor, hard.

"How could you, Junia? How?"

"I was injured in battle—badly. I would have died except for a Telumzan soldier who rescued me and found a Tnias family to nurse me back to health. Every day I thought about you and planned to flee before the snows fell. But then I saw the love the family processed for each other."

"We had love."

Julie stood. "What we claimed as love was only a dim shadow. Love is not selfish or proud, but patient and kind. I thought only of what I could get for myself, and for that, Urbane, I am truly sorry. I wish I could change all the times I have wounded you."

Her lover's body trembled in barely contained rage. "Will you swear to Zuzumza or choose the enemy's god over me?"

Struggling, Julie looked away. "I love you, Urbane, but I would not have known true love unless I first felt it from Yahweh. He is love itself, pure and unadulterated."

Determined not to lose his lover, the officer tried a different approach. "What about your career? Your glory? And hatred? You burned with revenge—seeking to destroy your father and brother."

"I still have no love for them, but neither do I seek their deaths. There are more important things like…tending widows and children."

"You have indeed gone mad—squandering your time with the weak."

"It is a weak god who commands his followers to kill those who cannot raise a hand in their own defense. Zuzumza fears the faith of even a small child."

Enraged by her slander, Urbane raised his hand to strike, stopping only an inch from her face. Hand wavering, strong emotions tore through him—love for a woman and hatred for a god colliding in a fiery cyclone. Instead of hitting, the hand slipped behind Julie's head, holding his lover firmly as he kissed her soft lips, letting pent-up passions from the last six months pour into her enticing mouth. His other arm wrapped around her back, pulling their bodies together.

The woman pushed against him, but Urbane's grip tightened, as if physically holding their relationship together. The princess was a trained killer, and the major knew if she truly wanted to escape, she would find a way. Her struggles became less as passion consumed reason. When her body finally melted against his, arms enclosing his broad shoulders, Urbane knew Junia was his again. He guided her to the bed, both falling on the thick mattress as their kissing intensified.

The door suddenly burst open. "Major Herron!" a frantic officer shouted. The lieutenant dashed in then froze, looking awkwardly at the ceiling.

Partly rising, Urbane fixed the soldier with a cold stare. "I asked not to be disturbed."

Nervously the soldier sputtered, "It's the… uh… the locked doors…I mean cells…"

"Be quick!"

Lieutenant Boute took a deep breath to steady himself. "The prisoners have escaped, sir."

Urbane stood up. "Escaped? How many?"

The soldier looked uncomfortable. "I believe all of them, sir."

"Impossible. How could they have gotten out of their cells?"

"We don't know. The doors are still locked, but the cells are empty. I have organized a search of the entire fort, but they can't be found."

"Send troops into the city and surrounding countryside. Let no man sleep until they're found." As Lieutenant Boute nervously hurried away, Urbane faced the woman sitting on his bed, once again the menacing Gogian commander. "Where are they?"

"I…I don't know." Julie stood, still dazed at what almost happened between Urbane and herself.

"You must know something!" Urbane had a murderous look. "Prisoners don't simply turn invisible and walk through lock doors."

Attempting to calm him, Julie spoke the first words that came to her mind. "There's an ancient story told of two innocent men who were beaten then put in a dungeon. Instead of being miserable and complaining, they sang praises. Yahweh saw the love in their hearts and freed them. The captives' chains dropped from their hands and feet. And they walked out of prison, passing in front of guards who couldn't see them."

Urbane studied Julie for a moment, unable to believe the story yet not able to dismiss it either. Finally he stormed out of the room with a threat. "For your sake, you better hope they're found."

Alone, Julie stood for several minutes in the middle of the room, slowly taking in everything that had just occurred. Relief flowed through her—the others were free! She was certain that no matter how hard the soldiers searched, her friends would not be recaptured, for when Yahweh performs a miracle, it cannot be undone.

But her joy soon turned into bitter disappointment—she was still a prisoner. Had Yahweh passed her by because she was weak, about to give in to Urbane? If the guard had not came in when he did, she would have completely surrendered. The Gogian dropped to her knees in agony. Was she so corrupt that Yahweh discarded her the first time she gave in to temptation? To burn in the Great Abyss because she was unworthy of the splendors of Shalom? In her short but oppressed life, she had committed tremendous crimes against his people. Why would any god save his enemy?

Face covered, Julie wept. She cried out her pain of abandonment to Yahweh. It may have been minutes or hours later, but sometime during the woman's prayers, invisible arms surrounded her, strong and loving. Warmth flowed through her, pushing back despair, while comprehension filled her mind. Yahweh had saved the refugees physically but rescued her from falling spiritually. Was not one miracle as great as the other? When Yahweh issued a miracle, it would not be undone. Julie felt that her whole life had reached an apex of a long awaited destiny, and though it meant death, she was ready.

Midafternoon when a tired and frustrated Urbane entered the room, one look at the woman kneeling on the wooden floor was enough for the Gogian to realize Junia was lost to him forever.

Chapter Twelve

Insects buzzed lazily in the hot sun. A small stream wound its way through green fields and thickets. On its banks, women washed dirty clothing, laying them on rocks to dry, while children played in a nearby meadow. Refugees pleasantly worked alongside citizens of Lasko who had opened up their homes to the destitute foreigners. The Brentwood emigrants stayed in close contact with each other, hoping missing family members would soon be found. Others refugees headed south or east, looking for new places to settle.

Rose dipped a shirt underwater then raised it up, only to submerge it again. Working kept her mind off her missing family—for short periods of time. Beside Rose, Vasia chatted non-stop about every subject imaginable—except her missing husband and son. Rose forced her mind to only think about the wet cloth in her hands.

Several children cried out and the women glanced up to see if anyone had been injured. Kids jumped excitedly, pointing towards the road. The ladies shadowed their eyes with their hands, examining the lane. Ben and several older kids began running down the road.

Petals dashed to her mother. "They're here, Mommy!"

"Who? I don't see anyone." Rose scanned the dusty highway.

"Behind the trees. I know it's Daddy and Watt and everybody."

Rose attempted to calm her daughter, knowing it could be any group of travelers, but her own heart pounded in hope. *Please, Yahweh,* she prayed, *let it be our families.*

All the women climbed the stream's bank and gathered by the road, scanning the horizon. Finally one figure then another emerged from behind the thicket, and still more. Vasia began screaming joyfully and dashed towards the travelers. Rose ran beside her, tears running down flushed cheeks. Soon Jon and Watt tightly embraced her while Danielle quietly cried. Tired but happy, Matthen handed over the sleepy toddler to Jenik's ecstatic wife. Nearby Bentic and Vasia kissed passionately while their numerous giggling children bounded around them.

Everyone talked at once, stories jumbling and mixing together. It was some time before the families settled on the grass and Simeon, the chosen speaker, narrated their miraculous escape. He was interrupted many times as others added comments.

Halfway through the story, Jenik and other husbands arrived, causing the tale to be retold from the beginning.

In prison, the Tnias had been singing praises after Julie had been taken away. Suddenly two shiny entities appeared in the cells. As the captives stared in amazement, the Mal'ak told them to follow. One bent over Simeon, and taking the injured man's hand, commanding him to rise. The elderly man stood up, completely healed. The cell doors swung open by themselves, and the prisoners filed out while the oblivious guards continued chatting with each other at the far end of the chamber. The cell doors closed and locked behind the last captives.

As the refugees followed the Mal'ak through the courtyard, they walked as if in a surreal dream, feeling no fear as they passed directly in front of soldiers looking in their direction but seeing nothing. Onward they traveled through the quiet city—not even a dog barked. A number believed they had died and were being taken to Agape. Several looked for Julie, expecting her to be rescued also. When the group reached the edge of town and the Gogian still had not joined them, Danielle turned around, determined not to leave her friend.

One Mal'ak stopped the teen, saying, "Yahweh has a mission for Julie. Do not worry. You will see her again in the future."

After the Lasko border was crossed, the Mal'ak gave the freed captives directions to find their families then disappeared into thin air. One lingered for a moment to give Matthan the sword Simeon had bestowed to Julie. Feeling as if they had just awakened from a dream, the Tnias looked around in amazement then joyfully headed east, walking through the night. They rested at dawn then continued through the morning and early afternoon until finding their families.

The Brentwood emigrants were only together for one more day. After gathering what little supplies they still owned or were donated to them, they said sad good-byes. Some had kinsmen living in Lasko or other nearby counties to aid them in beginning new lives. Others would travel until a location caught their fancy. A few, like Simeon and Sarah, stayed in the area to aid other refugees who dared to cross the border, dodging Gogian patrols. Rose would accept no destination except for Shalom—she refused for her family to be herded south again when the next country fell to the Gogian Empire. Feeling the same way, Vasia and Bentic decided to travel with the Bricks.

Danielle refused to leave, determined Julie would soon join them. So the two families waited. As the days slowly flowed past, restlessness filled the Tnias—it was time to press on. After a week, Rose gently talked with her daughter, explaining the logic. The farmers who had kindly opened their homes up to the refugees had their own growing families to feed and the emigrants needed to reach Shalom before winter. Danielle begged for more time but her mother said in two days they would leave.

The next day, Danielle and Matthan escorted the farmer to a nearby town to pick up supplies. The maiden visited every store, asking if anyone had seen Julie. She listened to local gossip, yearning for a clue. New refugees freely shared stories of horrors committed by the Red Army and their own daring escapes. The biggest topic of conversation was the execution of King Hermes. The people viewed his death as the symbolic end to the nation of Telumza. Downhearted, Danielle returned to the wagon where Matthan and the farmer stacked supplies brought in the marketplace.

Lifting a burlap bag filled with seed potatoes, the soldier asked, "Heard anything?"

"No," said the disappointed teen. "Just that King Hermes was killed and something about a Gogian princess turning out to be a Tnias. She's to be executed in Thorn. Maybe Julie's at a different border town. If we keep looking, I'm sure we'll find her."

Hearing about his king's death, Matthan stood in respectful silence for a moment. "King Hermes was a good man, and he'll be missed. Don't worry about Julie. She knows we're going to Shalom. I'm sure we'll run into her on the way."

"Yeah," mumbled the maiden, glancing at her empty hands. "It's just I can't leave without knowing what happened to her."

Matthan hefted another sack onto the wagon. "Yahweh's messengers said we'd see her again. Don't lose faith now after all we've been through." Grinning, he tweaked her nose and was rewarded with a smile.

"Strange about the Gogian princess," spoke the farmer. "I didn't think any offspring of Erastus could turn. Goes to show our god moves in mysterious ways—very mystifying indeed."

Determined to stay cheerful, Danielle added, "I wish I could see the Emperor's face when he discovers his daughter believes Yahweh is the Supreme God."

As Matthan picked up the last bag, a dim memory stirred in the back of his mind. Dropping the sack, he stood with mouth opened in disbelieving astonishment. Both the farmer and Danielle watched him in bewilderment.

"It can't...no...the dagger," sputtered the soldier.

"The what?" asked both onlookers together.

"I don't believe it! Impossible...yet it makes perfect sense."

The farmer commanded, "Get a hold of yourself, son, and tell us what you're blabbing about."

Matthan took a deep breath. "The first time I met Julie, she attempted to kill me with a dagger but missed. I pulled it out of the ground then threw it away. I never thought about it until just now, but it contained the royal insignia of the house of Erastus."

Danielle sharply drew in her breath while the farmer took off his hat and scratched his head in amazement.

Knowing the princess was to be killed, the maiden became defensive. "You might be mistaken about the symbol you saw. Just because she carried a dagger with an insignia doesn't make Julie a princess."

Matthan gently placed his hands on her shoulders. "Listen, Danielle. What do you think a Gogian princess would be like?"

"I...I guess angry, cruel, and vehemence—plain evil."

"Was not Julie all these things when she came to us?"

The maiden pulled away, unable to accept his words yet feeling truth in them. "The Mal'ak said we'll see Julie again."

"Yes, Danielle, in Yahweh's City."

Grief flooded through the teenager's tender heart. She turned her back to the men, body trembling, tears trickling down rosy cheeks. Matthan stepped closer and wrapped comforting arms around her waist. The maiden turned in his arms and leaned against his broad shoulders, no longer holding back her sobs.

~~~~~~~~~

Mounted horses plodded along the steep trail winding through forest-clad Hockquill Mountains. Quicker and safer paths existed but Urbane felt no concern for speed or comfort. The small troop of soldiers accompanying the major quietly joked and planned their first outings when reaching the capitol city, but they stayed wary of the tension between their aloof superior and his well-known prisoner. They wished for the long trek to soon end.

Hoarding the time, Urbane desperately sought a way to regain his lost lover. He attempted several angles, but every conversation ended with him losing control of his temper, unable to handle the mix of love and sorrow in Julie's eyes. Every step closer to Blackwall Palace strengthened the princess's determination—but kindled flames of frustration inside the major. He could not understand why Junia preferred a weak deity over all the glory and power she had earned under Zuzumza.

The day they rode through the cobble streets of Thorn, Julie expected fear to smother her. Instead, a supernatural peace surrounded her, keeping mind clear and purposeful. Curious bystanders whispered to each other, wondering about the tattered prisoner stately riding with head held high. Urbane—saving his most potent ploy for last—did not send a messenger ahead to announce their arrival.

In the courtyard of the palace, the major dismissed all but two escorts then lead the captive through familiar arched passageways and up broad stairs, finally arriving at an ornate door. Ordering the soldiers to stand guard, Urbane accompanied Julie inside, unbinding her arms.

"Look around you, Princess. This is your life." With a sweep of his hand, the major indicated the lavishly garnished chamber, thick rugs, gilded oak cabinets housing costly collectibles, a fashionable bed hidden by lacy veils. Time itself seemed to stop as Julie gazed at the familiar room that belonged to her—yet seemed to belong to a distant stranger. Everything in the chamber was either handpicked by her or was a gift from the many who wished to gain her favor.

Long forgotten memories from the princess's childhood danced through her mind, she playing with favorite toys, a stern nanny always watching. At the large desk she had completed assignments given by tutors or sketched birds and people seen from her window—quickly hiding the pictures when servants entered the room. On cold nights wrapped in thick blankets, she read books about oppressed protagonists who left on adventures and came back heroes. She identified so easily with them, envisioning her own victorious quests and winning her father's love— but that dream faded along with all beauty in her life. As a teenager, she only knew hatred and arrogance, fashionable clothes and parties. The only happiness in her dreary life was the sword practices with Rufus.

Urbane spoke, and Julie jumped, having forgotten someone else was in the room. "I was waiting for the right time to give you this." From his belt, he pulled out a dagger with the royal insignia and handed it to her.

Surprised, Julie traced the pattern with a finger. "It's the knife my father gave me when I was honored with the Medallion of Zuzumza. I thought it was lost."

The major's voice was thick with emotion. "It was found not far from your dead horse. I kept it, determined to deliver it to its owner in person."

The princess walked over to her desk and searched through her ivory jewelry box, pushing pass gold armbands, silver necklaces, and glittering pins. Finally she held up a blue velvet container, opening it to reveal the large gold Medallion of Zuzumza, the engraved image of the god reflecting sunlight. For a long moment she examined the medal, until another object caught her eye. Pushing aside costly adornments, she pulled out a wooden horse, with mane flying, which hung from a cheap metal chain. She laid it on the desktop beside the medallion and dagger. The princess studied the three objects that represented her life. The dagger symbolized royalty and power. The medallion spoke of glory and honor. The wooden horse was freedom and friendship. Urbane grew uneasy as Julie studied the three items.

"My brother gave me this horse when my mother was killed. He had to sneak out of the palace and searched half of Market Square before finding something 'worthy of you.' It was the only present given me in Gog with no strings attached." Julie clenched the necklace tightly in her hand.

"Look around you, Junia. Anyone in the empire would sell his own parents to be you, to possess your wealth and power. The empire itself could one day be your play toy. How can you give all this up for a senseless death?"

Pained, the woman closed her eyes. "There is a story of a man who, walking through a field, discovered a precious treasure. He sold everything he owned to buy that field in order to possess the treasure." She looked directly at Urbane. "The true value of a treasure is what you're willing to give up to process it."

"Is not your life more precious than a god?"

"What is gold and silver without love?"

Frustrated, Urban rubbed a hand through his short, black hair. "What about us? You claim to love me but prefer death than living with me."

Julie walked halfway across the room towards him, attempting to find words to express her emotions. "I love you, Urbane, with a love you yet cannot comprehend. I wish with all my heart I could wipe away all the pain inside you, replacing it with the serenity and peace Yahweh has given me." Her voice broke. "But I cannot do that. You must open your own heart to Yahweh."

The major stepped closer. "You are going to die, Junia—die. A signed contract and done deal, irreversible."

"We are both soldiers. Every time we rode into battle we knew it could be our last. We all die sooner or later. What counts is how we live our lives. I wasted so much of mine. I wanted to mold a golden god in my own image, thinking everyone was created to serve me. I was wrong, so wrong."

Urbane lightly brushed a strand of hair from her face. Once he had thought her sharp, haughty looks attractive, but the humble woman before him was poetic beauty beyond words, a rainbow after a summer storm. Part of him craved to possess that substance which had transformed her, but the stronger half of him was not willing to give up his career and life for a god—any god. Tears ran down Julie's cheeks. Having never seen the princess cry, Urbane touched them. Then gently he kissed her, not lustfully, but from a tender emotion harboring in his heart. For a brief time they were connected, their worlds in harmony—but the moment passed.

"I love you, Urbane." Julie took a deep breath. "I'm ready to face my father. I pray someday you will understand why I do this."

Urbane nodded, attempting to regain control of his raging emotions. He wanted to dash out of the palace with Junia, riding bareback into the mountains, never looking back at the wars and deaths that lay behind. Instead, he buried those tender feelings, once again a cold Gogian commander.

Chapter Thirteen

Lofty and mysterious, the Timbrel Mountain range rose sharply from the forest landscape. Each peak, taller than the last, seemed to pierce the sky itself. The enormous cliffs were visible halfway across the country of Lahad. Ragged and exhausted from months of traveling, two large families nervously stood before the rocky mouth of a cave located in southern Lahad, staring at the seven Mal'ak guarding the entrance. The immortal beings, dressed in sky blue tunics and golden trousers, looked human. The long trek's zenith came to this moment—the cold, hunger, dangers, and sacrifices no longer mattered—only their souls. The night before, the families had spent hours praying and singing. Carefully Yahweh's story was retold to the younger children, reminding them that only the pure in heart could pass through the caves.

Jon limped forward, unsure how to address the Mal'ak. "We, the Bricks and Ventix families, request entrance into Shalom."

A Mal'ak stepped forward, smiling warmly. "You are expected. My name is Nissima. I will be your guide."

Bodies relaxing, family members smiled in relief. Holding her youngest child, Vasia squeezed her husband's arm. Petals hugged her mother gleefully. Ben, tending the horses with Matthan, slapped the Tnias soldier a high five. Laughing, Danielle encircled several Ventix children with her slender arms while Watt hopped from foot to foot in excitement.

Nissima led the group through the broad entrance, passing the other guardians. Inside the cave, the horses pulled on their reins, stomping feet nervously, until Nissima touched each beast on the forehead. The animals quieted and followed like docile sheep. No torches were used—the Mal'ak's glowing body illuminated the infinite night. The craggy tunnel twisted and turned, splitting into many passageways, sometimes opening into spacious chambers arrayed in a vast display of stalagmites, but always the Mal'ak knew which direction to go. In the darkness beyond Nissima's light, shadowy creatures scuttled along walls, knocking pebbles lose. Horses twitched their ears towards the sounds, but Nissima's gentle voice calmed them.

For hours they journeyed through underground wonders, passing glowing crystals, gawking at strange rock formations, attempting to identify bizarre creatures hidden in the shadows, even crossing an ancient river on a large, flat barge. The children leaned over the sides, pointing excitedly at huge, white fish following the oars. Later, they rested and ate, drinking from a fresh spring and eating sweet, puffy mushroom and delicious, transparent fruit from pale-green plants that grew near phosphorescent crystals.

Filling content and blessed, Jon pulled out his guitar, strumming a few chords. In a clear voice he sang a familiar tune, slightly alternating the words to fit their long trek.

> *Yahweh is my shepherd*
> *I shall not be in want*
> *He feeds me fruits from translucent plants*
> *And leads me to quiet pools of fresh water*

~~~~~~~~~~

In the crowded Chamber of Juxtaposition, tempers were growing hotter than the gods' legendary furnace. Sitting at a long oak table, weary generals, lords, and advisors glanced uneasily at each other while their aides bustled about. Emperor Erastus half-raised from his massive ornate chair located at the front of the room and venomously attacked his oldest son's last statement. Phlegon answered in a calm, calculating voice that only angered his father more.

Catching Prince Rufus's eye, General Nereus quietly signaled for the young man to step in. It seemed to be the second-born's main duty these days to negotiate compromises between the two most powerful men in the empire. Though the Emperor's word was law, he needed to appease his appointed leaders who enforced the laws and kept him informed of the latest happens in his vast nation. Reluctant of change, Erastus refused almost all of the Crown Prince's innovative ideas of running the country, but Phlegon was cunning, waiting for the perfect timing in meetings to publicly challenge his father—who did not take kindly to his son's subordinations.

Standing, Rufus elegantly spoke, claiming Phlegon had given such intricate plans that a night was needed to deliberate. The monarch agreed—to the relief of everyone. As nobles filed into the hallway, a messenger scurried to the Emperor.

"Your Majesty, Major Herron wishes to deliver a Tnias prisoner, caught on the Lasko border, directly to you."

Impatient, the monarch brushed the aide away. "What is that to me? Just kill the barbarian."

Persistently the attendant followed. "Beg your pardon, sire, but it's your daughter Princess Junia."

That stopped the Emperor—and everyone else in hearing distance. The ruler turned slowly to face the aide. "She will be examined in the Great Hall of Kings."

The messenger nodded and hurried away. Nobles whispered the news to each other, and aides quickly spread the gossip. As the crowd dispersed, Rufus glanced towards his brother.

"This should be entertaining, huh, brother." Phlegon grinned sinisterly. "This must be our spoilt sister's most elaborate scheme for attention yet."

Rufus refused to answer but hurried towards the center of the palace. Arriving in the enormous, colonnade chamber, the prince observed that the three balconies levels were already crowded with onlookers. Erastus sat on his massive gold throne located on a raised dais. Heart pounding, Rufus pushed pass curious bystanders.

"Bring in the prisoner." The room quieted in the resounding echoes of the Emperor's voice, all eyes focusing on the double doors at the opposite end of the long chamber.

~~~~~~~~~

He gives me strength
He guides me in the right paths as he has promised

~~~~~~~~~

As two guards escorted a tattered dressed woman, the crowd whispered that a mistake must have been made. Surely this could not be the arrogant Princess Junia they remembered. The captive walked calmly between two guards, ignoring the excited crowd. Rufus stared in astonishment, recognizing his sister's face yet discerning that the woman was not the haughty teen he used to instruct in fencing. She was different somehow.

Urbane stopped the procession twenty feet from the throne. "Your Sovereignty, I bring you the prisoner Princess Junia who claims allegiance to the god of our enemies."

Emperor Erastus studied his daughter. "Interesting. I thought you died in battle months ago. What do you have to say for yourself?"

~~~~~~~~~~

Even though I walk through the valley of the shadow of death
I will fear no evil

~~~~~~~~~~

The onlookers eagerly stained to hear the captive's defense, and the woman did not disappoint them. Boldly she stepped forward. "I have learned that Yahweh is the creator of all—including Zuzumza. The god of Gog feasts upon hatred, spreading it through your people like a disease, but Yahweh is the God of Love, pure and holy. He cares for all people," she waved her bound hands at the audience, "and desires for each of you to denounce evil and come to him."

Shocked by the sacrilegious words, the crowd murmured loudly. Only Rufus watched in fascinating awe. This was the woman he always wanted his sister to become—viewing the citizens of Gog as a responsibility to shepherd, not pawns in a quest for power. He felt both the pride of a mentor who realizes that his student has just blossomed into a mature adult but he feared its high price.

~~~~~~~~~~

For you are with me
Your rod and staff comfort me

~~~~~~~~~~

As Julie spoke, Erastus became enraged. He marched down the steps of the dais, stopping only six feet from his daughter. Speaking in a beastly hiss, he demanded, "Do you swear fidelity to this god?"

White-knuckled, Rufus gripped a column. *Don't say it*, he desperately whispered in his mind. *Even if you believe it, don't say it. Live, sister, live—for me.* But he dared not speak his treasonous words aloud.

~~~~~~~~~~

You prepare a banquet for me
In the presence of my enemies

The Tnias did not hesitation. "I serve the One True God—Yahweh."

The audience gasped, knowing she uttered her death sentence. The Emperor's chest heaved, his body a shallow skin barely containing the enraged evil living within him. Standing near the throne, Phlegon smiled like a hungry predictor whose prey had just made a fatal mistake. Rufus felt the room spinning. He was trapped in a nightmare, powerless to stop the atrocity taking place before his eyes.

~~~~~~~~~

You welcome me as an honored guest
You fill my cup to the brim

~~~~~~~~~

Only Julie could see the reptilian red eyes, glowing in hatred, looked out from the Emperor's eye sockets. The monarch stepped to Urbane and pulled the soldier's sword from its sheath. Without a word, he moved near his daughter. Right arm drew back, hovering for a millisecond then plunged forward, like a hunger hawk diving downward for its prey.

The sword pierced his daughter's abdomen. It did not stop. The blade continued through the woman's body and emerging from her back.

"Noooo!" yelled Rufus. Without realizing that he was doing so, he ran towards his sister.

The demon king smiled. "So will be the fate of all who sell themselves to the God of Dung."

With a quick jerk, he pulled the bloody blade free and handed it back to Urbane. Julie crumpled to the marble floor. Most nobles and servants cheered. Someone began chanting Zuzumza name. Others took up the cry, their voices reverberating through the huge, arched chamber, but there were some who quietly looked away, troubled. On the second balcony, a silent dark-haired child stared in shock as her long-worshipped hero gasped for air.

Reaching his sister, Rufus dropped to the floor, cuddling the dying woman. He shouted at his father, "How could you? She is your daughter!"

Tilting his head, the Emperor studied his son for a long moment. Then he turned, addressing Phlegon, "Come. It is time for supper. I have ordered roasted pig."

Strolling beside his father, the Crown Prince exited the Great Hall of Kings, spitefully glancing once over his shoulder at the siblings who would no longer threatened his power. The audience dispersed, but Urbane remained rooted in the exact spot he had stopped earlier to address the Emperor, his wet-red sword loosely held in his hand.

Bending over his sister, Rufus demanded, "Why, Junia? Why did you do such a stupid thing?"

~~~~~~~~~

I know that your goodness and love
Will be with me all my life

~~~~~~~~~

The woman's eyes opened and she coughed blood. "For...for the first time...I did something...right." For a moment her eyes flicked around the room, but already her vision was dimming. "Ur...Urbane?"

"He's here." The prince glared at the major, demanding for the motionless man to speak. Urbane's face twisted in a volatile mask, but he remained silent.

"Ur...Urbane, I...I love you...and so does...Yahweh." She coughed blood again. Wrenching in pain, she briefly held her brother's eyes. "I...I love you...both." Her body convulsed in pain, eyes staring blankly. Then her body relaxed. The soul had flown.

~~~~~~~~~

I will dwell in the house of Yahweh forever

~~~~~~~~~

For a moment both soldiers stared at the peaceful smile on her face, then Rufus's body began to shake as unnoticed tears flooding down his cheeks. "Why? Junia, why?"

Urbane spoke, his tense voice betraying the hidden pain raking through his soul. He was a soldier of Gog, the servant of Zuzumza. There was no room for pity. "She made her decision. She preferred her god over you, me, even her own life. She knew the price she would pay for her *precious treasure*." Venomously, he spit out the last two words then turned, leaving the room without looking back.

Hidden in the shadows of a column, Princess Thasbow watched, barely eleven, forgetting nothing. Junia had never paid any attention to the child, but Rufus had sometimes played with her, coaxing her talents, giving advice. Yet it was the first-born daughter that the half-sister idolized, desiring nothing more than to be like her. Now her idol—her goddess—was dead.

Rufus held Julie, weeping. The prince's world lay shattered, leaving him nothing to believe in. For a long time, he cradled her head until he noticed a chain around her neck. His bloody hand held up a wooden horse. The animal, with mane and tail flying in invisible wind, galloped towards an unknown destination. The man removed the token and placed it around his own neck.

He slowly stood and walked out of the chamber, vowing to himself that his father had not lost one child, but two. *I will never enter this cursed palace again.*

~~~~~~~~~

Urbane marched past servants, ignoring their stares and whispers. *Walk. Just keep moving. Don't think about anything else.* But he could never escape the memories. Turning a corner, he spotted a stairway. He managed to make it halfway to the second landing before doubling over, retching his lunch. Sitting on a higher step, he tried to relax but his hands shook violently. The sword was still clutched in his right hand, glistening with wet blood—her blood. He was a trained soldier and stared death in the face a thousand times. *This is no different*, he told himself—but his body continued to tremble.

It's her own fault. She's the one who chose death. She could have called to Zuzumza, and the Emperor would have been merciful. It's her fault—she's the only one to blame.

He stared at the wet-red blade but it only seemed to laugh mockingly. His body continued to tremble.

~~~~~~~~~

It was night when the tired, but happy, families emerged from the lee side of the Timbrel Mountains. The cave's exit was located on a steep, grassy slope above the immense valley floor that stretched hundreds of miles until once again merging with the protective encircling mountain range. Looking westward, the Tnias stared in awe at a gigantic city, fantastic in shape, bright as the sun, taller than the clouds. Its glow illuminated the entire valley. For a long time no one spoke, feelings of wonder and rapture pulsing through them—eternity would not be enough time to take in the beauty of the legendary city.

Nissima spoke, breaking the trance. "Nearby is the town of Ephraath, which means *fruitful*. There homes await you. Bentic and Vasia, there is a farm with crops waiting to be harvested. There is no winter or severe storms here. You will be able to produce several crops a year. Jon, the townspeople have projects needing to be crafted. Rose, no longer will you treat the ill—no sickness exist inside Shalom. Your skills as a midwife will issue new life into this world."

"What about us?" asked Ben.

The Mal'ak smiled at the children, "You have school. There is much to learn. Many of you will cross into the lands of darkness again, fulfilling quests for Yahweh."

The children nodded, Watt believing school in paradise could not be *that* bad. Matthen squeezed Danielle's hand tightly. Nissima led the party downhill. Adults laughed joyfully. Several children started a game of tag, dashing between horses and adults.

For a moment Matthan and Danielle held back, looking towards the City of Light.

"Do you think she's there now?" asked the maiden.

The soldier smiled. "She's probably walking through a beautiful garden with Yahweh himself, dressed like a regal princess again."

Danielle leaned against Matthan's shoulder. "I know someday we'll see her again. Until then, we have much to do."

For a moment the youths looked into each other's eyes, remembering all they had been through, trials they had faced, friends left behind, childhood homes lost. Both had been tested by fire and changed forever. Without a word spoken, both knew one day they would challenge evil again—together.

Matthan lowered his head, kissing Danielle gently on her lips. The maiden closed her eyes, relishing her first kiss. Impatient, Sunshine nudged the couple with her head. Laughing, they hurried to catch up with the others.

PART III

"Indeed for this purpose I have raised you up, that I may show my power in you, and that my name may be declared in all the earth."

~Exodus 9:16

Chapter Fourteen

The late afternoon sun cast dark shadows on the Claw's balcony. Hidden in the archway, the grisly god Zuzumza rustled its leathery wings, unsatisfied. Hungry eyes watched doltish figures—human pawns—moving far below in the city. The god's empire stretched over half the continent, yet that was not enough. He would not be satisfied until the Timbrel Mountains crumbled and he placed the bloody head of Yahweh into Beelzebub's outstretched claws. Gods ruling the other landmasses claimed that followers of Yahweh had vanished almost completely. The few remaining believers were disillusioned and weak. Only those on the continent of Iona remained in the way of their plans.

Conquering countries was easy. Eradicating all Tnias was something else entirely. The isolated pockets of Yahweh supporters were as difficult to catch and destroy as fleas on a mammoth. Zuzumza's greatest asset was time. Give humans wealth, celebrations, and power. Let them swim in rivers of pleasure, enjoying the feasts of today, and Yahweh faded into a vaporous myth they mocked at parties.

It was the wretched, the poor, that clung to the stories of paradise waiting for them after death, but Zuzumza masterfully weaved the weapons of fear and tradition that ate through the generations until nothing was left but a fragile husk, withered and nearly dead, inside of Gog. Over time the newly conquered territories would also forget. The outspoken believers would be killed first then fear would eat the faith of the others. New traditions and myths would erase the past. All that was needed was time. And Zuzumza had no end of that.

~~~~~~~~~

Late night laughter drifted through the vast length of the grand ballroom of Blackwall Palace. Hours earlier the hall had been packed with nobles and officers celebrating the fall of Lasko, but most now slept in luxurious beds or lay passed out in corners. Only a handful remained awake in the wee hours of a new day.

Speaking in a slurred voice, Emperor Erustus raised his golden goblet high into the air, oblivious to the wine sloshing over the rim. "To my unconquerable kingdom, may Zuzumza rule forever!" The monarch drank, heedless to the fact that there was no one left to join him in the toast. "Wine! I need more wine." An attendant rushed to his side, filling the cup again.

Sitting nearby, Prince Phlegon watched his father like a predator. War days long past, the monarch's muscles had turn to fat, and the only things that interested him was drinking, festivals, and women. The Crown Prince was disgusted at the number of siblings he had, both legitimate and illegitimate. Despite the numbers, he had no competition, for they were nothing more than drones attempting to entertain their slothful father. Besides Rufus, none had been seriously tutored in politics. Thinking of his brother brought a satisfying smile to the Crown Prince's lips. Rufus was so popular that the dilemma of tradition being broken and the second-born being crowned had presented a real danger—until Junia's execution. The prince had been so traumatized that he had completely dropped out of the political arena.

Phlegon swirled the rich wine inside his cup, enjoying the image of his popular younger brother performing menial labor to support his plebeian wife and child. It was a delicious fate that the Crown Prince savored. A loud crash brought Phlegon back to the present. In a clumsy attempt to dance, the Emperor had knocked a table over.

"Out of my way, servant," barked the drunken monarch to the fallen table.

"Father, if you paid closer attention to what lay around you, surprises would never catch you."

The Emperor ignored the warning, grabbing a surprised maid cleaning the messy pile of overturn trays of food. He whirled the servant around the dance floor, thinking she was his latest wife.

Phlegon thumped his leg against the gold throne he was strewn out in, one leg over an armrest. Under his breath, the Prince muttered, "Soon, Father, surprise will overcome your foolishness."

The young man's eyes were drawn to the huge stain glass window located above the main entrance. An insatiability smile spread across his lips as the sky's blackness seemed to form in the window. The midnight substance solidified on the high ledge, unnoticed by the sleepy servants below. The apparition studied the room below while several attendants glanced around uneasily, feeling watched. With the speed of a striking serpent, the living nightmare launched itself from the ledge, spreading bat-like wings, and descended towards the dancing monarch.

The maid laughed hollowly, pretending to enjoy the drunken Emperor's advances. Her chuckle froze in her throat then turned into a scream of horror. A superheated cloud of thick smoke surrounded the man, enclosing his body. Stepping back, the frightened woman snatched her singed arms away from the black cloud. Erastus' screams of agony echoed through the chamber. Confused servants froze in horror, unable to believe their eyes. The unnatural smoke melted away, leaving behind the gleaming crown half buried in ashes and bits of charred bones. Inside the ring of the royal crown was the shrunken, shriveled head of the monarch, mouth opened in a silent scream. Among the hot ashes were two unburned high-fashion shoes still containing the feet of their owner.

The maid fainted. Other servants fled the room in terror, arousing the sleeping castle. Prince Phlegon, still sitting on the throne, raised his glass high.

"Long live the Emperor."

He drank deeply.

~~~~~~~~~

On the green fields of Abundance, several thousand people gathered, their attention on a raised stone platform where two hundred excited graduates of Salt Academy sat. Most of the students were dressed in traditional white garments, but here and there sunlight glinted off the polished armor of those who had chosen the military major. The crowd listened quietly as the dean spoke. Far in the distance, the bright glow of Agape created a halo effect around the ancient stage.

The shrewd dean did not speak words of elegance, for he knew too well what waited the graduates. "Today we send highly trained individuals with hearts of gold into a world of darkness and chaos. Our own hearts go with them, but it is Yahweh who will guide and protect them. They are a force that will cause the demons to tremble in fear, for they bear the whole armor of Yahweh. They battle not against humans but against wicked spiritual powers in this Dark Age."

With her eyes, Rose searched the rows of graduates until she found her daughter. Tension gripped the mother. She was losing her oldest daughter. To her the name Danielle implied a tender child, full of life and sweetness—not a determined woman sitting beside her ironclad husband, about to begin a trek to the most immoral and bloodiest country on the planet. Jon noticed his wife's pale face and squeezed her hand. Rose smiled and relaxed—somewhat.

On the stone platform, the dean turned to the students, indicating for them to rise. All two hundred Tnias stood as one. "Stand ready, with the Belt of Truth tied tight around your waist, with righteousness as your breastplate. Over the many dangerous miles, always walk in the Shoes of Peace, announcing Yahweh's message of love. At all times you must carry your faith as a shield. With it, you will block the burning arrows of the Evil One."

Danielle's mind strayed from the speaker. She glanced at the handsome features of her husband, drawing strength from his confident pose. Pulling from his experiences in the Telumzan army, Matthan had excelled at the academy, majored in Warrior of Light, and graduated valedictorian. Danielle scanned the area reserved for family. Soon she spotted her brothers, now teenagers, leaning forward eagerly, dreaming of their own future graduations. Petals seemed serene, watching her sister proudly. Jon sat regal as a king, but it was Rose that the oldest daughter focused on, remembering a conversation from the night before.

"But why the Empire?" Rose had demanded, voice slightly raised. "There are plenty of other countries, safer counties where Salts can be of service."

"Mother, we have been over this before." Danielle's tone was strained. "Both Matthan and I feel a special tug for Gog."

"Because of Julie?" Rose made the statement an accusation more than a question.

The daughter forced herself to relax. "Yes, in part it's due to her, but that's not the only reason. Yahweh has called us both. We can do nothing less than obey. He spared our lives in Fiennes for a special reason, and we intend to fulfill that purpose."

"Honey, we're talking about the Empire, the heart of all that is evil. If you open your mouth just once to proclaim Yahweh as the True God, you could be killed. How will dying so quickly serve Yahweh's purpose?" Rose found herself wishing that Danielle was a child again whom she could protect by sending to her bedroom. The older woman's voice softened, revealing the agony of her heart. "We won't even know if you're dead or alive."

Danielle understood her mother's pain. "I know, but we must trust Yahweh. His ways are prefect."

"What about when you and Matthan have children? So many things could happen to them. What if they are taken from you?" Rose would never see her own grandchildren or even know of their births.

The young woman refused to be discouraged. "Remember what you taught me, Mother? Train up a child in the way he should go and when he is grown, he will not depart from it. You have taught me well, Mother, now it's time to let me go."

"I know. But it is hard, so hard."

The dean's booming voice snatched Danielle back to the present. "Accept salvation as a helmet, and the Word of Yahweh as the sword to fight against temptation and traps. Most importantly, you must do this in prayer, asking Yahweh for help. Darkness will come but never give up. He will never leave us nor forsake us."

As the speech ended, the huge crowd burst into applause. Awards and diplomas were handed out among cheerful hoots. Jon swelled with pride when his son-in-law received several prestige awards. Both being soldiers, a close bond had formed between the two, Jon loving the younger man like one of his own sons. Three years ago when Matthan had asked for Danielle's hand in marriage, the father could not be prouder—until today. He understood and respected the couple's choice to travel to the Empire, but that did not remove the pain of the coming separation.

When Danielle walked across the platform to receive her diploma, her siblings stood up, screaming her name. Matthan received the same jubilant treatment.

After the last diploma was given out, Matthan walked forward to give the closing speech. The young man looked over the vast crowd before speaking. "Today we celebrate the end of one life and the beginning of a new one. Few of my peers were born in Shalom. We all know what waits beyond the protecting mountains, yet each of us has chosen to become a warrior for Yahweh, accepting the responsibility of being a ray of light in a hopeless world. We leave families and friends behind who we may never see again in this lifetime."

He paused for a moment, remembering Julie. He wore her sword strapped to his waist. "Some of us will be arrested, some tortured, and others required to give up their lives as we walk in those shoes of peace." Matthan took a deep breath before saying his last sentence. "This I do know—we will all meet again inside the City of Yahweh."

As the speech ended, the audience surged to their feet, clapping. Graduates walked down the stone steps, melting into the cheering crowd. It was a day of rejoicing, a day of celebration and parties, a day of somber good-byes.

Late in the afternoon, the Brick and Ventix families made the two-hour trip home in a wagon. Petals and Watt joked and played. Ben sat quietly beside Matthan, taking in everything with the eyes of a new adult. He was scheduled to begin his first year at the academy in a few months. Danielle kept a light spirit, jesting with young children, laughter barely a step ahead of unshed tears.

When the couple set out from Fruitful a week later, tears fell from many eyes. Riding on two horses and leading another packed with supplies, the couple called out their sad good-byes.

As Rose waved a final farewell, she felt as if a part of her heart had been wrenched out. Why did serving Yahweh have to mean separation and sacrifice? Why could not everybody live happily ever after in Shalom? But Rose did not voice her complaints. She knew the answers. Yahweh loved all, including murderers and rapists, so much that he continued to call forth witnesses—lambs to the slaughter. Why did it have to be her daughter and son-in-law?

Chapter Fifteen

Intricate levels of exquisite walkways below and above the cloud line connected artistically designed skyscrapers. The bright, smooth-lined structures were highlighted with rich blooming foliage, waterfalls, indoor parks, small lakes, and architecture achievements beyond the ability of mortals. Everywhere moved citizens of Agape—most human, some not. People of all races and backgrounds mingled happily together, joking, singing, playing, or working.

In one enclosed high-altitude park, an artist, surrounded by fragrant trees and songbirds, attempted to capture a child's image onto canvas. "Gilan, you must hold still," said the dark-haired woman, poking her head out from behind the painting.

The child automatically snapped into the position of the agreed pose. "I'm trying, but I'm too excited. A Mal'ak told me that my uncle will arrive soon at the Naphtali Gate."

"That's great, but please look towards the waterfall and not the fountains. I'm almost finished." As the portrait took shape, the artist's skillful hands filled in shadow and detail, creating a lifelike masterpiece. Finally, she called the child over to examine the picture.

Gilan gasped in delight. "Wow! That's me! Can I show my mom?"

The smiling woman handed the canvas to Gilan. "Here, it's yours, but be careful because the paint is still wet."

The child nodded and eagerly dashed off, proudly carrying the large canvas. Relishing the joy her talent gave others, Julie smiled as Gilan bounded away, blond curls bouncing. There existed a bond between woman and child since Julie had arrived in Agape, but neither remembered their only meeting which took place beyond the gold city walls—a dark night when the child's family had been slaughtered by the Red Army and Junia had personally cut the child's throat—an image which had once haunted the Gogian's nightmares. In Yahweh's paradisiacal city, nightmares did not exist. Neither did sadness, tears, or painful memories.

Carrying easel and her knapsack, Julie strolled through the huge park. Many passing people greeted her by name. There was a deep kinship among the citizens of Agape, deeper than that of best friends in the outer world. She paused to watch two playful otters in a pond. Their antics sent watching children into peals of laughter. Julie heard fast, upbeat music and followed the sound to a plaza surrounded by blooming trees. Passersby gathered around musicians playing instruments from several different cultures. Soon people filled the square with rhythmic dancing, worshipping Yahweh with feet and bodies.

Julie moved to join the celebration but was stopped by a Mal'ak who said, "Yahweh wishes to see you."

"Me?" the young woman asked in surprise. "You mean Yahweh himself?" The deity regularly walked among his people, and Julie had seen him from a distance on several occasions. Yet it was extremely rare to be summoned by Yahweh.

"Yahweh invites you to his Throne Room."

Julie nodded, pondering the message, and sat on a bench beside several friends.

Cory Tubbs smiled and gestured towards his parents twirling to the music. "Ah, Julie, it's good to see you. Just look at them. Father says my mother dances just like the day they first met." For a moment Julie studied the youthful couple, spinning and ducking gracefully, remembering a limping elderly woman with tired eyes thankfully receiving food from a maiden. Now the lady once called Widow Tubb was a young brunet with sparkling blue eyes.

"Would you be my dance partner?" asked Cory, no longer haunted by the horrible memories of war.

"I would, but Yahweh has summoned me. Would you take my paints and easel to my home?"

Cory whistled. "Must be important. Sure, I'll take your stuff."

Julie thanked him then walked towards the central palace rising hundreds of yards above the other structures. Dozens of heavy trafficked bridges connected to the lower levels of the palace. The immense building was filled with marvels unknown in the outer world. Only the uppermost floors were closed to regular traffic. Julie's progress through the palace was slow due to pauses to chat with friends and admire the many wonders. She was in no hurry for time had little meaning to the inhabitants of Agape who never aged or needed sleep.

Finally she reached the greatest phenomenon of the palace that regularly drew thousands of visitors—a series of balconies, walkways, and spiral stairs surrounding a thunderous waterfall that fell a mile straight down into a vast pool on the ground floor. Julie paused for a moment, enjoying the sight of three large, overlapping rainbows mixed with tiny ones in the mist. She continued walking tirelessly upward until reaching a closed ornate door guarded by several Mal'ak.

Before she could speak, one walked forward. "You are expected, Julie. Follow me."

The being led her up several more flights of broad stairs and passageways. They reached a grand hallway divided by a trench of sparkling water. A huge arched doorway opened into the Throne Room. Julie followed her escort into the large, airy chamber of light and beauty. The source of the water in the trench—which led to the Waterfall of Rainbows—was the throne itself. A gentle stream flowed out from under the gold throne along a deep channel etched into the floor. Circled around the throne were seraphim, entities of fire in human form.

It was not the River of Life, the awe-inspiring seraphim, or the elegant arched roof which captivated Julie, but the creator of it all—Yahweh. The features of his face were that of an average man, but his eyes reached into the soul, revealing all inner secrets. From him radiated the very essence of love, feeling to Julie like a powerful, living river that she could swim in forever. She kneeled in front of her god.

He smiled, and Julie knew what it was like to witness a newly created sun shining over its unspoiled planets. "Arise, Julie, my beloved. You use the talents I have given you to benefit others. I am pleased."

She stood, basking in his presence. "I thank you for the gift of art."

"The talent was yours before birth, but as Junia you chose to focus on destruction, not creation." Seeing confusion crossing her face, he said, "Junia was the name you went by while serving Beelzebub."

"I served Beelzebub?"

"Yes, for a season." He rose from the throne and walked to a window stretching halfway up to the vaulted ceiling. "What do you see, Julie?"

The maiden studied the vistas stretching for hundreds of miles. "I see mountains, plains, fields, and the cities of your people."

"Beyond those mountains are more cities and villages." An immense sadness filled his eyes, bearing the weight of millions of lives. "I love the people there as deeply as those inside Shalom. I hear their cries of agony and feel their despair, yet they kill the servants I send to them carrying my messages of love and hope. They chose instead to chase after evil. I will give Gog one final opportunity. Will you carry my message to them?"

"Me? I am the least of your handmaidens."

"Do not be so surprised." Warmth and wisdom lined his face. "Over the millenniums I have sent forth those who have tasted death and brought here those who never will. The reasons why are beyond your understanding. I must carry this burden which is too heavy for mortals to bear." He did not speak in contempt but as a loving father protecting his children. "It is a difficult task which I have need of you, Julie. You must go into the heart of Gog and be my witness, my mouth. This quest I set before you, but you must decide if you will take it up."

Julie straightened her shoulders and replied without hesitation. "I will go."

"It will not be easy. You will be mortal and experience death again. You will wrestle with weaknesses of your flesh. Before coming here, you struggled with accepting forgiveness for the pain you afflicted against others, against me. This you must remember, Julie, as far as the East is from the West, so have I forgiven your sins."

"I will not forget."

"Take this as a sign that you carry my message."

A seraphim stepped forward holding a long ivory box.

Yahweh continued, "I will give you words to speak when it is time."

The entity of fire opened the box, revealing a long, thin sword beside its metal scabbard. Both were made from the same mixture of ore as the weapon Simeon had given Julie long ago—both incredible strong but lightweight. Etched across the blade were two words written in the holy language spoken only in Agape which translated *The Word*. The pommel contained no jewels, only an engraved picture of a flame. Julie first picked up the gleaming scabbard then wrapped her fingers around the weapon's hilt. Immediately fire surged along the length of the blade, hot and intense. She gasped in surprise and let go. As the sword fell back into the box, the fire vanished.

Yahweh explained, "I made this weapon. Only in the hands of those purified by fire will the sword reveal its true potential. In any other's hands, it will appear a normal blade."

Again Julie picked up the weapon, studying the living flame dancing around a core of steel. She slid the blade into its metal sheath.

"It is time for you to go, beloved. A difficult trial awaits you outside the city. Do not forget my words. Stand firm and do not fear. I am with you always, even to the very end."

~~~~~~~~~

Branches heavy with fruits hung over Julie's head as she walked along a main street. The fruit was ready for harvesting. The Trees of Life produced twelve crops each year, the fruit and leaves transported into the nation of Shalom, giving health to all who ate them. The crystal clear River of Life flowed lengthwise along the street of gold, dividing it into two lanes, bordered by the laden trees. Though she had been here on countless occasions, this time Julie memorized every splendid detail, not knowing when she would see it again.

With the Sword of Fire strapped to her side, Julie reached a huge opened gate. Two Mal'ak stood guard, though there was no need. Fragile bodies of mortals could not come within several miles of the city. Outside the gate, Julie continued to follow the riverbank through lush vegetation for a mile before turning north. The main branch of the river would continue south until disappearing in the labyrinth of caves inside the Tumbrel Mountains.

For hours the woman traveled. At first she felt no different than if she was still in Agape. Then she began noticing sweat on her skin and the cool breeze providing relief. As the day wore on, her body grew weary and her stomach rumbled. She paused to pick several apples and rested under a tree. As she munched the juicy fruit, her mind wandered. She thought about her friends in the City of Light. A smile danced across her lips as she again pictured Gilan awkwardly carrying the canvas. Lips became a firm line as she pondered the quest Yahweh had given her. Part of her wanted to stay forever in his throne room, worshipping, basking in his serene presence, but there were people to help. Their needs were greater than her own.

Her eyes drifted to people traveling along the nearby road. One muscular man triggered a long forgotten image of a Gogian soldier holding a bloody knife. Julie sat straight up, dropping her half-eaten apple. The barrier that protected the immortal humans of Agape from painful, haunting memories of the past no longer shielded the woman.

Yahweh said that I once served darkness, she told herself, *yet it is hard for me to believe that is possible.* She took a deep breath and let more memories from the past resurface.

At first she remembered simple, pleasant images. *A brightly colored bird on a windowsill. Contently drawing animals on paper. The smell of ointment her nanny wore. Paths in a cultivated garden she happily skipped along as a child. A boy giving her a wooden horse necklace.*

As faces and scenes danced through her mind, the pictures became darker, carrying an underlining sadness. *A dark-haired child—herself—weeping uncontrollably. Gossiping servants staring, whispering as she walked pass. Endless groups of richly dressed nobles with faces smiling but eyes cold. A proud, aristocrat boy pointing at her, laughing, calling out "crybaby."*

Julie trembled. The world was so dark!

It was only the beginning of the evil she had lived.

Swords crashing together, metal chipping. Screams of men and horses. Blood. Faces of the dying. A warrior princess watching emotionlessly as another soldier crumpled to the wet-red ground. Houses ablaze. Townspeople running in terror. Children lying dead in the streets. Her blade smeared with the blood of the innocent. Princess Junia of the Red Army.

Julie bent double, arms wrapped tightly around herself, vainly attempting to still her shaking body. *I am a murderer! A butcher.* Her mind rebelled against the images, recalling Yahweh's loving face. Briefly she held onto the memory of his image, but it faded in the wake of another horror.

A heavy man with eyes of fire. Face of liven hatred. Sword drawn, plunging forward. Pain. Intense pain. Falling. A scream somewhere. The man's mouth in a sneer—her father. His back to her as he walks away. Someone holding her, weeping. A handsome man standing coldly by. He cannot look at her.

Her mind realized in shock, *I was killed by my father. My father. The one who is supposed to love and protect me.*

Julie lay in a fetal position, sobbing. It was several minutes before she realized someone's arms encircled her. Looking up, she saw a beautiful glowing woman. Deep peace filled Julie, and she felt again what it was like to be in the City of Yahweh. With the help of the Mal'ak, the human sat up.

"The past is painful, child. It can be used as a powerful snare by the enemy, but Yahweh sets us free from it."

Julie remembering what Yahweh had said earlier. "We are forgiven as far as the East is from the West."

"Yes. It will not be easy, Julie, for you to face the darkness beyond Shalom. Because you have lived in perfectness, you can now see evil for what it is without any blinders. Beware, there are still traps waiting for you. Never lose focus of your mission."

"I will not fail Yahweh," Julie said with iron determination.

"A companion has been selected to help you. Continue north to the city of Anavah, which means gentleness. There she will find you."

~~~~~~~~~

Diners conversed over their meals. Julie sat in a shadowy corner, relishing the hot soup given to her by a friendly waitress. Tired, hungry, and without any currency, she had arrived at Anavah two hours ago. For a long time she wandered the streets, looking for the promised traveling companion—to no avail. The townspeople were friendly, though some stared a little too hard at her. When the sun set, Julie finally entered a restaurant and asked a waitress if she could work for a meal. The woman had taken one look at her and declared that the meal was free.

Now as Julie munched on a roll, she wondered what to do next. She had no clue how to find this mysterious companion. Her body ached from walking all day. Perhaps she could trade manual labor for a night in an inn. She could not tarry long in Anavah waiting for the unknown person. Glancing around the room, she noticed several heads quickly turning in other directions. It had been like that since entering the restaurant—people staring at her but pretending not to. She picked up the bowl and sipped the last drops of soup. Not as good as fruit from the Tree of Life but still delicious.

"Is this seat taken?"

Julie looked up to see a woman in her mid-thirties dressed in comfortable wool trousers, blouse, and a traveling cloak. "Ah…no. Feel free to sit down."

The slim, dark-skinned woman made herself comfortable, taking off her cloak, revealing long braided hair. A look of determination and fire smoldered in her brown eyes. Julie also noticed a long sword strapped to the stranger's waist.

The visitor ordered food before addressing Julie again. "So I guess you're the one in need of a traveling companion?" The woman spoke in a monotone voice, scrutinizing Julie.

"Yes, I am. Did Yahweh send you?"

"I was told by a Mal'ak to look for someone who stood out. I guess you can't get any more obvious than that." A confused look crossed Julie's face. "You're glowing."

"I'm what?"

"Glowing. You know, like Yahweh's City. Like the Mal'ak who live there."

Julie studied her own hand. To her surprise, it did give off a faint glow. That would explain why people had been staring weirdly at her.

"Name's Roshell Ly'hico. Thought perhaps you were one of the Mal'ak yourself…" Roshell frowned as Julie placed her hand under the table then peeked under, delighted to discover that the glow was brighter. "…but I can see you're not."

"Do you think it's permanent?" asked Julie, fascinated as a child.

"What? The glowing? How should I know?" There was a trace of anger in Roshell's voice. "I'm here because I was ordered to come."

"Did the Mal'ak tell you what we are to do next?"

"Tell me? I thought you had the plans. I was busy leading a group of orphans across the Ulmjon border when the Mal'ak shows up, tells me to drop everything and come to Anavah." Roshell paused as the waitress placed soup and drink on the table. "It's not that I don't mind visiting Shalom. Who wouldn't? But I've too much to do, directing a series of orphanages, organizing refugee camps, challenging selfish government officials. I say it's their fault that Gog has taken so much land. Told the Mal'ak all that too."

"What did he say?"

Roshell suddenly became interested in her food. "Hmm…soup's too hot." The woman stirred the steaming contents for a minute before answering. "Told me to turn all my projects over to my assistants and head south. So here I am. Now tell me about this great mission we're about to embark on."

"We are heading to Thorn," said Julie with as much emotion as if she was speaking about the weather. "By the way, what year is it?"

Puzzlement crossed Roshell's face. "It's been three thousand four hundred seventy-eight years since the creation of Shalom. You mean Thorn—the home of the Emperor?"

"There's only one Thorn. I don't know that chronological scale."

A deep frown settled on Roshell's lips. She could not believe that Yahweh would take her from rescuing refugees to baby-sitting a youth on a suicide mission who did not even know what year it was. "How old are you?"

Distracted, Julie answered, "I'm...uh...was twenty-one when I was killed. How many years has Erastus ruled?"

That removed all doubt to Roshell that the stranger across from her was deranged. "Phlegon is Emperor. Has been for three years now. What do you mean by 'when you died'?"

"How long did Erastus rule?"

Roshell shrugged, "I guess thirty-eight or nine years. Who are you, by the way?"

Using her fingers to count years, Julie absently replied, "Name's Julie. What's Prince Rufus doing now?"

"Never heard of him. You clearly said, 'I was killed when I was twenty-one.' I have an excellent memory."

Julie looked up from her fingers. "If Erastus ruled for thirty-eight years, that means I've been dead five."

"Death seems to have done wonders for your skin."

"I've been in Agape during that time."

Roshell gasped, unable to accept but unable to disbelieve the strange woman in front of her. "I guess that explains the glowing effect. So Yahweh told you personally to head to Gog?"

"Yes." Julie's eyes lit up with the joyous memory of talking with Yahweh.

"And you do realize how dangerous such a trek will be?"

"That's how I died the first time. What's the worst that can happen? I die again?" For a moment the women locked eyes, testing each other. "The question is—can you handle it?"

For a moment Roshell angrily glared at the shimmering human. She was tough as steel, had risked her own life countless times, stood up against nonchalant governments. Those who worked closely with her knew she never backed down from any challenge. Could she handle traveling into the core of hell on Tanlep?

A smile spread across the Ulmjon's face. "I think we're going to get along just fine."

Chapter Sixteen

The gray sky matched the dingy streets of Belton and Matthan's gloomy spirit. He walked slowly, passing peddlers, taverns, prostitutes, and poorly clad children. It had been a long, hot day working as a blacksmith's apprentice. Nothing he did seemed to please his boss. Every day he gave his best, knowing actions can be a witness for Yahweh when words cannot be verbally spoken—but still his employer was as grumpy as ever. Weeks had stretched into months, and Matthan's patience was running thin.

It was not just the blacksmith but everything about Gog. The people were cold, turning a blind eye to others in need. Just today he had witness three fights. The first was a merchant and trader slugging out their disagreement in the middle of the market. Later two heavily built guys had pulled a drunken beggar out of a bar, beating him as he cried for mercy. Matthan had intervened, receiving a few licks in the process. The drunk thanked him then asked for money before disappearing into another tavern across the street. Just a few minutes ago Matthan had spotted a man slapping a woman. The Salt attempted to help the woman but she spat at him, telling him to mind his own business. It was a normal day in Belton.

It was nearly two years since graduation from Salt Academy. Back then, everything had seemed wonderful and adventurous. Matthan and Danielle had slowly made their way north, finally settling in the capital city of the province Achaia. They had cautiously searched for other Tnias, but fear kept citizens from talking freely. People bought and sold under the images of demons. It seemed every shop had a statue of a local god. Zuzumza's ugly face was painted on government buildings. In certain areas, cages hung with ragged prisoners inside who supposedly had committed political crimes. High rewards were posted for any that reported a Tnias. In two years the young couple had not found a single Tnias. Achaia had only been under the authority of the Empire for ten years, but it might as well be Gog itself.

Matthan wanted desperately to share the reality of Yahweh's love with the empty souls he passed every day. If only he could show them a glimpse of Agape, their doubt of Yahweh's existence would vanish, but they could never enter Shalom unless first bearing Yahweh's secret mark on their souls. He could not even mention the name of the god he served without risking his and Danielle's lives. It was very frustrating.

The Salt turned down an alley, passing several dingy doors, before climbing a narrow flight of steps to his own tiny apartment. Danielle greeted him warmly with a smile and kiss. The long hours she worked each day as a seamstress took their toll, but her faith and gentleness never faltered. Not a day went by without Matthan thanking Yahweh for his wife.

"I beat you home today, so I cooked supper." Danielle set chipped plates on the rickety table Matthan had saved from a rubbish heap.

As she worked, Danielle hummed a tune her father used to sing. Briefly, Matthan felt they were again in Shalom, sitting in the brightly lit home of the Bricks, surrounded by laughter, jokes, and stories told by the children. As the couple ate their watery turnip soup and cornbread, conversation stayed light. Matthan sensed his wife had something on her mind, but she was not yet ready to share it. After the dishes were washed, the couple settled on their worn couch.

Danielle leaned her head against her husband's brawny shoulder. "I had a dream last night—I guess it was more of a vision."

"About what?" Matthan forgot the aches of his tired body.

"Well, I first saw people we know from our jobs. Then faces of strangers. The images flew pass faster and faster, then whole villages and cities. Suddenly I was seeing the whole Empire as if I was looking down at it from the sky. It was as if…" She paused for a moment, wishing she could describe the raw emotions the vision conjured. "…as if the nation was a living thing. All the people were part of a larger, living organism. And it had a heart. I saw it beating, but it was black as the night sky. Pumping and beating, but not giving life to the people. Instead, it was slowly poisoning them, stealing their essences, their very souls, yet they took no notice."

She looked unto her husband's eyes, hoping to see understanding but only finding confusion. "Matthan, the black heart is Thorn. When the heart is healed, the rest of the body will follow."

"How can the capital city of Gog be changed? We haven't made the slightest difference here."

"It's not the city that needs changing but the ruling powers of the Empire."

The tired man slumped against dingy cushions. "You had an interesting dream, Danielle. Leaders set the direction of their land. This has been known for centuries."

Danielle sighed in frustration. "It's not something that might happen but will happen. I feel clearly that Yahweh is calling us to the beating heart, to Thorn."

"To do what? Witness to the Emperor himself? Impossible. We'll be killed before entering the palace. Danielle, I see so much pain here, around us. I want to help now, but I don't know how."

"They can be reached only when the nation's heart is changed. The forces of darkness are too strong here now, and the people only know fear. But I believe Yahweh has plans for something special in Thorn."

Matthan stood up and began pacing the floor. His mind rebelled against the idea of traveling further north. They were barely making a living here, foreigners treated with contempt. If they could not change one life in Belton, what could they expect in Thorn, the seat of evil? He finally stopped pacing and stood in front of the only window in the dingy apartment. Danielle silently wrapped her arms around him, and they stood for a long time, each lost in their own thoughts and prayers.

Finally Matthan turned to his wife. "We have a long journey, so we've better start packing tonight."

Danielle hugged him tighter, wondering if she should tell him the other secret she harbored, one not shown in a dream. No, he had enough to be concerned about right now. He did not need to worry about the coming child she carried—yet. Getting to Thorn before winter was the priority for now.

~~~~~~~~~

Julie's glow did diminish. By the time they emerged from under the Timbrel Mountains into Misko, she appeared normal—though Roshell viewed her as anything but that. The new mortal was full of questions, eager to discover all she had missed during the last five years. Not only did Roshell's role include being a teacher, but also guide and provider. Already upset about leaving her orphans, Roshell resented traveling with the foreigner. Julie seemed friendly and curious, almost child-like in the endless questions she asked, yet casual comments indicated a darker personality lurking under the surface. Roshell had better things to do than babysit this strange maiden. What had Yahweh been thinking when he sent her on this quest?

The rich culture and history of Misko fascinated Julie, for she had never visited the southern counties. Misko now consisted of a series of islands and two large inland tracts of land. In ancient times the nation had covered the entire lower continent. Civil wars, corruption, and arranged marriages had regularly redefined borders of its provinces. Then came that fateful era when Yahweh walked among the people and they had killed him...yet he had overcome death and created Shalom, dividing the ancient realm of Misko into smaller countries. For the last few centuries there had been peace among these nations until now. The ruthless Empire had pushed itself to the very edge of Misko and Lahad, leaving only three counties still free on the continent. The situation was very bad indeed.

But it also brought a unity never seen before in Iona. Once, the citizens of the southern counties had almost all been dark-skinned while northern and middle regions consisted of two lighter races. Now that was changed, for so many had fled south in front of the Empire's destructive wake that the three free counties had become an enormous salad bowl of refugees with their cultures mixing together. The sudden rapid increase of population could have triggered social upheavals, but fear of Gog smelted the old and new into a sharp blade with one common enemy.

Everywhere Roshell and Julie traveled in Misko, they saw a booming economy—blacksmith, merchants, and farmers barely able to keep up with demands. The Queen of Misko had watched for decades as her neighboring countries fell one by one. She had observed their mistakes and was determined not to repeat them. After Ulmjo fell, a brief but destructive raid lead by an overzealous Gogian general convinced Queen Verist that the Empire could not be defeated by human effort alone, so she pledged her life to Yahweh and strongly urged her people to do likewise. Then she formed a fresh alliance with the nations of Lahad and Kentniko. The Chancellor of Kentniko, a long-time Tnias, sent thousands of troops north to aid his northern comrades. Citizens began calling the three nations the Triad.

Too soon Roshell and Julie reached the guarded border of Ulmjo which they crossed under the cover of a moonless, cloudy night. The differences between the two countries were like day and night. A dark cloud of oppression covered the land and its inhabitants. People were wary, rarely making eye contact, never smiling. Members of the Red Army seemed to be everywhere. Along major roads, bodies hung from trees and poles, filling the land with the stench of decaying flesh.

As the horses plodded along, neither Tnias spoke. Roshell gripped her reins white-knuckled, jaw set, barely containing the rage burning inside. Ulmjo was the land of Roshell's birth, and pain pierced deeply into her soul. Her people were murdered while the land was being raped of its natural resources. Julie's grief was just as intense, but on a different level. She bore the crushing knowledge that her people had created the destruction.

Mid-afternoon, Roshell turned the horses onto a less traveled road, explaining she needed to check on her foster parents. Though the woman tried to appear calm, Julie noticed Roshell was jumpy. Two hours later, they arrived at a small town, appearing first as pleasant and inviting, but people quickly averted their eyes from Roshell or said a quick greeting before hurrying away. The woman pretended not to notice their inhospitality. Shortly after leaving the town, they arrived at a homestead with fields loaded with ripening crops, a few chickens scratching for insects.

Nervously, Roshell dismounted and walked to the log house, unconsciously reaching for her sword. Reaching the open doorway, the Tnias's body became rigid and a scream of rage ripped from her lips. "The damn butchers! I will tear them apart with my own hands!"

Julie left the horses untied as she hurried to Roshell's side. Glancing through the doorway, she spotted several bloated corpses on the floor. Gingerly she placed a hand on Roshell's shoulder. The older woman shook it off, refusing comfort. She marched outside, seeking something to lash her anger against. An old fencepost served that purpose as she kicked it over and over.

"Why, Yahweh?" she screamed to the sky. "Why them? After all they've done for you, why?"

"I'm sorry, Roshell." Julie said gently as possible. "Their trials are at an end. They are in a better place now."

The Ulmjon laughed bitterly. "How many times have I heard that cliché? How many times have I said it myself?" She gave another hard kick to the weathered post, sending a crack along its width.

"I'm not using a cliché, Roshell. Agape is real—I was there. Right now your family is celebrating, perhaps even talking with Yahweh himself."

"Don't lecture me about reality. I saw that city everyday while I was at the Academy. But neither can I forget what lies in that house, my home." Roshell became still, attempting to regain control of her rage. "They gave me a home, a real home. They took me in when everyone else just saw a defiant street kid. They gave me a second chance. And now those Gogian monsters have killed them. They take others' lives into the palms of their hands then crush it, without mercy, without remorse. All of them deserve the bottomless abyss of fire." Lashing out with her fist, Roshell hit the post, knocking a large segment to the ground.

Silence filled the yard except for a clucking hen calling her chicks to eat a worm she had discovered.

Julie spoke in a soft, pained voice. "I was once one of them—the Gogians."

Roshell looked up sharply but remained quiet.

"I killed without a conscience, just like the ones who killed your parents. Then I was injured in battle and taken in by a Tnias family. There I saw love for the first time. I learned that even when I cursed Yahweh, he loved me. Your parents know serenity, but their murderers do not. They pretend what they are doing is right, but inside darkness consumes them. At night, faces of those they killed haunt their nightmares. There is no rest, no peace."

"They don't deserve peace but condemnation!"

Julie looked away as if physically slapped. "You don't know what you say."

Roshell opened her mouth to speak, but held her tongue, realizing her words had condemned Julie. Yahweh had pardoned the maiden's crimes and even exalted her to the few who would die twice. Roshell was in no position to challenge the deity's decision. She felt no grudge against Julie, but neither could she forgive those who had killed her surrogate parents. "Come on. There are shovels in the barn."

Not until after the dead had received a decent funeral could the living talk again. Sitting by a warm fire, eating supper, Roshell reminisced about her life. She had been abandoned at four and wandered the streets of a large city for five years until a couple, visiting relatives, took pity on her and brought her to their house in the country. She loved having a family but felt insecure, afraid she would be kicked out if she did something wrong. It was a tough, ongoing struggle for everyone, but eventually Roshell accepted that she was genuinely loved, no matter her behavior. At thirteen, Roshell discovered an abandoned child in a ditch who she brought home. Helping one was not enough, for every dirty child she saw was like looking into a mirror of her own childhood. Several years later, she moved to the city and created, with the help of her surrogate parents and their relatives, a small orphanage. She learned fast and burned with passion to help every hurting child. Heeding advice, she attended Salt Academy in Shalom, but dropped out after two years, too impatient, frustrated that children were slipping through the cracks of society while she studied books.

In the following two decades, she helped create a series of children's homes and aided with many other projects, leading her to successfully challenge several governments' policies. When it became apparent that Ulmjo would fall, she had organized the migration of all orphans, homeless youths, and workers in the refuge houses. To walk away from it all in order to go to peaceful Shalom on Yahweh's order was the hardest thing she had ever done. If she had returned to Ulmjo instead, she may have gotten her parents out in time. They had stayed to the last minute, helping others.

As Roshell talked into the wee hours of the morning, the beginnings of a strong bond formed between the two women. Both burned with the vision of carrying love to others—Roshell to youth, Julie to the Empire. One question remained unsaid, could Roshell handle being a missionary to her enemy?

~~~~~~~~~

Phlegon surveyed his council of lords and military officers in the Chamber of Juxtaposition. Several squirmed in their seats, uncomfortable by his bold gaze, others whispering among themselves. The Emperor let his voice boom, calling the meeting to order.

"Congratulations, generals, you have done well." He raised his glass high in a toast of victory. "Only three countries left to be stomped into submission. Then the continent will be ours."

As the men drank, General Tryphena offered another toast. "To the quick victory of Gog."

The monarch turned his cool gaze on the speaker. Tryphena was too ambitious, had made too many mistakes recently. "This is no time for speed. Our greatest challenge lies before us."

Angry at being chastised in front of his peers, the general objected, "Sire, it is only three small countries compared to our vast bulk. Their armies have no chance against us."

Colonel Rahan attacked his superior. "If they're so defenseless, why did you lose three entire regiments in an unordered charge into Misko after Ulmjo fell?"

"I was…using the element of surprise."

"You attacked before Ulmjo was completely secured and while your forces were scattered. Did you think that Misko would not be prepared after years of warning?" The younger man pushed his argument, relishing pointing out the older man's weaknesses after years of being forced to obey his foolish commands. "The only thing you succeeded in was nudging the Queen of Misko to join forces with Lahad and Kentniko."

"So what?" shouted Tryphena. "All three will fall!"

"Gentlemen, the war is supposed to be outside this room." Phlegon addressed the officers as if talking to children. "My concern is not the unconquered territories. They will fall in good time. General Nereus, would you be so kind as to explain to the younger officers who our real enemy is?"

Every eye focused on the war hero, retired from active military service and now a prominent member of the council. The gray-haired man stroked his beard for a moment before answering. "Do you mean the fighting jackals who skirmish over every scrap of conquered land or the parasites who infest that land?"

The Emperor laughed. "You are very perceptive, General. While soldiers gloat over their victories, Tnias slip through the cracks and multiply. No matter how many territories are conquered, we will not win until every last one of them is eradicated. Gentlemen, this is not a war about land, but a battle for souls." He slowly looked each council member in the eyes. "Do I make myself clear?"

146

Men nodded in agreement. Only Rahad was bold enough to ask, "Then when do we attack Misko and Lahad?

"General Tryphena will strengthen the forces on our southern border. In the spring we will attack."

"In the spring?" broke in Tryphena. "That's eight months away! We need to attack now, before they grow in strength."

The Emperor's predatory eyes focused on the general. The room became deathly still. Unlike his father, Phlegon disposition did not include tantrums—his cold, calculating fury was far more dangerous. "Your insubordination is beginning to bother me. You are permanently relieved from your position."

Disbelief spread across Tryphena's face. "You…you can't do that. I was a war hero in your father's time."

"Then die like my father." The monarch nodded to General Herron. Urbane rose from his seat and walked to his former superior. Tryphena partly rose from his seat, still babbling indignantly. With his left hand, Urbane firmly grabbed the man's head, while his right hand slid a knife across the demoted general's throat. No one in the room protested, but several intently studied their notes without glancing around.

Ignoring gurgling from the dying man, the Emperor continued with his plans. "*General* Rahad will lead my southern forces. General Herron, I give you the task of wiping out all Tnias within our borders. Use any means necessary."

Reseated, Urbane nodded, accepting the responsibility without any show of emotion. Phlegon dismissed the council, scrutinizing each one as they exited. Most were ambitious men only looking out for themselves—perfect pawns. Only two officers stood out from the crowd. Nereus was known for his wisdom. His loyalty to Gog and his men was unquestionable. Unfortunately, his concern was stronger for people than for the Empire. Phlegon preferred the general on the field instead of his Cabinet. In a few months, he would strongly suggest to the council that it was time for the aged war hero's permanent retirement. Many parties and fine speeches would be given for Nereus, maybe another award or three presented, then he would spend the rest of his peaceful days out of the Emperor's way.

General Herron was another matter. United with conniving Junia, he had been a serious problem who might had eventually made a bid for Emperor. That had changed upon the princess's death. Urbane blamed Yahweh for the death of his lover. Revenge had forged him into a cold machine whose only purpose was to kill Tnias—the perfect tool for Zuzumza. After all, there was no greater test of loyalty than a man turning in his own lover.

Chapter Seventeen

The journey through Lasko was not as dismal as Ulmjo. Only a few unburied skulls lying in front of stone gods and several fresh heads spiked on city walls marked the gruesome reign of the Empire. Roshell knew the province fairly well for she had been an advisor for a government committee creating a chain of orphanages when Lasko had been an independent country. She chose a major road leading to Meccan. Arriving at the capitol, they plodded through the crowded streets, passing through the shadow of an enormous statue of Zuzumza connected to a crowded temple where many came to offer sacrifices. Soon Roshell found the three-story building she had been seeking but hesitated going in when she spotted a sign over the door reading, *Meccan State Orphanage*. The cheerful wave of a familiar woman in a conjoining playground finally convinced Roshell to ring the brass bell.

The door opened to reveal a young woman who greeted Roshell with a jubilant hug then led the visitors down the hall to the director's office. There was another round of hugs as Julie was introduced.

"I can't believe you're still here, Joni!" Roshell said. "After all the destruction we've seen, I wasn't sure if a single Tnias was left."

The fortyish director smiled. "It's been tough, but with Yahweh's help, we are making it. Please, sit down."

It was then that they noticed the Gogian flag in a corner and a large picture of Zuzumza hanging on the wall behind Joni's desk. Immediately both stiffened. Sensing their nervousness, the director said, "It's the only way we could continue. We have to feign going along with the Emperor's policies."

"Including teaching their doctrines?" Roshell's hand tightened around her chair's armrest

"Yes, when government observers are visiting the classrooms," Joni responded. "But at night we talk to them about Yahweh."

"Doesn't that confuse the children?" asked Julie.

"They understand that we must pretend in order to protect their lives. We teach them Yahweh is the One True God."

"That is compromising!" Roshell stood in anger. "You have the demon's image in your building. Do the kids say the Allegiance Pledge to Zuzumza every morning?"

"When there are officials here. We have no choice."

"Yes, you did! You could have fled to Ulmjo."

"Then to Lahad. Next Kentniko. Always running, never making a stand. My staff and I decided to stay here, to make a stand where we're needed most. Every one of our orphanages is overfilled. The majority of the kids who come were not Tnias and never would have known Yahweh's love if we had fled south. Hundreds of children have found redemption because we made our stand here."

"By compromising!"

"No! If the Tnias are to flourish under persecution, they must do so by cunning and stealth. The dead cannot feed the hungry."

Roshell opened her mouth to speak again, but Julie gently put a hand on her arm, silencing the older woman. "I am glad to see how Yahweh has blessed you during these dangerous times."

The director relaxed. "Thank you." To Roshell, she added, "You haven't changed one bit. That temper of yours will get you in trouble someday."

For a while conversation stayed light as Julie explained their mission further north. Joni smiled in amazement. "How ironic, Roshell, that after all your complaints about how we run our orphanages, you are going to Gog's capitol."

"It's not by choice."

Invited to spend the night, the travelers gratefully accepted. After supper, they helped wash dishes then joined the nightly service held in the packed attic. Children, teenagers, and staff joyously sung in unison, their simple voices filling the stuffy room with harmony. Here Julie sensed the same sweet Presence that inhabited Agape. Slowly Roshell's anger dwindled as she listened to teenagers leading the devotion, their faith shining. Maybe youth could lead a double life without distorting their images of good and evil. Maybe.

That night, Roshell was unable to sleep. Silently she left the room filled with two rows of sleeping children on bunk beds. She paced the hall for a while then stopped in front of a window, studying the nighttime view of the now quiet city. A couple of drunks wobbled along the street. In the distance, a twenty feet statue of Zuzumza towered over the surrounding buildings, demanding every eye's attention. The full moon was hidden behind it, creating an ominous, lifelike silhouette.

"I could not sleep either." Though Julie's voice was low, Roshell jumped.

Embarrassed, the Ulmjon forced a smile. "At least the kids are sleeping peacefully here. I keep thinking about the children I left behind. I should be smuggling more out of Ulmjo, but instead I am here. Why?"

It was a long moment before Julie answered. "You were wrong when you told Joni that you have no choice. You didn't have to come. You can still turn around."

Roshell was quiet, thinking. The Mal'ak had not asked her to come but spoke as if it was a fact. It was true that she could have refused, but to do so would have been disobedient to Yahweh. As a leader, she often told people what to do and expected them to obey. Sometimes they disagreed, but she was the one who understood how one person's duties affected the whole structure. Now, resentfully, she had given her responsibilities to others to follow a plan she did not understand.

Julie broke the silence. "Yahweh's ways are perfect. There is something waiting in Gog that only you can accomplish, but it remains hidden except between you and Him."

Roshell sighed. "It's probably to create more orphanages." Troubled, she brushed a braid away from her face. "I can't do that—not like here. I refuse to pretend to support a government that I abhor. I will not compromise. I will not hide."

~~~~~~~~~

Crops ripened and harvesters spent all day in the fields. The hum of insects and playing children filled hot summer days. In Telumza, no bodies hanged from trees. To the casual observer, life went on as it always did, but Julie could sense the costly toll the feign peace stole from the people. Smiles were fake, warmth long forgotten, neighbors not trusted. Terror no longer crushed the people's spirit—the original occupation of Gog did that. Only a husk of a once great nation was left. Grief, regrets, guilt, and reminisces of the past was the legacy handed down to children.

Julie was tempted to visit Brentwood but knew no one of importance to her would still be alive. The travelers skirted the edge of Noable Desert. High sand dunes brought back memories of armies and fighting. Of Urbane chasing her under the stars, catching her, tumbling down a sandy bank, kissing…Julie shook her head to clear the image. *What is he doing now? Is he even still alive? Stop it,* she chided herself, *he is out of my life permanently.*

Finally they crossed a range of low mountains into Gog itself. Within a day they reached the fertile Plains of Wheatland. Roshell was tense, feeling naked and venerable so far away from her southern homeland. Julie, though, felt alive for the first time since leaving Shalom. This was her land, her people, her culture. Never as Junia had she appreciated the land or noticed the common citizens. Now she embraced the endless landscape of green plains and thick forests, dotted with farms and towns. Gog was a part of her as she was a piece of it.

Towards evening, overloaded clouds poured down turrets of rain. The Tnias took shelter in the first available inn. Located in a mid-sized town, the inn was a popular hangout, and its ground level consisted of a large tavern. The sounds of boisterous patrons and upbeat music soon pulled Julie from her upstairs room. She watched the rowdy dancers from a railed landing, remembering when she had once been part of the drinking and merriment.

"Thinking of old times?" Roshell held out a steaming mug of soup. "I got supper."

Both stirred their scalding meal, watching a fight break out below, which ended just as quickly as it began. Several prostitutes passed the Tnias, leading clients to nearby rooms.

Julie asked, "Why did you never marry?"

"I'm celibate."

"Due to your decision or a command from Yahweh?"

The older woman sipped her soup before answering. "I never woke up one day and decided I would never marry. As a teen I flirted with several guys I liked, even had a major crush at the academy. For a while our friends considered us 'a thing,' but eventually we realized our callings were different, so we parted as friends. I even took part in his wedding a year later. Never thought about marriage much after that. I mean, I'm never in one place more than a few months. A husband and family would hinder my work. Instead of being the mother to a few kids, I feel like the mother of thousands."

"But do you ever miss…male companionship?"

"No, any woman who shows herself capably of using a sword is rarely not surrounded by them." Seeing the earnest look in her comrade's eyes, Roshell spoke frankly. "Sometimes when I'm with married friends, I wonder what it would be like to have someone by my side, a real home, and my own children. But one look at a scared kid I'm helping, and I know I'll never trade my life for anything else."

Julie nodded and sipped several spoonfuls of broth. "What about sexual desire?"

Roshell frowned. "You're abrupt."

"I'm serious."

"Yeah, I noticed. Look, I just keep myself busy, my mind focused on my work. I stay away from dangerous situations which may lead to future problems."

"But what about temptations that are right in front of you."

"Then you run, Julie. You have to stay prayed up and focused on Yahweh at all times for you never know when the enemy will strike or which weapon he will use. A tree with strong roots can't be moved. Keep your thoughts pure and when temptation comes, flee from it."

"That's easier said than done." An awkward silence fell between them. Julie finished her soup before speaking again. "I once had a lover before becoming a Tnias. When we finally met again, I almost turned from Yahweh to him."

Roshell sipped the last bite of her soup "What's the chance we will run into him?"

Julie's eyes took on a faraway look. "I don't know. Like me, he was a soldier. He could be dead by now."

"If you meet him again, can you handle it?"

"Yes. I will never turn back into what I once was. That person is dead. Still, I wonder about him. For so long, I didn't know what real love was. When I understood, it was already too late. Roshell, my last dying words were to him."

The Ulmjon was about to speak again, but a large fight downstairs drowned out all conversation as men slugged out their rage against opponents they had been laughing with only moments ago.

Chapter Eighteen

"So that's your home?" Roshell tried not to sound impressed with the spectacular view stretching for miles. The Tnias had paused on the mountain trail several thousand feet above the valley floor. Southward lay two fair size towns, several villages, and hundreds of farms. Northward was the great sprawling city of Thorn, the huge palace easily recognizable even to a stranger. The entire capital was enclosed by a thick stone wall. A constant maze of traffic flowed through the open gates.

"Hundreds of years ago, what you see between these two mountains was all there was of Gog. That changed when King Achozeiz made an alliance with Zuzumza." Julie explained, drinking in the vista.

Used to a hot southern climate, Roshell felt the chilly Hackquill Mountains was a place best left forgotten. "Too bad it didn't stay contained within this forsaken nether world of rocks. Make a pact with a demon and there goes the neighborhood."

"To the ends of the continent."

Agitated, Roshell said, "The Triad will not fall."

"So said my Telumzan friends about their country."

"Telumza's king didn't follow Yahweh." The strong mountain breeze blew several braids of hair across Roshell's face, and she brushed them away.

"The royal family of Achaia did follow Yahweh along with other long forgotten counties. They all are part of Gog now."

"How can you say such things? You of all people—you lived inside Agape."

"I'm only stating facts. I didn't mean to offend you." After living in the City of Yahweh, Julie viewed everything on a supernal level and was slow in realizing others still lacked that insight. "There is a significant difference between the fallen counties and the Triad. The ones that fell were already under Zuzumza's control. Though some of the rulers and citizens were Tnias, most of the people followed their own desires, worshipping their own gods. The Triad is different. The three nations are full of refugees who talk boldly of the horrors they have seen. No longer blind to what they face, the people have realized their wood and stone images cannot defeat a real, living evil."

"So are you now saying the Triad will withstand the Red Army?"

"I don't know. The strength of the Empire is tremendous and the soldiers are skilled veterans. The people of Misko, Lahad, and Kentniko have the fighting heart of a furious leviathan. What I believe is that it will be the bloodiest war ever fought on Tanlep."

"So this war will decide the spiritual fate of the entire planet? I should be on the front lines—not here."

"Roshell, you are on the front line." Julie slapped her reins, and her horse started down the steep trail.

Frowning, the older woman followed. She preferred the excitement of snatching innocent children out of the very mouth of the beast or fighting a visible enemy with a strong sword. Not hiding in the very bowels of the creature you wanted to kill. Again she questioned Yahweh's wisdom in sending her to Thorn.

Unable to reach the valley floor by nightfall, they camped in a shallow cave, the dirt floor showing signs that it was a regular layover for travelers. Roshell was awaken twice in the night by rats crawled across her. *Great*, the woman thought, *just like back home on the streets of Fastate.* Noon the next day, they finally reached Thorn. Getting into the bustling city was easy. The watchmen at the busy gate paid little attention to two mounted women dressed in worn homespun clothing—their weapons concealed and Julie's face hidden in the shadow of her hood.

Julie led the way along the crowded streets, eagerly pointing out familiar buildings, famous landmarks, and favorite shops. The Gogian was as excited as a child in a toy store, smiling at the astonishment Roshell could not erase from her own face. Outside Shalom, the Ulmjon had rarely seen buildings higher than three floors—and those were mansions and castles. In Thorn, there was row after row of five to eight story buildings, even in the poorest districts where the structures were built close together with narrow allies acting as divisions. Sectors for the high-class contained a vast diversity of architectural marvels, cultivated gardens, temples, and plazas. Thorn was nothing like Roshell imaged it would be.

Julie explained, "The enormous sum of money King Achozeiz offered for the best design for his new castle attracted architects from around the planet. Naturally only a few could work on Blackwall, so the first Emperor put the others to good use designing the ultimate city that would please the gods. What you see is the results of nearly a thousand years of labor."

Tall buildings were only the beginning of the amazing achievements of the proud Gogians. "The present city is built on the ruins of several smaller cities which were destroyed millenniums ago by enemies long forgotten in history. See that store over there? It has two levels underground. Engineers built the present city overtop pervious buildings. About five hundred years ago, someone came up with the idea of building the city, not upward, but downward. It was only successfully achieved in Market Square. In some places, businesses are located forty feet below ground. It's called the Underground and some of the most unique shops in the Empire are found there. I used to visit often with my friends—well, I actually never called them my friends, nor they me. South Underground is where you will find the lewdest areas—selling of children and pleasure drugs." A troubled sadness settled on the Gogian, and she ceased talking.

Every street corner seemed to have a temple, each uniquely created to outshine the last. The greatest one was the Mausoleum of Zuzumza, enormous and airy, with a towering statue of its patron god built into the front of the building. As they rode past the temple, the scantily dressed prostitutes sauntering on the broad marble steps, young children mixing with older harlots. Roshell could barely contain her fury. She wanted to rescue the children by grabbing one and dashing off on horseback through the crowded plaza, but she did not know the area or have a safe house. Silently she vowed to find a way to help the violated children

Out of money, the two Tnias headed towards Reed Sector, the poorest area in Thorn, to find a cheap place to stay. It was less likely Julie would be recognized there. Still near Market Square, they stopped at a stable and sold their horses, carrying their few supplies in backpacks. Walking along the crowded streets, Roshell noticed people staring at her dark skin, immediately identifying her as a foreigner.

"Relax," said Julie. "If anyone asks, just say you're a servant of a noble running errands. No one will think twice about it."

"That's easy for you to say."

Rounding a corner, Julie froze. Across the street four soldiers were lining up workers from a small clothing business. Most of the employees were old, worn women, spent from a life of manual labor. Two soldiers served as sentries while the other two slowly went down the line, asking each worker which god they served. Several passersby stopped to watch.

"I didn't think they performed these type of searches so far north," Roshell whispered.

Squinting against the setting sun, Julie studied the workers, focusing on a young woman in the line. "It's only done if an informant snitches. If the Reforcers find a Tnias, the informant gets paid."

"Let's move before they start questioning bystanders."

Roshell turned to backtrack, but Julie grabbed her arm. "Make a diversion!"

"A what?"

"A diversion. Do anything, but quickly. You must get the soldiers' attention." Before Roshell could say another word, Julie casually began walking across the street.

"She's crazy," mumbled the Ulmjon. "She's going get us killed our first day in this forsaken city." Seeing that Julie would reach the interrogation line in seconds, Roshell did the first thing that popped into her mind. She started screaming.

"Help! Help!" Passersby glanced her way, making a wider berth around her. The soldiers paid no heed. Raising her voice, Roshell walked directly towards the two sentinels, attempting to look helpless and confused—a difficult task for her. "Help! I've been robbed! Please, you must help me."

One of the soldiers responded in a bored expression, "We're busy. Go find someone else to pester."

"It was my lord's money! I was taking it to the bank. If you find it, I'm certain he'll reward you well."

The sentries glanced at each other. One asked for a description of the thief then ordered her not to move. Both soldiers bolted down the street. Roshell smiled, knowing if there had been a real robbery, the victim would never get the money back even if the soldiers caught the thief.

Julie had reached the line of workers while the remaining soldiers looked towards Roshell. Julie clasped a hand of the youngest employee and whispered, "Come."

The maiden looked confused but obeyed without question. The Reforcers were still distracted, and it looked like they might escape unnoticed until a woman further down the line started yelling, "There she is! You're letting her get away!"

Immediately Julie ran, holding the lady's hand tightly. The two remaining Reforcers drew their swords and followed in hot pursuit. For a moment, Roshell stood frozen in the middle of the busy street, wondering what to do. Realizing it would be almost impossible to find Julie again in the huge city if separated, Roshell bolted after the four retreating figures, grumbling as she ran.

As the deadly race wound its way through packed streets, Julie took sharp turns, knocking over obstacles in an attempt to slow their pursuers. Barely able to keep up, the maiden gasped in ragged breaths. Effortlessly the Reforcers jumped over fallen vegetable stands and tables, pushing people roughly aside. Racing behind the other two, Roshell was slowed by pedestrians standing around, gawking. Suddenly a man emerged from a butcher's shop and ran beside her. Out of the corner of her eye, she noticed he was dressed in a dirty apron and commoner's clothes. Their eyes locked for a brief second, each realizing the other was not a threat. Side by side they chased after the rapidly disappearing Reforcers.

Around corners, pass loaded wagons, through crowds gathered around vendors and entertainers, the six people raced. Julie realized the maiden was at the end of her strength and could not run much further. The skyline opened ahead. Both gave an extra effort, knowing Market Square lay just ahead—and hopefully safety. They could disappear among the bustling crowds. Suddenly the lady slipped. The Reforcers pushed their way through a throng and appeared several feet behind them. Julie grabbed a watermelon from a stand and threw it with all her might. She hit one soldier who went down, knocking the other man off balance. Quickly Julie yanked the maiden to her feet, turned a corner, and bolted through the nearest doorway. They passed startled customers and clerks, dashing through a storage room then into an alley. Recovering their feet, the soldiers stayed on the main street, presuming that the fugitives had continued towards the marketplace.

Both women leaned against the cool brick wall, gasping for breath. The maiden stared in amazement at Julie, about to speak, when suddenly she spotted two figures pounded pass the alley's entrance. The woman ran to the street, yelling. Recognizing his name, the man turned around and dashed into the alley. A tired Roshell followed. The couple embraced, tears running down the maiden's cheeks. Julie stood quietly with a look of serenity, knowing this meeting was not by chance.

Roshell leaned against the damp wall, attempting to catch her breath. "Julie, the next time you decide to pull off a stunt like that, I'll hang you myself. What do you think you were doing?"

"Saving the life of a very good friend whom I am indebted."

"So it is you!" Danielle came within three feet of the Gogian, uncertain. "I thought maybe I was already dead and you were a Mal'ak coming to take me to Agape."

Shocked, Matthan gasped, "We thought you were dead—executed by the Emperor."

With a twinkle in her eye, Julie said, "I once was dead but am now alive."

Recognizing the well-known line from Yahweh's Word, a big grin spread across the man's face, and he embraced his old friend. Danielle followed with her own hug, repeating over and over, "It's a miracle, an incredible miracle."

"If you're finished with your little reunion," cut in Roshell, "we need to get out of here—hopefully alive."

She walked to the opposite end of the alley. After looking in both directions, she motioned for them to follow. They sneaked through the back streets and allies, avoiding more trouble. As the sun set, they rested in a city park.

"So is it a boy or girl?" asked Julie, placing a hand on her friend's flat stomach.

Danielle laughed. "It's in Yahweh's hands. I'll be pleased with either—or both."

"So when is the due date?" Before her death, Julie had been too consumed by desires for power to consider becoming a mother. Children were something she and Urbane might have had in the distant future. Seeing her friend lit up from an inter glow of motherhood stirred instinctive feelings inside Julie which she did not know lay dormant inside her.

"In just over six months." Danielle gave her stomach a loving pat.

Standing several feet away from the park bench the ladies sat, Matthan and Roshell conversed. The father-to-be drank in the tranquil scene. The stillness of the park, strong scented night flowers, exquisite moths pollinating blossoms. It seemed so natural, so normal for women to be discussing the miracle of life that he forgot the dangerous reality they faced—for a moment.

Roshell had barely contained her temper as they had fled the back streets to the park. The old friends constantly wanted to talk about the adventures that had befallen them since their last meeting, but the Ulmjon kept pushing them onward. It was not until they stopped in the park to rest that she realized the couple were foreigners like her, and faced the same bigot attitudes of the arrogant Gogians. When Matthan mentioned they had both graduated from Salt Academy, Roshell's aloofness finally faded. For the first time since leaving the South, she was among peers. She found Matthan to be a quick-witted soldier with a good head on his shoulders and tenderhearted Danielle had a special love for children.

Matthan said, "They will place a spy by our house. There's no way we can go back. Maybe tomorrow I can relocate Sunshine to a new stable."

"Where are we to stay tonight?" Danielle asked.

Julie knew their money would not support very long four people and one hungry horse—Matthan would never sell Sunshine. "We have no home or contacts. This is our first day here."

"And already we're on the most wanted list," mumbled Roshell.

"We've only been here a few weeks ourselves," said Matthan.

Suddenly a sense of danger ran down the southerner's spine. Instinctually she crouched, drawing her sword. A huge, dark shadow passed over them. Roshell and Julie looked up, and gasped in shock. Matthan and Danielle immediately dropped their gaze.

"Quickly, look at the ground!" commanded Matthan.

Roshell obeyed, but Julie could not tear her gaze away. She walked forward several steps, transfixed, hand partly raised as if to touch the high, flying nightmare. Matthan ran forward and roughly turned her to face him. Her eyes stared unblinking, unfocused. The monstrous creature seemed to have flown directly out of the mythical stories she had grown up with. Hands on her shoulders, Matthan roughly shook Julie until her body relaxed and she came back to the present. The oppressive atmosphere in the air suddenly vanished. Night birds began singing and insects chirped.

"What was that?" demanded Roshell.

Matthan opened his mouth to answer but Julie cut him off. "It is Zuzumza, God of War. The same god that turned this valley into the Empire of Gog."

"There is only One True God," Danielle reprimanded.

"It is the archdemon which devours this city." Matthan looked towards the empty night sky. "Sometimes it appears during the day. When it does, people look anywhere but at the sky. They know it's there but won't acknowledge it. They say it has the ability to read thoughts, so people try to avoid attracting its attention."

"I cannot believe it shows itself in broad daylight. That's never happened before." Julie was more herself again.

"Call it demon or god, it is not as powerful as Yahweh. It will meet its end someday," Roshell said. "Now we need to find a place to stay. I don't know about you, but it's been a long day. I'm exhausted."

No one spoke for a few minutes while each pondered their situation. A cool breeze rustled leaves above the homeless Tnias, hinting of the coming winter.

After praying silently Danielle said, "What about the Greencliffs? They might let us stay for one night."

Answering the newcomers' curious looks, Matthan explained, "The Greencliffs are an elderly couple who own a watch shop. Through a slip in conversation, Danielle discovered they are Tnias. Since then we've visited them several times at their store.

"How many others are there in Thorn?" asked Roshell.

"Don't know. The Greencliffs are the only ones we've discovered so far, and they're as wary as rabbits, just like everyone else in this city. Still, they're our best shot."

Down quiet streets lined with trimmed hedges, they headed north through the richest areas of town. The few people they saw paid them little attention. Matthan turned east, leading the group through the middle-class Dejeon Sector until reaching an area were the tall, narrow brick houses were built close together, giving the old homes the appearance of being smaller than they were.

Joatham Greencliff opened the door to Matthan's knock. The clockmaker's face was aged and his hands callused from years of hard work. Frowning, he invited them in, casting a wary glance towards neighboring houses.

Passing a stairway which went up three floors, he led them into a cozy den with thick cushioned couches and a blazing fire. Danielle and Matthan kept up a light

159

conversation, but Joatham stayed tense. Sensing his aloofness, the couple gave up the idea of asking for shelter for the night. Slow thumping on the stairs announced that someone was coming down. Josias Greencliff entered the room.

"I thought I heard voices." Wrinkles covered the aged woman's body, her milky skin splotched with blue veins. "I guessed it was our son Onias and his girlfriend entertaining some of their friends. We rarely get visitors anymore."

Danielle gave the frail woman a hug. "I'm glad to see you're in better heath."

The elderly lady chatted freely about her five grown children, complaining about their rare visits, except for her youngest, which still lived with them. "Unfortunately, his girlfriend also lives with us." She glanced accusingly at her husband.

Feeling uncomfortable that she was sharing so much in front of the visitors, he grumbled, "It's better they live together here than in the Reed district where she's from."

Ignoring her husband, Josias went on, "I pray every day Onias and Sandra will get married and that the rest of my children will realize they need Yahweh."

At the mention of the deity's name, Joatham shifted his weight nervously. When they had met the young couple before, they seemed genuine in faith, but the government could be laying cunning traps that his too trusting wife was walking blindly into. He studied the swords of the two strangers who came with the young couple. Both women had the rugged look of soldiers—or Reforcers.

Josias continued. "It seems every generation is worse than the last, disdaining what we teach them. Not only are our children lost, but our grandchildren too." She sighed. "I don't know what to do. Every time I talk to them, they ignore me or listen like I'm an imaginative child who needs patronizing."

As the women chatted, Julie walked to the mantle, seemingly interested in a beautiful centerpiece clock. She rubbed her hands over the smooth wood, feeling prophetical words dancing on the tip of her tongue, just like the time she spoke in the town meeting at Brentwood. Her courage failed. What if the things she saw in her head were untrue? But to be silent might mean missing a miracle.

Taking a deep breath, she turned and faced the others. "Do you have contact with other Tnias?"

Josias was about to answer, but Joatham cut her off. "No, we keep to ourselves."

"Unfortunately what you say is true. Though occasionally you meet with other Tnias, your faith is weak and you feel alone. You secretly tell yourself that Yahweh can't forgive your mistakes or the catastrophe sins of your nation. You believe that Yahweh has turned his back on you and abandoned the last Tnias in Gog."

Joatham's lower jaw dropped in speechless astonishment—and anger. What right did this stranger have to talk like this to him in his own house? How did she know his secret thoughts? He was not sure if she was even human—perhaps an immortal messenger he read about in Yahweh's book. "You…you speak too boldly to be a spy."

"I have bolder things yet to say. Though you sometimes wondered if Yahweh even exist, Yahweh has always cared about you. The prayers you thought he never heard have pieced his heart deeply. The mistakes you asked forgiveness for have long been erased."

The pride of the old man wilted, leaving him feeling naked and transparent, not in front of the mysterious woman, but in front of the deity he barely believed existed.

"Now accept his forgiveness, Joatham, and know he will never leave you or abandon you. There is a great work to be done in Thorn, and you and your wife have a role to fulfill. From this day forth you will be called Kowkab Chacah, the Stars of Hope."

"We are old and my wife is sick more than she is well."

"Has not Yahweh blessed you with wealth and a large home with empty rooms? Are there not cries of pain from those in the streets? As a sign for your lack of faith, I have this message for you." Julie drew her sword. Hot flames leaped along its polished blade.

Gasps of wonder filled the room from the five onlookers. Roshell rose and took three steps forward. Danielle clasped Matthan's arm, himself staring in amazement, unable to believe his eyes. Only Josias was unconcerned about the strange weapon. A look of rapturous joy basked her face as she witness a transformation in her husband as he gawked in awe at the Sword of Fire. Julie tilted the blade towards herself, giving the hilt to the elderly man. As he griped the handle, the fire vanished. He rubbed a finger gingerly over the still warm blade, his mind slow to accept the wonder he had witnessed. He had stopped believing in miracles long ago.

Julie pointed at the etched symbols on the blade. "The Word is sharper than a two-edged sword. It can't be taken away or changed. It is time for you to trust in the words you read—those that you hide in a compartment under the seventh step of your stairs."

Though worn from a hard life of work and worry, hope sparked in Joatham's eyes. "I'll take you to our meeting tomorrow night."

As Josias lead the four visitors upstairs to bedrooms, the sword was passed around.

Matthan ran his finger over its smooth surface. "So Yahweh gave this to you himself?"

"Yes."

"And you were really dead?" asked Danielle for the second time.

"Yep." This time Julie laughed.

"When you said that line about once being dead but now alive, I didn't think you meant it literally." Matthan was just as stunned as his wife at the sudden turn of events. For years they had lived under the hopeless atmosphere of the Empire, never losing faith but feeling the slow grind of darkness taking its toll. Now suddenly a long lost friend shows up, dares a fast pace rescue, performs a miracle or two, and the next thing they know, they are about to make contact with the long sought Remnant.

Roshell was not impressed. "First she glows. Now her sword does. What next? Her footprints?"

Ignoring the Ulmjon, Matthan and Danielle pounded their friend with an endless parade of questions. Josias listened, talking it all in. Finally they parted, heading to various bedrooms Josias had selected for them.

Over her shoulder, Roshell called out, "If you need a light in the middle of the night, just call Julie."

Frowning, Julie fell in step beside her friend, worrying about the jealousy she saw building inside Roshell. "I am the least of all people. If you knew me before I died, you wouldn't recognize me. Hatred and pain consumed me. I destroyed others' lives and felt no remorse."

"Yes, yes, I know the rest. You pledged your soul to Yahweh, died a martyr, and now you're a living saint."

"I'm mortal just like you and will die again someday. I too wrestle against weaknesses."

"And suddenly have prophetic insight." Roshell stopped walking. "Do you know what will take place tomorrow or the next day? Can you read my thoughts right now?"

Julie glared at her, almost saying something she would regret later. Instead, she forced herself to take a deep breath. "I control no powers. I'm a servant of Yahweh, just like you. He chooses who he will."

"And of course, he chooses a Gogian demon child to be his spokesman." Julie winced, as if physical slapped. "What will you do next? Send an earthquake to destroy Blackwall Palace or pull out your fiery sword and the Emperor will suddenly become as gentle as a kitten, professing Yahweh?"

Troubled, Julie turned away. "Stop before you dig a hole you will never escape from. Your jealousy makes you sound like what I used to be."

"What other secrets do you keep?" Roshell lashed out, angry at being reprimanded by the youth she had been providing for over the last several months.

The two women glared at each other. Early in the trip when Roshell had shared so much about her own life, Julie had almost spoken about her life as a Gogian princess—almost. But she had sensed the underlying rage Roshell felt for the Empire. It had been hard enough for the Ulmjon to accept that Julie had once been part of the Red Army. What would Roshell do if she learned she was traveling with the sister of her most hated enemy?

"What I know must not be revealed until Yahweh chooses to do so." With that, Julie entered her bedroom and shut the door, leaving Roshell alone with her bitterness.

~~~~~~~~~

Dim lantern light illuminated raw sewage flowing along ancient trenches. Five people followed Joatham through the underground labyrinth of decaying filth, hordes of rats, and slippery walkways. The stench was overpowering. Roshell lost her balance and grabbed the moist wall for balance, grimacing as her hand touched slime. Putrefied liquid poured from a pipe overhead. Attempting to dodge, Danielle would have fallen into the waste moat if Matthan had not grabbed her arm. Hearing a loud crunch of a large roach's exoskeleton cracking under her foot, Julie shuddered, briefly thinking of the marble floors she used to walk on.

"The sewers are not my idea for a sanctuary," grumbled Roshell.

"Nor mine," chatted Josias good-naturedly despite her easy tiredness, "but it's safe down here. Don't worry, we don't actually meet in the sewers."

Holding high the only lantern, Joatham gave a history lesson as they walked. "There was once an ancient river which flowed through this valley, cutting channels through the limestone, creating caves. When humans first settled here, they used the caves for shelter and storage. Eventually a series of cities were built on top of earlier ruins. When the engineers of King Achozeiz redesigned what was to become Thorn, they used the natural tunnels and old city ruins for their sewage system. Then it lay forgotten for half a millennium until Market Square's Underground was developed, but the rest of the system was in too poor shape for renovation. Several of the workers on the project were Tnias and realized that here was the perfect spot to worship in safety." He waved a hand to indicate their surroundings

They now traveled on a crumbly brick walkway that had once been a street. Closer inspection of the walls revealed decayed skeleton fronts of rocky structures that may once have been businesses. Their roofs had long ago collapsed and the buildings had been filled in with dirt and rock. The visitors felt like trespassers, intruding on a page of history long ago vanished from the minds of the human race—a place only ghosts treaded.

They paused to jump a three-foot gap to another narrow walkway. Josias would have fallen if not for her husband's strong hand pulling her to safety. "We rarely come down here anymore. We're both getting too old for this," she gasped.

Soon the fetid stream broadened into a small river. They crossed an ancient stone bridge, slippery from lichen. Several rocks had fallen from the span and the Tnias found themselves looking down at the raw waste flowing under their feet—a bit unnerving. It was a relief to everyone when Joatham finally turned down a rocky tunnel leading away from the rancid stew. Several more turns along rough-hewed passageways leading steeply downward brought them to an immense natural chamber originally created by the extinct river. Beautiful stalactites covered the ceiling and stalagmites rose from the floor, sometimes connecting to create pillars of living rock. Over the millennium, the walls at the lower end of the cavern had been enlarged and the floor smoothed out to create an amphitheater complete with slanted floor. Large rocks served as benches.

Matthan whistled, the sound echoing several times. "Never have I seen a more magnificent place of worship!" The others were equally impressed.

Joatham followed a well-worn path through the field of slow growing stalagmites until reaching the smooth, lantern lit area that served as the sanctuary. Despite the vast cathedral, only two dozen people gathered on the rocky seats, all middle aged or older—the Remnant of Thorn. They greeted the Greencliffs but turned wary eyes towards the newcomers. Joatham and Josias introduced everybody by name.

"They have traveled all the way from Shalom to visit with us," concluded Josias.

"From Shalom?" People gasped in surprise. Contact had been lost with the outer world for countless generations.

"That's a long way to come just for a friendly visit," said Eleazer, head of the Remnant. He was portly and bald with a jovial attitude in the face of hardship that had earned him the respected position.

Julie said, "We have come with a message from Yahweh which I would like to share."

"Hopefully it comes with some encouragement. There's rarely good news here in Thorn."

The meeting began with singing. There was no music, but as untrained voices echoed through the vast chamber, it seemed as if a choir of Mal'ak had joined. As Julie sang, she wondered what to say to these people who lived in a barren world of darkness and constant threats. To her eyes only, the chamber suddenly became dim, as if the dancing flames of the lanterns had lost their power of light. In the darkness, individuals shined, some brighter than others. In that brief moment, Julie realized Yahweh had preserved a remnant for this moment, this time. Some had completely lost faith but came for companionship and hope that others offered. Some had never stopped trusting in Yahweh's goodness, no matter what tragedies had befallen them. Those who glowed dimly along with the brightly lit ones, together, would create a force that even the gods would tremble from in fear. All that was needed was for the spark to be ignited.

Eleazar gave a short devotion from his tattered Book of Yahweh then invited Julie to the front. She passed the various size rocks that served as benches, seeing the Remnant as they saw themselves—old, worn, persecuted, controlled by fear. Their minds trapped in snares as strong as any physical chain.

She paused to borrow Eleazar's frayed book, so damaged by age that the words were barely visible. In a loud voice she read, "My people will know that I am their Lord when I break the bars of their yoke and rescue them from the hands of those who enslaved them." She closed the book. "Yahweh has heard your prayers, and his heart breaks in sorrow. He never left you. His Presence is here, now."

Several people on the front row rubbed their eyes, thinking the smoke from the lanterns was getting to them. It seemed as if the woman had a faint glow about her.

"Yahweh cannot be contained in a room or inside one person. He is El Olam, the Everlasting God of all ages. It is time for you to make a stand, believing in the stories you have long read in this book. These heroes were no different than you—ordinary people who put their trust in Yahweh. What stops miracles from happening now?"

Several people gasped in surprise. The speaker's skin glowed as if from an internal fire. One woman poked her sleepy husband in the side, while others whispered to neighbors to see if they saw the same thing.

"It is lack of faith. Your children and children's children think you worship a dead god. Yahweh wants to send a fire which will rage through Gog, burning and purifying."

Even those half blind from age could now clearly see the light that radiated from the woman. It was brighter than the lanterns and expanding with each word she spoke.

"He wants to give hope to those in darkness, heal the sick, give the destitute homes. Even the dead will walk among you. Miracles will happen, but it can only be done through you. Believe. Trust. Surrender your fear, your pride."

As the last words were spoken, light exploded through the chamber, becoming a mighty living river of love and peace. Several yelled in surprise, some bowed in prayer, others silently crumpled to the stone floor. Only the four who had been in Shalom understood what was happening. The invisible current swept through the souls of the Remnant, a stream of power mortals could only surrender to or flee from. Those who abandoned themselves to the Presence felt themselves transported, standing directly in front of their God of Love. Time lost meaning. Privately sins were confronted and spiritual chains broken. Weeping filled the cavern as souls found release and new purpose. Julie moved among the people, praying, ministering as needed. Weeping joyfully, Danielle joined her. Matthan lay on the floor, lost in the Presence. He finally sat up, putting his hands on the shoulder of a frail man kneeling beside him. A surge of electrical power flowed through the Salt, and the old man looked up.

"I can see! I can see!" The elderly man jumped up and began running through the rows, cane held high. It was only the beginning of miracles that would take place among the Remnant.

Roshell was the only one who seemed unaffected by the pulsing supernatural power. Seeing the other Salts helping people, she approached a kneeling woman. Before Roshell could reach the woman, she ran into an invisible barrier. She pushed forward with all her strength, but it was as if a transparent stone wall had suddenly been built between her and the weeping woman. Trembling with anger and fear, Roshell turned and walked away, not stopping until hidden behind a large stone column.

"Yahweh," she challenged the air. "Why do you treat me like this? Have I not spent my life helping others? I've sacrificed everything for you."

The only sound was of distant weeping and happy shouts. She glanced around, looking for an answer, disturbed that the entire chamber was lit up as if a sun burned inside it. Peeking around the edge of the moist column, she watched the Remnant being transformed before her eyes. Eleazar danced jubilantly while Josias stood with arms raised. Joatham was part of a group, holding hands, praying. Suddenly Roshell's focus was jerked to a large man facing her, arms crossed, legs apart, standing where the wild, jagged floor met the hand-smoothed area. His handsome carved features seemed like a bronze statue come to life. The Ulmjon swallowed, recognizing the man as the Mal'ak who had given her the message to meet Julie.

Words filled her mind. *I will judge between one sheep and another. Is it not enough for you to feed on the good pasture? Must you also trample the rest of your pasture with your feet? Is it not enough for you to drink clear water? Must you also muddy the rest with your feet? Must my flock feed on what you have trampled and drink what you have muddied with your feet?*

Roshell dropped to her knees in agony, remembering her curses against the murders of her foster parents, her prejudice against Gogians, her burning jealousy of Julie. All the good she had done over the years was rotten fruit in front of a god who saw her heart. Tears ran down her cheeks as shame filled her. Instead of helping Yahweh, she had become a hindrance—and was now blocked from doing further work for him.

Gut wrenching words of repentance arose from her lips. Her body seemed to become light, feeling as if it rose into the air. No longer could she feel the cold, rough floor. She tumbled end over end in a powerful current of love. The hatred and jealousy which harbored in her heart were scrubbed away. Images of children flashed passed her eyes—Gogian children with hopeless eyes. She loved them, caring for them as much as the southern orphans she knew. She had found her purpose.

Chapter Nineteen

Over the centuries, little changed for the Remnant except there was less in each new generation. It was difficult to believe mythical stories of an ancient, distant god when all around were magnificent temples that friends visited. Some sensed an aching void inside, wishing there was more to life than work, entertainment, bitter relationships, and self-gain. In the cold, underground cavern, a fire had been lit in the middle of dry, wither twigs. It smoldered, burning, sending sparks to other dry patches, building into a raging wildfire that refused to be contained, bursting forth at such a rapid pace that even Julie was amazed.

Normally the Tnias only met once a week for the journey underground was too strenuous for most—and many of the elderly no longer came at all. Now they had been given a glimpse of paradise and forever changed. They decided to meet again in three days, planning to find all the Tnias who were not at the meeting and tell them something marvelous was happening. They left expecting miracles, and none were disappointed. Nearly a hundred Tnias gathered in the rocky chamber several days later, starving for something greater than the harsh reality they lived. Elders came, trembling and wheezing from exhaustion, determined to witness Yahweh's power before dying. Several grown daughters and sons came with their parents, some to appease, others out of genuine desire to discover if the stories of Yahweh were true. Julie was pleased to note one young couple even brought their children. Unless there was Tnias among the youngest generation, Beelzebub would win the battle in the long run.

Entering the vast cavern, newcomers stared in amazement at the chamber lit up like day from an unknown source, the atmosphere warm and inviting. There was an invisible living Presence in the room. Some recognized it immediately and embraced it. Others felt afraid, transparent, glancing around to see if anyone knew their dark secrets. The meeting did not follow any preset format. People were on their knees praying hours before it was supposed to begin. Spontaneous singing burst from joyful lips and eager people told miraculous adventures that had happen to them.

A woman named Manira had been shopping in a store when a robber pulled a knife on the young store clerk. Helpless, Manira watched the trembling teenager give all the money to the shouting man. After yelling a few more obscene threats, the thief vanished out the door, and the youth slumped to the floor crying. Manira comforted the teen and reported the crime to authorities. The next day she stopped in to check on the young lady only to find the storeowner about to fire Terra because he thought she was making up the robbery story to cover stealing the money herself. Manira retold the story to the owner and offered to walk the bashful teenager home. Embarrassed, Terra was forced to admit she was homeless, so Manira insisted the teen move in with her. As Terra warmed to the older woman, she began asking why Manira went out of her way to help a stranger. Terra attended the meeting that night and became a new believer in Yahweh.

Manira's story was only the first of many. The Remnant had learned, instead of hiding, to reach out to those in need. Most stories were not as dramatic as Terra's, but people were curious and inquisitive when someone took time to help them in the look-out-for-yourself city.

The meeting never ended. Singing and stories went on into the wee hours of the morning. Slowly individuals drifted away to head home through the odorous maze. Others fell asleep on the floor or in smaller nearby chambers. Some stayed up all night, lost in the Presence, time forgotten. Days blended together as people came and went, prayed and slept, hunger for what the Empire and Zuzumza could not give them.

Julie, Matthan, and Danielle kept busy aiding as needed. Roshell helped often, but would disappear for long periods, needing to spend time alone. All four were viewed as the leaders of the new movement and fondly dubbed Salts, even though the word was traditionally reserved only for those who had graduated Salt Academy—Roshell was a dropout and Julie had never attended. With the help of Joatham and a friend of his who was a retired Reforcer, Matthan and Danielle recovered their sparse possessions along with the Sword of Justice Matthan had hidden in their apartment. Sunshine was safely quartered in a new stable.

Onias and his girlfriend Sandra showed hostility to the four strangers who had suddenly moved in with the Greencliffs. The son, a student at the local university, helped with the family business and worried about his parents spending so much time with the strangers. There was an increase in visitors knocking on the door, money and supplies disappearing. Onias would have reported the four to the Reforcers except his parents might also be arrested in an investigation. He tried talking with his father, but the elderly man only smiled and said it was his duty to help the poor.

Sandra was also perplexed. Josias had always criticized everything she did, looking down on her for being from the Reed Sector—not good enough for her son. The criticism stopped. Josias began going out of her way to be helpful. One day Sandra discovered Josias going through closets, pulling out clothing seldom worn, claiming she was given them to the poor. The young couple were bewildered. Determined to get to the bottom of things, Onias took up his dad's suggestion of visiting the underground sanctuary.

The next day they journeyed through the underground. Both Onias and Sandra were appalled to discover the elderly coupled literally traveled through the sewers. Jaw set, Onias decided when they got back, he would somehow put an end to his parents' ridiculous treks, even if he had to lock them up someplace while Reforcers searched the house for the Tnias strangers. Reaching the well-lit grand chamber, Onias scanned the jagged walls, looking for the source of the bright light—but finding nothing. Scattered around the cavern were more people than he expected. Several children started a game of tag but were quickly reprimanded by a woman. Disturbed, Onias studied individuals praying near the lowest end of the chamber, recognizing a Zuzumza priest, a retired Reforcer, and a couple he went to school with. This was bigger than he thought.

Looking to his right, Onias spotted Sandra hugging a sister she had not spoken with in over two years. They chatted like best friends. A shudder went down his spine. He should not have brought Sandra, but she had insisted on coming. His parents and the four interlopers scattered among the rock benches, greeting others. Onias observed how people responded, smiling and freely chatting about this illicit deity. A death sentence aboveground.

An hour later, Sandra was on her kneels weeping, her sister on one side and Josias on the other. Onias sat on a rock, frowning, knowing that the plague that infected his parents now gripped his girlfriend. He would have fled the cavern if he did not fear becoming lost in the reeking labyrinth. *This must be stopped*, his mind screamed. *I must remember the right path when we leave so Reforcers can handle this.*

The singing ceased. In the silence, Onias glanced towards the lowest end of the chamber. The one called Matthan stood there, sword on hip, book in hand. As Matthan spoke, several individuals fell to their kneels, weeping. Others shouted in agreement. As the ancient text was read, loathing tore through Onias for the Salt and the words he uttered. The Gogian had always thought himself reasonable, always guided by logic, caring little about gods and their destinies over man, living life the way he wanted. For a reason he could not explain, the heresy spoken here bothered him deeply, leaving his soul trembling. Who was this man who claimed there was a God of Love, far more powerful than Zuzumza, the Ultimate God, who had raised Gog out of the dust of the earth?

More singing followed, eerie from the echoing effect of the rocky chamber, referring to images Onias could not understand. The hairs on the back of his neck stood straight up and chill bumps ran down his arms. The harmonies rose in zest,

170

reverberating through the cavern, seemly alive, piecing through him, carrying him to a zenith where he would either fly or fall. *I have to get out of here!*

Even as he stood in panic, heart pounding, the singers quieted. A teenager stood at the front. The youth was thin and frail, scared to be in front of so many people. For what seemed an eternity, she trembled, unable to speak.

Finally she found her voice. "Manira has already told you my story about how I was homeless and now have a place to live. But there are many more like me who…" The teen's voice faltered and tears ran down her cheeks. "They…they need homes too. They sleep in snow and fight for food. It's no place for children. We need help." She covered her face and wept in front of three hundred strangers.

Several in the audience stepped forward to comfort her. Some shouted suggestions, while others pointed out problems with the ideas. Roshell stood, and the chamber became quiet. Onias clenched his jaw.

She seemed poised and confident, in her element. "Look around you. You have been blessed. Now is the time to pass it along. I have explored many of the connecting passageways. You already use some of the rooms for sleeping. Why not turn them into dormitories and classroom for the homeless and those needing shelter from dangers above? Create an orphanage." Heads nodded in approval. "It will take a lot of work and donations. We will need beds, clothing, food, and volunteers."

Roshell tried to say more but was drowned out by people yelling things they would donate. The audience became loud and boisterous, excited about the prospect. Roshell and a growing crowd moved to the back of the amphitheater, soon disappearing down a passageway to develop plans without disturbing those who still worshipped. Joatham, Josias, and Sandra were among those who left.

Time dragged by for Onias. The singing irritated him, and the weeping made his skin crawl. What was wrong with these people? Losing patience, he walked down the passageway he had seen his family vanished through. Following the sounds of voices, he finally came to a crumbly brick street where most of the buildings on each side were still standing. Down the middle of the ancient road, fresh water ran in a deep but narrow trench someone had dug long ago. People bobbed in and out of buildings, throwing out ideas about how to repair damage and what each room could be used for. Roshell was busy writing ideas down on parchment, using a crate for a table.

Sandra spotted Onias and gave him an excited hug. "Have you ever seen anything so wonderful? Onias, we're going to sweep the alleys of Reed, giving homes to the kids I used to pass everyday on the streets. Can you image your mother talking with the homeless? That will be a sight!"

"No, I can't. Nor you. What has gotten into you? These are the enemies of our government. You would lose your scholarships and could even be killed if the Reforcers knew you were helping."

Sadness filled the young woman as she realized her lover stood on the other side of a great gorge. "Listen to what you're saying. We are helping others. What's wrong with that? If the government thinks helping those in need is wrong then it's evil, not us. In those university classes, you and your friends were always spouting off about what is wrong with our society but never offering solutions. Well, here they are, like it or not."

He pulled her to the side of the aged street, away from any eavesdroppers. "Not like this, Sandra. They follow a false god."

"What is Zuzumza? Has he ever done anything for you?" Onias refused to meet her eyes. "I saw how you responded in the Great Chamber. You felt him too."

"Felt who?"

"Yahweh. He was in the cavern, you know. He's everywhere, even above ground. You can't escape him. In your eyes, I see the fear you have of him. You know he's real."

"You beginning to talk nonsense like my parents."

Her eyes flashed, reminding him why he fell in love with her. She was the only woman bold enough in classes to challenge the ideas of his friends.

"I dare you to spend one hour praying to this *false god*. If I'm talking nonsense, then nothing will happen except you'll feel a little silly. If I'm right, then you'll have an experience you will never forget."

"This is stupid. Let's just go home. Tomorrow you will see that this was all just emotions."

"I'm not sleeping in the same room with you again until we're married."

"What? We've never discussed marriage."

"Josias explained to me why what we were doing is wrong."

"Sandra, you *never* listen to my mother."

"Your mother has some wise advice. Look, I've got work to do. Remember what I said—spend an hour in the Great Chamber." Before he could say anything else, she turned away, joining her sister.

Angrily Onias walked along the passage. How could she, of all people, become one of them? She had fought hard to escape the slums and attend the university. Her level head in debates had made her popular among intellectual students. Now she had suddenly gone crazy, and he refused to take another minute of it. He walked through the Great Chamber, passing deranged worshipers, and exited the way his parents had originally brought him hours earlier. He grabbed a lantern and kept walking, determined to retrace his steps. He turned down this corridor then that one, slipping several times on the moist stone, unsure which was correct, but his outrage gave speed to his feet.

I will turn them all in. First I'll talk with Sandra, alone. If she won't listen, then her blood is on her own head. An hour later, dirty and exhausted, he finally admitted he was lost. *This shouldn't be happening to me. I'm top of my class.* He kept walking.

Then the lantern's wick flicked out, leaving him alone in the dark. Terror gripped him. He could hear water dripping and the scurry of rats. Somewhere down a side passage, a creature squealed in terror, but the cry was cut short. Teeth crunched on bones. Panic pulsed through the man. He ran, keeping one hand against the moist wall. Suddenly the wall ended and he fell into a channel filled with reek liquid. He swam to the other side, and pulled himself up, exhausted.

There was a squeak of a rat then pain shot through his hand. He jerked upright, instinctually putting the dirty, injured finger in his mouth, only to gag on the vile taste. An animal ran across his leg. He jumped up, terrified. He could not stay still, but moving was just as dangerous. He yelled for help until hoarse, slowly moving, keeping a hand against the slimy wall for guidance. His mind played tricks. Twice he thought he heard someone answer his calls, but it turned out to only be his echo. There were strange sounds of creatures moving in the dark, and he envisioned huge monsters with hungry, gapping jaws. Hope vanished and he began thinking of death.

He remembered Sandra, missing her calmness. Did she know he was in danger? What were her last words? *Yahweh. He's in the cavern, you know. He's everywhere, even above ground. You can't escape him.* He shook his head. The Tnias' god could not help him. *What is Zuzumza? Has he ever done anything for you?* Why did her last words to him have to be about gods? He was desperate, more frighten than he had ever been his entire life. Being lost in the sewers was far worse than an exam you forgot to study for.

Into the pitch darkness he yelled, "Whichever god saves me, that one will I follow!" His voice echoed back several times, and he cringed in its resonance. In the silence which followed came only the infinite sounds of dripping water and squeaking rats. He kept moving, stumbling over unseen debris.

When his eyes finally saw a dim light, his mind did not register it until after it had disappeared. He stood, pondering if what he had seen was real. His ears picked up the shadowy whisper of what may have been a human voice. He shouted, the walls bouncing the sounds back in distorted waves. Then there was silence. A dim light appeared in a passage across a putrid canal. Onias shouted and the light became brighter. It took a moment before the man's eyes could focus on who held the light.

It was a woman holding a fiery sword. His heart pounded, for he thought that Junifelia, Goddess of Death, had come to claim him. Then he recognized his father walking behind the woman, and he called out joyfully. It was several minutes before the rescuers could find a way to cross to his side of the canal. Joatham reached out to hug his son, but Onias pulled back.

"Don't touch me. I'm filthy."

"I don't care." Joatham pulled his son to him.

The young man stood stiffly for a second then his pride melted. He began to weep, confessing his plans to turn the Tnias over to the Reforcers. Julie moved off so father and son could talk privately. After some time, the two walked to her, Onias with a new look of hope in his eyes.

Chapter Twenty

Reed Sector consisted of six and seven story apartment buildings built within inches of each other, shabby businesses, the smell of urine in hallways, weeds the only plants daring to grow among the rubbish filled sidewalks. Angry shouts, crying children, and occasional screams of fear rent the air. Each dank alley was a self-contained world of crime, hopelessness, and horror.

Clothed in a warm coat, Sandra walked beside Roshell through the dingy streets, pointing out where one gang's territory ended and another began. They had made several expeditions before, but Roshell would not send volunteers into the dangerous ghetto until she understood the rules and language of the streets that were different but not far changed from the southern slums of her childhood. The volunteers would be trained thoroughly, always traveling in pairs or triplets. Roshell seemed to weave effortlessly between the gangs, stopping to talk here and there. On the rare occasions when threatened, all she needed was to ominously place a hand on her sword and her adversaries would back down.

Today Julie and Onias had decided to come, but both felt very out of place among the garbage-strewn streets. It was a world far removed from their own. Julie thought about the elegant palace she had grew up in and the cultivated park which served as her backyard. She had taken it all for granted, only focused on her love-starved life. From the middle-class, Onias always had what he needed, never sparing a thought for those who did not. His parents had paid for his expensive schooling. He hung out with the most popular peers, attended plays and sport competitions, and courted the prettiest ladies. When he first asked Sandra to join him on an outing with friends, he believed himself charitable to be publicly seen with someone from Reed Sector. As their relationship bloomed into something more, Sandra rarely talked about what it was like growing up in the most dangerous area of Thorn, and Onias had never asked.

This morning, on the spare of the moment, he decided to join Sandra and Roshell—but now wished he had not. He was overwhelmed and sickened by what he saw. Toddlers playing in fresh horse droppings, a mother screaming at a frightened boy who had just scraped his knee, scrawny children digging through garbage looking for food, young men leering at women walking past. A seedy whore—nothing like the enticing temple prostitutes—called to Onias, causing him to flinch. The harlot, like far too many in the sector, was shriveled and wasted from years of addiction to drugs. How had Sandra kept her sanity growing up here? They had been together for nearly a year and half, and he thought he knew her. Now he realized he knew nothing at all. More than ever, he respected her for the determination that had raised her from the ghetto to attend Achozeiz University. She had competed with top students in the city to win scholarships that paid for her tuition. In the ghetto Sandra's demeanor was so completely altered that Onias could barely recognize her. She walked with an aggressive swagger, warning lecherous men she wanted nothing to do with them.

Sandra glanced over her shoulder and gave Onias a grin, pleased he had chosen to come along. He returned a weak smile, pretending the stench of a foul man slumped against a wall was not making him sick to his stomach. Suddenly screams ripped through the air. Passers-by glanced towards a narrow alley but kept walking. Roshell bolted across the street and headed down the dark passageway, closely followed by the others. From a side passage, a man ran pass them, knife in hand. In that split second, all four saw a crying teen holding the remnants of a ripped garment in front of her bare body. Blood trickled from a cut on her cheek.

Julie instantly pursued the criminal, but felt a check in her soul. If she caught the man, what would she do? Cleave him in half? Yahweh had not sent her to Thorn to slay rapists but to offer love. She turned back, finding Onias bent double, throwing up his breakfast. She placed a hand on his back to steady him while glancing down the side passage. The teen, perhaps fourteen years old, was in shock, letting no one come near her. She kept frightened eyes on Roshell who talked in a reassuring tone. Sandra bent on her knees, and slowly scooted forward, asking simple questions, occasionally looking towards Roshell for silent advice. The shaking youth finally managed to get out that her name was Violet then burst into sobs. Sandra held her, rocking the teenager like a child. Roshell took off her outer cloak and placed it around the girl's thin shoulders. It was sometime before the three rose from the dirty ground, and walked to the end of the side alley.

The Ulmjon met Julie and Onias' questioning looks. "We're taking her to the Haven."

"What about her family?" asked Onias in a quiet voice, his breath a white fog in the cold air.

Sandra whispered, "She's a prostitute. This time someone preferred to take instead of pay."

"Oh," was all he managed to say, feeling awkward.

They walked down the street, paying little attention to curious eyes. Surprisingly, the leering group of guys who had hassled them earlier now watched silently with respect. Turning down a particular alley, they removed a sewer grate. Violet hesitated entering the darkness, but after reassurance from Sandra and Roshell, she climbed down.

Violet was the first of many who would make the menacing trip through the sewers on faith that a paradise greater than her desolate world lay beyond.

~~~~~~~~~

Winter's first snow covered Thorn in a cold, beautiful blanket. Children played carelessly, throwing snowballs, building miniature forts. Older people hid indoors, wearing thick coats when forced outside, knowing freezing blizzards would arrive soon. Winter in the north was always brutal. Deep below the frost line, construction and renovation continued, giving the Haven a busy atmosphere of a small town. Minira had sold her home and moved with Terra permanently into the underground, both volunteering as housemothers for the new orphanage which was quickly filling with scrawny children and scarred youths, each struggling with haunted pasts. The caverns also housed a number of battered women and their children fleeing abusive males.

Today the Haven was busier than normal due to the wedding of Onias and Sandra. Eager for a reason to celebrate in the perilous times, hundreds of Tnias bustled through the passageways. Women prepared steaming food, keeping firepits burning. As food cooked, men hauled rock and dirt, sweat pouring off them in the cold caverns. An architect and two engineers directed the construction, overseeing the new shafts which would soon release smoke harmlessly into the sewers from the firepits. Matthan guided Sunshine, pulling a small cart filled with rubble, through narrow tunnels. Few horses could take working in the underground, away from sunlight and fresh grass, but Sunshine loved her master so deeply she would follow him even into the Great Abyss.

A call went out and work creased as people hustled to the Great Chamber. Eleazar united Onias and Sandra in marriage while proud family and friends watched. Dalphine, Sandra's sister, could not contain her glee. The feast began, lasting for hours. Julie found herself surrounded by orphans demanding a story. She glanced around seeking help from Danielle, but the woman was busy cleaning dishes and wiping spills. Seeing she was on her own, Julie led the young children to a quiet chamber and talked about the first thing that came to her mind—Yahweh's City. The kids listened intently as she described the city's wonders and beauty, puzzlement showing on many faces.

"What do flowers look like?" asked three-year-old Jonu.

"Like those weeds which bloom in spring, stupid," said her older brother, Lonees.

Julie gave him a scolding look before continuing, "Flowers are the parts of plants which bloom in bright colors."

"Oh," said Jonu, still confused.

"How can weeds be pretty?" another child asked.

"Flowers are pretty," answered Julie, "because of their many colors. They can be found on trees, bushes, or weeds."

"They've never seen a tree or a bush. I ain't either, for that matter," said Lonees.

"You have never seen a tree?"

"None grow in Reed. Where could they? In the garbage heaps?" The boy laughed at the idea.

Julie studied the children, clothed warmly, their thin bodies starting to fill out from fulfilling meals. Just a week ago, they roamed the streets searching through trash for food. "Have you ever been to the city park?"

"The park's only for rich people. Ha, some of us never even left the alley we were thrown into. It's too dangerous to travel down the block because then you're in someone else's territory, and he may decide to beat you up."

A small boy became tired of Lonees controlling the conversation. "How can the City of Love be all light?"

Julie tried her best to explain. "It is like a sun burning inside the city."

"How come it no burn up?" tiny Junu asked.

The princess sighed in frustration. How can you describe something when your audience has no experience for understanding it? Beauty did not exist in their harsh lives. A heavy sadness overwhelmed Julie. *Yahweh, how can I help them understand what I have seen?*

Show them, a silent voice whispered through her mind.

For a moment she pondered the words, then a grin spread across her face. She studied the natural chamber they were in. It was dry with only one entrance, three sided—one side almost straight, the other two convex—roughly forty, thirty, and twenty-five feet wide, all rising to a height of nearly ten yards. After stopping an argument between Lonees and a six year old, Julie told them her plan.

"Look at this wall behind me." The children focused on the rocky surface in puzzlement. "I will show you beauty. I will paint the city of Agape on it."

The younger children shouted in glee, and a few jumped up and down with no inkling of what Julie actually meant. Anything new was exciting to them. Only Lonees sat cross-legged, unimpressed. "What good that's gonna do?"

"Watch and see," the once immortal responded with a twinkle in her eye.

As the children dashed off to rejoin the celebration, Julie scrutinized the walls, developing ideas of what scenes to paint and the amount of material needed. A scaffold would have to be built for she intended to use every square inch, including the smooth domed ceiling created naturally by the extinct river. Special plants and herbs would need to be purchased for the dyes. It would take tremendous work and long hours, but excitement pulsed through her veins as she visualized the finished mural. She would paint scenes never before seen by mortals' eyes.

~~~~~~~~~

Brown vines clung to columns surrounding the palace courtyard. Trimmed hedges and flower bulbs were buried under a foot of snow. Urbane strolled along the walkway, deep in thought, paying little heed to the lanky man talking nonstop beside him. Liverton was captain of the Reforcers in Thorn. Seeing his superior officer walking around the courtyard, the newly appointed man saw the perfect opportunity to impress the general—except Urbane preferred to be alone. As Liverton chatted about his newest ideas, the general pondered the problems of wiping out all the Tnias in the new territories.

Urbane had just gotten back from a long expedition in the south where he had visited with many colonels and majors, listening to their complaints and problems. Many had boasted that no religious heretics remained in their areas, but the more sincere ones openly discussed the impression that many Tnias remained hidden despite the measures to eradicate them. As expected, the newest province, Ulmjo, had the worst problems. Tnias were constantly trying to cross the border both ways, and many probably succeeding. The heretics had become bolder since the three unconquered counties had suddenly become religious and banded together. The heretics no longer feared death. Using the same methods as General Nereus, Urban had encouraged his men, speaking of how they pleased Zuzumza with their hard efforts and must not become discouraged so near the end. The officers had responded warmly to him and pushed themselves harder. As the first snows covered the north, Urbane had traveled back to Thorn to aid the council on planning the next invasion. Like Phlegon, Urban felt a delay was needed to strengthen the Empire and planned to advise a year's wait.

"So which strategy should I use?" asked Liverton.

The question pulled Urbane back to the present. "Which ever nets the most fish."

Urbane tried not to appear irritated. The captain fit the mold of a Reforcer officer—ruthless, hungry for glory, and a coward. They avoid the dangers of battle by volunteering for jobs a real soldier would be offended by, sitting in offices while sending subordinates to hunt down easy victims. Though Urbane saw the need for Reforcers, he looked down on the government branch, preferring the vast power of the Red Army. With the right people in charge of the military, it became a dangerous and potent beast. Nothing could stand in its path.

As Liverton discussed his favorite scheme, Urbane let his eyes drift across the courtyard. Suddenly his body became rigid. Intensely he studied a figure strolling on the other side of the courtyard. She noticed his stare and quickly exited through an arched doorway. The captain stared curiously at the general then peered in the same direction the other was looking. There was nothing to be seen but empty walkways and a snowbound garden with a frozen fountain.

Urbane started walking again, pretending nothing had happened, cursing under his breath, angry at his own reaction. It had only been one on the many princesses living in the palace. Thasbow, he recalled—a quiet, shadowy teenager. In that one second, one infinite moment in time, he thought the figure was Junia. Instinctively, his heart had pounded and warm desire had filled him.

Five years. It's been over five years but just one glance is enough to make me feel like a school boy again, he chided himself.

Several occasions when loneliness had been greatest, he had slept with other women, but all he could think about was the fiery princess whom he had fallen in love with. No one else measured up. He went through deep periods of depression, finding relief only in exterminating those who had poisoned her mind. Every Tnias who died under his leadership was a memorial to Junia.

~~~~~~~~~

Princess Thasbow pulled a fur-lined hood over her loose, flowing black hair as she hurried through corridors leading to the Royal Garden. He had been staring at her—that monstrous general who had arrested her sister and let her die from his own blade. How could he? Anger flushed anew through the teenager. She hated him even more than she hated her parents—which was considerable.

Erastus had never bothered to even learn her name. Rollana, her mother, was as gorgeous as she was foolish. The woman had only been officially married to the Emperor two months before he divorced her for another, but she had remained his concubine, coming whenever he called, even after she remarried. Thasbow had been bounced between her stepfather's villa in the west and Blackwall Palace, dragged along on her mother's whims. Her stepfather despised her, seeing her as a reminder that Rollana sometimes bedded the Emperor. Upon Erastus' death, Thasbow had refused to journey back west with her mother. After an angry fight, the two parted and had not spoken to each other since.

Reaching the Royal Garden, Thasbow walked along the cleared paths, feeling as frozen as the snowbound world surrounding her. Life in the palace was miserable and competition ferocious. The desire for power and glory ruled nobles' lives. The women, including those already married, were out to snare the richest men or the latest war hero. Men battled over beautiful woman to sleep with but only wanted to marry those with a title and money. Weaving it altogether was the uncontrollable, omniscient force—gossip. Thasbow knew some of the darker things said about her. She was not worthy of the title she had been born with, a useless shade with a brainless concubine for a mother. She pretended not to care, keeping to herself and avoiding social engagements. In Gogian high society, a noncompetitive person had no value.

The princess walked past sentinels guarding the entrance to Royal Garden. Only nobles, officials, and their families were allowed to stroll along its cultivated paths through exotic plants, ornamental gazebos, marble statues, and greenhouses sheltering rare tropical plants of the South. Instead of entering, she wandered through the much larger city park, passing laughing skaters on the lake. Thasbow instinctively moved away to less popular areas. She had been like that since Junia's death. As a child, she had looked for a role model to pattern her life after. She found that in Junia. The first-born princess had hidden her title and secretly rose through the ranks to win the highest medal of honor. Throughout the Empire, many maidens had admired Junia and emulated her. Over the last six years there had been a rapid increase in the number of women who joined the Red Army.

Thasbow may have followed in Junia's footsteps of becoming a soldier if not for the heroine's dramatic death she had witnessed. It had been the focus of conversations for weeks afterwards. Many highborn women had been jealous of Junia's success and gleefully spread dark rumors about the fallen princess but admired Urbane for his dedication to the Empire. He was insured a promotion, perhaps colonel, they claimed.

There had been some who identified with Junia, mainly those with no title, who blamed the Tnias for poisoning her. It was claimed she was captured, tortured, brainwashed, and finally released to die at the hands of her own people. Fear—and hatred—of Tnias increased. Thasbow believed none of the stories. She had seen Junia's last stand, heard her bold words and dying gasps. Urbane had told Prince Rufus that Junia had made the decision herself and knew the price she would be required to pay. Those words followed Thasbow as she fled from the balcony, haunted her dreams at night, and darkened her thoughts during the day. She separated herself from humankind, becoming a shadowy ghost among the living, rarely talking to others.

Surrounded by bent trees encased in ice, the sixteen-year-old was just as frozen, trapped inside a legacy she could not escape.

~~~~~~~~~

Danielle walked along a dark tunnel then turned down a side passage that almost immediately opened into a large chamber. Millenniums ago, an underground river rushed through the rocks where the woman walked, cutting new paths among the softer limestone, pounding water pushing against weak earth, occasionally creating dead ends where turbulent water circled until finding release back into the main channel. Danielle paused at the entrance of the domed room, lit only by a few lanterns turned low to prevent smoke from tarnishing the walls. She observed the wooden scaffold and a woman, high up, oblivious to all but her work.

"Hello, Julie." The sudden echo made the artist jump. "It seems like ages since I've seen you."

"I didn't realize you were there." Julie only looked down for a moment before continuing.

"How long have you been at it today?"

"Since early morning." The artist dipped her brush back into a clay bowl containing paint.

"It's past midnight now."

"Really? It does not seem like it."

"Did you even eat supper?" Danielle stood with hands on hips like a scolding mother, her own stomach beginning to swell from her unborn child.

"Hmm. The children did bring food a while back. I guess that must have been supper."

"You need to get some rest."

"Alright, I'm coming down." The Gogian gathered brushes and bowls, lowering them to the dirt floor on a plank fastened to a rope. She clambered down after them. Though tired, she washed the utensils and bowls in a basin before the paint dried.

Danielle studied the wall containing a large yellow blob surrounded by dark contrasting colors. "It's…uh…looking interesting."

Julie gave a tired laugh. "The kids are always popping in, thinking I'm a wizard who's going to magically create enchanted pictures. Unfortunately, it doesn't happen quite that fast."

The Telumzan worried that the end results would be stick figures and kiddish backgrounds. "I've been wondering, when did you learn to paint? I mean you never showed interest in art before."

"When I was in Agape." Julie began tightening lids of jars containing fresh paint.

"Oh. So does everyone suddenly take up art?"

"No, but people have the opportunities to develop talents they never did while alive. Many are born with special abilities that are never used or pushed aside for other pursuits. As a child, I use to draw and could have been fairly good at it if I had someone to encourage me. Instead, because of pride, I put my focus into fencing which led me to join the army. I chose destruction over creation."

As both walked towards the exit, Danielle pondered her own talents, wishing she had learned to play the guitar like her father. "There was something I was wondering, Julie. Could you do more good by helping with the orphanage and other projects instead of isolating yourself here day after day?"

Julie sighed, fatigue settling over her like heavy snow on a roof. "Each of us has talents. Some we are born with, others develop over time. Yahweh asks us to use them to bless others. You and Matthan have caring hearts, giving comfort to the hopeless, never giving up on the worst of us. Roshell is a natural-born leader, a great organizer, able to guide people into doing things they never thought possible. She knows how to handle the roughest areas of this city. I offer the gift of beauty. So many have only seen harsh ugliness. They don't know what true beauty looks like. When trials come and people wonder if Yahweh cares, the mural will be a reminder that they are loved, in good times and bad."

Danielle nodded, understanding. "During the worst moments of doubt when Matthan and I lived in Belton, we reminded each other what Agape looked like, knowing we suffered so that others might have a chance to live there." She was quiet until they reached the ancient road bordered by buildings. "Matthan and I have been wondering something. We've tried to ask several times but you always cut us off. Are you a princess?"

"Yes, my father was Emperor Erastus. There are some, including Roshell, who would judge me without listening to the message I bring. That is why I don't speak of it."

"Then Matthan and I will remain silent until such time you deem it necessary to reveal it."

Chapter Twenty-one

Wind howled, blasting snow through the deserted streets of Thorn, burying doors and windows under huge snowdrifts. Many people stayed indoors, but energetic youth, traders, and those bored with being trapped headed to the Underground. The shops, warmed by furnaces, remained opened in the worst of weather. Anything could be brought: food, animals, clothing, unique gifts, sex, drugs, and people. The underground market was the pride of the citizens of Thorn. It attracted the high-class from across the Empire. Many had luxurious apartments in the expensive sectors where they lived during the harsh northern winters, splitting their time between Blackwall Palace and the Underground.

Roshell pulled her hood tighter around her face and walked around an embracing couple kissing deeply, oblivious to the passersby. Always busy, she had not bothered to visit the underground market before, but she needed to get away from the Haven for a while. She had expected the Underground to be dark and seedy. Instead, the decorative stone walls had been plastered and painted white, reflecting light. Mirrors where used to transport sunlight into huge chambers where numerous booths were set up—though today only bright oil lanterns were used due to the blizzard. Everywhere there were people buying, selling, or just hanging out. Street performers drew crowds and richer visitors paid to see plays in a large amphitheater. That structure, like many others, had entrances above and below ground. A hidden system of coal burning furnaces kept the entire subterranean market warm and inviting. The southerner wondered if it was possible to create such a system for the Haven, something she would appreciate very much.

Remembering Julie's warning that the seedier area of the Underground was east, Roshell headed in that direction. She did not go far before broad marble steps attracted her attention. Bold letters chiseled in stone told her the Mausoleum of Zuzumza was located directly above. Nearby several booths offered a variety of animals for sacrificing. Roshell climbed the stairs, passing several temple prostitutes dressed in revealing outfits. The decorative passageway spilt into several branches, a sign pointing out directions. The Ulmjon headed to the main worship center.

Her first view of the vast chamber stretching to a dizzying height was of awe and horror. Huge ornamented columns rose many stories up to join the arched roof. Built into the marble walls were statues of varies gods. At the end of the room was a towering idol of Zuzumza. Located between his legs were two enormous doors leading into the most sacred chamber. A long line of people, many holding animals for offerings, waited for a priest to call them through the doors. Incense burned, filling the air with exotic scents. Thick cushioned couches were arranged in circles and crowded with people talking or making out. On the north and south walls, temple prostitutes disappeared through gold doors with clients. Sometimes children went through the doors with men. High above, the gemstone eyes of the stone god Zuzumza watched it all.

Roshell became queasy. She was in a temple of abomination, a shrine dedicated to the god responsible for the death of her parents and many friends, a god who cared nothing for the lives it destroyed. A male prostitute approached her, wearing only a colorful loincloth. His smiled salacious and wriggled his hips. She quickly turned and joined the long line waiting to see a priest. Looking around, she spotted lecherous men flirting with half-clad children. Anger raged through her. She had to leave before she did something irrational. The Ulmjon turned towards the exit but froze in shock. Two soldiers were standing directly behind her in line. *Could things get worse?*

"That blond one looks interesting." A lanky soldier spoke to the man beside him. Out of the corner of her eye, Roshell spotted a captain badge on his Reforcer's uniform. "Are you sure you're not interested?"

The second man, muscular and tall, held two pigeons in a cage. "I've come to pay homage to my god, not to seek pleasure."

The harshness in his voice made Roshell glance in his direction, but she quickly jerked her eyes forward after noticing general's stripes on his shoulders. *Things are worse.* She breathed deeply, calming herself. No one would expect a Tnias here. *Why am I here?* She would stay in line a few more minutes then causally leave as if she had something else to do.

The thin soldier continued, ignoring the other's tone. "Go, please your god. I'm here to please myself. There are some juicy ones by the third column."

"A real man does not *vex* children." The general did not try to hide his disgust.

The captain laughed. "You've killed children many times."

"They were Tnias who were put to death immediately. I never permitted my men to defile themselves."

"There is no difference between you and me." Merriment filled the captain's voice. "They were created to serve our whims." He left the line and walked towards two young girls leaning against the base of a broad column. As he talked to the kids, they huddled together with frightened eyes. A priestess rose from a couch where she had been leading a debate and approached. She coaxed the children, taking the hand of the oldest, who looked around eight, and put it into the man's large hand. The child pulled backwards and the priestess sharply reprimanded her.

Roshell could take no more. *Help me, Yahweh*, she prayed silently while casually strolling past marble columns and groups of people. Pretending to be walking towards the doors of the antechamber, she came near the captain. Suddenly she stepped sideways and kicked the man in the back of his knees, sending him tumbling to the ground. As he started to rise, she brought her elbow down sharply, sending him back to the marble floor. Quickly she picked up the youngest child and took the hand of the second.

"Come. I'll take you some place safe." The youngest clung to Roshell, but the second pulled back uncertain.

"They're mine! Let go!" The priestess grabbed the free hand of the other girl.

The captain shook his head and started to rise.

Roshell's time was running out. "In the name of Yahweh, get out of my way!"

At the name of the god, the woman stooped, hissing in fury—and let go of the child's hand. Roshell bolted with the children, but she only took a few steps before the captain pushed himself up from the floor and rushed forward. In one liquid movement, Roshell dropped the oldest child's hand and drew her sword which had been hidden under her long cloak. The soldier realized too late she was armed but could not stop his forward movement in time. He impaled himself on the blade. A bystander screamed, and the temple suddenly became quiet as everybody looked in Roshell's direction.

"She's a Tnias! A Tnias!" screamed the priestess in hatred.

Several people moved to intercept the culprit, but she pulled her sword from the dying soldier and waved it threateningly. They backed away, some yelling obscenities at her. Out of the corner of her eye, she spotted the general dashing towards her, sword in hand.

She ran, the older child barely able to keep up. The Ulmjon's eyes met those of other children she passed. "Come, if you want freedom!" Several bolted after her in the confusion.

With the general gaining fast, Roshell and her entourage made it to the passageway heading downward to the underground exit. The stairs slowed down the children. One girl screamed as the general pushed pass her, reaching for the dark-skinned woman.

Yahweh, help! Roshell pleaded.

Suddenly the officer slipped and fell, barely missing two girls. Cursing, he tried to rise, but pain shot through his ankle and up his leg. A child jumped over him and vanished after the others. The man forced himself to his feet, wincing in pain. He held the railing tightly. Several prostitutes and passersby glanced his way, but the foreigner and temple children were gone.

Through the smelly underground maze, Roshell led the seven young refugees. She talked constantly, trying to smooth their fear, promising hot food and warm beds. The youngest, named Tasia, clung to her, crying, hiding her face in the woman's hair. A seven-year-old held tightly to Roshell's hand, leaning against her leg during rest breaks. Behind walked the older girls, uncertain why they had left the mausoleum but terrified to go back. It seemed like an eternity had already been spent in the sewers and yet the labyrinth did not end. The children shivered in the cold and trudged onward.

Suddenly the children found themselves in a dry, well-lit cavern with people milling around. Roshell led the way pass crates and miscellaneous projects, towards the area set aside for the orphanage. The Ulmjon noted there was an unusual large crowd around a weeping woman sitting on a wooden box. Something was up, but the children were her first priority. Entering the chamber that served as a dining room, Roshell introduced her charges to Minira and Terra.

Minira invited the children to sit and ordered more plates to be brought. The temple refugees glanced towards Roshell who gave them a reassuring nod. Soon six of the girls were stuffing themselves as if they had not eaten in days. Other orphans glanced shyly at them and several started conversations. Tasia refused to eat, keeping a death grip on Roshell's leg. Vainly, the woman tried to pull the child gently away, only resulting in the girl crying.

Violet, the teen prostitute Sandra and Roshell had helped in the ally, bent down on one knee beside the child. Thin and dispirited, Violet usually kept to herself. In a soft voice, she whispered to the youngster, "Hey, it's okay. I've been through it too. No one's going to hurt you here. What's your name?"

The child sniffled, "Tasia."

"Nice name, Tasia. I'm Violet. Will you come and eat with me? I'll let you sat on my lap."

The youngster thought for a moment then nodded, reaching out a trusting hand to the teenager. Violet picked the child up and carried her to the table.

Smiling her thanks, Roshell headed towards the Great Chamber. Julie emerged from a side tunnel, spattered with paint.

"Something's up," said the Ulmjon.

"Yes, Sandra just informed me. There's been a raid on Doctor Ijohn's clinic. A number have been killed and the rest fled here."

There was a sinking feeling in the pit of Roshell's stomach. Ijohn was a retired physician who had recently turned an apartment in the Reed Sector into a clinic. A lifelong Tnias, he was highly respected by the Remnant. "Is Ijohn dead?"

"I believe so." Julie would have said more but they had reached the supernatural lit chamber crowded with people whispering in frightened voices. Danielle and Josias comforted a woman Roshell had earlier seen weeping. Greeting them, Sandra and Onias took a seat beside Julie and Roshell.

Matthan spoke with Eleazar then walked to the front of the amphitheater and waited until the crowd quieted. "Today we have lost a number of good people, including Doctor Ijohn. They will be deeply missed. Though we mourn for them, know they now celebrate with Yahweh. We must continue onward in their legacy."

"Legacy?" said a wild-eyed youth in the dangerous stage between adolescence and adulthood. He was thin, dressed in worn clothes, his hands clenched in anger. "My father died serving the Empire as a soldier. My mother worked constantly but could barely keep food on the table. My little sister was sick so my mother took her to the clinic. Now they're both dead along with my two brothers. What legacy is that? Tell me."

Sandra leaned over and whispered to her neighbors, "His name is Manideck. They say he rescued eleven in the raid by leading them to the top of the building and crossing to another rooftop by creating a plank bridge." Sadness thickened her voice. "But he still could not save his own family."

Matthan hesitated, seeking the right words to comfort the grieving teenager, but Eleazar spoke first. "Son, your mother had strong faith in Yahweh. She will always be remembered for her tender heart, mending clothes for those without money."

"And what good did that do her?"

"She is in Agape now. All of us will die, sooner or later. What counts is how we live our lives. Your mother was a cherished woman who we all will miss deeply."

Voice breaking with unshed tears, Manideck said, "All of you can just plod along like nice, obedient sheep directly to the slaughter house." He shook his head in denial. "I refuse to! I will fight until there is not a drop of blood left in me. And all of you are fools if you don't do likewise."

Roshell stood. "I agree with you, Manideck. We are at war. To pretend otherwise will lead to our annihilation. Today I left a remembrance in the Mausoleum of Zuzumza that will long be talked about. I freed seven children and killed the captain of the Reforcers." Surprised gasps and several shouts of approval filled the air.

"I wish I had been there," said Manideck.

Julie's skin felt clammy. She understood better than anyone the repercussions such an act would create. Danielle sought Matthan's eyes across the room, both preparing each other for what was to come.

Eleazar was the first to challenge the Salt. "We are used to living under threat, but we cannot fight our enemy. Restrictions have been lax in Thorn due to overconfidence. What you did today could destroy all the good we have accomplished so far."

Roshell refused to back down. "I know my actions will lead to greater persecution. But neither can I sit back and let these abominations continue. There comes a time when we must fight."

"If they realize there is a growing body of Tnias in their capitol city, the Reforcers will stop at nothing to destroy us."

As both Roshell and Eleazar's words sank in, many in the crowd began to murmur, some demanding by what right she had to declare war for them all. Many of the new Tnias were not ready to face death. The fate of Doctor Ijohn and the others were fresh on their minds.

As fear and anger swept across the room, Danielle whispered to Julie, "You were once dead. You must have some insight to help us."

The Gogian hesitated, unsure what to do. She stood and slowly walked downward to the front. *Yahweh, give me your words to say. There is so much fear.* Julie took a deep breath as people quieted. "As many of you know, I died several years ago and went to Agape. Yahweh sent me back here, to the city of my birth, to tell you that he loves you."

Excited whispering broke out, many expecting another miracle like the last time she spoke

"My friends, don't be amazed because I stand before you but be excited that you also will one day visit Agape. For whom much is given, much is required. Don't be afraid of those who kill the body and after that can do no more. Instead, fear him who, after killing the body, has power to throw you into the Great Abyss. Yes, I tell you, fear him." It became so quiet in the enormous chamber that water could be heard dripping. "Are not two sparrows sold for two copper coins? Yet not one of them is forgotten by Yahweh. Indeed, the very hairs of your head are all numbered. Don't be afraid, for you are worth more than many sparrows. We are in the midst of a war. You always have been. Unknowingly, most of you had been an enemy to the True God who loves you. From the day you were born, you were a soldier in a spiritual war that has raged for millenniums. Now you serve Yahweh, but that doesn't free you from the battle. You must choice today who you will serve, and follow your master unto death."

Julie swept her eyes over the silent audience. Some looked away, troubled. To the younger generation, serving a new god had been exciting, an adventure, but now that faith could cost their lives. Many were not ready for that. From the middle section of the rock benches, the retired Reforcer officer stood up in a traditional salute, his eyes focused upward. Julie's throat constricted in deep emotion. Standing near her, Matthan saluted in Telumzan style. Others across the amphitheater stood, pledging in their own ways their allegiance to Yahweh. Those timid took courage from neighbors, children proudly standing beside parents. Not one person remained sitting.

Voice choking, Julie turned to Matthan. "It's your turn. Prepare them for battle."

The Salt stepped forward and let his voice boom forth. "There is much you have already accomplished, yet much more is required. The lost wait for someone to free them, to show them true love. This is our first priority. The Haven must remain a place for the dispirited to heal, a resting place for those in need. We must take great precautions protecting it from raids. No longer can we afford to bring visitors down unless they have first sworn their lives to Yahweh. We will post sentries to guard the sewers and use passwords."

People nodded and shouted approval, some calling out further ideas. Matthan selected a group of the wisest individuals to aid him in developing plans and met with them in a smaller chamber. The rest prayed long into the night.

~~~~~~~~~

The headquarters for the Reforcers was a plain, ancient brick building located at the edge of Market Square, four stories tall with two basement levels containing cells for prisoners—though rarely inmates stayed long for the death penalty was the favored punishment. Urbane marched through the entrance, passing clerks who suddenly became very busy at their desks. He continued up the stairs, popping his head into several offices, demanding for the occupants to meet with him now. A small, nervous crowd soon gathered in the conference room, wondering what the general was up to. As Urbane took a seat at the head of the large table, several glanced around vainly seeking Captain Liverton.

Looking at Lieutenant Patrobas, Urbane demanded, "What were your men doing today?"

For a moment, the lieutenant looked uncertain. He never liked the general of the Red Army. The two military divisions had long been at odds with each other. Patrobas felt that Reforcers went through training as rigid as a soldier's and were an equal match for any Red Army cadet. "Going on information by informants, we led three searches. One proved false, another only found an elderly, bedridden woman who was put to death on the spot. But the third raid was a jackpot. Turned out a retired doctor was running a Tnias clinic. Four were killed and three others wait for execution below." Pride filled Patrabas's voice as he spoke about what his men had accomplished, knowing none of the other teams had found even one antagonist.

"How many escaped?" Urbane asked.

"Escaped?" Patrobas readjusted his body in the wooden chair. "We were not expecting to find so many heretics so we were short on manpower."

"How many did you fail to catch?" commanded the general in a slow, hard voice.

"Perhaps six or more. They barred the door to a room and went out the window onto the ledge. By the time we broke down the door, they had vanished. We searched the entire building room by room, but no more heretics were uncovered."

Urbane's frown deepened. "Captain Patrobas, you should have placed sentries at every stairway and kept several guarding the exits on the ground and sub-terrain levels."

Uncomfortable, the officer tapped a finger on the table. He did not like being criticized in front of his peers. "Sir, we were following protocol. We had no idea there would be more than three or four."

"You should have been prepared for anything. Your greatest mistake is underestimating the enemy—a mistake Liverton will not make again." Every eye in the room focused on the general. "The captain was killed today in the Mausoleum of Zuzumza by a female foreigner."

Gasps of surprise and curses filled the air.

"In the name of the Ultimate One, how could this happen?" said Patrobas.

"In the most holy of places!"

"By a woman, of all people."

Urbane waited until the officers quieted. "Today the heretics have defiled our most sacred temple, spilling blood on consecrated ground. These outlaws are not human but parasites. When one insect stings, a hive is usually nearby. Gentleman, it is time to take the same measures in Thorn as we do on the frontier."

Several men uneasily glanced at each other, unwilling to change from their lazy, luxurious lifestyles. They were paid well to send subordinates on raids, while they supervised from the sidelines. Urbane scrutinized the officers, carefully choosing the next captain. Patrobas was an ambitious man, often the first through a door on raids, challenging his former captain's indifferent altitude, demanding the most from his men.

191

"Patrobas, as the new captain, you must revitalize the Reforcers."

The man was taken by surprised, immediately changing his opinion of the general. "What are some of your ideas, General Herron?"

"Random searches, especially in the poorer areas of town. Enforce the ancient Rule of Acquire where buyers must claim a god's name when purchasing items. Have undercover officers patrolling Market Square and fine any clerk who forgets to ask. The same must be done at all city gates. No one leaves or enters the city unless they swear by Zuzumza or a lesser god. And increase the rewards for informants."

Captain Patrobas nodded. "All this will be done and much more. All Reforcers..." he glanced at the officers seated around the room, "...will go through a vigorous retraining. Relaxed protocol will not cause us to underestimate the enemy again."

Chapter Twenty-two

Horses trotted through broad, snow-covered streets, pulling an elegant carriage. The women inside were dressed warmly in fancy fur dresses, chatting about the latest gossip—all except Princess Thasbow. Wearing a simple gray dress and long overcoat, she silently looked out a window, watching buildings pass by, wishing she had walked to Market Square instead of agreeing to travel with Lady Mahan. She could tolerate a short ride with Mahan, but the young woman had not mentioned Lady Cassandra was also coming.

Aristocratic and gorgeous, Cassandra used her inherited talents to rise to the top of the social structure. Everyone wanted to be considered her friend, yet few could stand being around her long. One minute she might act like your best friend, the next moment your worst enemy. She was all smiles and warm questions, memorizing every answer to use as weapons in the future. Despite her known faults, she was still the most popular and sought after guest at social engagements due to one fact—she was the favored concubine of Emperor Phlegon. So far the monarch had remained unmarried, keeping his focus on the development of his nation, but everyone knew that sooner or later he must marry to produce a legitimate heir for the throne. And Lady Cassandra was the most likely candidate.

Thasbow sighed, wondering if the ride would ever end. Normally a coach took ten minutes to reach the square, but Cassandra had insisted on visiting several associates and inviting them on the outing. An hour and a half later with seats crowded, they still had not reached their destination. Not that they cared. The women tried to out shock the others with the juiciest stories.

"I heard that the Emperor is unsatisfied with the Reforcers," Lady Mahan said, casting a glance towards Cassandra to see if the powerful young woman approved. "They still have not wiped out all the heretics. There seems to be a small but steady trickle of them. It's whispered that the problem continues to grow worse."

"Maybe General Herron's head will roll," laughed Lady Richmon who was wintering in Thorn with her husband. She still held a grudge against the general since he had been the lover of her now dead archenemy. "It is his responsibility to rid the Empire of them."

"Yes, the Empire, not Thorn. That is Captain Patrobas's job. Out of the goodness of his heart General Herron is helping after the tragic murder of Captain Liverton."

"Goodness of his heart? Dear Lady Mahan, I thought you *knew* the general?"

Mahan blushed in anger and embarrassment. It was common knowledge that she had spent one night, and only one night, with the commander. Thinking she had nabbed the most sought after bachelor at the time, she had bragged about the night with friends who then told their acquaintances. Disgusted, the general had nothing more to do with her.

"The Emperor is pleased with General Herron's performance." Every eye turned towards Cassandra, expecting her to tell more. One of her common ploys was to remain silent until others had recounted all they knew. Then she would offer bits of information, smoothing over hurt feelings, acting the part of a wise queen. "That is why he keeps giving General Herron more responsibility. There is not a more devoted person to Zuzumza. Who else would turn in his own lover? Herron is the Emperor's most trusted officer."

The women nodded, accepting her word as truth. Lina Richmon was pleased at the negative reference to Princess Junia. Feeling like a caged animal, Thasbow felt relief when she spotted the first businesses of Market Square. The coach driver directed the horses into a large stable then helped the women step down from the carriage. Cassandra led the way to stairs leading to the Underground, chatting about which stores they would visit and what she wanted to buy. Thasbow followed for a short distance then slipped away, not bothering to even say goodbye.

For a while she wander aimlessly, casually picking up items then setting them back on shelves, with no memory of what she had just held. Her mind was on the conversation in the carriage. *How can they praise that monster? Honorable because he turned in Junia. They are just as hideous as him.*

Reaching one of the large underground chambers containing dozens of closely packed booths, Thasbow selected a piece of fruit. "I'll take this one," she addressed the seller.

"Nice selection, madam." Reaching for her coin, the clerk added almost as an afterthought, "Whom do you serve?"

Thasbow frowned. *Another one of those stupid Reforcer rules.* Part of her wanted to say Yahweh just to see his reaction, but instead she answered, "Junifelia, Goddess of Death." She felt a slight glee from the clerk's disapproving frown. Her sister had been named after the goddess.

"Unusual choice," remarked the clerk, sticking the coin deep in his pocket then turning to another customer. It was a woman holding a young child by one hand.

The youngster picked up an apple, and the seller held out his hand expectantly. The lady placed a coin in it then turned away. The clerk called out in a bored voice, "Wait, lady. Who do you honor?"

The young mother glanced back at him. "The Ultimate God."

The seller nodded then turned to another customer. Having decided against buying a scarf, Thasbow pushed her way through the crowd, falling in step behind the woman and her child munching on the apple. Suddenly a muscular man, dressed in a commoner's outfit, halted the lady by blocking the two lanes of pedestrians moving between the crowded booths.

In a commanding voice he demanded, "Who is the Ultimate God?"

Great, he is a Reforcer, thought the princess in annoyance, wishing she could push pass.

The woman hesitated, glancing at the child looking at her with frightened eyes. The lady bent down to her son and whispered in words so low that only Thasbow was close enough to hear. "Go find your Daddy. Don't come back, no matter what."

Impatience, the Reforcer repeated his question while drawing his sword. Thasbow felt people pushing from behind, several grumbling about the traffic jam. When she glanced back towards the woman, the child had vanished among the colorful stalls.

The lady on trial took a deep breath then spoke in a strong voice, "The Ultimate God is Yahweh."

With a mocking grin, the armed man tilted his head. "Wrong answer."

Without further warning, his sword plunged into the woman's stomach. She bent double in pain then fell to the stone floor as he pulled the deadly blade out. Someone nearby screamed. Thasbow gasped and tried vainly to move backwards. Blood splashed onto her shoes and the hem of her dress. The crowd became deathly quiet. For a long moment no one moved or spoke, then people turned and quickly tried to retrace their steps away from the scene.

Knowing there could be more Tnias nearby, the Reforcer questioned everyone still trapped in the tight circle surrounding the dead woman. Thasbow was the third one he asked.

"Zuzumza," the princess answered without hesitation this time.

It took ten minutes before she could escape from the tangle of booths and people. She took the first tunnel she found, hurrying pass stores and shoppers, finally stopping because her stomach threatened to lose its breakfast. She sat on a bench, her body shaking uncontrollably. It had happen so suddenly. Too sudden. One minute the woman had been standing. The next she was dying on the floor.

"Princess Thasbow, darling, what is wrong? You look so pale."

Glancing up, the sick teen saw Cassandra and her entourage, their hands filled with bags and parcels. She closed her eyes, wishing they would disappear.

Spotted the blood on Thasbow's shoes and dress, Mahan became concerned. Placing her packages on the ground, the woman sat beside the teenager. "Are you hurt? Injured?"

"No, I'm fine." Responding to Mahan's genuine anxiety, the princess relaxed slightly. "A woman was killed in front of me. Killed in the blink of an eye."

Lady Richmon gasped. "Oh, my. Did they catch the murderer?"

Thasbow glanced at Lina Richmon but looked directly at Cassandra as she answered. "They are the murders—the Reforcers. There is no glory in killing a helpless woman. She was just like you and me. Shopping, enjoying the Underground with her family. She was a mother, but now she is dead."

The ladies glanced at each other, uncomfortable with Thasbow's words. It was not like her to say much at all, let alone put down one of their government's most venerable military branches.

Mahan placed an arm around Thasbow's shoulder. "You have just seen something horrible and under a lot of stress. We will take you back to the palace where you can rest." She glanced towards the other women. "In shock people say things they do not mean."

Cassandra smiled like a spider that had just spotted a fly caught in its web. "Yes, people do say things they later claim they did not mean. We need to get you cleaned up. I just bought a pair of shoes that should fit though they will not match your outfit." She sat on the bench, keeping her packages between her and the young princess. "Lady Richmon, please throw these soiled shoes away."

Lina took a step back in horror, but obeyed when Cassandra cast her a stern look. Gingerly with two fingers, she carried the bloody shoes to the nearest trash bin.

Thasbow let the women worry over her, feeling like a kitten being handled by too many selfish children, wondering how she could slip away again. On her own, Mahan was a kind woman, but around others, she quickly bent to the opinions of those most popular.

After a few minutes they started walking in the direction of the stables. The women debated if Tnias should be kill directly in front of innocent bystanders. Lady Richmon voiced her opinion that it was wrong to subject properly breed citizens to such a barbaric sight. Cassandra pointed out that the killings purpose was to instill respect in crude commoners who needed to be reminded where their place was. The Tnias heresy was considered a low class problem caused by the poor wishing to believe in a mythical land full of rich promises.

Thasbow became more appalled as she listened. Unable to take any more, she said, "You go ahead and shop. I need to…spend time in prayer at a temple."

"Of course, we understand," Lady Cassandra responded smoothly.

Mahan opened her mouth to say something, perhaps offering to come with Thasbow, but the teen quickly marched off. Behind her back, she could hear low whispering among the women and guessed what was being said. Several would call her a poor child abandoned by her witless mother, doomed to a life of tragedy. Probably Cassandra, in just half a sentence, would cunningly insult every relative of Thasbow except, of course, the Emperors.

I don't care, the teenager told herself as she wound through the decorative tunnels, thinking maybe she would actually seek a temple to pray in. Perhaps some overlooked goddess would feel sympathy towards a friendless princess. Sometime later she entered a small shrine dedicated to Lonevelia, a foreign goddess who was said to have fallen in love with a mortal man. When he died, she cast herself into the ocean, crying endlessly for her lost love, creating powerful rivers of turbulence under the sea. It was said that sailors prayed for her to bring them safely home again to their lovers. Thorn was not located anywhere near the sea, so few visited the quiet shrine.

Being her first visit, Thasbow entered shyly, wishing she had brought an animal for sacrifice, but there were none for sell near the entrance. The brick room was small with several tall oil lamps casting the only light. Curtains of thin lace served as wall ornaments and half covered a door leading to prayer rooms. There were several padded chairs in the room. The only occupants were two men moving a couch across the room and a priestess giving directions where it should be placed. Sitting the couch down, the men straightened. The priestess gave money to one then asked for a chair to be repaired in another room. The men turned to follow, but the one who had received the money stopped when he spotted Thasbow. For a moment the strong, black-bearded man studied her intensely. The teenager felt uncomfortable under his scrutiny and decided to leave.

Before she reached the exit, he asked, "Thasbow? Princess Thasbow?"

She turned and asked in a wary tone, "How did you know me?" Suddenly a distant memory clicked and her mouth flew open in astonishment. "You're not…I mean are you? You can't be… can you?"

The man laughed. "I get many reactions, sister, but I think yours is the most welcome."

"I heard you were doing manual labor—I mean working for a living on a job…that pays wages. I did not expect to actually see you…but it is good to."

Thasbow stumbled over words, afraid everything she said could be taken as an insult. What do you say to the second born prince who now lived like a commoner?

Rufus laughed. "Actually I'm a manager of a furniture factory. Tried to take a lesser job, but I'm a little too well known in Thorn. I make enough to feed my wife, two children, and Henna's many relatives who come for extended visits. Come. Sit. I would love to hear everything that is happening in your life."

Shyly the teenager settled in a chair across from the war hero, not knowing what to say. She knew he was still highly regarded by both nobles and commoners. Normal citizens loved him for turning his back on his title and working among them. Soldiers and council members admired his valiant leadership abilities. When Emperor Erastus died, many had wanted to crown Rufus. Rumors said that key government officials had met with him in secret, pledging their support if he would publicly step forward to claim kingship. To the bitter disappointment of many, Rufus had refused, knowing it would plunge his nation into a bloody civil war.

Thasbow was reluctant to talk about her own life. "I was…am out with Lady Mahan and Lady Cassandra. They're shopping someplace or perhaps gone to see a play."

"From what I have heard of Lady Cassandra, she is the perfect match for my brother's arrogant temperament."

The adolescent held her breath in shock. No one in their right mind insulted the Emperor, no matter how much they hated him. But Rufus was not just anyone— he had been honored with the Medallion of Zuzumza.

"So what brings you to this out-of-the-way shrine?" Rufus was very perceptive of people and knew something was deeply bothering her. He noted the blood stains at the bottom edge of her hem and the bright purple shoes that clashed against her gray dress. No high-class lady would dare be seen in public in such a mismatched outfit.

Thasbow narrated the tale that had led her to the sea goddess's shrine. Rufus listened intently, occasionally asking questions. Slowly she relaxed, realizing whatever she told her half-brother would not become gossip on elite lips at parties. She told him much, much more than she originally intended. All the pent frustrations and anger over the years came out, including the argument with her mother that had split them apart for three years. Gossipers said Rollana had abandoned her daughter. Thasbow had never told anyone that she had insulted and yelled at Rollana until her mother had broken down and fled away in tears.

"You remind me very much of our sister Junia." Memories stirred raw and fresh in Rufus's mind. Himself crying, holding Junia's limp body. His sister, his failure. He had wanted to save her from the dark influence of the arrogant nobles. Instead, the troubled young girl had following in his own footsteps, turning into a cold, merciless soldier. It ravaged her soul. But in the end something had changed her during those missing months on the front. The sister who died was not the same one who had once practiced sword drills with him. For over five years he had been haunted by that last scene, her face, her words. But the secrets she harbored died with her.

Thasbow was caught off guard by his comment. Her face revealed the deep, secretive fascination she held for her dead sibling. "Do you really think so?"

"You have the same build, same eye and hair color, and similar problems. She used arrogance to cover up her pain while you hide behind yours." *And it could lead to your death as it did hers.* Iron determination filled him. Where he failed with Junia, he would not with Thasbow.

The teen's face saddened. "I would prefer to be her. She was afraid of nothing. She never let anyone tell her what to do or cared what others thought about her."

"Yes, that is the image she projected. But beneath her hard armor were fragile feelings and much pain. All she really wanted was love and acceptance." He eyes stared blankly at a lacy wall as his thoughts drifted to the past. "Something changed her in the end. For the briefest of moments I saw a sensitive, mature individual. She found what I have always been seeking."

Thasbow shifted uncomfortable in her chair, not understanding what he said yet sensing there was something sacrilegious in his words. Part of her was fearful to talk about anything that might upset the gods especially in one of their own temples, yet there was a question that had nagged her for years. Seizing the only opportunity she may ever find, she leaned close to her brother and whispered, "Do you think he...I mean the heretics' god is real?"

In a low voice near her ear, he answered, "If Zuzumza is real then so is Yahweh."

Thasbow's breath caught. His statement went against everything she had been taught. Yahweh was supposed to be a mythical god only believed by superstitious low class. The possibility that he was real sent chills down her arms. Sitting in the darkened shrine made her feel that the god might suddenly materialize behind her.

"Is he as powerful as the stories claim?" she whispered.

"Perhaps. But if he is, I cannot figure out why he has not destroyed Gog. We have certainly done enough against him to warrant it."

His words frightened the teen. If the speaker had been anyone else besides Prince Rufus, she would have ran away, glad to escape with her sanity, but he was one of the most respected men in the Empire. His words must hold truth.

"Can he be met, talked with?" Her words were barely audible.

Hopelessness filled the man's haunted eyes. "Why would a god have anything to do with his enemies except revenge?"

The workman, carrying a toolbox, came through a door closely followed by the priestess. "Sir, the chair is fixed, but the altar will need to be taken to the shop."

Rufus nodded and addressed the priestess. "We will bring the wagon tomorrow, if weather permits." To Thasbow, he asked, "Would you like to eat dinner at my home? Henna loves having guests over."

For a moment the teenager hesitated. She hungered for true friendship, and some sleepy inner part of her relished his boldness and freethinking views. "Yes, I would love to."

Chapter Twenty-three

For several days the clouds departed. For a while, life returned to the surface streets of Thorn. Eager children dragged parents or governesses to the city park to skate on its popular lake. Sometimes schoolmasters, needing a break, brought their entire class. And the Salts brought the disquieted youths from the underground. The children deserved to see more than stone walls and lanterns as their only light. Five charges were put with each volunteer adult who chose different routes to the park.

Behind Julie five youths played and laughed, as if their past had never existed. Lonees threw a snowball at his sister but missed, smacking young Tasia on the head. The six year old yelped in surprise, but her self-appointed guardian Violet was quick to retaliate. She scooped up a hand full of icy snow and threw it. Her aim was bad and ten-year-old Mickhan received a shower of snow. Julie laughed, only to be cut short as three snowballs flew towards her. Wiping snow from her face, she noticed three Tnias groups had already reached the frozen lake.

Hundreds of people frolicked on or near the enormous lake, which had several islands, including one large enough for a grove of trees. During warm months, picnickers often paddled out to it. Now orange flags marked off areas of the ice deemed too thin for skating. Julie led her merry troop to the lake, nodding silently to Sandra, Minira, and Terra who were already teaching their charges how to skate. The plan was to keep the groups separated. Julie continued around the lake, finally meeting Roshell who was putting rental skates on her children. The Gogian took her charges to the hide-covered skate wagon, helped each youth select the right size then paid the vendor. She spotted Matthan and Danielle's groups a short distance away.

A new problem quickly presented itself. None of the southern Salts knew how to skate nor how to teach the youths. Roshell glared at the ice as if it would suddenly open up and swallow everyone whole. Feeling their guardian's apprehension, her charges became timid of the lake. Realizing she would have to instruct all four groups, Julie stepped onto the ice and made several tight turns, warming up after years of absence. The children stared at her.

"It's easy," she said as she sprung into the air, twisted, and landed on a different foot. Several of the children oohed in surprise. Julie made a wide circle, gathering speed, then jumped into the air, performing a complicated double axel. Using her brake, she came to a sudden stop in front of Roshell's group. "There's nothing to it."

Roshell grumbled, "If we were meant to dance across the ice, we would have been born with skates on our feet."

Matthan stepped onto the ice, determined to present an encouraging example for the children. He promptly fell onto his backside among peals of laughter. Catching his wife holding her sides in uncontrollable mirth, he said, "I thought you were supposed to be on my side?"

"I am. You're doing a fine job, darling."

Julie skated to Matthan and helped him stand. Holding his hands while moving backwards, she instructed him how to move his feet. Not wanting to be left out of the fun, the youths scrabbled onto the ice, many quickly falling, others moving shakily across the slippery ice. Julie moved among them, offering advice and helping the fallen regain their feet. Only Roshell and Danielle remained on the side. Roshell refused to look like a clumsy fledging, and Danielle's thick coat hid her swollen belly. Time flew quickly pass. Many of the older children took easily to the ice. Even those who spent more time falling than skating were reluctant to leave when it was time to depart.

As the groups separated, Julie took her charges northeast along a path she often walked in earlier days. Her mind drifted into the past, remembering skating with siblings and her nurse as a child. Later, she raced against highbred girls, competition as fierce on the ice as it would later be for boyfriends. She had been so proud the day she had won first place in the junior division, only to give up skating the next year after she came in second.

Suddenly Julie was jerked back to the present, her mind just now registering someone she had seen several minutes ago. Looking behind, she spotted a couple with two young children disappearing through a gate into the Royal Garden. Heart pounding, she walked along a path parallel to the brick wall surrounding the elite park. She had to see the man's face again!

She turned to her charges. "I need to check on something. You are to remain in this area and not talk with anyone. Violet, you are in charge until I get back. Do not wander off."

The teen nodded, and the children watched Julie vanish into a thick grove of trees. Lonees looked Violet in the eyes, wondering what was going on. Jonu spotted a squirrel. Squealing in delight, she chased it up a tree. Tasia joined the younger child in dancing under the tree, daring the animal to come back down. Mickhan packed another snowball and hit Violet in the head. Soon a snow battle raged through the clearing.

~~~~~~~~~

Julie climbed the tall stone wall and jumped down, pulling the hood of her coat over her head. Keeping in the thickest foliage, she worked through the cultivated park until spotting the couple. They moved casually, stopping here and there to let the children play. Excitement filled the concealed woman. *It is him! Rufus!* She wanted to dash to him, but the couple moved along popular paths, passing high-class nobles, some who greeted them, others quickly averted their steps. The central area of the park offered no cover, and Julie was forced to walk along the path, face hidden in the shadow of her hood. Several people glanced at her which caused her heart to pound. She took a path towards a less visited section and hid in a grove of evergreen trees. Disappointment filled her. She was so close to her brother yet still unable to talk to him.

Pass the trees was a small meadow and frozen pond. Sadness overwhelmed Julie as she remembered sword practices with her brother in the field. Back then she dreamed of winning glory in war. The world had been hers to conquer, to own. She thought she had known all there was to know about life. Rufus had reprimanded her, trying to open her eyes to the larger world, but she had remained blind.

Yahweh, give me a chance, just one, to speak with him.

There was a laugh of a child. Looking around, Julie realized that Rufus's family was walking on the path she had just taken. Reaching the meadow, the children dashed into the field of snow, giggling. Hand in gloved hand, the couple strolled towards the tiny stream which joined the iced over pond. Remembering a heated argument years ago, Julie studied the woman who had been a brick wall between her brother and herself. Henna was tall and physically fit from years of walking the streets as a peddler, though she had gained some weight from birthing two children. She had long reddish-brown hair and sharp eyes, revealing a keen mind. Time had done justice to Rufus. His shoulders had broadened. Dark beard and moustache were trimmed, giving him a distinguish appearance.

Julie stepped out from behind the trees and walked across the snow towards her brother. She was twenty feet away before he glanced in her direction. She pulled back her hood.

His body became rigid. "Henna, take the children and go to the great fountain. I'll meet you there soon."

Concerned, his wife looked between her husband and the stranger, reading in his eyes that a sinister adversary stood before him. Henna called the reluctant children to her and walked back along the brick path, glancing over her shoulder twice.

When they were out of sight, Rufus address the stranger in a harsh voice. "Who sent you? General Rahad or Herron? One of the lords?"

"No human sent me, Rufus," Julie answered gently, walking nearer.

"I have no time for political games. You can tell whoever hired you that I'm not interested in any deals. I'm appalled that they would snoop to blaspheming the memory my sister. Let her rest in peace, something she never knew in life because of them."

"You are wrong. Junia met someone who changed her life and gave her peace beyond anything you have experienced." Raw emotion choked the speaker's voice. "I am she."

"How dare you!" spat out the man. "Junia died in my arms! My arms. Her blood was on my clothes. I saw her last gasps of air. Leave now! Or I will have you arrested."

"Rufus." Julie spoke his name with deep sadness, wishing she could hug him, erasing his pain. "My last words were 'I love you both.' I spoke to you and Urbane. He stood there, just stood, while I bled from his blade. But you did not desert me, beloved brother. You were always wiser than I, telling me there was evil destroying our land, destroying myself. My journey has been long, but I have come to tell you that you were right."

"That is enough! Stop your atrocity." Rufus's anger boiled. How dare this woman talk like his sister, stirring up the pain anew. "You are not my sister. Her body was burned, and her ashes thrown across the rubbish heap."

He had been devastated after Junia's death. Splotched with her blood, he had wandered the streets of Thorn after finally leaving her lifeless body, not knowing or caring who saw him. Somehow he had found Henna, her warm arms encircling him, holding him as he wept. He left the city with her and stayed with her large family. For days he barely talked or ate. She refused to leave his side. Restlessly he chopped firewood and hauled water, anything that channeled his anger. Eventually he gained mastery over his rage, finding healing among the closeness of Henna's family. The couple wed a month after Junia's death.

"My body perished but not my soul. For five years I was in Agape, Yahweh's City. He sent me back to tell you that he loves you."

For a moment the man did not speak, part of him wishing he could believe her words. "So the Tnias sent you. Woman, guard your words or they will be your death sentence."

"I have already died once. What do I have to fear?"

Rufus shook his head, denying what she said. "I will only tell you one last time—leave or I will call the guards."

The woman stepped forward, feeling the Presence throbbing through her. "Under you shirt you wear a metal chain. Attached to it is a wooden horse you gave me as a child. I used to wonder where the horse was running. Later I didn't care, as long as it was away from my father. You no longer care either. You have lost hope for yourself and your people. Today you must choose where the horse will run—aimlessly through the darkness or towards the light of Yahweh."

Staring at the woman, Rufus pulled the necklace out. He grasped it tightly in his hand, galloping horse with mane flying, wood darkened from bloodstains. He had no need to look at it. He had stared at it too many times. "You are more than what you seem."

She stepped nearer. "I am exactly who I say I am."

Rufus felt a warm, spring breeze surround him, blowing his hair, carrying scents of flowers and rich earth. The wind became stronger, yet branches of nearby trees remained motionless. He could feel it through his thick coat, flowing deeply pass his skin, piercing his soul. It was eerie yet inviting, peaceful and delicious like a thousand carefree days of summer rolled into one. And he knew he was in the presence of an unseen god. The same one he had fought against in battle and had overseen the deaths of its people. His hand holding the horse began to shake and his legs became rubbery. Slowly he sank to his knees in the snow.

Julie bent on the frozen ground beside him. "He loves you and will forgive you of your sins. All you have to do is ask."

For a long time the prince could not speak, only sit with his head bowed before a god greater than anything he had known before. Finally, he said, "Tell me, Junia, about this City of Light. Is the legend true that it is taller than the clouds?"

Julie smiled at his use of her name. She described in rich detail Agape. Rufus drank in every word like a man marooned in a desert. Hope returned to his life, and joy sparked in his eyes. When worried Henna appeared a while later after finding someone to watch her children, she did not find the husband she knew. Instead, a jubilant stranger rushed to her and embraced her. He had the same face but the pain was gone that had haunted him for years. In disbelief she looked back and forth between Rufus and the dark-haired woman as both told her a story so fantastic not even her favorite childhood fairytales could equal it.

Finally she gave Julie a sisterly hug and said to her husband, "Your god is my god."

~~~~~~~~~

The frigid wind whipped across the park, shaking snow from tree limbs. The children tossed snowballs at each other, giggling. The younger ones began to tire.

"I'm cold," complained little Jonu to her brother.

"Me too," said Tasia, shivering.

The older kids glanced around, wondering where Julie was. She had been gone far too long. Without a word, Mickhan walked into the grove of trees where she had disappeared. The other four looked at each other, uncertain. Knowing it was her duty to keep everyone together, Violet called after Mickhan several times, but he paid her no heed. Angrily she marched after him with the other three trailing behind. They found him staring at a wall.

"What's behind there?" asked Mickhan.

"How am I supposed to know?" said Violet.

"She went over the wall. See. Her footprints end here." Mickhan pointed at the ground.

Lonees stood beside the older boy and touched the wall. "I remember we passed a gate a little ways back. We could get through that way."

"We're to wait for Julie in the field. Let's go," commanded Violet.

The two boys started off, but not in the direction the teen indicated. They followed the high stone wall to the left. Violet followed, demanding the children obey her.

"Hey, it's cold," complained Lonees. "Jonu and Tasia need someplace warm. So do I. Maybe there's a shop or building on the other side we could hang out in."

Violet considered what he said. They were all freezing despite the multiple layers of clothing and coats they wore. "Okay, but we must be careful."

The five youths walked through the snowy woods, tired after a long day of excitement. Abruptly the trees ended and they found themselves standing beside a large iron gate guarded by two sentries. Violet gasped in fear, but Mickhan marched forward, only thinking of shelter.

The younger sentry blocked his way with a long spear. "Hey, kid, you cannot enter the Royal Garden."

Mickhan stared at the weapon only an inch from his face and could think of nothing to say.

Violet answered for him. "We...uh...didn't know it was the Royal Garden. We'll be on our way now." She tightly clasped Jonu's hand and began moving along the brick path. Tasia followed a few steps behind.

"Wait," commanded the older, rougher looking soldier. "Who do you serve?" It was protocol to ask all who attempted to enter the gate.

The children looked at each other with frightened eyes. Lonees and Mickhan slowly began backing towards the thick foliage on their right. Violet followed their lead.

The younger man sighed, thinking they were just peasant kids terrified at seeing real soldiers. The older guard pointed his spear towards Tasia and barked, "Who is your god?"

The six year old stared at him timidly. Finally she stammered, "Yah…Yahweh."

Violet stepped forward and clamped a hand over the child's mouth. The two boys bolted into the trees, running like a rabid dog chased them. Seeing her brother flee, three-year-old Jonu followed.

Voice trembling, Violet sputtered, "She's young and doesn't know what she's saying."

The younger guard dropped to one knee. "Child, you have just committed a serious crime. Yahweh is our enemy."

"She'll know that next time," said the teenager, still covering Tasia's mouth.

"Let her speak for herself," demanded the older, hasher man.

Violet moved her hand. The sentry who was eyelevel with the child asked, "Is Zuzumza good?"

"No," answered the confused child, wondering why Violet was trying to stop her from speaking the truth. "Zuzumza is evil. Yahweh is good."

The older soldier leaned his spear against the wall and pulled out his sword. "Move out of the way Tranton."

The younger man stood, keeping his body between Tasia and the armed guard. "Bension, she is only a child."

"She has broken the law twice now and must pay the penalty."

Violet grabbed Tasia's arm, dragging her backwards. "She won't do it again. I promise."

Bension attempted to move pass Tranton, but the younger man blocked him. The older guard gave a hard push, sending the cadet crashing to the ground. Roughly he grabbed the child. Violet screamed. Tranton rose from the icy ground and drew his own weapon.

"Get a hold of yourself," commanded the older sentry. "To defend a Tnias you will lose your career, perhaps your life."

The cadet felt trapped. He had not joined the Palace Guard to kill young children, but neither could he stop what was happening. Bension pointed his sword at the trembling child's stomach.

"What is going on here?" demanded a deep voice.

Guards, teenager, and child looked toward the stout man standing with his family. His wife was pale, holding the hands of her children tightly. Both sentries saluted.

Bension explained, "Your Highness, we are enforcing the law. This child is a Tnias."

The nobleman placed both guards under his scrutinizing stare. "This is supposed to be a safe environment for my family. I will not have them subjected to public executions."

"I am sorry, sir. We will take care of business someplace more private."

For a brief moment Rufus let his gaze rest on the pale teen and trembling child. "I do not think this frail girl will cause the fall of the Empire. Did you have children, soldier?"

The man was caught off guard. "Yes. Yes, sir."

"Then let this child go."

Bension shifted uncomfortable. The military hero was asking for him to break the law, but if he did not obey the prince, Rufus could find a way to end his career—or life. Nobles were well-known for doing so when angered. Slowly he lowered his weapon and released the child. Tasia ran to Violet who hugged the child. Henna exhaled the breath she had unknowingly been holding. Her own children's pale faces regained color.

"Good choice," responded Rufus, memorizing the faces of both guards. He led his family pass the guards. Making brief eye contact with the teenager, he gave a slight nod of his head to the left. For a moment she looked confused then quickly chose the left path, hurrying away with Tasia's hand grasped tightly. Rufus's family took the trail to the right.

A short distance down the path, Violet spotted a hooded woman with three frightened children beside her. Now that the danger was over, the teen's body started to shake. She embraced Julie, crying. Tasia buried her face in the woman's coat.

"It's over now, honey. You are safe." As the teenager's sobs slowed, Julie apologized. "I'm sorry, Violet. I should not have been gone so long. I had to speak to a man—the same one who saved your life."

About to leave the park, both she and Rufus had seen the guards interrogating Tasia. Making eye contact through the trees, the two silently communicated a plan. Then Julie had climbed over the wall, almost falling on top of the two terrified boys. Puffing, little Jonu had blindly ran into her. Calming the frightened children, she had led the group out of the woods, praying her brother could rescue the other two.

"Let's head home," Julie said. Violet nodded, still unable to speak.

Chapter Twenty-four

"Heard you left the kids alone in the park." Roshell's voice was menacing, daring her statement to be disputed.

Julie glanced towards the Ulmjon as they walked through the snowy streets of Lephin Sector. The area had originally been designed for the upper class, but over the years it had disintegrated. Some of the apartment buildings shared fenced communal yards. Occasionally there was a tiny park with a few trees. The two Salts were heading to the home of Sandra's sister, Dalphine, supposedly for a small birthday party, a cover for a Tnias meeting. Many elderly attended such meetings for the underground trip was too strenuous for them. The secret gatherings also served as a testing ground to weed out spies before they were introduced to the Haven. Newcomers were not taken underground until they had attended at least three meetings and been approved by elders of the Remnant.

Julie answered, "I had to speak with a man I once knew. Another opportunity may not have presented itself."

"You put the lives of those children in danger. They come before your reminiscing." Her hand briefly slid to her sword, hidden under a long coat.

The Gogian sighed, used to Roshell becoming a furious leviathan when defending children. "Look, the man I talked with pledged his life to Yahweh along with his wife. He was the one who rescued Violet and Tasia."

The scowl stayed on Roshell's lips. "Saved by a miracle of Yahweh. Never, Julie, never leave vulnerable children alone in a dangerous area. You could have innocent blood on your hands."

Julie winced as dark, gruesome images from the past flashed through her mind. She forced them away. "I already do."

Realizing her words had been taken wrong, Roshell switched topics. "So who is this rescuer? When do we meet him?"

"He is a noble and an old friend of mine. He would like to visit the Haven soon."

"He has not gone through the tests yet."

"I trust him with my life. And he is too well-known to attend gatherings. It would draw suspicion."

They entered a seven-story apartment building. On each side of the structure was a fenced yard shared with its neighbors. They climbed three flights of stairs and walked along a hallway to Dalphine's quarters. Sandra greeting them. The apartment was originally designed for the upper class. The rooms were large and airy with many arched windows. They placed gifts on a table and mingled with the guests. Josias Greencliff chatted happily, explaining that her husband had to attend other matters. Onias was nearby talking with Manideck who had moved in with Dalphine's family after the loss of his own. There were a number of children and teens playing or swapping stories while parents talked about more serious matters. Among the Tnias were three newcomers—a married couple and one middle-aged man—ready to be tested for membership into the Remnant.

Julie wished Matthan and Danielle could have joined them. Danielle's pregnancy made the difficult trip through the sewers exhausting. She spent most of her time helping Minira and Roshell with the orphans in the Haven. Matthan was always busy on projects. Today he and Joatham were delivering clocks and visiting a few shut-ins, giving them food. Julie herself had been spending too much time underground painting. She needed this break.

The meeting started with a time for silent prayer then Onias led a devotion. He stood before the others, nervous and jittery, for it was his first time speaking in front of a group. Eyes shining, Josias and Sandra listened proudly. Next came joyful laughter as Dalphine opened her many presents, then the guests attacked the food. Several teenagers invited friends downstairs to another apartment where they could relax away from parents. In a quiet study, the Salts began testing each newcomer. The married couple was quickly approved. The heavyset, middle-aged man answered their questions correctly, yet they both felt his words were too smooth, perhaps rehearsed. After they dismissed him, they remained in the bedroom, debating what should be done.

Manideck burst into the apartment, breathing hard, followed by two pale teens. "They're coming! We've got to get out, quick!"

Hearing panicked voices, the Salts emerged from the study.

Breathless, Manideck continued, "I saw them outside the window. Just like last time, but there's a lot more of them now."

A number of people rushed to the windows, including Roshell and Julie. The street was crowded, too crowded for the cold weather. And most were men dressed in long overcoats, some chatting, others reading or leaning against benches—all waiting. Julie ran to a window looking into the grassy alley. Several men stood there too, talking among themselves. Julie's trained eyes spotted large objects bulging under the overcoats—hidden weapons. The men were waiting for a signal. The middle-age man just interviewed by the Salts stood at another nearby window, cleaning his glasses.

The signal!

The men in the tiny park entered the side door—all but one who walked towards the fence and spoke with someone on the other side. Julie jerked around and caught Roshell's eye. With a brief tilt of her head, Julie indicated the heavyset man beside her. Roshell nodded once then walked across the room towards him.

Julie climbed onto a table and spoke in a strong, commanding voice. "Everyone stay calm. The raid has just started. They will be heading to this apartment first then will search the building room by room."

People began talking in panicked voices, gathering family members together. Kids cried, and a woman babbled hysterically. Sudden silence filled the room as every face looked towards Roshell. Her sword was pressed against the throat of the startled spy.

"I should kill you right now and send your soul to the Great Abyss," she growled at him. He remained silent, only staring at the sharp blade with large, frightened eyes. "Instead, I will let you receive payment for turning us in. Every person whose innocent blood is shed today will be on your soul. May their faces haunt your every thought for the rest of your tormented existence, through life and beyond." Sword pressed against his back, she led him into a far bedroom and locked the door.

Julie continued, "Dalphine, how close is the building behind this one? Can we create a bridge to it?"

"N…no. The courtyard is larger there, with a few trees." The woman could barely stay focused.

"The only way out is through the doors on the bottom floor," said her husband, Mondren.

Julie gritted her teeth. The buildings on the east and west were too far away also. Every exit would be blocked. They were trapped. Their only choices were to hid in various apartments, hoping not be discovered, or to fight their way out. People would die either way, but few would elude a meticulous Reforcer search. Frightened neighbors would be quick to turn Tnias in. Attempting to break out was equally as dangerous. She and Roshell were the only ones trained for combat.

Roshell walked back into the room. "We don't have time for elaborate plans. We flee now. I'll lead the front. Julie, you take the back. We go for the backdoor. There'll be less guards." She looked over the scared people and silently said a prayer for protection.

Julie nodded and addressed the Tnias. "You must remain calm and quiet. Your lives depend on this. When we get pass the blockade, scatter. Do not head to your homes. Make sure you are not followed then make your way to the Haven."

Parents hugged children. Husbands and wives kissed, not knowing if it would be for the last time. Josias quieted the hysterical woman. Prayers tumbled out of trembling lips. Several young children wept uncontrollably.

Manideck said, "There are others in an apartment on the second floor. I told them to stay there until I came back."

"Good, Manideck," answered Julie, remembering that he had kept his head and saved eleven people from an earlier raid, despite the fact his mother and siblings had been killed. "I need you to go back there now. Walk casual and don't run if you see a Reforcer. Lead your friends downstairs to the back door. We will meet you."

The teenager nodded and was out the door without further word.

Drawing her weapon, Roshell stood beside the closed door, waiting, giving Manideck time to make it to the stairs. Julie walked among the frightened people, trying to organize them. She placed Sandra and Onias in charge of two sections. Sandra remained calm, despite her fear. Growing up in Reed Sector, she had been in dangerous situations before. Onias's eyes were large with fear, but he boldly stood by his mother, determined to protect her and the others at any cost. Several men grabbed brooms, pokers, vases, anything that could be used as a weapon.

Opening the door, Roshell dashed down the hall. Quickly the long line of Tnias followed as best they could. Roshell skipped the closest stairwell and headed towards the backend of the building. Before dashing down the stairs, she looked over the railing, seeing several men far below. Sword in hand, she bolted down. She made it to the landing of the third floor before encountering the soldiers. They were ready for her.

Roshell fought like a tiger, one sword against four on the narrow landing, but there was little room for maneuvering. Dalphine's husband battled with an iron poker, blocking several sword thrusts. Another Tnias attacked a Reforcer with a broom. With one blow his opponent cut through the wooden stick, slicing into the young man's chest. A nearby woman screamed. Roshell yelled in rage and dashed forward. Her sudden charge caught one man off guard, and he crumbled to the floor holding his side. At the same time, Roshell felt a blade slash across her ribs. She swung at her attacker but missed. Two soldiers aimed for her unprotected back.

It would have been the end of her except Julie had pushed her way through the Tnias. In frustration she had watched the battle taking place below, knowing Roshell and the untrained men could not hold the front. And more Reforcers, hearing the sound of battle, were coming up the stairs. If she tried to help, the backend of the line would be undefended. Another strike force, coming down from the floor above, could reach them at any moment. She chose the visible enemy.

Pushing her way pass terrified women and children, she pulled out her sword before reaching the landing. Immediately flames leapt along the steel blade. She swung, her heated blade cleaving through both bone and flesh of both soldiers who were focused on killing Roshell. They fell in gasp of pain. The fourth soldier turned to attack her, only to be knocked out cold by Mondren's iron poker.

Julie glanced at Daphine's husband, noticing blood flowing from several deep wounds. "Get to the back and guard it!" she ordered then dashed downstairs after Roshell. There was no time to tend injuries.

The two women rushed into the next wave of Reforcers. Julie took the lead, using her forward motion to add force behind her blow, beheading one man caught off guard. A second opponent lasted only a few seconds in the confusion. Roshell took out the third soldier. They passed the second floor landing without trouble. Halfway down to the first floor, they encountered more Reforcers. Side by side the two women fought, finding it difficult to put force into the swings of their blades on the narrow stairwell. Roshell received several wounds as she attempted to block blows, but Julie fared better as her opponents were intimidated by her surreal sword. Fortunately, there was only room for two Reforcers to combat them at a time. But there were more waiting to take the place of fallen comrades.

Swish. Thud. Julie wrenched in pain as a sharp dagger flew through the air, sliced across her shoulder, and impaled itself into the wall. Soldiers further down the stairwell refused to be kept out of the deadly fray.

Sounds of combat came to them from the stairwell above as Mondren and several men attempted to defend the back of the line against more opponents. Dread filled Julie. They were trapped at both ends and could hold neither much longer. People in the middle would be slaughter like sheep.

In the middle of the group, Josias was doubled over, wheezing, barely able to breathe. Onias held her frail shoulders, repeating, "Yahweh, help us," over and over. Around him came the sounds of sobbing kids, occasional screams, desperate prayers, and coughing from the elderly bothered by the heat of the crowded stairwell. Sandra stood on the second floor landing, her sister and young family pressed against her. Realizing both ends of the group were trapped, Sandra did the first thing that came to her mind. She opened the second floor's door and peered through. There were no soldiers. The ones that had been stationed there had earlier rushed up the stairs and been killed by the two Salts.

Sandra yelled over her shoulder for the others to follow and ran down the hall. People flowed out behind her, relieved to be away from the nightmarish stairwell.

Reaching another hallway, Sandra glanced to her left, seeing the leg of a soldier vanishing behind a further corner. She turned right and headed towards another staircase. Her stomach seemed to be in her throat as she ran. One phrase repeated itself in her mind, *Don't let soldiers be there. Don't let soldiers be there.*

Finally she spotted the broad steps of the side staircase. Unlike the back stairwell, there were no doors separating the flight from the hallway. And there were no Reforcers. She bolted down the steps, but slowed on the middle landing, signaling for her sister and others to wait. Below she heard talking and a groan. Keeping low, she scooted downward. The sight that met her eyes stole away hope. In the bottom hallway the group of youth Manideck had led was lined up against a wall. Soldiers walked in front of them, swords waving menacing. Insults and crude jokes were directed towards the youths. Two teens attempted to keep a feeble grandmother on her feet, but she slumped, exhausted. A guard threatened that if she could not walk he would kill her where she stood.

Manideck stepped away from the wall. "Leave her alone. She's old and sick."

The guard moved within a foot of the young man and sneered, "I think I'll leave you for last so you can watch the others die. Then I'll make sure your own death is slow and torturous." He slammed his fist into the adolescent's stomach. As Manideck doubled over in pain, the man brought his knee up, hard, into the teen's face. A girl standing beside Manideck screamed. The soldier swung the handle of his sword at her.

Sandra reacted on instinct. She threw her only weapon, a vase she had picked up in the apartment. It crashed against the man's head, sending him toppling to the floor. Immediately three Reforcers dashed up the stairs towards the new attacker. Sandra knew in that split second she was going to die. She felt no fear, only sorrow that her niece, nephews, and sister would be next, and there was nothing she could do to save them. She stood still, waiting with eyes closed. She sensed movement then the clang of metal hitting metal. Opening her eyes, she saw the Reforcer's sword blocked by a blade of fire.

Julie pushed hard, catching the soldier off balance. He fell backwards down the steps. A guard on her left managed to strike a glancing blow to her side. He paid for it with his life. Further down the stairs, a third soldier swung at her feet. She jumped over the blade, sending her own downward into his shoulder. He screamed in pain. With a kick, Julie pushed him down the stairs. Reaching the bottom of the staircase, she braced for the wave of soldiers who awaited her. Some hung back, fearful of the fiery blade. The enraged man Sandra had hit with the vase was the first to reach Julie. She sidestepped his charge and severed his sword hand at the wrist, leaving him writhing on the floor in pain.

Others attacked. Each fell. Julie reacted on instinct, once again the untouchable warrior princess of old. The remaining soldiers fled in panic. Yelling for the Tnias to follow, she led the way to a side exit into the garden. A high iron fence separated the small park from the street. Sandra stopped the group at the door of the building as Julie attacked guards. Twisting and blocking, swinging and paring, she moved across the snowy courtyard in a deadly dance. Battle lust filled her eyes and excitement ran through her veins. She laughed as men fell helplessly before her supernatural blade. When she realized no one was left to fight, she felt disappointment.

Seeing the enemy vanquished, Sandra dashed out, closely followed by a steady stream of frightened Tnias. They ran across the snowy grass, passing dead and drying Reforcers. The fence's gate was locked so people streamed through the back and side doors into the next apartment building. Several youths climbed over a metal fence near the further away apartments. Manideck stood inside the courtyard, helping others over the barrier.

Julie turned to join them, but Reforcers guarding the front of Dalphine's apartment building had reached the fence and were attempting to climb over. The princess jabbed at them through the iron bars, sending them crashing to the ground in pain. Wild exultation pumped through her as she strutted in front of the barrier, laughing. The Reforcers dragged or limped away from the fence, terrified of the strange woman with the sword of fire. Surely she was not human. Another man came around the front corner of the building, and the line of soldiers parted for him. Julie's world suddenly froze, everything vanishing except for one man standing poised and confident on the other side of the fence. Urbane.

Their eyes locked. His face filled with astonishment and disbelief. Unconsciously Julie took several steps towards him, lowering her fiery blade, heart pounding, still enthralled in battle lust. She studied his tall form, broad shoulders, handsome face, and military uniform. Memories stirred, and forgotten passion swirled through her. Urbane, the lover she tried not to remember—the man she never stopped loving. If the fence had been absent, she would have run and embraced him in a tight hug, forgetting hard earned lessons and the lives counting on her now.

"Julie! Your help would be vastly appreciated!" Roshell yelled, bleeding from several cuts, attempting to keep the Reforcers from exiting the door. One man, Kentim, still fought beside Roshell with a sword taken from a fallen Reforcer. Heading across the frozen courtyard, two men supported Mondren, barely alive, suffering from deep wounds.

Jerked back to the present, the Gogian princess took several steps backwards, once again a Salt.

"Junia wait," Urbane partly raised a hand, reaching for the memory of the woman he loved.

"Julie, I need help!" Roshell called, blocking a sword thrust.

The princess could not tear her eyes away from the lover she had not seen in over five years. Kentim, fighting beside Roshell, groaned as an opponent's sword pierced his shoulder.

Roshell desperately screamed, "Julie, now!"

The Gogian whirled, fiery blade up. In three strides she reached the doorway and cut off the attacker's sword arm. Roshell propped up injured Kentim and headed across the courtyard. Julie kept the door blocked, not a difficult thing to do for the remaining soldiers were afraid of her, believing she was sent by the gods. Several men came out of the backdoor of the apartment building. She raced after the soldiers, reaching them before they could attack Roshell and the injured man. The Reforcers could not stand long before her fury. A deadly guardian, she protected her friends' backs as they entered the new building, then barred the door from the inside. But not before she took one finally glance at the far fence. Urbane still stood behind the fence, watching her intensely.

Chapter Twenty-five

It seemed to take an eternity to find an opening into the smelly tunnels. By then, they were about to drop from exhaustion. They collapsed onto the slimy stone floor, several feet from raw refuse flowing through a channel. They were only six—the ones who had fought furiously to protect the flank of the Tnias trapped in the apartment building. Mondren slipped into unconsciousness, and two men who had carried him were weak from their own injuries. Roshell and Kentim were both close to passing out from pain and exhaustion. None could walk another step or fight if the Reforcers found them. That left Julie, bleeding from two deep cuts and haunted by the image of Urbane, as the only mobile person. Weariness settled over her like an inviting blanket on a cold, winter day.

She attempted to care for the worst cuts of the weakened Tnias, but there was no medical kit and her own side throbbed with every movement she made. Barely audible, Roshell ordered Julie to find help before they all died from blood loss. Julie obeyed, walking as fast as her injured body would allow through the dark tunnels, using her flaming sword as a torch. She soon met a search party. Several refugees had already made it to the Haven and had alerted the people there of the raid. More guards were immediately posted and groups began searching the tunnels for Reforcers and wandering Tnias. After giving the men directions to find her injured friends, Julie sank to the cold floor. Dimly she was aware that someone tended her wounds. She slipped into a dreamless sleep, not even awakening when she was placed on a stretcher and carried back to the Haven.

Two days later she awoke sore and stiff. When she tried to move, sharp pain seared her side. Danielle appeared in her line of vision, telling her to lie back down for she had stitches in her side and shoulder. Julie asked how others fared, discovering that Mondren had passed away before the searchers had found the injured group. Kentim, the man who had fought beside Roshell, died a few hours later. In all, seven had been accounted either dead or missing.

The next day was the Festival of Peace. For months the holiday had been planned. It would be the first time in known history that the sacred day would be celebrated in Gog—even though the festival would take place secretly underground. Excited children made decorations that hung from strings. Colorful lanterns cast bright patterns in the caverns. But the raid overshadowed the festival. Peace did not exist above ground or in peoples' minds. A memorial service was held for Mondren, Kentim, and the other five. Julie was able to attend though Roshell was still bedridden. Held tightly by Sandra, Dalphine wept uncontrollably, her children huddled against nearby Josias. Two coffins, containing the bodies of the men who died underground, were placed at the front of the Great Chamber. Both Matthan and Onias spoke at the service. The latter broke down twice before he could finish his prepared speech. After the service, the feast was held, but people were quiet, subdued. In the back of each one's mind was the thought that next time it could be themselves lying in the coffin.

"Teach me to fight, Julie, so I can avenge the deaths of my family and friends."

The Salt looked up from her supper. Manideck stood before her, hands clenched into fists. His young, handsome face burned with determination.

Julie placed her plate of food on the crate she was sitting on. Preferring to be alone with her thoughts, she had sought a quiet corner away from the crowded tables. "Revenge is not the answer, my friend. We must love our enemy. Do good to those who persecute us."

The young man glared at her in shock. "How can you say such things? You just killed a host of them. They are butchers, and we must defend ourselves. You could train an army. Then we would hunt down the Reforcers, cleanse our streets, and eventually take over the palace."

"Fire cannot destroy fire. Violence is not the answer for violence."

"Matthan said almost the same thing, but I thought you were different. I saw you cleave men down with your sword of fire. Nothing could stand in your way. Nothing." A hungry look filled the youth's eyes. "Violence and power is the only thing these butchers understand."

Disturbed, Julie looked at her half eaten plate of food. How many children would be haunted by the bloody images they had seen? Several had watched their fathers die in front of them. The Salt stood. "You are right that violence and power are all they understand. They will never learn differently if that is all they see."

She turned away from the frustrated youth. Wincing in pain, she headed down tunnels towards the dome room with the partially finished murals. The tall scaffold took up much of the chamber. Scattered on the floor were jars of paint, brushes, rags, mixing bowls, and other colorfully spattered objects.

Working half the long winter, she had finished one wall and started on the ceiling. The flat wall was a detailed green landscape with a river flowing from the shiny city of Agape, as if seen from miles away. Using a perspective technique, Julie had created the river to flow directly towards the viewer, growing larger until reaching the edge of the wall. There it stopped, but she planned to later paint the floor to seem as if viewers walked on the top of flowing water. On the still untouched convex walls, she planned to use their natural shape to create the tremendous waterfall that flowed from Yahweh's throne. She would place the waterfall where the two curved walls met, painting balconies and crosswalks filled with people and creatures representing cultures from across the entire world. It would probably take a year or more to complete the project. Just a week before, she had started working on the dome ceiling that would show Yahweh's throne room. The waterfall would appear to flow from the throne and fall down the wall to the pool on the floor, connecting with the river painted on the flat wall.

Today she studied the dim, yellow paint mapping out where the completed throne would be placed. Yahweh's unfinished face was faint and smeared, as though viewed through a distant fog. She closed her eyes and slumped against an unpainted wall, feeling tired and disconnected from her master. Faces of those she killed or mangled in the raid played across her mind. The images melted into faces of Tnias she had slaughtered in years past. Her hands had already shed too much blood. What right did she have to take more? Even to protect life.

Her reaction in the raid terrified her. She had relished the sensations of power to control life, to give or spare it as it pleased her, just like when she was Princess Junia commanding the Royal Cavalry. Then there had been Urbane. Why did she have to see him at the worst moment when she was closest to becoming what she had once been? Did Yahweh mock her? No, she knew better. She had been warned that she would wrestle against her own weaknesses. And that was what scared her most.

Looking up at the high ceiling, she studied the blurred face of her god. "Never again, Yahweh, will I take the life of any human, ever."

~~~~~~~~~

Through the dark city dashed two horses pulling an elegant carriage. The driver refused to slow for pedestrians, and a drunken man barely had time to jump out of the way. When the horses reached Market Square, they quickened their speed over the vast, snowy field of desolated cobblestone, racing along Market Lane under the skeletal limbs of bare cherry trees, finally halting at a sinister four-story building, headquarters of the Reforcers. Captain Patrobas stepped from the shadows of the building and opened the door of the carriage to help General Nereus step down.

"Thank you, General, for coming." Relief showed on the captain's face.

The retired Cabinet member, slightly stooped, placed both hands on his carved cane. "Your message said it was urgent."

"Yes, yes. Let's talk in my office." Patrobas led the way into the brick building, through hallways, and up several flights of stairs. Finally behind closed doors, the captain felt safe to explain the problem.

"I admire General Herron for his loyalty, courage, and wisdom. He has followed in your footsteps—the same as I—of leading men by example, not dictatorship." Patrobas took a deep breath, bracing himself, before discussing the problems of the man who had promoted him into the position of captain. "But something has happen which may ruin his reputation and, perhaps, his sanity. You're the only one I know that he looks up to, so I turn to you for help. The men have already begun spreading rumors, though I have threatened to court-martial any Reforcer found gossiping. If something is not done soon, General Herron will fall into disgrace."

The retired commander listened carefully. He viewed Herron as an excellent, battle-smart officer, though cold and distant. "I might be able to help if I understood more about the problem."

"Well, it all started three days ago. After a disastrous raid where half the team was killed or injured, he stormed through this building without saying a word then locked himself in his office. There was the sound of objects slamming against the wall and glass breaking. He hasn't come out since, nor will he talk with me. Sometimes he accepts food, but it comes back half-eaten. I could think of no one else to call but you."

Nereus sighed, absently stroking his thick beard. Sometimes it was hard for soldiers to accept defeat, especially ambitious officers with a long run of success. "What caused such a high number of causalities?"

The captain looked uncomfortable. "Well, the men reported there was a glowing spirit with an unnatural sword of fire sent by the gods to protect the heretics. Some less reliable rumors claim a ghost stole the general's soul."

"A guardian from a god?" A transformation came over Nereus's face. "I would like to see General Herron now."

Patrobas led the way to the fourth floor, stopping in front of a heavy oak door. Nereus tapped with his cane. No answer. He rapped louder, this time with his fist. Only silence could be heard.

"General Herron, this is General Nereus. I would like to speak with you."

For a long moment there was no answer then someone stirred. The two men heard crackling as broken glass was stepped on. The lock turned slowly, and the door opened to reveal a haggard, unshaven man. The room behind Urban looked like a hurricane had blown through. Chairs were overturned, small objects thrown across the room, walls and cushions stained from broken wine bottles.

"You're not looking well, General," said Nereus in a fatherly voice as he entered. Patrobas remained in the hallway.

"I'm getting by," Urbane said as he picked up a padded chair for the older man to sit in. For himself, he cleared a torn leather couch of its debris.

"I see." The two men studied each other for a few heartbeats. Then Nereus spoke, "You are reputed as being a dispassionate and fair man, dedicated to the Empire."

Urbane's mouth twisted into an ironic smile. "Until now."

"Your men worry about you, especially Captain Patrobas."

Troubled, Urbane stood up and walked to a window. With his back to the elderly war hero, he asked, "What did he tell you has brought on my sudden aliment?"

"That you saw a guardian of the gods which might have stolen away your soul."

Smiling bitterly, Urbane turned towards the general. "I saw Junia."

"Princess Junia?" Nereus's eyes widened. He had been among the crowd the day she died.

"There was a fence which separated us, but I saw her clearly. She held a sword of fire, her body…her perfect body…radiating a golden light. She stood in a fighting stance—one that I taught her—striking down highly trained men as if they were helpless infants, protecting the cursed people of her beloved god."

"Was this an illusion? A vision sent by the gods?"

The younger man gave a hollow, bitter laugh. "I wish it had been. I went through the building, viewing her leftovers. The wounds from her weapon are like none I have ever seen before. The blade cuts and cauterizes in one blow. The men who survived were in extreme pain but lost little blood. I examined one man whose sword arm had been chopped off clean at the elbow. The stomp did not bleed. Believe me, General. She was real, too real."

"I believe you, son. Sit down. I'm going to tell you a story that those who lived through rarely talk about. As a zealous private, my regiment was ordered to destroy a village controlled by Tnias. The only problem was that the swollen river was impassable and the bridge guarded. We attacked, thinking we would quickly overrun a handful of armed farmers. But somehow, our two hundred soldiers could not get pass the blockade of crates and overturned wagons. I was sent in a frontal charge twice and barely escaped with my life both times. When night came, we called it quits until morning. Next day, I was sent with a small test group to attack the barricade. In ten minutes all seven Tnias were dead. I looked at their young faces, some not older than sixteen, wondering how they prevailed against us the day before." He looked towards Urbane for an answer.

Urbane shrugged his shoulders. "You fought a larger group the day before, and they strolled away under the cover of darkness."

"Wrong guess. It was a full moon, and we had a broad view of the area beyond the bridge. Archers kept watch in case anyone moved beyond the protection of the barricade. Care for another try, soldier?"

General Herron shook his head, intrigued despite himself.

"The ones on the bridge were buying time for the village to be evacuated. There was not a single person or animal left in the town. We planned to follow their trail and hunt them down, but the minute our feet touched the ground on the other side of the bridge, a severe thunderstorm sent us running for shelter in the nearest abandoned buildings. Of course, when the hail and rain finally stopped, there were no signs left to indicate which direction the villagers had taken.

"I have never told this to anyone before, but that day I began to suspect that the god of the Tnias was not a myth or as weak as we had been led to believe. Over forty years I have served Gog in the military, rising in rank, fighting and later commanding hundreds of battles, overseeing the collapse of nations, ordering the execution of tens of thousands of civilians because of the god they pledge to. But every so often, I've witnessed the impossible—the Tnias call them miracles. I've seen some of my best plans go awry for no logical reason. I've seen weather obey the prayers of a seven-year-old child. Our seasoned scouts accidentally crossed into our own border on a clear night and burned one of our own villages. Trained war horses panicked at the sight of one youth blocking a pass. The list goes and on."

Urbane looked at the aged general as if seeing him for the first time.

"Over the years, I've come to realize that I was not fighting against mere humans, but a powerful force. Every victory was granted only with permission from this unseen god. Every defeat I suffered somehow fitted into this god's purpose. I cannot explain the logic behind this but felt it in my bones as truth."

The younger man shook his head in disbelief. "You have gone soft in your old age. Zuzumza is the one who grants victory. Speak this way with anyone else and you would be condemned as a heretic."

"That, Herron, is why I only share my insight with you. You also have seen the unexplained wonders of this god—the dead fighting to protect the living."

"And what am I supposed to do, O Wise Bearer of the Medallion of Zuzumza?"

The old man sighed, feeling the weight of tradition and responsibility. "What I always do—pretend I have seen nothing extraordinary. Continue to fight under the banner of a god who gives death but cannot control the elements."

As Nereus stood up to leave, Urbane said in a haunted voice, "I cannot forget what I have seen."

222

The older man looked his progeny in the eyes. "Neither can I. The question is what are you going to do about it?"

Urbane took a deep breath then vowed, "I will hunt down this spirit called Julie with the face of Junia. I will destroy it or die trying."

The retired general nodded gravely. "I have already traveled down the path you now walk. There is nothing at the end but numbing hollowness and bloody memories—the fate of every soldier."

Captain Patrobas worriedly met Nereus in the hallway.

"You will find your commander back to his old self, more fervent than ever."

The relived Reforcer missed the undertone in the speaker's voice. "My gratitude is boundless, General."

Nereus waved off the man's thanks. Reaching the street, he decided to walk home, needing the time to think. Though it had only been two months since his permanent retirement from the Cabinet—thanks to Phlegon's insistence—he refused to just walk away from the problems of his government. His life had passed so quickly. His children grew up, married, and had kids of their own while he fought on foreign soil. Two sons followed in his footsteps and had paid the ultimate price. Since his own wife's death, his youngest daughter Colark had worried about him, finally talking him into moving in with her family. She was probably pacing the floor right now wondering what was keeping him out at such a late hour. The one good thing about retirement was he had plenty of time to spoil his grandchildren.

Suddenly a strong hand grabbed Nereus and pulled him into an alley.

"Give us your money!" commanded a rough-looking man, waving a knife.

Indignity filled the elderly officer as he studied the two hoodlums confronting him. This was the capital of the nation he had shed his own blood for. "Do you know who I am?"

"Who cares? Your money is the same as any other," smirked the second mugger.

"I am General Nereus."

"And I'm the Emperor," laughed the first thief, pushing the tip of his knife against the old man's stomach. "Now pass over your belongings before I rip them from you."

Angrily, Nereus grabbed the robber's wrist, forcing the blade downward while bringing up his knee into his opponent's groin. As the bandit doubled over in pain, the second man hit Nereus from behind with a club, sending the older man tumbling to the ground. Recovered, the first mugger kicked the elderly man viciously in the side. Nereus groaned, his shattered pride hurting worse than his ribs. As other kicks pelted his body, he stared at the dead end of the alley. Perhaps it was a hallucination caused from pain, but he saw an apparition emerge from the ground.

As one robber reached down to search their victim's pockets, a stranger appeared from behind, bringing his hands, combined into a powerful fist, down on the robber's bare neck. The bandit went down. Reacting fast, the stranger kicked the club from the second mugger. Angrily the robber charged the stranger, catching him in the middle. The two men tussled on the ground, rolling back and forth. Nereus regained his feet, only to be grabbed by the second bandit. He jabbed his elbow into the man's soft stomach, gaining release. Enraged the robber threateningly waved a knife in his right hand.

The man who had appeared from the ground managed in the scuffle to grab the stout stick he had earlier kicked from his opponent's hand. Pushing away from his attacker, he stood and brought the weapon crashing against the enemy's knee. The robber dropped to the ground in a scream of pain. Spinning quickly, the stranger hit the second bandit in the back of the head. The hoodlum fell, unconscious.

Nereus and the rescuer dashed out of the alley, not stopping until several blocks away. They collapsed on a bench in front of a noisy tavern. Breathing hard, the general studied his savior. The stranger was a foreigner dressed in a worn coat and dirty boots.

"I thank you for the help," said the elderly man after regaining his breath. "But who do I owe my gratitude to?"

The stranger offered a handshake in greeting. "Name's Matthan. I happened to be passing through and saw those hoodlums kicking you. I couldn't stand by and just watch."

"You fight well. A soldier?"

"Yes, spent a year on the front."

"And likes to travel in sewers." Surprise flashed across Matthan's face. "I saw you come out of the ground and noticed your shoes are covered in muck. I guess there is a sewer grate at the end of the alley."

Matthan laughed. "You don't miss much, do you? You seem a soldier yourself."

"I am—or was. I'm retired now. My reflexes have slowed or I could have taken those robbers myself. So what has you stomping around sewers this late at night?"

The young man hesitated, unsure how to proceed. "I was on an errand for my supervisor."

"And who is your supervisor?"

It was a long moment before Matthan answered. "I serve Yahweh and believe in helping those in need. I am proud to be called a Tnias."

"You realize I am your enemy, Matthan? Telling me this could lead to your death."

"I know, but I believe in doing good to those who persecute me and my people. Would you have preferred me—your enemy—to walk by or stop to help?"

Nereus felt uncomfortable under this young man's bold challenge. He had ordered many Tnias to their deaths but knew he could not turn in this man who had risked his own life to save him. "I appreciate the help but do not understand why you would risk your life for me."

"That is because you live in a greedy world looking out for only what it can gain. I represent an untainted God of Love. To understand him, you must turn away from selfish desires and look with spiritual eyes. He is waiting for you, always has been. It was not by chance that my path crossed yours tonight."

Nereus stood, uncertain, haunted by the words he had spoken to General Herron earlier. *Do what I always do—pretend I have seen nothing extraordinary. Continue to fight under the banner of a god who gives death but cannot control the elements.*

Had Yahweh really sent this young soldier to help him? Why would this god care for an old, discarded general who killed his people? One thing Nereus did understand—this would probably be his first and last opportunity to talk openly with a Tnias. If he walked away, his questions would never be answered.

"This is not the best place to talk. Let's go to my home and discuss this more."

"I would enjoy that."

~~~~~~~~~

Julie entered the small chamber that served as an infirmary. Minira, Terra, and youth surrounded Roshell's bed. Violet, feeling awkward and shy, held out a vase filled with colorful paper flowers made by the children for the bedridden hero.

"These are given to represent life which..." For a moment the young teen's memory faltered, and she glanced at Terra for help. The older adolescent mouthed the words. Violet continued, "...which comes from planting seeds. May you bear a thousand fruit."

"It's also a remembrance of spring coming," added Lonees, determined to get a word in.

Sitting up on the rough straw mattress, bandaged Roshell smiled her thanks. "The spring and its warmth I eagerly look forward to. Minira, could you place this lovely present on the crate? Perfect."

As the youths left, Julie walked to the bed. "It's good to see you awake again."

"I feel like a pin cushion," grumbled Roshell. "I think my seamstress doctor mistook me for a worn garment. I have more stitches than my own coat."

"And blessed to still be alive," said Danielle, entering with a tray of food. "No infection has set in. In a few more weeks you should be as good as new."

"If I survive being captive to a bed that long."

"Better than a prisoner of the Reforcers," retorted the very pregnant woman, sitting the tray on a rickety table near her patient.

Julie laughed. "Roshell, you are forgetting two well-known rules—never argue with someone bringing you food, and never, ever disagree with an expectant mother."

"And who wrote those rules? I don't remember them in Yahweh's Word," countered the invalid.

Matthan burst into the room, face jubilant. Danielle kissed him deeply, relieved, for he had been missing all night. Though she kept her fears to herself, every time her husband went above ground, she worried he would be caught.

"Ahem." Roshell cleared her throat. "There are other people in this room— including someone hungry and sick."

"The most wonderful and miraculous thing happened!" Matthan's eyes shined. "Yahweh guided me to exit the sewers in an alley where a man was being robbed. I was able to help him, and he wanted to know why I did so. I shared my faith. He invited me to his house where we talked into sunrise about Yahweh. He now serves a new master!"

Matthan's excitement spread. Danielle gave her husband a tight hug. Julie grinned. Roshell, who forgot the aches of her body for a brief moment, gave a nod of approval.

The elated Salt continued, "He is a retired soldier named Jerron who lives with his married daughter. He wants me to meet her and her husband. In a few days I'm to go back and hopefully speak with the entire family."

At the mention of the man's name, Julie's lips became a firm line. "Was his full name General Jerron Nereus?"

Mathan faced her. "I didn't ask him what military position he held."

"What did he look like?"

"Tall, broad shouldered, slightly scooped, gray hair, uses a cane."

"Did he have a small scar on his left cheek on the jaw line?"

"Yes. Yes, he did. I realized from his conversation that he was an officer. A general! I should have guessed. Do you know him, Julie?"

The former Red soldier weakly sat in a wobbly chair. "Who does not? He just happens to be the most respected man in the entire Empire, right beside Prince Rufus."

Roshell asked, "Was his conversion genuine or could he be sitting you up?"

Matthan took his time before answering. "Real. I saw a hungry for knowledge, a haunting pain in his soul. He regrets many of his past decisions but saw no way to choose differently at the time. When I left, he was a changed man—hopeful, ablaze with ideas. For a while I will be the only one to have contact with him and his family until they have pass the tests." Danielle squeezed her husband's hand proudly.

Roshell turned to Julie and said, "Since we're discussing who's who, what's the man's name who had you mesmerized during the raid?"

A shadow crossed Julie's face. "I don't know who you are speaking about."

"Don't give me any of that selected memory stuff. You couldn't tear your eyes away from his handsome face on the other side of the fence. Your hesitation cost Kentim his life."

Staring at a rock wall, Julie spoke in a flat voice. "His name is Urbane Herron. He was once my lover."

Danielle and Matthan gasped in shock, both remembering being held captive at the Telumzan border. Shivering, Danielle again felt the cold knife pressed against her throat and the major's deep voice calmly ordering the execution of twenty men, women, and children including her father and brother.

"Urbane Herron?" Roshell searched her memory. "Do you realize he is now a general—the same one who chased me in the temple? He is the one the Emperor has charged with eradicating all Tnias in the entire Empire. You sure know how to pick them, Julie."

"That is enough, Roshell," commanded Matthan in a dangerous tone. He knelt beside Julie who had buried her face in her hands. Silently Danielle watched, appalled at the thought of Julie coupled with that horrific monster.

Face hidden by long, black hair, Julie said, "He was a sergeant—my sergeant. We had the same goals, the same dreams. We were a perfect match. As he was promoted, so was I. Together we fought against…" Her voice broke. "There is so much blood on both our hands…so much." With the collapse of the emotionless dam that she had hid behind, uncontrollable sobs of grief and regret burst forth.

Matthan held the weeping princess. "It's in the past. Remember, Julie, you're not the same person. You have been forgiven by Yahweh himself. You are not responsible for what Herron does now."

"He's right, Julie," added Danielle, forcing away horrifying memories of the past. She knelt beside her husband, taking the princess's hands into her own. "Don't forget Agape. You saw Yahweh with your own eyes. How many of us dream of such a thing? There is no blood on your hands anymore."

"Yes, there is!" Julie looked up. "During the raid I killed soldiers—my peers. They are what I once was. Whenever I take a life, I deny that person the opportunity of redemption."

"They're the enemy," spoke Roshell from the bed. "They died so innocent people could live."

"The innocent would be in Agape right now walking on streets of gold. The men I killed burn in the Great Abyss. Never will they have the chance to know peace. I have sentenced them to a fate far worse than death. Never, never again, will I take the life of another, even if guiltless must die."

Matthan gently said, "If you feel that is Yahweh's commandment for you, then you must obey. I will support you."

Julie sighed, her tense body relaxing. The heavy weight she had carried on her shoulders for days vanished. Deeply she was thankful for her friends' support. But she knew Roshell did not understand. The Ulmjon could not see imperial soldiers as anything but monsters.

~~~~~~~~~

Chatting with Henna, Thasbow excitedly swung a heavy basket filled with food as they walked along a street where dirty snow was shoveled against buildings. Between teenager and mother trotted Henna's two children, Juke and Nadine, equally excited about visiting their cousin's house. The plan was to meet Rufus, who had been repairing furniture all morning there. Thasbow enjoyed getting away from stuffy high society and spending time with Henna and her many down-to-earth relatives.

Reaching the four-story apartment, Henna knocked on her cousin's door. A cheerfully, heavyset woman opened it. She hugged both Henna and Thasbow then pinched the cheeks of the two children. Andean introduced her children and husband. Nasben grunted a hello as he held up one end of a couch. Surrounded by tools, Rufus's lower body was sticking out from under the tilted piece of furniture. Juke and Nadine dashed off to play with younger cousins. Rufus emerged from under the couch, kissed his wife, and hugged his sister. As Henna and Andean headed into the kitchen to prepare the meal, Rufus motioned for Thasbow to follow him down a long hallway.

The brother asked, "Do you remember our conversation about Yahweh? That he is real and hates his enemies?"

"Yes," answered the teenager cautiously. She enjoyed spending time with him but felt uncomfortable when he spoke heretical.

"I was wrong about several things. Yahweh is real, but he is not distant nor feels hatred towards us. I have something I want to show you, something wonderful which your eyes will not believe."

Worried, Thasbow studied her brother. There was a twinkle in his eyes, and a mischievous smile on his lips. "What is it?"

"It is better for you to see than for me to explain."

With that he opened the door to a room serving as a cozy den. Family heirlooms, ancient furniture, and portraits filled the room. There were two tall windows with thick, heavy curtains; one was pulled back, sending a brilliant ray of light into the darken den. Within the sunbeam stood a slim, black-haired woman, dressed in a simple tan cloak, seemingly golden from the light. Thasbow caught her breath in shock. She took several hesitant steps into the room then glanced back at her brother. He entered, shutting the door behind him.

"It's really her," he said. "Go ahead, she will not bite."

The adolescent made it half away across the room, staring, fascinated by the woman who looked identical to her sister. The sunbeam created a halo of light round the stranger.

The woman spoke warmly. "Hello, Thasbow. It has been a long time. I am sorry I was not much a sister before."

Thasbow trembled. "Junia is dead. I was there, on the second floor balcony, watching."

"Yahweh is the God of Miracles, Thasbow."

"Are you…I mean you must be a goddess then."

The stranger stepped forward out of the sunbeam. "No. I am mortal, just like you, and will die again. Yahweh sent me to share his love to Gog—to you."

She held out her arms, and without further hesitation, Thasbow ran to her. For a long time the two siblings held each other tightly. With one hand, Julie gently ran her fingers through her sister's long, black hair—the same shade as her own. Her heart was overwhelmed by deep feelings too powerful to speak. How could she have scorn Thasbow and her other younger siblings? With that one hug, an unbreakable bond formed between the sisters.

The princesses sat on a couch, grinning Rufus in a chair nearby.

"Thasbow, everything I stood for before I was brought in front of our father was wrong. I was deceived, as you are. Zuzumza is a creation of Yahweh who chose hatred and jealousy over love. And one day he will pay dearly for all the pain he has inflicted."

"Whatever you believe, Junia, so will I," proclaimed Thasbow.

"Think carefully. Following Yahweh is the most serious decision you will ever make in your entire life—even more important than whom you will marry. It may cost you your friends, possessions, and even your life."

The young princess thought about superficial palace life, false friends, and her absent mother. Her life had been empty before Rufus had taken her under his wings. She glanced towards her brother. He gave her a reassuring nod. Obviously he now followed Yahweh along with Henna. Probably Andean and her husband did too. Thasbow remembered the woman in the Underground killed directly in front of her. She had long pondered why the woman had been willing to die for a distant god. Now she began to understand.

Taking a deep breath, the teenage replied, "Never have I seen anything good come from gods or goddesses before. Yet Yahweh has sent both of you to me. He really cares. I will follow him until death."

"Believing in his existence is the first step. Next you must ask forgiveness for the wrongs you have done. He will forgive you and help you overcome the bonds of sin."

Thasbow thought of the pain she had caused her mother. "That is a hard thing you ask, but I will do it."

She knelt on the floor with her sister and prayed. Unsure how to talk to the deity her royal family had long mocked, words floundered from her lips. She remembered the scornful words she had spoken to her mother the last time they had been together. Slowly she began telling Yahweh about her troubles. An unnatural peace filled her, and she relaxed, revealing the raw wounds of her heart to him. Healing began.

When she finally stood, Thasbow said, "I need to write a letter to my mom."

Chapter Twenty-six

Urbane briskly walked along the catwalk between towers of Blackwall Palace. The dizzying height did not bother him, nor did he pause to admire the magnificent view offered of the entire valley with its bustling capital city, outlying towns, snow covered pastures, and mountain slopes clad in trees simmering like diamonds from the sun reflecting off their ice encrusted limbs. A poet could write for a lifetime and still not capture the full beauty of Gog Valley. Urbane only focused on the Emperor strolling beside Lady Cassandra. The general fell into step behind the royal couple, waiting to be acknowledged.

The trio passed sentinels keeping watch at each tower. Dressed in thick furs, Lady Cassandra chatted about the kingdom, dropping hints that an heir was needed to continue Phlegon's exploits. The Emperor absently listened, finally pausing in a dark shadow cast by the highest tower. He dismissed his concubine, saying he had business to discuss with his general. As Lady Cassandra walked away, she glared at Urbane, envious that Phlegon gave more attention to his officers than to her.

The Emperor studied the city stretched out below while Urbane waited patiently a few steps away. "Thorn is the culture center of my Empire. It was designed to show the world what Gogians could achieve. For centuries visitors from across the world have come here to see the city's architectural feats for themselves. They go home, telling the world the wonders they have witnessed. All of Tanlep thinks of Gog and trembles. What happens here in my capital affects my entire Empire." With piercing eyes, he turned towards Urbane. "So, General Herron, how does my city fare?"

Any other man would have flinch under the Emperor's challenging stare, but Urbane evenly met the monarch's gaze. "The heretical plague grows."

"And why is that? Is not Gog supposed to be free from superstition? If our homeland is infested, how will our provinces prosper?" Phlegon asked in a too calm voice like distance thunder reverberating before a storm.

"We have learned much recently from a spy which infiltrated the network before being discovered. The heretics believe four foreigners arrived here from Shalom. Salts they are called. These radicals stirred up the few remaining Tnias. Many from the slums believe their lies. They have a nest or haven which my men are searching for." Urban omitted the small detail that one of the Salts looked exactly like Phlegon's executed sister.

A frown deepened on the Emperor's face as he listened. "These Salts," he spoke the title like a curse, "must be hunted down and terminated. Their deaths will cause the collapse of the heretics' frail beliefs."

"I have been using all of the Reforcer's resources to fulfill that goal."

"That is not good enough, General. I commission you to use the same tactics that are used in the provinces. No mercy must be given. Use public executions to strike fear into the hearts of the people. Keep cages in Market Square to imprison the defiled. Stake heads on the city walls and streets posts. I will have my scribes create flyers which will be placed across the city, praising those who turn in heretics. We will make heroes of informants. In public I will present them with gold as a reward. Fear and greed will desalt these heretics."

Urbane bowed, pleased with the power granted him. "Your command will be done, My Lord."

~~~~~~~~~

An elderly man loosely held the reins of a horse pulling a cart through melting snow, a reminder of the coming spring. The man kept his eyes downward to avoid the faces of beheaded Tnias nailed to trees along the street. He had made the mistake of looking once. Now forever etched in his memory was the lifeless eyes staring at him of his best friend Eleazar, leader of the Remnant. Joatham had almost retched, but he could not spare even that reaction. It would have raised questions of anyone observing him. For three days he had refused to leave his home. It had taken all of Joatham's meager courage, a sober visit from Matthan, and a heartfelt prayer with Yahweh before he went back to work at his watch shop.

Too much needed to be done for him to hide. As raids increased, survivors fled to the Haven, afraid to return to their homes where they might be arrested. Others came because terror kept them from facing the horrors of the upper world. Rocky chambers and tunnels quickly filled until there was not enough food or living space for the refugees. Charities were hampered, leaving street kids sleeping in alleys and elderly shut-ins hungry. Along with the Salts, Eleazar had preached to the people that they must keep laboring above ground to carry Yahweh's word to the hopeless. But Eleazar was dead now.

All of the profit from the Greencliff's business went to buying food for those in the Haven. Still it was not enough by a long shot. Onias came to his parents one day and declared that the money saved to pay for the rest of his education would be better used to feed the hungry. That was the day that Onias truly understood the loss of giving up everything—including dreams—to help others. Both Sandra and Onias planned not to attend the university the next term. Instead, Onias followed in the footsteps of Eleazar, determined to become an ecclesiastic. Sandra and Onias continued to visit with people in the lower-class sections of town, helping where they could. Josias' health kept her home, but she mended clothes and cooked food that was delivered to others in need.

Sunshine's hooves sunk deep into slush. Ears cocked, she eagerly listened to birdcalls and sniffed the scent of fresh dirt from someone tilling a flowerbed, grateful to be out of the dark tunnels. She preferred galloping cross endless green plains with Matthan, but she liked Joatham as well. He always had a carrot or apple for her.

Reaching a large furniture factory, the elderly man directed Sunshine through a wide doorway. A foreman ordered several workers to unload two huge clocks carefully padded in the back of the wagon then directed Joatham towards a flight of stairs. The elderly Tnias labored up the steep stairwell and entered a small office. The manager greeted him pleasantly, placed a jingling bag of coins in Joatham's hand, and invited him to rest by a small wood heater. Soon the two men were swapping stories about family life as if old friends though neither had never met before.

Suddenly the foreman burst into the room. "Sir, Reforcers are here!"

Joatham paled. A shadow of fear also crossed the factory manager's face, but it was quickly replaced with iron determination. Followed by his foreman, the supervisor marched down the stairs. Fear immobilized Joatham. Hiding among dark shadows, he peered out the office window overlooking the factory floor. He watched as Reforcers lined up workers. Several tried to sneak away through backdoors, only to be led back to the main group with swords pressed against their backs. Distrusting the dank smell of the armed men, Sunshine neighed and pawed the ground.

The factory manager marched up to the Reforcers and angrily demanded, "Who is responsible for this outrage?"

"I am," spoke a captain. "It has come to our attention that several heretics are employed at this workshop."

"Your search is stopping production and costing me money, Captain. And I will have to train replacements for any you kill. The rest will be so upset by what they see that quality will decline."

"They won't be killed here. Don't worry…unless you happen to be a Tnias."

"Be careful what you say," spoke up the foreman boldly. "You speak to Prince Rufus."

Astonishment replaced scorn on the captain's face. Like many young officers, he was deeply influenced by stories of Major Rufus and General Nereus, but he still had a job to do. He continued in a respectful tone, "What is more important, Your Highness? Letting heretics ran rampant or losing a little money?"

"I assure you, Captain, that I do not hire traitors. These are loyal people who keep this country's economy blooming. They buy products and food for their families."

"I will be the judge of their loyalty." The captain questioned the first employee in line. "Who do you serve?"

The gray-bearded man stared at the sword in the captain's hand. The worker had been one of several caught attempting to escape through the backdoor. In a trembling voice, the elderly man responded, "I worship El Olam."

Captain Patrobas frowned. "I have not heard of that god."

"I am a foreigner, sir, from across the great sea."

The officer continued down the line, stopping in front of a middle-aged woman with tan skin and slanted eyes. "Who is your god?"

"Sir, it is El Shaddai." The robust lady boldly met the captain's glaze. "I am also a foreigner. The first man you spoke with is my father."

Patrobas moved to the next person in line.

Without waiting to be asked, the dark-skin man said, "I serve Rapha, God of Healing."

The captain's frown deepened as he glanced over the workers. "It seems, Prince Rufus, that almost all your workers are foreigners who worship strange gods."

"It is hard for them to get jobs in Thorn. I find them excellent workers who go the extra mile for me from gratitude. And who work for cheap wages. Can there be a better arrangement, Captain?"

The officer frowned but continued questioning every employee without a single one answering to Yahweh.

"Now can my workers get back to work before I lose a full day's schedule?"

Captain Patrobas glared at the prince, suspicious that something was going on but unable to prove anything. "I have just one more question. Who, sir, do you serve?"

The foreman opened his mouth to complain that the captain was in no position to question a prince, but Rufus held up a hand for silence. Turning to Patrobas, he answered with full dignity, "The god I worship is named Adonai. Now I ask that you and your men leave."

The Reforcers reluctantly filed out of the building while workers remained in place, broad smiles spreading across worn faces. When it was certain that the religious police were gone, several burst into laughter.

Warmly Rufus addressed his employees. "Good job. You have lived through your first raid, but do not become too relaxed. There are couches waiting for coverings and desks needing varnishing."

As cheerful workers returned to their tasks, Joatham met Rufus at the bottom of the stairs. "Sir, I also serve Yahweh. I realize your entire factory must be filled with Tnias, but how did they manage not to deny Him and still live?"

The prince scrutinized the elderly man before answering. "My sister knows many names for Yahweh in a language native to Shalom."

"Your sister is wise."

"She is unlike any other."

~~~~~~~~~

Clothes spattered from paint, Julie exhaustingly walked through the lantern-lit tunnels. She had wanted to sleep in this morning, but several teenagers were counting on her. A few weeks ago, Violet and two others had asked to become her apprentices. Each day, she taught them techniques which they practiced on parchment while she worked on the murals. Last night she had visited with her brother and his family, staying up extremely late. Now she wanted to skip the nightly worship service but needed to talk with the elders about a new idea. During last night's conversation, someone's question led her to name all the titles she knew referring to Yahweh. Rufus came up with the idea of using the foreign words as a defense tactic against Reforcers. With so many local and foreign gods, it might work if the police had no proof that the interviewee was a Tnias.

Entering the Great Chamber, she sighed. It was packed as usual and would be difficult to find those she needed to talk with. A better idea would be to speak with Matthan or Roshell, asking one of them to announce a meeting tomorrow for the elders. And she could get some needed sleep. Winding through the throng, she bumped into Danielle who smiled a greeting though her eyes revealed deep tiredness. Since Doctor Ijohn's death, Danielle was often called to tend the sick. In crowded chambers, so near sewage, plagues regularly threatened to break out. Neither did it help that she was pass eight months in her pregnancy.

"Have you seen Matthan?"

"He is supposed to be here soon. He's bringing someone new down." Danielle glanced around anxiously, searching faces. Spotting Roshell chatting with a small group, the two Salts walked over.

Joatham greeted the two women. "I like to introduce you to Mahn, his wife Annie, and their two children. Mahn saved an entire factory of Tnias this morning."

Julie turned pale, recognizing her brother's family. Often Tnias used aliases as protection in case someone was caught and tortured. As Julie shook hands with Rufus, she shook her head indicated a silent *no* to his unspoken question. It was dangerous for her brother's identity to be revealed even in the Haven. Phlegon would stop at nothing to find and destroy his siblings if rumor reached him of their traitorous beliefs. Henna also looked questioning at Julie but pretended to have never met the Salt before. Young Juke and Nadine hugged Julie tightly around the legs, but Henna managed to distract them before they could address their aunt.

Joatham restarted a detail narration of the day's events. Thanks to Joatham, the idea to use different names for Yahweh was already circulating through the crowds in the vast chamber. Before the story was finished, Matthan showed up with three guests—an elderly father, his daughter, and her husband. As Joatham introduced them, the father's face turned pale and his eyes widened when he spotted Julie.

Rufus cut Matthan's introductions off before astonished Nereus could speak. "Is there a private place we could speak?"

"Yes, of course," answered Matthan.

He led the large group to a chamber reserved for meetings with the Elders. They settling on wooden chairs and crates scattered throughout the room. Henna started a polite conversation with Colark and her husband. Nereus remained standing, tightly gripping the back of a chair, unable to tear his eyes away from Julie.

Smiling warmly, Julie spoke to the general. "It's good to see you again."

Trying to appear calm, Nereus glanced towards Rufus. "It is not a big surprise to see you here, but could you explain how your sister is alive when I saw her die?"

"Sister?" exclaimed Roshell and Joatham at the same time, realizing something secretive existed between all the newcomers and Julie. Matthan and Danielle glanced at each other.

Rufus held his sister's eyes for a moment before answering. She gave a brief nod, giving him permission to speak her secret. "Junia died and spent five years in Agape. Then Yahweh sent her back to Gog as his messenger."

"After she died? How is that possible?" Nereus looked between the two siblings in disbelief.

Julie answered, "Yahweh works in mysterious and powerful ways, General. You being here is a miracle none of us could have foreseen."

The retired commander attempted a smile. "Only a powerful god could bring an enemy prince, princess, and general into fellowship with his people. I'm glad I am not fighting against him anymore. I would not trade places with the Emperor for all the gold in the world."

Both Roshell and Joatham wore flabbergasted expresses. Matthan grinned, unable to determine if the two were more shocked by Julie's royal bloodline or that two of the most influential men of the Empire stood before them as comrades. Danielle chuckled, holding her bulging stomach, forgetting her weariness. Rufus, Henna, Colark, and her husband joined the jovial mood. Juke and Nadine looked around in confusion, not understanding what the grownups found funny. Julie smiled, happy to have her friends and family united in fellowship.

When the group broke up to attend the service, Roshell pulled Julie aside. "So how long has Matthan and Danielle known you're royalty?"

Cautiously the Salt answered, "They figured it out about the time I was executed."

"And when were you planning to tell me? I thought we were in this together."

"I was waiting until you were capable of handling the information."

"What is that supposed to mean?"

"That you are prejudice against the upper class and soldiers of Gog. I'm in both categories along with my brother. You were barely able to accept the knowledge I was in the Red Army. Would you have come north with me if you knew I was the sister of the Emperor?"

Feeling betrayed, Roshell moved away several paces, keeping her back to Julie. It was difficult to control her anger, but she attempted to be honest with herself. "I would have turned around immediately. But why did you not tell me here?" Roshell faced her friend. "Over the last months we have worked closely together, sharing the same dangers, same toils. Why did you still keep your identity a secret?"

"Maybe I should have told you sooner. Truthfully, I do not like thinking about my past, yet I cannot escape from it. Roshell, you have never killed the innocent. You don't know what it is like to bear that weight, what it costs me every day. It is far easier to keep your conscience dead than face the guilt. To admit being wrong after hurting so many lives is a ticket to insanity. I can never do enough to make up for the evils I have done, never."

Seeing her friend's distress, Roshell forgot her own anger. "Hey, General Nereus and Prince Rufus are now soldiers for Yahweh. Who would have predicted that? It's a brilliant strategy."

Julie took a deep breath, forcing herself to relax. "Like me, they will be haunted by what they have seen and done until death. In Agape, peace and forgetfulness awaits them. I ate, laughed, even danced with the same ones I killed. There is peace here also. I know that. Yahweh has forgiven me, forgiven us."

"Look, Julie—or Junia, there is no blame in Agape, neither should there be here. Yahweh has pardoned you of all crimes. No one has the right to point accusing fingers at you. Not me, not anyone. That is one of the things Yahweh has taught me by sending me to the place I hate most. Neither will I hold anything against Prince Rufus or General Nereus. If your Urbane or the Emperor suddenly did an about face, I would accept them also—though it would take a lot to convince me that they were genuine."

Julie smiled at Roshell's frail attempt at humor. The rift between the two women now healed.

Chapter Twenty-seven

The fragrant smell of blooming trees and flowers filled the air. Spring was upon the world in full force. Princess Thasbow paused under the canopy of blossoming cherry trees growing on each side of Market Lane. Deeply she breathed in the rich smell, thankful anew the life Yahweh had given her.

"Come on, we do not have all day," Lady Mahan grumbled. "Lady Cassandra expects us at noon at Draken Café—not twilight."

The royal teenager pushed away rising resentment, reminding herself she was now a spy. Her whole life she had never done anything of importance—until now. Much information could be gleamed from the gossip of Cassandra and her associates. Several times Thasbow had been able to pass on information to Rufus and the Salts about upcoming Reforcer raids and plots. Lives had been saved because of her—Princess Thasbow. For the first time in her life she felt worthy of the royal title.

Spring brought life to Market Square. No longer was it a huge open field of snow-covered cobblestone. Everywhere were booths, entertainers, wagons serving as mobile businesses, tempting food odors, and crowds surrounded by more crowds. Through the commercial hub cut Market Lane, the heavy trafficked road bordered by flowering cherry trees. Located in the enormous square were also two small parks where people rested on benches and children romped on playgrounds.

Today their destination was Draken Café that bordered one of the parks and offered an excellent view of the entire square from its top two floors. The richest customers paid an extra price to eat under shaded canopies on the roof. As the two women neared the restaurant, both noticed a wooden guillotine that had recently been constructed. A chill went through the teenager's body despite the noon heat. A brightly painted sign announced times public executions would be held. Bothered by the sinister sign, Lady Mahan shivered and hurried pass. Reaching the fancy café, a waiter led them up to the rooftop where Lady Cassandra and Lady Richmon were already seated. The high, unobstructed view was worth the extra price.

"There you are," smiled the royal concubine, a little too easily. "I thought maybe a handsome Reforcer had caught your eye, and you forgot all about our lunch engagement."

"How could we forget?" apologized Lady Mahan. "It is always the greatest honor to dine with you."

Forgiving their tardiness, Lady Cassandra signaled the waiter to take their orders. As Thasbow munched on exquisite stuffed mushrooms, she listened for information relating to Tnias, but conversation fluttered from who was sleeping with whom to the rising cost of fur. When the main dishes arrived, the women sipped wine as they ate, continuing the chitchatting. Just as they started on rich desserts, a loud blast of a trumpet caught the ladies' attention. Glancing towards Market Square, they saw a large crowd gathering around the guillotine. Several Reforcers stood on the high platform while others led several prisoners from a large wagon through the throng. Pale, Thasbow felt as if her heart had frozen forever in the middle of one long, horrified beat.

"Ah," exclaimed Lady Cassandra, "I was hoping we would get a chance to witness an execution. That was why I picked Draken Café."

"How dreadful," mumbled Lady Richmon. "I think I just lost my appetite."

"If it bothers you, just look the other way," reprimanded the royal concubine. "I am here to prove to myself that a lady can handle the sight of blood, just like a man."

Lady Mahan nervously glanced towards the others. She had no desire to see an execution but neither did she want to offend Cassandra. "It should be…interesting."

"I'm certain it will be a sight you will never forget," smiled Cassandra.

Thasbow remained silent, afraid her voice would give away her aghast emotions. Unable to tear her eyes away from the guillotine, she watched as a prisoner was directed to kneel and place her head through a slot. A sharp blade rose high in the air, reflecting sunlight. It hovered for a moment then fell, its sickening thump piercing Thasbow to her very marrow. Spectators cheered. The red-slick blade climbed again to its high perch, waiting hungrily.

"Having trouble eating, Princess?" asked Cassandra in a honeyed voice. Though her face was all smiles, her eyes studied Thasbow like a hungry cat.

The teenager realized with a shock that her hand holding her spoon was shaking. Looking towards cool Cassandra, Thasbow understood that a dangerous trap had been laid just for her. Maybe there had been too many Tnias avoiding raids, perhaps Thasbow had let something slip in an earlier conversation, leading Cassandra to suspected Thasbow of being an informant. Now one wrong word or gesture would mean the princess would soon become another victim for the insatiable blade.

Trying to appear natural, the maiden forced calmness into her voice, "This is only the third time I have seen someone die. If you remember, the first two times left me very upset. I was very young when I witnessed my sister's death and suffered from nightmares for years afterwards. I believe public executions traumatize children and should be banned."

"I agree." Lady Mahan glanced at Cassandra, hoping no offense was taken.

"There is no need for these barbaric practices here in our capital," said Lina Richmon, going along with the debate, despite the pallor of her face. "It reveals that our proud nation has become…" The woman's voice was drowned out by an agonizing scream. The sound ended with a loud thud from the guillotine's blade.

Hoots and cheers arose from the square. Lady Richmon covered her mouth with a laced napkin. Lady Mahan stared at her uneaten pie. Thasbow felt bile in her throat. With tremendous effort she overcame the urge to vomit. Cassandra took a bite of rich chocolate cake, relishing the taste.

A third Tnias praised Yahweh even as the red blade fell. The fourth preached to the gathered throng, demanding for them to repent from evil. The crowd jeered and laughed at him. Next the guards selected from the wagon a woman holding the hands of two young children. She did not wait for the guards to drag her, but calmly climbed down then turned to help her children to the ground. The frightened children huddled against her legs as they walked between guards along the cleared path to the guillotine. The executioner indicated for the woman to lie on the bloody bench. The lady stepped close to the black-hooded man, speaking words only he could hear. Reluctantly the rugged man nodded, giving permission for the children to die first. The mother bent down, whispering to each child as she hugged them. If there were tears in her eyes, Thasbow was too far away to see. Strangely, the crowd became deathly quiet. Two guards gently pulled the children away from their mother, placing both on the bench with their heads through the large notch.

Thasbow could take no more. "I apologize, Lady Cassandra, but I have had enough nightmares already."

Without a further word, she rose from the table. She had only gone three steps before Lady Richmon followed. Lady Mahan looked between the departed women and the smirking Cassandra, finally following Thasbow. All three headed down the carpeted stairs, the echoing *thud* of the blade ringing in their ears.

Reaching the first floor, Lady Richmon spoke, "My niece is about those kids age. I cannot believe that Cassandra. You would think she had Erastus's blood in her."

"That is her plan," said Thasbow, "if she marries the Emperor."

Lady Mahan, white as a ghost, said, "I hope she was not offended by us leaving. I think we should wait for her on the first floor."

The three women found an empty table. Lina Richmon and Mahan attempted to keep a light conversation going, but Thasbow slipped into a solitary shell, wrapping iron bonds around her wild emotions. While Lina ordered wine to calm her nerves, Thasbow excused herself, saying she had shopping to do. Exiting the restaurant, she headed in the opposite direction of the guillotine, fleeing from the rowdy yells of the crowd as another preaching Tnias offered exciting entertainment.

As she wound through the quiet booths, the teenager noticed many people were deliberately not looking towards the beheading. They studied the ground as they hurried along or stared too hard at merchandise. *Thump.* A clerk and customer jumped, the seller absently repeating his last phrase for the third time. A mother covered the eyes of a young child as she hurried the toddler away from the square.

Strange, the princess thought, *how just a few hundred feet away from a mob screaming for blood, the people are subdued.* Deep in thought, Thasbow came to the edge of the square where she was violently jolted back to the present. She believed she had just witnessed the greatest horror imaginable. She was wrong.

A crowd was gathered around a large iron cage. Inside huddled five people, filthy from garbage the throng had pelted them with. A young child in the cage yelped as a fruit hit his arm then hungrily picked up the soggy grape. He took a big bite of the rotten food, only to immediately spit it out. Watchers giggled. The child began crying as two youths threw nuts against his bruised skin. A thin female prisoner wrapped her body around the youngster in an attempt to protect him. There was no place to hide as all the walls of the stockade consisted of iron bars. Another captive lay on the dirty floor, not moving, flies feasting on rubbish covering him. An exhausted teenager swatted at the insects, determined to protect her father. The fifth Tnias sat motionless in the middle of the cage, his skin open and raw from a recent beating. Bored, the youths yelled vulgar remarks, making the exhausted maiden blush. The mother tightly held her child, refusing to show emotion to the specters.

Shocked, the princess watched in anger. The captive teenager turned her teary face towards Thasbow. Silently they studied each other. They were the same age, had the same hair color—perhaps both shared the same dreams of romance, children, a golden future. A tomato flew through the air, snapping the teen's face sideways.

"Stop it!" Thasbow yelled at the man who had thrown the vegetable. "They are people!"

"They're animals," snorted the man. "Maybe you're one of them, too."

Heart pounding, the princess held the harsh man's gaze. Suddenly she turned and ran, not stopping until she was several blocks away. No one pursued her. In an alley, she pressed her wet cheek against the cold brick wall, needing the support of something solid. Why did Yahweh not save his people? Why did he let them suffer?

242

Thasbow's frail faith melted like butter on a summer day. The world was just one huge madden cesspool of torture and hatred. How could a god of love be real? The teenager thought of the two people she did believe in—Junia and Rufus. They had experienced cataclysms yet still believed in one All Powerful God. How?

She attempted a prayer. "Yahweh, I do not understand anything. Why do you not stop what is happening?"

A silent voice whispered, *It starts with one tiny seed.*

Startled, the teenager looked around, but she was alone in the alley. Was she hearing things?

Faith of a tiny seed can move mountains. The words formed in her mind as clearly as if someone was standing right beside her, talking.

Deciding she had definitely crossed over into insanity, Thasbow challenged the invisible speaker, "A seed cannot save those Tnias in the cage or bring back those killed."

An unprovoked image filled Thasbow's mind, one she had never seen before. A forest somehow inside a vast building. Incredible vibrant music. Jubilant people twirled and danced to the rhythm, laughing. Three of the faces Thasbow recognized. It was the mother and her two children killed at the guillotine. While the young children played a game, the mother danced with a broad-shoulder man. Without being told, Thasbow knew it was the woman's husband.

The princess had never personally experience anything supernatural before beyond seeing her dead sister alive, yet somehow she knew the vision revealed a glimpse of the City of Yahweh. "That's them, the family I saw die. They are happy now. But what about those Tnias in the cage?"

Start with one seed. The words echoed then faded.

"What seed?" There was only silence. "Hey, do not stop talking now. What can be done? Hey!" Realizing she would receive no answer, Thasbow felt a bit foolish talking to thin air. Did things like this happen often when dealing with Yahweh? Having nothing else to do, she attempted to figure out the riddle. "Seed means faith, somehow. Does that mean I am supposed to have faith? Faith that they will be rescued? Or that I am supposed to rescue them myself? What do you mean?"

The only sound in the quiet alley was a rat scrambling through garbage. A cat pounced from shadows, barely missing the rodent. Stalker and prey disappeared behind rubbish cans. The princess grimaced and quickly hurried out of the alley. Uncertain what to do, she aimlessly wandered through businesses, unable to shake the image of the filthy teenage girl looking at her with beseeching eyes. But what could she—a palace bred noble—do? Attend parties, scalp information from gossipers, parade the right outfits and words to charade as a princess in a world she had long despised. That would not save the lives of the Tnias prisoners.

What would Junia do? The maiden asked herself. *Find a way to free them herself, of course.*

Thasbow searched among booths and stores, pretending to be interested in merchandise. When two fruitless hours passed, she lost patience. *Yahweh*, she prayed in anger, *show me what I seek or I will return home.*

Nothing happen. Shoppers walked pass without glancing her direction. To her left were merchant stalls, a blacksmith's shop to the right.

"Make way! Make way!" barked the bored voice of a mounted guard, forcing shoppers to divide into two lanes. Behind him, a large wagon rumbled under the power of two strong horses.

Thasbow sidestepped into the shop to avoid being trampled. As the wagon passed, she noticed large wrapped bundles lying in the back—human shape and bloody. The teenager felt sick at her stomach but could not tear her eyes away.

"Can I help you, miss?" A deep voice made the maiden jump.

"What?"

"Can I do anything for you?" The speaker was a muscular man, biceps huge from decades of hammering molten metals.

Etched into a worktable beyond the large man was the symbol she had been looking for—the Tree of Life. It was a rude sketch of a tree with twelve round fruits hanging from its branches—a fruit for each month of the year the tree bloomed. Julie had told Thasbow that the sacred picture had come to secretly symbolize the Remnant. Most Tnias carefully placed some version of the tree in their homes and businesses as a signal to other believers. It may be painted, drawn, or even be a living miniature tree with artificial fruits tied to its limbs, but the tree had to contain twelve fruits of some sort.

It took Thasbow several seconds before she found her voice. "No…I mean yes. I'm looking for harnesses."

"We have plenty. A few might be fancy enough even for you." The man laughed. Thasbow smiled halfhearted. "Manideck, show this gentlewoman our stock."

Scowling, a tall youth, only a few years older than the princess, waved for her to follow. He weaved among sturdy racks of farming equipment, weapons, and plows. Finally he stopped in front of an assortment of harnesses. Thasbow pretended to study several of them, attempting to work up enough courage to speak.

Abruptly she turned and asked, "Are you Tnias?"

The young man's frown deepened, and anger flashed across his eyes.

"I am not a spy," Thasbow added quickly. "I am one too. I saw the symbol of…"

"Shh. Are you trying to get us both killed?" Manideck glanced towards several customers in the store. Raising his voice an octave, he added, "We have several new ones in the back. Come, I'll let you pick from the best."

Passing the blacksmith hammering on a horseshoe, the youth led Thasbow to a storeroom. "You never, ever mention Tnias, Yahweh, or the Tree of Life in the open. You got that?"

"Yes. This is my first time, you see."

Impatiently Manideck cut her off. "What do you want? I have much to do."

"There is this cage in the square with Tnias inside."

"I know about it."

"Then you will help me free them?"

The young man laughed. "You are indeed naïve. The cages are constantly guarded by Reforcers dressed like commoners. They are on the lookout for people like you who let their emotions give them away."

"Look, I thought all Tnias were kindhearted. How can you not care?"

"Because today one of my best friends and her two children died to entertain blood drinking leeches."

Thasbow inhaled sharply. "I might have seen her today. She was tall, dignified, with dark brown hair."

Manideck's face completely altered. "You watched Dalphine die? Her children…how did they face it?" Through he tried to keep a blank expression, his trembling voice betrayed intense emotions.

The princess was unsure how to speak about the horror. "If it helps, she died well. She asked the executioner to let the children go first. The crowd was deeply moved. It was the only time they became quiet."

The apprentice turned away from Thasbow and pressed his forehead against a wall. It was a long time before he spoke. When he did, his voice was choked with tears. "My family was killed near the beginning of winter. I was there, helping others escape but unable to rescue my own family. I can still hear the screams of my mother as she watched my siblings die in front of her. Dalphine and her husband took me in, gave me a home. Mondren was the one who got me this job. Then there was a raid at their house. Mondren fought bravely but was wounded. The Reforcer vultures never got a chance to torture him. He died peacefully underground. I vowed to myself to protect his family."

His haunted eyes looked at the young woman. "But as you can see, I failed in that, too. I learned about their arrests this morning."

"I am sorry. I watched someone important to me die also. I know this may sound crazy, but I fled from the executions to an alley where a voice talked to me. And I saw a vision of your friend dancing with her husband in Agape. Their children played nearby."

Mondren studied the maiden, probing for truth in her story. "Do you often hear voices?"

"No. This is the first time. But I know it was Yahweh." Thasbow held her head high. "He told me I must start with a seed of faith, so I am going to free those prisoners in the cage, with or without your help."

~~~~~~~~~

Night shadows closed around Manideck like a living blanket. He embraced them, using their darkness as camouflage. He hunkered behind a rubbish can in an alley, waiting for the maiden. There was no doubt in his mind she would come. He had spent most of the day working under the scrutinizing eyes of his boss, Gramercy. Since the news had arrived that Dalphine and her family had been arrested the night before, the blacksmith worried Manideck would do something crazy. In fact, Manideck had immediately attempted to bolt out of the shop in a blind rage, ready to tackle every Reforcer he saw until he freed Dalphine. With arms of steel, Gramercy had grabbed him, refusing to let go until Manideck calmed down. It had been a rough struggle, ending with Manideck breaking down into hot tears— fortunately the shop had not opened yet. He had managed to keep his emotions in check until the unnamed maiden walked in. Manideck had worked diligently in front of the blacksmith but secretly collected tools needed for breaking locks.

At the end of the long day, Gramercy had given the teenager a long stare. Manideck shivered, feeling that his forbidden thoughts could be read.

"Will you be okay?" the large man asked.

Manideck shrugged his shoulders. "Yeah, I'm just going to get a bite of food then find a place to stay." The apartment Dalphine and her family had recently been living in would be watched.

"There's a safe house near here on the corner of West and Sharpton. Code word is *blue sky*." The blacksmith's scarred face softened. "May Yahweh keep you safe, son. I want to see you here bright and early tomorrow."

"Yes, sir." Manideck hurried away before the man guessed his dangerous quest.

The youth was jerked back to the present by the sound of someone stumbling over something in the dark. Manideck stepped out from his hiding place, causing the maiden to jump at his sudden appearance.

"Sorry, didn't mean to frighten you," he whispered.

"I am a little jumpy. That is all." The teenager tried to keep her voice steady, but a slight quiver revealed her fear. She pulled her dark brown cloak tighter around her slender body.

Manideck studied the maiden in the dim light, guessing it was her first dangerous foray. "Look, I don't have anyone waiting for me at home. If I live or die, it doesn't matter. You're highbred and will be missed. Now that I'm committed, I'll go through with this no matter what. But you don't have to."

"Yahweh started me on this quest, and I'm not about to quit now." This time her voice was firm.

"Alright, but the chance is higher that we'll both die than free these prisoners."

"I've seen enough people die while I stood helplessly by. I'm not backing out when I finally have a chance to save somebody." Her eyes resolutely held his.

"Know how you feel." Manideck nodded, pleased to see her determination. "Let's go then." At the mouth of the alley, he paused. "I don't even know your name."

"It is Pr….Thasbow. Just Thasbow." She quickly darted out of the alley before another word could be spoken.

Silently they walked through streets, now deserted in the wee hours before dawn. Reaching Market Square, they paused, studying the endless rows of empty booths. Anywhere among the ghostly stalls and flapping canvas could be lurking Reforcers. Keeping close to the ground, they crept between dark shadows. Too soon they reached the large cage set upon a raised platform. No booths were placed within thirty feet of the stockade—thirty feet of open space were anyone crossing would be visible in the moonlight.

Manideck turned to his companion and whispered, "You keep watch here. When those clouds cover the moon, I'm going to cross the clearing. If you see anything, meow once like a cat."

Thasbow barely had time to nod before the square was plunged into darkness by thick, fast moving clouds. Immediately Manideck scuttled across the cobblestone as fast as he safely could without creating a sound. The clouds thinned, leaving him exposed a yard from the black shadows of the raised cage. Praying no guard was glancing his direction, the youth dash the last three feet and pressed his body against the stone platform, once again invisible. He surveyed the surrounding booths, breathing a sigh of relief when he saw no movement. Quietly he crept along the base of the platform to the iron door, grimacing when he stepped on soggy fruits. A sweet-rotten smell clung to the still air. Waiting until the clouds again blocked moonlight, he raised his head up to peer into the cage. Several motionless forms lay on the dirty, wooden floor. Pulling out several tools, he attempted to pick the lock but had to duck down as bright moonshine filled the square.

"Who's there?" whispered a faint voice, barely audible from the cage.

"A friend," answered Manideck in an equally quiet voice. "Have you seen any guards?"

There was a ruffling sound as the speaker moved closer. "No, but we heard them drinking and joking in the blue tent, third from left. They have been silent for some time—perhaps passed out." Her voice was hoarse from several days of no water except from eating fruit thrown into the cage.

"Good. Be my lookout as I figure out this lock."

A maiden's shadowy face pressed against the bars above him. For a moment they studied each other. Finding comradeship in the young man's eyes, she nodded once then disappeared out of sight. As the world was once again plunged into darkness, Manideck kept his body low while stretching high with his hands to reach the lock. Abruptly the thin rod slipped from his fingers. Metal clanged against metal. He froze. No sounds came from the suspicious booth. Taking a deep breath he continued with his work, pausing several times when the moon peeked out from behind its fluffy coverings. A rush of victory filled him when the rod finally turned inside the lock.

The maiden quietly aroused the other sleeping prisoners. Coming back to Manideck, she whispered, "My father and another man are too weak to walk."

"We'll support them. I have a partner on the other side who can help." With a feeling of dread, the young man realized no signal had been worked out to call Thasbow to him, and he feared risking too many crossings across the cleared cobblestone.

"She goes first," said the maiden. A woman holding a child to her bosom carefully crept out of the open door. She leaned against the platform, trembling.

Manideck crept close to her ear. "Wait till the clouds cover the moon again. I have a friend on the other side. Tell her to come here. Then go as fast as you can. Don't look back. There's a safe house at West and Sharpton. Code word is *blue sky*."

The woman did as he asked. Within a few minutes a concerned Thasbow huddled beside the filthy cage. Manideck was inside, helping an injured man creep to the exit. The teenager Thasbow had seen earlier propped up her father in the shadows of the platform. The injured man groaned as Manideck lowered him through the door to the ground. The maiden glanced anxiously towards the suspicious booth.

With hand motions, Manideck directed Thasbow to help the father and daughter while he aided the other man who was close to passing out from pain of reopen wounds. They waited for what seemed an eternity for a cloud thick enough to transform the world into stark blackness. Their burdensome trek across the cobblestone clearing felt like a mile instead of thirty feet. The maiden had little strength left to support her father so Thasbow felt most of the man's weight against herself. Manideck had the most difficult task, for his charge could barely put one foot in front of another.

"Stop where you are!" barked a voice from among nearby booths.

For the briefest moment, Manideck considered bolting. Both he and Thasbow had a good chance of losing their enemy in the darkness. But that meant abandoning the three prisoners—something he had vowed never to do again.

Two armed men emerged from the shadows where they had been hiding. One was dressed in the official uniform of the Royal Guard; the other was wearing a Reforcer's black leather armor.

The soldier scornfully said, "Did you think you could really escape? How pitiful."

Hope banished, the captive maiden burst into muffled sobs. "Not again. Oh, Yahweh, please not again."

"Back into your cage, you filthy animals. Exactly where you belong," barked the Reforcer.

None of the Tnias moved. Remembering defense lessons Roshell had taught him, Manideck calculated if he could take out both soldiers while the others made a dash for it. The only problem was all three escapees were too weak to go far on their own.

Gloating in victory, the guardsman ordered the other sentry, "Go wake Don and Cox. Tell them that while they were sleeping, I caught their jailbirds flying the coop."

The Reforcer hesitated, glancing uncertain at the five criminals held at bay by one-armed soldier. "Just because you're in the Royal Guard doesn't give you the right to order me around."

"Did I drink or fall asleep on duty like you idiots? Go, now! Before I file a report about you like I will for Don and Cox."

Angry at being threatened, the Reforcer sulked across the clearing. Manideck braced himself, waiting to spring at the soldier as soon as the other guard was out of sight.

The remaining sentry lowered his sword. "Flee, quickly. You only have a minute or two before they come back. I'll say you attacked me."

Shocked, none of the Tnias moved.

"Why are you helping us?" asked Manideck.

"Because my allegiance is pledged to a higher power than the Emperor. Now go, quickly. Soon this place will be crawling with Reforcers."

The relieved escapees hurried across the clearing and disappeared among the booths. Tranton smiled briefly, giving thanks to Yahweh. It had bothered Tranton so much seeing the mistreated prisoners that he had volunteered to be a guard, praying for an opportunity to help. Tranton's lips moved silently in a prayer for their protection. Then he dropped to the ground, letting his head hit the pavement, hard, pretending to be unconscious.

The Tnias limped along the streets and alleys, trying to put as many buildings as possible between themselves and Market Square. Supported by both his daughter and Thasbow, the weakened father fell several times. The man Manideck aided plodded slowly along, unaware of his surroundings. In the distance, excited shouts filled the night as recently awoken Reforcers poured out of their headquarters, eager to search for the missing prisoners. The fugitives quickened their pace, but the two injured men soon reached their limit. The group rested in an alley, hearts thumping wildly as they listened to sounds of pursuit drawing closer. Several Reforcers ran pass the alley's entrance.

Manideck waited until the footsteps died away. "We must keep going, now."

The maiden said, "My father can't walk another step."

"We are almost to a safe house were you will get food and rest. If we stay in this alley, they will find us sooner or later."

Reluctantly the young woman helped her father to his feet. The group exited the alley on the opposite side of where the Reforcers had passed. Halfway across the new street, they heard a shout, "There they are!"

"To the nearest alley!" yelled Manideck.

The Tnias redoubled their effort to reach the dark passageway. Glancing behind, Thasbow caught the terrifying image of six armed Reforcers dashing down the street. Even if the tiny band reached the alley before the soldiers, they could no longer hide or outrun their opponents. Fear tightened around the princess's heart. She was going to die tonight. *Yahweh, help.*

The fugitives reached the alley. The Reforcers reached the fugitives. Shouts rang forth. Swords crashed. Someone screamed. With a shock Thasbow realized that person was her. She was not dead—not yet. Two armed men had emerged from the shadows of the alley and blocked the Reforcers from entering the narrow passageway. Two against six. The strangers were strong, quick with their swords, but so were the Reforcers.

Blocking a sword thrust with his own weapon, one of the protectors yelled over his shoulder, "Run, quickly!"

"I won't leave you, Gramercy," responded Manideck, ignoring the groans of the injured man he supported.

The blacksmith sidestepped another blow. "Your priority is the prisoners, son. Don't stop, no matter what." The muscular man winced as a blade sliced his shoulder.

"Nooooo!" screamed Manideck, rushing forward. The man he supported topped to the damp ground.

Thasbow grabbed Manideck's arm. "We must honor their sacrifice. We must flee, now!"

The maiden and her father hurried to the other end of the alley. Manideck glanced towards the retreating family and the barely conscience man lying on the ground. The sounds of the fighting pulled him. He could not just walk away again, leaving others to die. Haunting memories rushed pass—he leading families out of the window of the doctor's apartment while he heard his own mother scream, a young sister crying.

"I can't go," he whispered in a barely audible voice.

"I am." Thasbow bent down, attempting to pull up the injured man but she lacked the strength.

Cursing under his breath, Manideck grabbed the other man's arm. Together the two teenagers half dragged the weaken Tnias out of the alley and across the next street. Behind them the sounds of fighting grew dimmer. Reaching a restaurant on the corner of West and Sharpton, Manideck pounded on the door. It immediately opened and a robust woman quickly let them inside. Without speaking a word or lighting any lamps, she led them into the storage room and down a secret staircase. The drab underground chamber contained a number of Tnias eating around a rough table. Others slept along the walls, bundled in ragged blankets.

The two teenagers gave their charge over to the plump woman who had let them in. She led the rescued man to a pile of straw were he collapsed into deep sleep. A happy but exhausted maiden and her father grinned their thanks from the floor at Manideck and Thasbow. At the table sat the last two escapees—the young mother and her son eating heartily.

The storeowner approached Manideck. "Did you spot Matthan and Gramercy? They went to help you after the woman came in with her son and told us what you were up to."

The teenager could not meet the owner's eyes. "Yeah, they found us. They held up the Reforcers so we could escape." He clenched his fist in anger. "I'm going back out to find them."

"No!" yelled Thasbow, clasping Manideck's shoulder. "You will be killed."

"I'm not going to let them die!"

The chubby owner moved in front of the narrow stairs, blocking the teenager's path. "Son, you have helped save five people tonight. You are exhausted and need rest. Going back out will only lead to your death. If anyone can beat the odds, it's Gramercy. He and the Salt will come out of this alive."

For a long moment the teenager and the heavyset woman studied each other. Frustrated, Manideck finally headed to a corner to sleep.

Thasbow sat down beside him and sought words to comfort him. "Your friends will be okay. I believe that."

Manideck gave an ironic laugh. "I've lost too many people close to me to believe that anything good still exist. Gramercy has been like a father to me ever since…" Overwhelming grief drowned out his last words.

The princess refused to give in to fear. "I lost the person I loved most, too. My life was dark for years. Then a miracle happened. Now I believe anything is possible."

Manideck gazed at Thasbow for a long moment before looking away. His body trembled but he refused to shed the tears he held inside. Wanting to comfort him, Thasbow hugged him, uncertain. For a moment he kept rigid, then broke down, weeping.

Eventually he pulled back, now calm, "I'm wrong. Beauty still does exist."

The maiden blushed and suddenly became deeply interested in her hands.

"Don't change, Thasbow, no matter how cruel this world becomes."

"I…I'll remember that. Goodnight." The teen stood up and headed across the room to sleep beside the newly freed mother and child.

Chapter Twenty-eight

"Could you repeat that one more time?" Roshell kept her voice calm though her heart rate had just doubled. In the midst of the Haven, busy Tnias strolled pass Roshell and Onias.

"It's right here on this parchment. I read it five times myself hoping it was a mistake." Onias waved the flyer in the air. "There is no mistake."

"Read exactly what it says."

Onias frowned, wishing the words would spontaneously reform themselves in some miraculous new pattern. By now, he had read the flyer so many times he had it memorized. "Heretics have no place in our society. The leader of the illegal cult, Matthan Denett, has been arrested by our commendable military police, the Reforcers. Denett will be publicly executed tomorrow at noon in the coliseum along with five other criminals." The final words clung to the inside of Onias' throat, reluctant to come out. "You and your family are invited to this momentous event. The Emperor commends your hard work in the moral cleansing of our society. Together we can make a better nation for our children."

"Better nation for our children?" Roshell grimaced. "How did the Reforcers find out who Matthan is?"

"My guess is torture. Or perhaps a spy identified him." Onias suddenly lowered his voice to a whisper. "Danielle just walked in. No one has told her yet."

The southerner turned and studied the busy midwife. Danielle's slender frame was distorted due to the large bulge of her belly. Danielle paused to cheerfully chat with a young couple who were also expecting a child soon. Both women's eyes sparkled with the glow of motherhood.

"I can't destroy her happiness," whispered Roshell. "How does anyone say that your spouse is about to be executed?"

Onias remained silent. He had no answers.

Spotting her friends, Danielle waddled over. "I grew up hearing the complaints of expecting mothers. I thought half of what they said was made-up. Was I ever wrong. You don't look so good Roshell. Is something wrong?"

"I…um…think you should sit down."

"What's happened? Is it Matthan?" The young mother-to-be's face clouded with anxiety.

Roshell and Onias glanced at each other.

"What has happened to him?"

"You should sit down," repeated the southerner firmly.

"I don't care about sitting. What has happened to my husband?"

The southerner took a deep breath, "Matthan has been arrested."

To Danielle the cavern suddenly dimmed and the floor moved as if it had become a ship riding out a severe storm. Her legs slowly sunk beneath her.

Onias grabbed Danielle before she fainted. Roshell pulled a crate over to serve as a chair.

"There is more." Roshell wanted to get all the information out as quickly as possible. "He is to be publicly executed at noon tomorrow."

"Tomorrow? Then he is still alive." Hope filled the young midwife. "He can be rescued. Roshell, you must organize a group. Julie and her brother can help. There are others who could get information."

"Danielle, honey, I don't know if that's possible."

The fanatic wife clasped Roshell's hands. "You must save my husband. He can't die without seeing his child's face. Our child needs his father. I need him too."

Roshell swallowed. "I'll promise you this, I will do all I can, even if it means trading my life for his."

~~~~~~~~~

A few hours later a small group of volunteers gathered in the small, rock-hewed chamber serving as the council room. All were men with stormy pasts who had developed strong bonds of loyalty for Matthan over the preceding months. Several had military backgrounds that cemented their friendship with the formal Telumzan officer.

Roshell entered, dressed in comfortable leather armor, giving the appearance she was ready to take on Beelzebub himself. She felt the opposite. Scanning the room, she noted Julie was absent despite two messages sent. Spotting Prince Rufus seated across the room, Roshell breathed a sigh of relief. At least one thing was going right.

Forcing a smile of confidence, she addressed the group. "Men, we have sixteen hours to create a successful plan to rescue six prisoners being held in the Reforcers' headquarters. If we fail, they die. If we succeed, several of us will surely die. That's the tradeoff. If you want to walk out now, no one will hold it against you."

She paused, waiting. The volunteers glanced at each other. No one moved.

A muscular, tattooed man named Gian spoke up. "Matthan pulled me out of some tough troubles, and Gramercy is like a brother to me. I'm not about to turn my back on either of them now."

Other men voiced their agreement.

Despite the fear she could not shake in the pit of her stomach, Roshell smiled. "Now all we need is a plan."

"Mind if I say something?" All eyes turned towards a casually dressed man with handsome features.

"Be my guest." Roshell was careful not to address the prince by name.

"The prisoners probably have already been moved to the arena where they will be kept in cells underground until brought forth for their execution. They will be well-guarded."

"So we fight our way in tonight," suggested Gian.

Rufus shook his head. "My advice is to wait until almost noon tomorrow."

"Wait till noon? That's pushing it close." Roshell was interrupted by the chamber door opening to admit a teenager. "We're in a meeting right now, Manideck."

"I know." The teenager planted his feet, bracing for an argument. "I've come to join your outing. Before you start in on how young I am, know that I've lived through three raids and rescued over a dozen people. Gramercy was my boss, my friend, and a father to me. The Scared Word says there is no greater love than laying down your life for another. I'm ready."

The Salt scrutinized the young man. With a curt nod, she said, "Take a seat."

~~~~~~~~~

The artist dipped a worn brush into dark blue paint then dabbed it onto a tin plate. She dipped the bristles into a clay bowl containing white paint. With the two-tone brush, she swirled the blue and white pigments together on the tin plate, creating a medium blue.

"Have you heard a word I've said?" challenged Roshell, standing at the base of the scaffold.

"Yes," answered Julie without glancing over the edge of the high wooden plank she lay on. "You, my brother, and a number of others will attempt a suicide mission to save six lives. Somehow even my young sister is involved in the plot." Gently she brushed blue bristles across the rocky surface of the dome ceiling.

Exasperated, Roshell raised her voice. "We're talking about Matthan, someone who once saved your life." She had been counting on Julie to be one of the leaders in the rescue attempt. Instead, the princess had isolated herself in this chamber of half completed murals. "And it's not suicidal. I really think we can pull this off. What we need is your skills in fighting to cover our getaway."

"Have you ever noticed what happens when you mix dark and light colors?" Julie dipped her brush into the blue paint.

"What does that have to do with anything?"

"Everything." The princess leaned over the side, extending her paintbrush so Roshell could see its color. "Take the primary color white. Mix any other color with it. What happens?"

"Do I look like a painter to you?" Realizing Julie would not continue until she received a serious answer, Roshell reluctantly muttered, "It turns darker."

"Right. When even the smallest traces of pigments are mixed with white, the color is altered forever. Light mixed with darkness creates new shades of darkness. Peace enforced by violence doesn't bring about peace."

Roshell sighed. "I know you took an oath not to kill again. I'm not asking you to break it. Just scare a few guards with that fiery sword of yours. Half of my volunteers have never held a weapon before. I need someone with experience to lead the second team."

"There is my brother." Julie continued her work.

"Rufus and your sister are the tickets to get us inside the arena. Then we split. Their names stay in the clear. No one will even know they helped us." There was a long pause as Roshell waited for an answer. The only sound was the gentle tap of a brush against the side of a bowl. "We are talking about Matthan, Danielle's husband. You know, the father of her soon-to-be-born child."

No response. Roshell lost her temper. "Will you get your nose out of the paint for a minute and listen to me!"

Julie's smudged face appeared over the plank. "Do you really think I am heartless, Roshell? You are asking me to do something I swore I would never do again. I care deeply about Matthan and Danielle. I understand exactly what Matthan feels right now. The fear, the waiting. I know death for I have tasted it. And I have experienced what lies beyond. Matthan will become a martyr, a hero. While we struggle every day, he will be in paradise."

The Ulmjon refused to back down. "You're colder than even I could image. You didn't leave behind a child who would never see your face or a spouse subjugated to insufferable loneliness."

The artist turned away before Roshell could spot the tear running down her cheek. Urbane. What had he gone through after her death? Had loneliness twisted him into a soulless killing beast? In her mind, she had viewed a thousand times their

256

last moments together. Could she have said something differently? Julie took a deep breath to calm herself. Since the beginning of her second life, her greatest fear was being face to face with Urbane again. Then suddenly they had met at the worst of times. It was brief, yet his image stayed with her day and night. She desired to see him again, sharing with him all her experiences: what Agape was like, seeing Yahweh face to face, basking in the deity's love. There was so much she longed to show him. But would he listen or kill her? Silently, Julie bowed her head and prayed for guidance.

Hurried footsteps in the adjoining passageway grabbed both women's attention. Hair flying, Violet burst in. "Danielle's gone into labor!"

"What!" exclaimed both Roshell and Julie at the same time.

"Danielle's in labor." The worried teenager's face was speckled from paint from working earlier that day with Julie. "Minira's with her now, but she's asking for you both."

"I thought she wasn't due for several more weeks," said Roshell.

"She isn't, but I've heard her say before that stress can cause early childbirth." Violet quickly moved to grab the paints and brushes Julie was lowing by rope. Expertly the teenager sealed paint jars while Julie clambered down the ladder. Within minutes the cleaning process was finished, and the three women headed out of the chamber.

Screams ripped through the wee hours of the morning, echoing down passageways that had not seen sunlight in millenniums. Danielle panted while Julie dabbed her face with a wet cloth. Roshell sit in a corner, body rigid until the screams ceased. When the southerner had first entered the room, she had been a nervous ball of energy, restlessly seeking tasks to do—and quickly getting on the wrong side of Minira who was serving as midwife. Minira kicked Roshell out, but later let her back in with the agreement that the southerner would stay out of the way. Violet brought in boiled water from the kitchen.

A high pitch yell sent silvers down Roshell's spine. "I don't think the torture chamber of the Emperor could equal this torment."

Julie shot the Ulmjon a dirty look.

"I will remind you, Roshell, that if you continue to speak, I will throw you out—again." Minira threatened like a general.

"And people wonder why I chose never to marry," muttered Roshell as another scream resonated through the small chamber.

"Violet, get the blanket," commanded Minira. "I see a head."

Though labor had lasted for hours, the actual birth only took a few minutes. An exhausted but beaming Danielle was soon cooing to her new son held gently in her protective arms. Smiling broadly, the other ladies gathered around the bed.

"His hands are so small," said Violet.

"He has his father's eyes," beamed Roshell.

"And his determination," added the proud mother.

Looking the infant over, Minira said, "He's fit as a fiddle and ready to take on the world. But first he needs a good meal."

Only Julie remained silent. Loneliness consumed her as Danielle nursed her child, the link creating a bond that would last a lifetime between mother and son. *If I had not been so selfish, perhaps I might have been a mother now.* No children depended on her, needed her. No lover kept her warm at night.

"Matthan eagerly looked forward to this day," said Danielle, sadness creeping back into her voice.

Roshell said with steel determination, "We will bring your husband back." She locked eyes with Julie, "Won't *we?*"

The princess looked at the tiny infant suckling hungrily. Matthan should have been here to see his son's first breath. "With Yahweh's help, we will bring him back to you, Danielle."

Chapter Twenty-nine

A carriage bumped along the stone road, passing excited crowds heading towards the arena. Nervously Thasbow watched the people pass, mainly commoners enjoying taking a day off work.

Prince Rufus leaned over and whispered into her ear, "Relax. You must appear natural."

The teenager forced a smile, wishing she had the skills of her older brother. He always seemed in control—in the battlefield or playing with his children. Perhaps her tension was due to the strange woman sitting in the seat across from her. Thasbow had only occasionally seen dark-skin people from a distance, never close-up. Usually they were servants or sailors, but this one had the look of a warrior, savage and menacing, though she was dressed in a simple handmaiden's dress. Beside the southerner was a thin man dressed as another female servant. The whole picture would have been hilarious if not for the stark seriousness of their mission. Both *maids* kept their eyes downcast, playing the role of lowly servants.

Needing to see a more friendly face, Thasbow poked her head out a window. "Are we almost there, footman?"

Keeping a strong grip on a railing, Manideck leaned close to the window. "It's not much further, my lady, where you will see the most historical execution in all of Gogian history." He winked. "At least it will be by the time we leave."

Rufus interrupted the youth's mirth with a stern warning, "I suggest that footmen focus on happenings outside the carriage instead of inside the carriage or someone will be walking."

Thasbow looked crestfallen though Manideck grinned as he withdrew from the window. A few hours ago at the final meeting, Manideck had been informed he would be escorting a princess and Prince Rufus to the arena. When he had reached the carriage, his eyes had almost popped out of their sockets at the sight of Thasbow dressed in a lavish velvet dress standing beside the famous war hero. It left the young man on a giddy high.

The driver was forced to slow the horses for the road had become more congested. As they passed Citizen's Gate, the crowded commoner's entrance leading into the huge stone arena, Thasbow strained to spot Julie and her team among the hundreds of pedestrians—an impossible task. A few minutes later, the coachman turned down a narrow, tree-lined road and stopped in front of the elegant, vine covered nobles' entrance. Manideck quickly jumped down and folded out several steps attached to the bottom of the coach. Rufus was first out, walking regally. As Thasbow exited, blank-faced Manideck held her hand. She wanted to wish him good luck but knew Reforcers were watching. The two servants rose from their seats to follow, but Thasbow absently dismissed them with a wave of her hand. Manideck jumped onto the back of the carriage as it pulled away from the curb.

A gentle breeze sent a shower of pink petals swirling through the air from the cherry trees lining the cobbled road. Taking Thasbow's arm in his, Rufus walked to the arched gateway guarded by four sentries. Out of the corner of her eye, the princess noticed Lady Mahan was climbing out of another coach.

A guard humdrummed, "Turn all weapons in here."

"I carry none," responded Rufus with a touch of indignity in his voice.

The sentry stepped forward to do a brief pat down.

"My word should be enough!" The prince retorted.

The guard sighed, "Today I've already heard a hundred threats from arrogant nobles like yourself who claim they're best friends with the Emperor. Now unless you're His Majesty himself, we've been ordered by General Herron to search every person who enters these gates."

"Hello, Princess Thasbow," called the cheerful voice of Lady Mahan, taking her place in line behind the royal siblings. "Prince Rufus, what a surprise to see you at a public function."

The sentry snapped to attention. "Prince Rufus, I'm sorry I didn't recognize you! You and your party may go through immediately." The other guards saluted as Rufus, Thasbow, and smirking Lady Mahan strolled through the archway and down a brightly lit tunnel leading to the first-class seating.

~~~~~~~~~

Pulling away from the elegant nobles' entrance, the heavy built driver directed his horses toward the nearby long tunnel leading to the largest parking lot in the city. The paved field was designed to handle the enormous volume of visitors to Market Square. It was customary for coachmen to drop off their first-class patrons then wait at Arena Parking until signaled by a runner that it was time to pick them up again. It was also a hangout for taxi drivers on break since there was ample space to water and rest their animals. Arena Parking held no interest to Roshell, but the long tunnel leading to it did. The passageway actually went completely under the massive arena and came out on the other side—and as Gian predicted, it was dimly lit.

Perched in the high driver's seat, Gian slowed the coach when halfway through the tunnel. The two *maids* inside the carriage had already stripped off their dresses. The thin man, now dressed as a coachman, climbed out of the cabin and swung himself up into the driver's seat. Clad in black leather armor, Roshell pulled herself through a window just in time to see Gian jump to the ground then press his large body against the shadowy stone wall. Gian's size had made it impossible for him to pass off as anyone but the driver, yet he was an essential component for the next stage of the plot. In his youth he had worked as a custodian at the arena.

Manideck thumped three times against the body of the carriage then leaped to the ground. Roshell jumped next. Under the coach, two men dropped from their hiding place to the ground. They waited until the wheels of the wagon passed then swiftly rolled out of the path and flatten themselves against the wall. No one moved as another carriage passed by, the driver too busy drinking from a bottle to notice them. Quickly Gian led the group to a narrow, rarely used side passage. Midway, a rusty iron gate blocked the corridor. Within two heartbeats Manideck had the lock picked. When the group had gone far enough into the unlit passage not to be seen by passing carriages, weapons were pulled out of bags carried by Congter and Micran, the two men who had hidden under the coach. In complete darkness, the Tnias bowed their heads for one final brief prayer. Each had already spent time that morning in the Great Chamber, preparing their soul for the dangers which awaited.

Keeping their left hands against the wall for guidance in the dark, the four conspirators followed Gian, relaying on his dusty memories two decades old. He had been right in that the ancient passageway was rarely thought of and more rarely used. After several twist and turns, Gian brought them to a halt at a corridor lit by a few oil lanterns fastened to walls. They were nearing the prison cells. Proceeding cautiously through a rank smelling hallway, the Tnias passed caged animals used as entertainment in the arena. Some beasts ignored the Tnias while others jumped against bars, snapping hungrily.

Gian whispered, "Sometimes they don't feed the animals for a week or more. When released into the arena, they will attack even their own mates in a hungry frenzy."

Manideck muttered, "The creatures are more humane than their beastly guards."

Hearing footsteps approaching, the five Tnias froze. A worker came around a corner, carrying a large pail of raw meat. "I'm coming, you mutts. Keep down the racket."

As the keeper passed Gian hidden behind a large cage, the large man brought his fist crashing onto the worker's head, knocking him out.

Roshell picked up the worker's keys and unlocked an empty cage. "Put him in here. Gian, which way?"

The middle-aged man pointed to the far end of the hallway. "That's the quickest way. They're probably in the adjoining corridor, but it will be guarded."

"Good." The southern gripped her sword tightly. "I was wondering when the real action would begin."

"Wait." Manideck stepped near Roshell, taking the keys she held. "I have an idea."

~~~~~~~~~

Captain Patrobas briskly marched through the labyrinth of passageways under the arena. All his men were in position, prepared for the worst. While General Herron was overseeing final details above ground, Patrobas had made it a point to be the honored supervisor who would lead the prisoners to their deaths. As he stepped into a large antechamber, the three guards dropped the cards they were playing and snapped to attention. For a moment the captain scrutinized the rock-hewed room. There were several entrances to the chamber, but only one had a bolted door made of iron. Beyond it was the cellblock.

"As you were, gentlemen," said the captain, completely at ease with his men. "Continue your game. It will be sometime yet."

The Reforcers relaxed and sat down. One young rookie invited Patrobas to join. Several minutes into the game, he asked, "Sir, when are we supposed to bring up the prisoners?"

"A squad will be here shortly, son," the captain answered as he placed a card down.

"I thought they die at exactly noon. I win again, Jake."

Lieutenant Jake threw his hand of cards down in disgust. "Haven't you gone to executions before, kid? First the mayor's got to give his big speech then the Emperor. Next come animal fights to get the crowd all worked up by watching the beasts kill each other. Then after the executions there'll be races."

"Why couldn't I have been off today," complained the second private. "I could've won some good money betting on the races."

"You should watch what you say in front of your supervisor," the lieutenant warned.

The rookie nodded towards a short hallway. "Looks like they're already moving the beasts upstairs."

The other three men glanced towards the door the first guard indicated. A snarling animal, all bristling hair and fangs, stood in the doorway. The men watched idly, expecting to see the keeper yank on the beast's chain any moment. Instead, the creature continued to slink down the passageway, pausing to gobble up a small piece of raw meat thrown in front of him by Manideck hiding in the adjoining corridor. The animal walked forward to eat another piece.

Patrobas said, "Looks like one of them has escaped. You two go chase him back into his cage."

"I'm not paid to chase animals," protested the second private.

"You are now," said Lieutenant Jake. "It won't do to have one of the nobles' children attacked. It'll be your neck on the guillotine."

Both subordinates pulled their swords and slowly approached the carcajou. Growling, the animal lowered its head. As the soldiers drew closer, the creature suddenly lunged. The first guard screamed and jumped backwards, the beast's teeth snapping shut an inch from the man's leg.

Patrobas and Jake threw back their heads and laughed.

"Come on, my children could do better than that," taunted the lieutenant.

"Well, why don't you show us how to capture this pussycat then," challenged the second private through clenched teeth.

The lieutenant frowned, refusing to lower himself to chasing escaped animals.

"Delighted," Captain Patrobas answered instead. He believed the way to get quality performance from soldiers was for leaders to set the example. "As a boy, I had to deal with these scavengers all the time back on the farm when they tried to steal chickens." The officer boldly stepped forward, drawing his own weapon. "If you make a carcajou think you are tougher than he is, then he'll retreat."

"Yeah, right," muttered the lieutenant.

As the Reforcers focused on the snarling animal, none noticed four figures emerging from the shadows of another doorway. Roshell, Gian, Micran, and Congter rushed across the small chamber and attacked. Micran knocked the second guard unconscious before the man had a chance to turn around. Gian pushed the startled first sentry to the ground then pressed his sword against the man's back. The officers were not taken so easily. It took several minutes for Congter to subdue the lieutenant. Patrobas and Roshell appeared to dance across the room as each dodged the other's swift blade. In the confusion, the carcajou leaped between the fighters and fled towards a quieter room. Patrobas jumped backwards to dodge the beast, only to find himself firmly grabbed from behind by Gian. Roshell knocked the officer's weapon from his hand then pressed her own blade against his throat.

"We'll take your keys now, Captain," smiled the southerner.

Manideck entered the room from the hallway the creature had first appeared.

Taking the Reforcer's keys, Roshell asked Manideck, "Will that beast come back and attack us?"

The teenager laughed. "Hardly. He's too busy munching on a pail of meat I left for him."

Roshell nodded then unlocked the iron door leading into the main prison block. Beyond was a long corridor with several dozen wooden doors. "Matthan, where are you?"

A face pressed against the bars of a nearby cell door. "Roshell, is that you? What are you doing here?"

"We're rescuing you, of course." She unlocked his door.

Stepping out of the rank smelling cell, Matthan grabbed the wall to keep his balance as a wave of nausea hit. "There are others. Here. We must save them."

"We will. Can you walk?" asked Roshell, noting Matthan's black eye and bruises on his arms.

"Yes, I think so."

"Roshell, hurry, over here!" yelled Manideck, standing in front of another cell. "I think Gramercy is in this one."

As Roshell unlocked the door, lantern light revealed a small, dirty cell where the blacksmith lay on a mound of filthy hay, not moving. Worried, Manideck walked over and gently touched the man's shoulder. There was muttering then Gramercy slowly sat up, dazed.

"Is it time?" he asked through parched lips.

The teenager swallowed in shock, barely able to recognize his mentor. One eye was swollen shut and dried blood covered half his face. "It's time for freedom, Gramercy."

The man stared at the teenager. "Manideck? Did they capture you too?"

"No, my friend, this is a rescue mission to get you out."

"Let's go!" barked Roshell from the hallway, having unlocked the other cells. "Our time's slipping away too quickly."

Manideck helped Gramercy to his feet. Coming out of the cell, the teenager's anger boiled as he looked at the other freed prisoners. Several had been imprisoned for weeks and tortured repeatedly. One frail man kept his unmended broken arm against his chest. Gian and Micran escorted their Reforcer prisoners from the antechamber into the hallway. Congter dragged the unconscious guard over.

Roshell placed her sword against Patrobas's throat. "Undress. We have need of your armor."

The two officers glared angrily at her but obeyed. The young private was forced to strip the unconscious guard. Congter, Micran, and Manideck slipped on Reforcer uniforms while Roshell draped on a priestess cloak to cover her leather armor and weapon. As chains were loosely put on those who had no disguises, Manideck slipped into the cell where the four Reforcers were tied together. For a long moment, he looked into the frigid eyes of the captain while remembering his dead mother and siblings.

In a dangerous voice, the teenager spoke, "I sentence you for the crimes you have committed against the innocent." He raised his sword with deadly intent.

"Stop!" commanded Matthan, rushing into the cell. "Son, don't bloody your own hands. Let Yahweh be their judge—not us."

Angrily the teenager said, "How can you say that? They killed my family. They tortured you and the others out there. They deserve death."

The Salt gently pushed the teen's blade towards the floor. "By our standards they do, but Yahweh sees things differently. I agree with Julie. To kill them denies them the chance for redemption."

"Reforcers can't change. They're evil."

"Perhaps. But they're also men, some with families. Leave them. Our only concern should be getting out of here."

Reluctantly the teenager sheathed his sword then spat into the officer's face. "That's for my family."

Anger flashed through Patrobas's eyes as he watched the youth leave the cell. *Typical heathen. But why did the other stop him?* As Matthan was about to close the prison door the captain called, "Why spare my life, heretic? I'm the one who gave you the black eye."

"I know." The Salt looked calmly at the Reforcer. "When you were the captor and I the prisoner, I still had more freedom than you have ever experienced. Maybe someday you will understand."

The door banged shut, leaving Patrobas and the other guards wrapped in darkness.

"Hurry," barked Roshell. "We don't have much time."

Quickly the three false Reforcers marched their seven prisoners through the passageways. Chained Gian kept pace at the front, secretly directing the lead guard, Manideck, in which direction to take. Priestess Roshell brought up the rear, keeping head bowed, chanting—and praying. Their direction was not towards the ancient work tunnel under the arena for it would be too suspicious for soldiers to march prisoners out pass the nobles' entrance or the Arena Parking. If the escape was discovered, the tunnel and parking field would quickly turn into a death trap since the few exits could easily be blocked by the many roaming Reforcers on duty.

Dim daylight filtered through slits high up the wall, telling the Tnias they had reached the first sub-level under the arena. The stone walls and roof vibrated from shouts of the massive crowd above them. Heavy footsteps echoed through the passageway, announcing soldiers heading towards the escapees. Fear quickened every Tnias' heartbeat. A lieutenant appeared with ten Reforcers following in tight formation. Manideck saluted. The officer returned the gesture and kept going.

As the squad disappeared down the corridor, Gian whispered, "They're going for the prisoners. It won't take them long to realize what has happened and who did it."

"Then I suggest we speed up. Double time!" yelled Manideck.

Prisoners, priestess, and guards ran down the hallway. They were halfway up the steps to the ground level when shouts echoed down the corridor behind them. The escape had been discovered.

At the top of the steps, Gian paused, uncertain of the right direction.

Manideck spat out, "Now is not the time to lose your memory!"

"It's been twenty years. I never cleaned this section."

"Which way, man?"

"Left, I believe."

The teenager dashed left then came to an abrupt halt. They were at a large archway leading into the arena's tournament field. A number of citizens sitting on benches above the exit spotted the guard and the prisoner beside him and began shouting, believing the executions were about to start.

"Quick! The other way!" yelled Manideck.

At the tail end of the party, Roshell and Congter suddenly found themselves in the lead. The group dashed through a large tunnel which connected the stables to the arena. Grooms and riders watched in surprise as a priestess dashed past, followed by guards and prisoners, intermingling so closely it was hard to tell who was captive or captor. Taking turns at random, Roshell rapidly led the group pass stalls and storerooms. Gian was the only one who knew the right direction, but he was at the back of the group. Suddenly she found herself staring at a dead end. She halted, only to have Congter and several others run into her from behind, sending all four crashing to the floor in a tangle.

While pushing someone's boot out of her mouth, Roshell heard Gian shout, "This way!" The next thing the southerner knew, she was at the end of a line rushing into a small open courtyard where a startled groom was exercising a horse. Gian led the group into a passageway on the other side.

Behind the fleeing group, angry shouts rent the air as guards demanded from grooms which way the fugitives had fled.

"Shut the gates! Shut the gates!" yelled a Reforcer officer.

The command jumped from guard to posted guard stationed around the arena. The alarm cry traveled faster than the Tnias could run.

Chapter Thirty

The roar from the excited crowd in the arena could be heard in nearby Market Square. Traffic had lessened at the wide Citizen's Gate since it was past noon, but the broad fenced in courtyard in front of the ticket booths was still crowded with latecomers waiting to gain entrance into the arena. Julie blended with a group near the first gateway, pretending to watch a juggler but keeping her eyes focused on the guards posted at both ends of the large walled courtyard. Six soldiers frisked visitors before allowing them through the tunnel leading into the arena. Another six guards sharply observed newcomers entering the courtyard directly from Market Square.

Laughter pulled Julie's attention back to the crowd surrounding a juggler. The brightly painted entertainer pretended to wobble badly as he balanced on one leg, spinning a hoop on his other foot while juggling five balls. Suddenly he tossed the hoop high in the air, caught the five balls in his hands, then let the hoop land on his head. The throng clapped in amazement.

"Close the gates! Close the gates!" The command echoed down the tunnel, demanding immediate action from the guards.

Julie's heartbeat quickened. It was all over if either of the two gates of the commoner's entrance were barred. Reacting on instinct, Julie pushed pass several people in line then dashed through the large entranceway of the tunnel leading into the arena. The guards were momentary detracted by the alarm call and did not notice her merge with several other frisked townspeople going through the second gate. She broke from the line and ran towards the small gatehouse built into the side of the tunnel. Already a soldier was turning the crank to lower the massive portcullis. Pulling out her weapon, Julie entered the tiny room. The guard reached for his own weapon then froze, staring in horror as flames licked across the surface of his enemy's blade. Too well he remembered the rumor of a fiery goddess who cleaved a squad of Reforcers in half during a raid.

Julie sinisterly glared at the pale man. "Run. Run as fast as you can."

The trembling man nodded his head slowly as he edged towards the door. Once out, he bolted down the tunnel without looking back. Several guards noticed the fleeing gatekeeper and pulled their own weapons. Hiding away from the view offered by the open door, Julie stopped the falling gate and prayed to avoid a situation that would require her to take someone's life. Glancing through a tiny window, Julie could see across the courtyard where other Tnias struggled to keep the first portcullis from closing. While several battled the guards, one quick-thinking man had jammed a crowbar under the falling metal gate, halting the portcullis three feet above the ground. Julie spotted five nearby soldiers heading in her direction.

Suddenly chaos broke loose. The juggler, a Tnias conspirator, screamed at the top of his lungs, "Run for your lives! The prisoners have broken lose!"

Already jittery from the alarm call and the fighting at the far end of the courtyard, several hundred latecomers waiting in line panicked. A few dozen retraced their steps towards the far gate exiting to Market Square, but they found the way blocked by fighting Tnias and Reforcers. The mass attempted to bolt through the gate leading into the arena. The five guards ominously waved their swords at the citizens, yelling that no one could enter the stadium until searched.

Boom! A wagon seemingly stacked with innocent hay at the edge of Market Square suddenly blew up. That did it. Not even armed soldiers could calm the hysterical throng. Many fled under the second half-closed portcullis and dashed down the tunnel. Trying to obey their earlier orders, the soldiers pushed people to the ground, screaming threats at them, too busy to remember that the gatehouse guard had mysteriously abandoned his post.

~~~~~~~~~

"That jacket clashes with Lady Cassandra's dress. How ancient can you get?" criticized Lady Richmon, setting beside her husband one stone bench below Rufus's party.

"Perhaps she's attempting to bring back the Achozien period," giggled Lady Mahan.

Thasbow sighed in frustration. A few weeks ago she would have relished conversation that trashed her archenemy, but today her thoughts were on the secret raid—and Manideck. What if he was hurt or killed? Julie could hold her own, but Manideck was not a trained soldier. She wondered how her brother could be so composed, listening patiently to Lord Richmon drone on about a dull hunt that seemed to last longer than the history of Gog.

A sharp jab in Thasbow's side from Lady Mahan brought the teen's attention to the present. "Haven't you been paying attention? Look who is in the royal box, handsome as ever."

The princess glanced at a large balcony reserved for the royal family and their guests. Behind a podium, the mayor was deep into his speech about the power of the common citizen to eradicate evil. Further back, Emperor Phlegon and Lady

Cassandra sat in embellished gold chairs with proud nobles scattered about, all attended by servants with trays laden with fancy food. But it was General Herron that Lady Mahan indicated. He stood alone and aloof from the others, his eyes scrutinizing the soldiers below, occasionally hand signaling his commanders new orders.

Onlookers surrounding one tunnel suddenly began cheering.

Mahan cut off Lady Richmon's passionate conversation about hats. "Do you think they're finally about to bring the prisoners out?"

"Not likely," answered Lord Richmon. "The Emperor has not given his speech yet."

"Good," replied his wife, "I haven't yet told you ladies about the dreadful bonnets that are so popular on the East Coast. You would not believe what people do for the sake of fashion."

Thasbow clenched her fists in frustration. She felt like screaming at the absurdity of the whole scene. Innocent people were about to be killed, and the world went on like it was nothing. Sensing his sister's impatience, Rufus squeezed Thasbow's hand. She relaxed—slightly.

Suddenly a shrill shout was heard. The call was repeated by other soldiers yelling. Thasbow sharply looked at her brother. Had the plan gone awry or were the Tnias safely through the gate and long gone? A nearby explosion vibrated the stone benches the vast crowd sat upon, causing many to scream in fear. A panicked throng fled into the stadium from the tunnel leading to Citizens' Gate.

Urbane disappeared through the balcony doorway. Soon he reappeared from a tunnel on the lowest seating level, closely trailed by a dozen soldiers. Taking the shortest path, he leaped over the railing and dropped eight feet, landing with a roll on the sandy arena floor. Quickly he regained his feet and dashed towards Citizens' Gate. Without hesitating, the soldiers with him followed his example. The crowd calmed, taking comfort in seeing the armed men heading in the direction of the explosion.

"Wow, look at General Herron go," purred Mahan, eyes shining. "He'll have everything back in order before you know it."

I hope not, thought Thasbow.

~~~~~~~~~

Teeth clenched, sheathed sword banging against his side, Urbane ran across the hot sand. Behind him pounded a dozen soldiers, handpicked by himself. Along the rim of the giant sand bowl, dozens of Reforcers dashed along walkways towards the gate. Other sentries stayed positioned throughout the arena to keep the crowd calm.

Reaching the far wall, the general dashed through a small open tunnel that quickly joined a larger passage. Soon he and his men reached the broad commoner's entrance tunnel, now nearly deserted. He ignored frightened stragglers passing him, heading into the stadium. Forty feet ahead, eleven people scrabbled towards the outer gateway, three wore soldier outfits, one a priestess, and the others were obviously escaped prisoners. Immediately Urbane and his men pursued them.

Reaching the first half-closed portcullis, the fugitives ducked under. Urbane cursed. Where were the guards he had stationed here? Both gates should have already been secured. In answer, the general spotted one whimpering watchman huddled against a stone wall. Reaching the first portcullis, Urbane slowed to duck under the bars. As he did so, he spotted four sentries, pale, swords drawn, at the edge of the courtyard. *How dare they let the escapees run right pass them! After this is over, I will demote them to stable duty.*

Then he saw what the guards feared. A lone woman stood in the middle of the courtyard, a portrait of savage beauty, a warrior stepped out from the pages of myth welding a sword of fire. Junia. Hot rage flowed through Urbane's veins. This time only a hundred feet of open space separated them.

The soldiers following Urbane hesitated, remembering the apartment complex incident, but when the general boldly dashed forward, they followed. Without taking his eyes off the dead princess, Urbane flew across the courtyard, quickly cutting the distance between him and the fugitives. She did not notice him for her eyes followed the fleeing Tnias. When the Tnias reached her, she turned and ran with them, keeping near the back of the group. Urbane increased his speed, determined to attack them before they reached the second gate.

A nearby wine keg suddenly exploded in an enormous burst of flame. Knocked to the ground, Urbane quickly regained his feet, but the diversion had already succeeded. The fugitives reached the second portcullis and rolled under the three-foot opening. One muscular man paused to yank the crowbar from under the heavy gate. The iron bars fell with a heavy crash inches in front of the enraged general.

"Get the gate up now, if you value your life!" barked Urbane to the nearest panting soldier. He would not lose her this time. There would be no second defeat.

~~~~~~~~~

Hearing the portcullis bang to the ground behind her, Julie breathed a sigh of relief. At least Matthan and the other prisoners were free. But the danger was only half over. The Tnias had to scatter through Market Square avoiding the quickly advancing Reforcers pouring out of their headquarters located straight across from the arena. Most of the rebels on Julie's team had already melted into the nearby crowds. The only ones who remained held the reins of horses saved for injured prisoners. The beasts were quickly mounted.

"Get the gate up now, if you value your life!"

Hearing the familiar voice, Julie whirled in shock. Standing two feet away, Urbane firmly met her gaze with piercing eyes of simmering rage, again separated from his former lover by iron bars.

Gasping for breath, Roshell motioned to Matthan. "Only the best for you."

Sunshine neighed a friendly greeting to her master. Despite his pain, Matthan smiled and patted the horse's neck. "There's not enough animals here for anyone."

"Two to a horse. Go quickly," said Roshell. "Matthan, don't worry about anyone else. You have a wife and son waiting for you."

As another ragged prisoner climbed up beside Matthan onto Sunshine, the young Salt glanced sharply at the southerner, searching her eyes. A smile spread across his face and he slapped Sunshine's reins, disappearing among the stalls and booths.

Roshell gave a final glance to ensure that all who needed a horse had one. Only two horses and three Tnias remained. One being Julie standing by the gate, pale, still as stone. "Not again," muttered Roshell, spotting the formidable general on the other side of the gate. "Julie, let's go now!" Already the gate had been raised six inches.

The princess hesitated only a moment then ran to the nearest horse, already mounted by Manideck. She was barely seated when the teenager dug his heels into the horse's flank, sending the animal galloping across the vast square.

~~~~~~~~~

Urbane squeezed under the rising portcullis seconds later and headed for the nearest horse. The owner was readjusting supplies on the beast for his homeward trip.

"I'm borrowing this horse, now!" snapped the general.

The peddler angrily responded, "No, this is my pack horse."

"Wrong answer." Urbane pushed the old man to the ground and jumped onto the animal.

Jingling trinkets and fragile pottery bumped together as horse and rider galloped pass booths, merchants, and customers. Annoyed, Urbane unfastened the bags attached to the saddle. Pottery shattered on the ground in his wake. Teeth clenched, he forced the horse into a full gallop, dodging people, never for a second taking his eyes off the look-alike Junia racing ahead.

Reaching a blocked path, the teenager dressed as a Reforcer directed his animal to jump over a countertop then dash through a tent. Urbane forced his mount to follow, not even glancing at the enraged cook yelling about his trampled supplies. Tiring, the packhorse Urbane rode fought her bit, slowing. The general pounded his heels into her side, demanding more speed, but the elderly horse had already given her best. To Urbane's deep frustration, the gap increased between them.

Reaching the edge of Market Square, his targets turned down a main street. Pounding far behind, Urbane made it to the street, only to catch a glimpse of flying horsetail disappearing down a side alley. Finally reaching the alley, Urbane brought his trembling mount to a halt. The dead end was empty except for the panting horse the heretics had ridden. The general scanned the walls of the buildings. No ladder, one door bolted from the outside, only boarded up windows. There was no way for them to escape. Then he spotted the sewer grate slightly ajar.

In a flash, he dismounted and peered through the iron slats. Darkness stared back at him. Pushing the grating aside, he dropped to the slick floor below. Through he had no light, he continued forward, keeping one hand against a slimy wall as guidance. The dim light from the alley above soon faded into nothingness. As his eyes adjusted, he realized there was a faint glow ahead—and voices. Peering around a corner, he spotted the distant figures of the teenager and the woman with her glowing sword held high as a torch.

"This is the wrong direction," insisted the youth.

"Are you sure?" came the voice of the princess that supposed to be dead.

"Yes. We'll soon hit the Underground, which will help us little. It will be crawling with Reforcers."

Sword drawn, the general flattened his body against the wall, waiting, listening to the footfalls of his approaching enemy, gurgles of raw sewage flowing nearby, and a rat squeaking. As the unnatural light grew brighter, Urbane's grip tightened on his hilt. Like the ghastly appearance of a gargoyle, the general whirred around the corner, sword slashing, knocking the woman's weapon from her hand. Darkness immediately filled the passageway.

Urbane swung his blade again, feeling it slice through flesh. There was a yelp of pain then a splash. Light pushed away blackness, revealing the woman on her knees, having just retrieved her sword. The teenager foundered in the shallow trench, attempting to gain footing on the slimy floor, holding one bleeding shoulder. Urbane aimed his blade for the neck of his former lover. She rolled, barely dodging the deadly blow. Regaining her feet, she ran. Ignoring the injured youth who he could easily finished off later, the general pursed the ghost princess.

Taking random turns, she attempted to lose him, but he easily followed the light cast by her sword. Realizing this, she paused to sheathe her weapon. Ahead the passageway broadened into a tall chamber with dozens of different size concrete pipes spilling water into the grotto from a factory overhead. Dim sunlight filtered through a large grating fifteen feet overhead, casting deep shadows. Splashing through the shallow pool covering the rocky floor, the woman dashed towards the opposite passageway.

"Again you run," echoed Urbane's voice through the chamber. "You are too much of a coward to be Junia."

The woman paused two feet from the exit, head bowed. Slowly she turned to face him. "You are right. It is time I stopped running."

Heart thumping wildly, Urbane demanded, "Who are you?"

"I'm the one you called Junia."

"You lie. She's dead. I saw her die with my own eyes."

"How could I forget? Pierced by your sword, probably the same you carry now."

"You are not the woman I loved."

"Right again." Bitterness filled her voice. "I am the woman you let die. You turned your back on me as I lay in my brother's arms. I called to you, but you had too much pride." She paused to regain her composure. "My last words were, 'I love you and so does Yahweh.'"

Urbane shook his head in denial. "By the gods, you cannot be her! No one comes back from the dead."

"Yahweh did. He is far more powerful than you can imagine. Death is only a gateway to his presence."

"Enough of your sacrilege!"

Urbane charged forward, sword raised to strike. Instinctively, Julie pulled her weapon from its sheath, blocking the blow. Her enraged opponent slashed again. Water pouring from pipes overhead turned gold, reflecting the bright light of the fiery blade. A beautiful yet deadly dance twirled across the watery chamber. Twisting and dodging, stabbing and blocking, both opponents were equally matched. Urbane had strength, but Julie had agility. The princess fought defensively while Urbane pressed the attack.

Swords crossed inches from the opponents' faces, muscles straining. The general muttered, "You fight like the Junia I trained."

"Glad I meet with your approval."

"I also know her weaknesses."

He quickly rotated to the left. Thrown off balanced, Julie fell, the water cushioning her impact against the rocky floor. Urbane stabbed downward. The Tnias tried to roll, but the general's blade pieced between upper ribcage and collarbone, pinning her to the watery floor. Julie screamed in pain, and her sword hilt slipped from numb fingers. The grotto fell into shadow.

Keeping his weight pressed against his weapon, Urbane demanded, "I will not ask again. Who are you?"

Through clenched teeth, the woman yelled, "Once Junia, daughter of Emperor Erastus! Now Julie, Salt of Yahweh!"

"I've heard enough of your lies." The general pushed harder on his sword, pushing the tip of his blade through bone and out her back.

Almost unconscious from agonizing pain throbbing through her body, Julie's hand brushed against the cold surface of her sword. With the last of her strength, she grabbed the handle and jabbed upward. Urbane easily dodged the clumsy move, but Julie was freed from his blade. She attempted to stand, but slipped on the watery floor. The general quickly knocked the sword from his enemy's hand. In the suddenly darkness, Julie scrambled on hand and knees to the nearest wall, passing under miniature waterfalls from overhead pipes.

"Show yourself, coward!" demanded Urbane, searching the shadows.

Julie pulled her injured body into the first pipe large enough to hold her. Crawling several yards, she collapsed, weakened from pain and loss of blood. *Yahweh, help me*, the Salt prayed desperately.

Urbane's foot bumped against her sword lying under the water. Picking up the weapon, he studied its lifeless surface. "I have you unholy weapon. Without it, you have no power. You and your accomplices' reign of terror in Thorn is over."

Yahweh, what am I to do? He is lost forever to me and will continue to kill your people.

A silent voice whispered to her heart, *Show him love.*

Julie's survival instinct fought against the command. *He'll kill me.*

Who gave you life? Who created the world and all that lies within it?

The Salt winced. There was no arguing with Yahweh.

Urbane's voice resonated through the chamber. "Where is your god now? Can he save you? He never helped the hundreds of heretics I killed with my own two hands."

"He is here in the midst of my trials," answered the quiet voice of Julie.

Turning towards the sound, her former lover mocked, "Have you come back for your precious sword?"

"I have no need for it. He that is in me is greater than he that is in you." Slowly Julie walked under a waterfall into the dim light, grimacing as the pounding water hit her shoulder.

"You speak nonsense. Now are you prepared to die?"

"Yes. The question is, are you prepared to live? Live with the knowledge that you killed the only woman who ever truly loved you—for the second time?"

"Do not speak of love! You know nothing of what I feel."

"Do I?" Lightheaded from blood lost, Julie weakly dropped to her knees in the center of the chamber. "I know we both shared the same ambitious goals. I used you; you used me. But someplace in the midst of selfishness and desire, you did truly care for me, as did my brother Rufus. But I pushed everyone close to me away, including you. It took me a long time to realize the true power of love, but you were too far gone to understand." She firmly met his eyes. "You are still blind. Come into the light, Urbane. Find forgiveness and peace."

"I've had enough of this!" He tossed the mystic sword towards Julie. It landed with a splash near her. "Stand and fight."

"No. I will fight no more."

"Get up! Get up and fight! Or I'll cut you down like the dog you are."

"Go ahead. Every fiber in me will still love you."

Enraged, he dashed forward and swung his sword, stopping abruptly one inch from her neck. She waited silently, not attempting to dodge. Urbane's whole body trembled. He was reliving the same nightmare that had haunted him for nearly six years. The scene of Princess Junia's death. Sometimes in the dreams it was the Emperor who struck the killing blow—sometimes it was him. In the final few seconds, part of him always tried to stop the sword—but never succeeded.

Now reality and nightmares mixed. Though he tried to deny it, he knew in his heart that it was Junia kneeling before him, again waiting execution. She had the same brown eyes, same black hair, same perfect body, but not the same soul. She possessed something he had no name for or understanding of. A part of his empty soul cried for it while his logical mind claimed it did not exist.

Again he raised his sword, poised to deliver the deathblow. Julie looked at him serenely. Tender emotions harbored within her eyes, fragile as an unwritten poem. Urbane's sword arm shook so much that he had to steady it with his left hand.

"I love you, Urbane Herron," whispered the young woman kneeling in the water before him.

The general's legs turned rubbery, and he dropped to the watery floor. Without realizing it, he began crying. Grimacing in pain, Julie wrapped her arms around Urbane as he sobbed like a child. For a long time they held each other, finding comfort against the darkness of the world—until Urbane realized the stickiness against his chest was his lover's blood.

Pulling back, he placed a hand over the wound causing Julie to wince in pain. "I am sorry, so sorry."

"I have had worse," smiled the Salt, attempting humor.

Urbane glanced around at the falling waterfalls and dark tunnels leading further into the sewers. "This is not a sanitary place to dress a wound. I'll take you to a healer."

"No." Julie's voice came out sharper than she meant. Going above would mean possible contact with Reforcers where Urbane would either have to turn her in or die. "My world is cut off from above. If you wish to follow Yahweh, you must also separate yourself from the life you have known."

The general studied Julie for a long moment before answering. "How can I fight against a god who gives life to the dead? He has given you back to me. I pledge both my life and sword to your god."

The injured Salt laughed with joy. "How I have longed to hear you say those words."

Chapter Thirty-one

Exhausted, Julie collapsed on the floor of a small chamber consisting of a rickety table, several doorways, and an open wall revealing raw sewage flowing through a wide trench. The room, if it could be called that, served as a rendezvous point and contained a medical kit, fresh water, and a few oil filled lanterns. Following Julie's direction, Urbane retrieved the kit from its hiding place behind a false stone. Sitting on the floor beside Julie, he removed the cloth he had tied around her shoulder. Despite her determination, she yelped at the sudden pain. Carefully he ripped her shirt, exposing her bare shoulder. Fresh blood flowed from the open wound. He recoiled from the knowledge that he had caused the injury, remembering the rage that had surged through him.

Julie placed a hand upon his. "It's okay. I forgive you just as Yahweh forgives you of your many crimes."

Taking fresh gauze, he firmly wrapped entrance and exit points of the wound. "Why would he forgive me, I have done too much against him."

She shakily laughed. "Have I not shared in your sins? Did I not also take the lives of his people, drunk on their blood? Yet he still loved me enough to spare my life in the canyon, let me regain my heath among a caring family, and took me to paradise when I died. I deserved none of these things."

Urban securely tied the gauze. "Hopefully that will stop the bleeding."

Though her mind was hazed by pain, Julie continued her instructions, "Beelzebub will be greatly disappointed in losing you, my love. He will double his effort to win you back, saying Yahweh will never forgive you. He'll feed on your pride and desires. Never give in. Yahweh has promised that you will never be tested by more than what you can endure."

"I can handle any trial as long as you are by my side." Gingerly he touch her face, taint with pain. His mind still struggled with accepting that she was real. "You are so beautiful, princess."

She smiled, despite the throbbing ache. Bending over her, he gently kissed her warm lips, feeling he was coming alive after years of slumber. She was tangible and belonged to him. Nothing else mattered. Not kingdoms. Not gods.

"Stop where you are!" commanded an angry voice.

The general turned to see a dirty teenager dressed in a Reforcer uniform, one shoulder bandaged. "You again. I have no quarrel with you, son."

"But I do with you, General Herron. You're responsible for killing my family and friends." With his sword pointed at his enemy, the youth walked into the room. "Step away from Julie."

Still sitting on the stone floor, Urban held up his empty hands. "I am sorry for your pain. Sheathe your weapon and let's talk like reasonable men."

Julie sat up. "Manideck, he has changed. He's on our side now."

The teenager glanced at the Salt, remembering how she had been mesmerized by the general at Citizen' Gate. "He'll say anything to get you."

"You don't understand," insisted Julie.

Footsteps announced several others coming down a passageway. Entering the room, Roshell asked, "Manideck, have you found Julie yet?" She froze, seeing the youth's raised sword, face twisted in hatred. Following his line of sight, she spotted Julie sitting on the floor with bloody blouse torn and General Herron slowly rising. "I guess you have."

Gian and Matthan stopped in the passageway behind. Gian had earlier met the filthy, bleeding Manideck wandering in the darkness, stubbornly searching for Julie. They headed towards the rendezvous point for medical supplies, but Manideck had rushed ahead when he heard voices.

Standing, Julie broke the silence that filled the small chamber. "Roshell, Matthan, I would like you to meet Urbane."

"We've already met," responded Matthan, unconsciously touching his bruised cheek. "And the pleasure was not mine."

"Urbane now serves Yahweh."

"Like a wolf to a shepherd," snapped Manideck, taking another step forward, ignoring his own shoulder wound.

Julie glanced at the teenager then focused on Roshell. "Do you remember the conversation we had not too long ago? You promised to accept those who changed, no matter their crimes."

The Ulmjon frowned, preferring to forget her promise. *If your Urbane or the Emperor suddenly did an about face, I would accept them also—though it would take a lot to prove to me they were genuine.* She had not really believed the possibility would become reality—especially this soon. "Just an hour ago, General, you wanted to kill us all. How do we know you're sincere?"

Impatiently, Julie answered before Urbane, standing near her, could respond. "Believe me, he is genuine, Roshell." Feeling weakness wash over her, Julie placed a hand against the table to steady herself.

279

"As genuine as fool's gold." Muscles tense, Manideck moved to where the table did not block his target.

Matthan asked, "Julie, who injured you?"

"Urbane. But that was before he changed." She clenched her teeth against a new wave of pain.

Keeping his hands away from his sheathed sword, Urbane tried to relieve the tension. "Again I apologize for what responsibility I share in your family's death. I am guilty of much. Ten of my lifetimes could not atone for the pain I have caused." Though he spoke words of peace, the general's trained mind worked on calculating the distance between his opponent and himself plus the time it took to draw his own weapon.

"You can go to the Great Abyss," spat Manideck.

Dizziness hit Julie, causing her to fall. Urbane grabbed her before she hit the floor. Blinded by hate, Manideck misinterpreted the suddenly movement as an attack. The teenager charged forward, sword aimed for the general. In the split second before impact, Julie's foggy mind realized Urbane would not be able to dodge the blade for he was holding her, so she forced her body upward, taking the thrust instead. The sharp blade sliced between ribs, puncturing a lung.

Horrified, Manideck pulled the bloody blade from Julie's side, his mind in denial. The weapon dropped from his lifeless hand.

A bellow of animal rage roared from Urbane. He would have ripped the teenager apart with his own hands except he still held Julie. Slowly he lowered her body to the ground and placed a hand over her bleeding side. Roshell and Matthan rushed forward. Roshell grabbed the remaining clean gauze, using it to block the blood flow, but it was quickly saturated. She took off her priestess robe, tossing it to Gian who ripped it into strips. Urbane pressed the rough cloth firmly over the soaked gauze. Across Julie's limp body, Matthan met Roshell's somber eyes, both having seen enough injuries to know the wound was fatal.

Julie attempted to speak, but it came as a cough. Blood dribbled from her lips.

"Fight it, Junia! You cannot die again," ordered Urbane.

The princess painfully smiled at Urbane, attempting to hold his hand, but she was too disoriented to find it. He grasped her hand, squeezing hard. Her body convulsed then went still.

Manideck turned to flee, but Gian blocked the teen's path. Gently, but firmly he told the ashen teen, "Turn and look, son, at what hatred does. It destroys those we care about."

"I...I didn't mean to," the youth stuttered. "She moved in the way."

"To protect me." With murderous eyes Urbane stood, his bloody hand reaching for his weapon.

"No!" Matthan stepped in front of the general. "Julie would not want you to kill again. If you truly belong to Yahweh, put up your sword."

White knuckled, Urbane gripped the handle. His love was dead and every fiber in him wanted to kill her murderer. Julie's earlier words whispered through his mind. *Beelzebub will double his effort to win you back, saying Yahweh will never forgive you. He'll feed on your pride and desires. Never give in.* If her god had saved her once, he could do so again.

Slowly he released his death grip on the sword. Turning to Matthan, he barked, "How does Yahweh bring back his dead?"

Matthan and Roshell exchanged sharp glances. Both had witnessed many miracles but never a fresh corpse regaining life.

Cautiously Roshell answered, "He does so only when it fits into a greater plan."

"Her life does! I will not serve this god unless he gives me back Julie."

Gently Matthan reprimanded the grieving man, "Urbane, Yahweh will not be dictated to. He looks into our hearts. Nothing you say or think is hidden from him. He doesn't want you with strings attached. You must go to him with a humble heart, not demanding your way."

Angrily Urbane turned away and knelt beside Julie's body. Gently he pushed hair back from her still warm face, noticing the blood drying on her chin and the redden gauze wrapped around her shoulder. How could she forgive him after what he had done to her? Head bowed, he attempted to push away his pride. What did one say to the god you have fought against your whole life? Why would Yahweh answer him?

"I have no right to ask you for anything. I've sacrificed to Zuzumza, killed in his name. I have served the Empire my whole life, earning renown, yet my life has been empty except for Junia. When I was with her, I no longer felt alone. Then she chose you over me. I've hated you for that. I still do."

Roshell, Matthan, and Gian also prayed though their focus was not on Julie but for the deliverance of her lover. In a corner huddled Manideck, trembling, wishing the earth would open and swallow him whole. He had just taken the life of a consecrated Salt. The Remnant would hate him, despise him. Yahweh would never let him into Agape, exiling him forever from seeing his murdered family.

I'm sorry. So sorry, Yahweh, cried the teenager. *Have mercy upon me. Upon us.*

A soft wind blew through the chamber, overpowering the odorous sewage with the fragrance of newly blossomed flowers. Roshell and Matthan breathed deeply, remembering the endless spring days in Shalom.

Urbane only noticed that the darkness that poisoned his soul melted like ice before the sun. "I do not know how you can forgive me after what I have done. Still, I plead for you to give Junia back to me. Perhaps she is better off with you, yet I still need her, please. I will do anything. My sword is yours. My life is yours. Take everything I have, that I am."

Julie's body shook. She sat up, violently coughing up blood. Urbane held her until the spasms passed. Deeply she breathed in fresh air. Roshell wetted a strip of the priestess robe with fresh water and wiped blood from Julie's face. For a long moment, Julie leaned against Urbane, trembling. Roshell carefully examined her wounds. Blood covered Julie's ripped clothing, yet there was no trace of cuts on her side or shoulder.

"Welcome back to the world of the living." Relief showed on Roshell's tense face. "How do you feel?"

"Like I've been mistaken for a pincushion," said Julie shakily.

Matthan smiled, faith shining in his eyes. "Seems that Yahweh still has plans for you."

Urbane held Julie close, touching her hands and arms, needing contact with her to reassure his mind that she was real and alive. For a few minutes no one spoke. Julie noticed Manideck staring at her, his eyes wide with fear and awe. With Urbane keeping an arm around her waist for balance, Julie stood and walked over to the teenager.

Manideck looked at her with pleading eyes, "I'm sorry, Julie. I didn't mean to…injure you."

"But you did mean to kill Urbane, one of your own brethren."

"He's responsible for the deaths of my family. My friends."

"So am I, Manideck. I was part of the Red Army and took the lives of many innocent Tnias." Tenderness filled her eyes. "As Yahweh forgave me, so I forgive you. I only ask one thing in return, that you also forgive Urbane."

The teenager swallowed. Memories haunting him. Death screams of his siblings, his mother murdered, friends killed one by one until he remained alone. So alone. Now he was asked to forgive the man who symbolized all the pain and hatred his short life had known. It was asking the impossible. Yet heavier weighed the knowledge that he had killed a sanctified Salt now standing before him bearing no blame.

"I for…" Unable to continue, the youth looked towards Gian. The older man nodded encouraging. Taking a deep breath, Manideck tried again. "I forgive you for what you have done to my family and friends."

The general nodded, knowing how much it cost the youth. "I will spend the rest of my life atoning for what I have done."

"Well, now that's done," said Roshell. "How about we head to the Haven? Matthan still hasn't seen his new son."

~~~~~~~~~

Violet counted slowly with eyes closed. Children ducked behind crates and bags. Hiding under a dining table, Lonees shushed his giggling sister. Unable to decide on a location, Tasia dashed across the cavern just as Violet turned around.

The teenager pretended not to see the six year old. "Wow, everyone is hiding so well this time." Immediately several chuckles escaped from the youngest children, revealing their hiding places. Violet slowly moved across the rocky chamber, peeking behind cartons and barrels, sending screaming children dashing towards a large rocking chair which served as base.

Minira entered, carrying a tray of food. The tired houseparent placed the tray on the long wooden table. "Supper is nearly ready. Everyone wash up." Groans escaped from the children. "Quickly. Lonees and Violet, help Terra bring in the food."

As the younger children filed out of the room, Minira spotted several adults entering from a passageway. She smiled in relief. The atmosphere had been tense for the last twenty-four hours in the Haven since Matthan's arrest. Many who had gone on the rescue attempt were back along with five escaped prisoners, all now sleeping soundly. Wild rumors had circulated, saying Manideck and Julie had been chased by none other than General Herron himself.

Wiping hands on her apron, Minira approached the new arrivals, face turning ashen when she spotted the blood on Julie's ripped clothing and the man dressed in an officer's uniform. "Julie, I'll get someone to tend to your wounds."

"There is no need. I would like you to meet an old friend of mine, Urbane Herron."

Minira's eyes darted to the general, but she refused to greet him. "Matthan, Danielle has been eagerly awaiting your return all day."

"And I to see her," grinned the new father. With that, Matthan headed across the large cavern to a far exit leading to the sick ward. Manideck and Gian followed to check on Gramercy.

Joyfully Julie pressed against Urbane. "There is so much I have to tell you, show you. I don't even know where to begin."

Minira gave Roshell a worried glance.

"How about getting a bath and new clothes," interrupted Roshell. "You look like the walking dead. And Urbane, you need to lose the uniform. It's going to be hard enough for people to accept you without being reminded of what you stood for."

"I'll show you our home," purred Julie.

"No, I will," Roshell said in an authoritative voice. "Take care of yourself first."

The princess opened her mouth to argue, but a brief nod from Urbane quieted her. "I'll see you at supper then." She trotted away with concerned Minira.

Roshell led Urbane down crowded corridors, passing crowded sleeping chambers housing multiple families. Everywhere bustled people busy at various tasks. Women sat in circles on the rocky floor sewing or knitting. In one corner, an instructor attempted to teach twenty wiggling students to read—using only one frayed book. Rich odors drifted from the main kitchen. People greeted Roshell but stared at Urbane in grim silence. During the short tour, Urbane viewed the Haven with the eyes of a trained assassin, forming schematizes in his head, analyzing assets and weaknesses, judging the military strength of its people.

"We keep the orphanage separate from the rest to give the kids a feeling of family," explained Roshell. "Originally we planned for the Haven to be a safe place for street kids and battered women. Instead, thanks to the Emperor and you, hundreds have been driven underground. Most are partial families, missing a member or two that have been executed. There is not enough food, clothes, or space for them all. And since we are connected to the sewers, diseases regularly break out."

"We never imagined how organized you were." Urbane spoke politely as if he was in the palace. "Nor until this day could I understand why Tnias held onto a god that only brought death and fear."

"It is Zuzumza that brings death and fear. Yahweh is love and peace." They halted in a small room piled with used clothing. "You won't find anything fashionable or of the high quality you're used to."

"I do not mind," responded the general. "I was raised on a ranch, the son of a farmhand."

"Oh, I always thought you were a noble who joined the army for the adventure."

Sensing her hostility, Urbane said, "I know you would as soon put a dagger in my heart just like that kid earlier. And other refugees feel the same. I see it in their eyes. I cannot change the past, but I can work on changing the future."

"You speak elegant words, Urbane Herron. It's easy to see why you made it to general. I have long learned not to trust in others' words but in their actions. When

I see you helping those you hunted, feeding the starving, and mourning when they die, then you'll earn my trust. Until then, watch your back when I'm around."

Urbane smiled in admiration. "It's good to see not all Tnias are gutless." Before the Ulmjon could retort, he added, "Is there anything else I need to know?"

"Yes, you have better be careful how you treat Julie. Until you are married, there will be no sex. Is that clear?"

This time the general laughed. The southerner, ablaze in righteous fury, reminded him of a mother scolding youngsters for eating candy not yet stolen. Roshell's frown deepened, and Urbane forced the mirth from his face. "Quite clear."

"When in love, it's easy to serve a new god. Time will show your true heart. See you at supper." Roshell nodded to a nearby man sorting clothing. "He's all yours now." She marched away, leaving Urbane with the man in charge of distributing clothing.

The evening moved like a whirlwind to the general. Around him were hostile forces. People staring at him, quickly averted eyes when he glanced their way—no friendly hellos or amiable greetings. He was a stranger in a world that wished he never existed. Urbane moved along the dimly lit passageways, finally locating the large chamber that served as the dining hall. He stood near a wall as hundreds of Tnias sat down at various mismatched tables, chatting with friends.

Doubt resurfaced. *What am I doing in the den of my enemies?* It had happened so suddenly. Searching for weeks to destroy the shade of Junia, only to discover the impostor really was her. Logically he should have destroyed the traitor and gone on with his life, but he could not be her executioner—not again. Then she was abruptly taken from him again then restored by the god he had fought against his whole life. Urbane meant the pledge he had spoken to Yahweh, but it was difficult letting go of a lifetime of memories serving the Empire.

Julie appeared and Urbane's worries faded into vapor. She was dressed in casual tan blouse and dark green slacks, long hair pulled into a ponytail. Her face was radiate, as if all the wars on the planet had suddenly come to a complete halt.

Smiling, she strolled over and took his hand. "Why do you look at me that way?"

"You are beautiful, no matter if you are dressed like a princess, soldier, or commoner. I have missed you so much."

"And I you."

They lost themselves in each other's eyes, the distance between them vanishing as Urbane pulled her closer and kissed her warm lips.

"Ahem," said Roshell loudly, glaring at the couple who slowly pulled apart.

Dinner flew by. The food was plain, and few dared to speak to him. Urbane focused on Julie, but there were blunt reminders that he was no longer in the palace.

As he reached for a second roll, Julie stopped him. "There is not enough food for us to have seconds, and we must soon leave for the second group will be coming in to eat." As they stood, she added, "Only breakfast and dinner are cooked. There is no lunch."

As they headed out of the dining hall, they bumped into Matthan and Danielle holding her new son. The young couple were in complete bliss—until Danielle realized she was looking into the face of a man who had once ordered her death. Matthan had told her the complete story, including Julie's second death, but it was still difficult for the new mother to accept Urbane.

Forcing a smile, Danielle said, "It good to meet you again, Urbane."

"I am sorry, but I do not remember meeting you before."

"I was only one in a group of twenty you order to be executed on the border of Telumza. My father, one brother, and my future husband were also your prisoners."

"And so was Junia. I remember that night very clearly. I still do not know how you escaped."

Julie laughed, entwining Urbane's fingers with her own. "I have many stories to tell you. Come. There is something you must see."

~~~~~~~~~

As the room filled with cheerful conversations, Manideck sat alone, eating a meal he did not taste. The events in the tunnels swirled through his head, giving him no rest.

"There you are!" Thasbow's face lit up as she spotted the youth. She quickly settled onto the bench beside Manideck. Once seated, the princess felt awkward like a skittish schoolgirl, unsure what to say.

The maiden's genuine welcome briefly cast a sunbeam in Manideck's dark world. "How did it go from your angle?"

"Not too bad. I've been worried for hours not knowing if you got out or were caught. The arena was in chaos. No one was allowed to leave. We had to watch most of the races before Rufus found an excuse to get us out. Lady Richmon and her husband told so many boring stories that I felt like jumping in front of a chariot." Thasbow continued with more details until she realized Manideck's mind was elsewhere. "What happened with your team? I have just arrived but overheard some strange talk."

Manideck stared at his food, reluctant to speak. Without asking, he trusted that the Salts and Gian would not gossip about the ghastly events that took place at the rendezvous point. Still the implication of taking Julie's life weighed heavily on him. Julie had forgiven him, but Manideck could not forgive himself. He had thought he was a good person, having saved lives numerous times. Today was the first time he faced the rage that smoldered inside him—and he did not like the monster he saw.

"We followed the plan. The second team kept the gates opened till we got out, then we all hightailed it to safety."

Thasbow lowered her voice. "I heard General Herron chased you and my sister into the sewers. Now he is suddenly a Tnias. Surely that is fiction of loose tongues?"

"No," answered Manideck slowly. "The Salts believe he is genuine."

"That cannot be. There is not a colder, heartless murderer in all of Tanlep— except for my father and Phlegon. I was there when Herron gave his sword to my father to kill Junia. I have seen the banquets given in honor of his victories and heard his speeches praising Zuzumza. He is one of the few men that Phlegon trusts. It must be some trick. Herron would never turn."

Absently Manideck mixed vegetables with gravy. "The impossible does happen."

"How can you be sure? Junia may be fooled. Love does that." Anxiety filled the maiden's pretty face. "The whole Haven may be in danger. Reforcers may be marching through the tunnels right now."

The young man placed his hand reassuringly on Thasbow's clenched fists. "I saw what happened firsthand. Believe me, Yahweh has performed the impossible. The Haven is safe."

The maiden studied Manideck's face for a long time, noting the set chin and hard eyes. He was not the same free-spirited youth she remembered from this morning. Something had happened which troubled him deeply. She wanted to ask but her female intuition told her to wait until he was ready to talk.

~~~~~~~~~

"That is the face of Yahweh?" Awe filled the general's voice as he gazed up at the painted deity on the dome ceiling.

"As close as I could make it," answered Julie, checking to see if her teenager helpers had properly cleaned up before heading to supper.

"He looks so lifelike. And the city, the waterfall, even the trees. When did you learn to paint?"

"In Agape," replied the princess matter-of-factly, washing several brushes.

287

Urbane looked around in astonishment. Though only partly completed, the chamber gave him the feeling of stepping out of a dank cave into paradise. Peace seemed to flow from the pictures and seep into his marrow. Glancing again at the lifelike face of the god, Urbane felt that Yahweh was looking directly at him—no, through him, seeing his most private thoughts. The deity's face did not frown but smiled with kind eyes.

Finished cleaning, Julie studied Urbane, noticing his fascination with the mural. "I created this so others, when troubled, can remember the awesome future Yahweh has waiting for them—for you."

The general sat on a large crate, gazing at the mural of rich green fields and deep blue sky surrounding the lustrous City of Yahweh. "What is it like to die?"

Julie sighed then settled on the opposite side of the crate. She studied the rough outline of what would soon be a detailed mural of people from many races on balconies and bridges watching a waterfall dropping thousands of feet. "It was different for me each time. The first time a Mal'ak flew me to Agape where I was welcomed by people who knew me. One was an elderly widow I met in Brentwood who now dances with her husband. There were many others—all that I killed with my own hands. They didn't condemn me but embraced me warmly."

Before going on, Julie pressed her back against Urbane, leaning her weight against him. "Today was much different. I felt my soul depart from my body, light and painless. I watched everything from the ceiling, tried to call out to you when you went after Manideck."

The general shuffled uncomfortable. "Did you hear my prayer?"

"Yes, every word." She quickly went on, sensing Urbane's uneasiness when his heart was exposed. "I cannot explain it, but I knew I was not going to Shalom yet. In the same way, I also know that the next time my soul and body part, it will be permanent."

For a long time, silence filled the mural chamber, each lost in deep thought. Finally Urbane turned and wrapped his strong arms around Julie. "Thank you. I needed this."

Relishing the moment, Julie whispered, "I can't believe you're here, really here."

"Neither can I." Tenderly he stroked her silky hair. "I have missed you so much." He kissed her lips, gently at first then more firmly. Her arms wrapped tightly around him, drawing him in. For a brief moment wars and governments were forgotten.

Julie pulled away. "It should be time for the nightly meeting to begin. Come."

Hand in hand, the couple walked down the passageways to the crowded Great Chamber. Urbane peered at huge, moist stalagmites, wondering how the massive room was lit as bright as day.

"Is it by mirrors?" he whispered to Julie as they sat on a rough-hewed boulder.

The Salt smiled mysteriously. "No. It's by Yahweh's power."

The crowd quieted as a frail looking teenager walked to the front, signaling the beginning of the service.

"That's Terra," explained Julie, "Once she was homeless. Now she works with the orphanage and is one of our best singers."

Soon musical voices echoed through the vast cavern. Having never sung since his youth, Urbane listened. The raising harmonies touched an elemental part of his soul he never knew existed, creating a longing for a god and city he had only today seen in a painting. The songs ended as a young man stood up at the front.

"Onias," informed the Salt by his side. "He is one of our primary speakers since Eleazar's death."

Urbane attempted to listen to the young man's sermon, but it was full of strange words and symbolism that the general could not comprehend. His mind wandered to counting the Tnias, noting the exits, and calculating how many soldiers would be needed to subdue a throng this size.

Julie squeezed his arm. "He's talking about you."

"What?" Urbane was jolted back to the present.

"Have you not been paying attention? Onias speaks about forgiving your enemy, loving those who despise you, turning the other cheek. He's telling everyone to welcome you with open arms."

"He has no right to talk about me to this group."

"Word travels quickly in crowded caverns, my love. There is not a Tnias in the Haven who remains blind to your presence. Many are afraid and angry, but Onias is reminding them of Yahweh's commandment to love everyone, including our enemies."

The general's frown deepened. Nearby people openly stared at him, and chill bumps ran down his arm. He was in the midst of a thousand people who had multiple reasons to kill him. The walls seem to shrink. Stalactites became divine spears ready to crush his body.

"He's asking you to come to the front." Julie's voice was muffled as from a great distance.

"No," Urbane shook his head, trying to clear his mind. "I need to get out of here."

"You're going to the front, like it or not."

Regal as a queen, Julie grabbed Urbane's hand and led him between rows of stone seats. Instead of jeers, clapping filled the vast amphitheater. When the couple reached the front, Onias gave the general a firm handshake.

"Welcome, Herron. Yahweh has answered my prayers tonight. May you be the first of many Red soldiers to join us." Raising his voice to the crowd, he said, "Come, let us welcome our new brother."

By ones, twos, and dozens, Tnias stepped forward to welcome the wolf into their flock. Instead of stones and daggers, Urbane received pats and hugs. As blurred, smiling faces passed by, one suddenly stood out—the aged face of General Nereus.

Shocked, Urbane exclaimed, "General, I never expected to see you here!"

"Nor I you. Few had been more harden or as dedicated to Zuzumza as you. It is with great joy that we welcome you to the side of light. If you serve Yahweh with the same zest you gave the Emperor, great things will be accomplished through you."

A bearded man behind the aged officer added, "My family has longed prayed for this day, General Herron. My sister has never looked happier. You have better take great care of her."

Urbane's eyes widened even further in amazement. "Yes, sir, Prince Rufus." Turning to Julie, he whispered. "The finger of Yahweh has reached further than I ever imagined."

Next came Manideck and Thasbow. For a moment the two couples studied each other, then Manideck reached out his hand, spanning the deep canyon between tormenter and victim, firmly gripping Urbane's rough hand. Thasbow was more reluctant. She glanced from her sister to Urbane, noting the happiness both shared. Finally she stepped forward, shaking the general's hand and hugging her sister.

Chapter Thirty-two

Candlelight twinkled in windows. A cool night breeze played with Julie's dark hair as she gazed across the city from the rooftop of the Greencliffs' tall home. Three days. Three days of complete bliss, of laughter, of joy, of sharing her heart and deepest thoughts. Never in the days of old did the couple get along so well, enjoy each other's company without strife or jealousy. With a sigh, she wished Urbane was by her side now. Matthan and Urbane were at a secret meeting in the Reed sector, talking with a priest who wanted to know more about Yahweh. Part of her resented being separated, even for a few hours, from Urbane. Seeing her brooding, Roshell had talked the princess into coming with her to visit Josias, recently bedridden due to declining heath. Julie looked out across the tops of thousands of houses, business, and temples. Someplace out there was her love, now toiling for Yahweh.

Julie, a voice whispered in her mind.

Distracted, the young woman glanced around the rooftop, thinking someone had called her name. She only saw Sandra's plotted plants, a picnic table, and wooden chairs.

Julie, the voice again whispered. *Look*.

The breeze stilled. The princess glanced across the city, feeling she was looking at a painting instead of reality. Candles no longer flicked. Horses pulling carriages were frozen in place.

"What do you wish to show me?" she asked, feeling the hair on the back of her neck prickle.

The view of the city rippled then faded into a scene of an ocean. Distant waves crashed against a shoreline she had never seen before. Over a hundred mighty warships plowed through the water. With a shock, Julie identified the navy as Gogian

As the shoreline grew closer the voice murmured, *Kentniko*.

Julie's pulse raced. Kentniko was the southernmost country on the continent of Iona. According to Roshell, the Tnias king had sent most of his troops to the northern border of Lahad to aid his allies. Kentniko was not prepared for an attack of this magnitude. The scene again rippled, revealing another ocean, this time the distant mountains of Timbrel rose from the plains of Misko. The navy of Queen Vevist fought valiantly against a Gogian fleet twice its size.

The princess's legs weaken, and she dropped to her knees on the rooftop. Now she knew why the Emperor had not attacked in over a year. He had been massing a navy that would catch his opponents off guard. They had been expecting a land attack on the border of Ulmjo and had committed the majority of their troops there. Emperor Phlegon was bypassing the frontline altogether with a swift strike to the hearts of his enemy. First defeat the small patrol fleets of the Triad, then Gogian troops would push rapidly inland to capture the capitols of Kentniko and Misko. Chaos would follow. The Triad crushed. Alone, Lahad would not be able to stand against the might of Gog.

The scene shifted again. Below zoomed forested hills, farmland, and towns along the southern border of Ulmjo—and tens of thousands of soldiers. Sunlight glinted off the armor of troops locked in deadly combat. Gogian swords clanged again Lahadian battle axles. From the sky rained deadly arrows and stones from catapults. The lofty Timbrel Mountains zoomed into the distance and again Julie saw troops furiously fighting in the jungles of Misko. Everywhere was death and destruction.

"Yahweh, you must stop this," Julie pleaded. "This cannot come to pass or all is lost."

I have a message for the Emperor. You must take it to him.

Her heart quickened. Surely she had heard wrong. "No, I already faced my father and died. I cannot face Phlegon." She did not fear death itself, but she did fear never experiencing being a wife and mother, of not finishing the murals, of leaving her apprentices' training incomplete. There was too much work to be done, too little of life she had yet to experience.

Again the scene changed. War raged across meadows and forests of Lahad. Swords crashed, screams of the dying filled the air. Horses galloped over dead bodies of women and children. Smoke rose from burnt villages. Once she would have been one of the butchers, gloating in the destruction, now she trembled in the terror of what was to come.

Shaking, she told her god, "I will do whatever it takes to prevent this."

A cool breeze kissed the tears running down her cheek. Looking across the city, she saw twinkling lights and trotting horses, laughter drifting from an open window nearby. All was like it had been. A dark object passed over the moon, casting the city in deep shadow. Glancing up, Julie spotted the swift God of War darting across the sky. Quickly she hurried across the roof and down the stairs.

~~~~~~~~~

"Toss me another onion," commanded Roshell, chopping vegetables as furiously as she tackled everything in life. A white bulb sailed through the air and the southerner easily caught it.

Sandra went back to stirring a pot. "Onias should be up soon. He's always been a late raiser. Joatham's in his study. He's taking too much on himself, and with Josias sick, he's going to die of worry."

Roshell spooned eggs and chopped onions into a heated skillet. "A good meal is what this family needs."

The door swung open and Julie entered.

"Good morning," called out Sandra, but her cheerfulness died when she saw Julie's face.

Roshell glanced up. The girlish, happy maiden of the last few days was gone. A somber woman, reconciled to fate, stood before them, eyes puffy from crying. "Looks like you had a rough night."

"I did." Julie sat in a chair and stared blankly at a cup of water Sandra placed in front of her.

Roshell settled across from Julie and waited. Finally losing patience, she challenged, "So are you going to tell us what happened before my hair turns gray?"

The princess took a deep breath. "I had a vision from Yahweh. Emperor Phlegon created two vast fleets which will attack lower Misko and Kentniko at the same time."

Sandra stopped stirring the food.

Roshell forgot to breathe. "Are you sure about this?"

"Unfortunately, yes. It gets worst. The upper borders of Lahad and Misko will be invaded on the same day."

The southern slumped in her chair. Memories of friends, co-workers, and children swirled through her mind. "Four places at once. I didn't think Gog had such resources after all these years of fighting. The Triad can't hold out long."

"My father stripped conquered territories of all their resources and excess food. It kept the new lands in submission and strengthened Gog. I knew we had a strong navy, but my brother has tripled its size."

Unable to bear more, Sandra said, "Yahweh will not let the Triad fall. Many believed the other nations fell because they turned away from Yahweh, but most of the leaders and citizens of Lahad, Kentniko, and Misko have pledged to him. Yahweh will not desert them."

Roshell shared the same belief, but felt no comfort remembering the invasion of her own country of Ulmjo, family and friends dead. The Red Army was a well-organized machine that brought death to all it touched.

"Yahweh has asked me to do something." Sandra and Roshell looked expectantly towards the Salt. "I am to deliver a message directly to my brother Emperor Phlegon."

"What?" exclaimed the southerner. "You'll be sentenced to death—again."

"I know, but I must obey Yahweh."

"There must be another way," Sandra said. "Just write the message down and pay someone to deliver the letter."

"I have already considered that possibility. In a fit of rage Phlegon may kill the courier, even if it was one of his own soldiers. I will not have more innocent blood on my hands. No, I must be the one."

Sandra shook her head, not accepting the news.

Roshell was more resigned. "If Yahweh says it must be done then you must obey. Your bigger problem is how will Urbane take it."

~~~~~~~~~

"I knew about his plans," Urbane calmly spoke at the end of Julie's story. "I helped him create them. Within the next few days, I was to head south to Ulmjo to oversee the final land attack."

"You knew? Why did you not tell us?" Julie stood near a stack of crates in an isolated storage room where they could talk privately.

"For what purpose? Everything has already been set in motion." The general chose his words cautiously, treaded the edge of the gap which still separated how he and Julie viewed life. "What can you do? Send a warning to the Triad? It would take weeks for a messenger to reach the south, and most likely he would be killed trying to cross the border between two armies ready to shoot at shadows."

"We can still try."

"You do not understand. Even if the southern rulers knew what was to come, they would not have time to reposition their troops. They are already outnumbered and inexperience. They will lose."

Agitated, Julie turned away. She had enough military experience to know he spoke the truth, but it bothered her. Part of her wanted to jump on a horse and dash south, but doing so would accomplish nothing. Taking a deep breath, she told him the hardest part of what Yahweh had revealed. "I am to take a message personally to my brother."

"See the Emperor? He will put you to death immediately."

"I know. But I must obey Yahweh."

Numbly he glanced around the small storage chamber, desperate to find a way to erase the words he had just heard. "I forbid it. You cannot go."

"You forbid?" Annoyance flashed through the princess's eyes. "On what authority do you forbid me? You are not my god. Nor my husband—yet."

"I will not let you go on a suicide mission. You said yourself the next time you die will be final." Urbane's own anger rose to the surface. "Do you really think I can sit by and let you die again?"

"I am going tonight and that is final." She marched towards the exit.

Reacting quickly, Urbane grabbed her shoulders, twisting her around, and firmly kissed her on the lips.

Angrily she pushed him away. "Is that your answer for everything?"

"Your solution is to always do things your way, with no regard for the feelings of others. Of course, I should be used to that by now." He turned his back on her.

An awkward silence filled the small room. It took Julie several minutes to overcome her fury. "What you said is unfair. I know I did things that hurt you, but I am no longer that conceited princess. Do you think I want to die?"

Urbane rubbed a hand through his short, cropped hair. "Neither do I want you to. Without you, there is no reason for me to live."

Julie's face softened as she came nearer. "Yes, there is. Yahweh has not transformed you just to abandon you a few days later. He has a purpose for you just as he does for me. We both must follow that plan."

The general clasped Julie's hands. "And that plan is for both of us to face the Emperor."

The young woman studied her fiancé's face. "Are you sure?"

"More so than in my whole life."

~~~~~~~~~

Blackwall Palace bustled in celebration. Nobles paraded in their best outfits while servants hustled to attend their every need. Exhilarating music resounded through the enormous Hall of Kings, bouncing off three floors of columned balconies. Beating drums announced the arrival of performers. As lights dimmed, dancing couples quickly cleared the central floor as acrobats somersaulted into the room. While twirling torches, darkly clad jugglers formed a border around the open dance floor. Costumed dancers performed to a bone-piercing beat the story of Achoziez's Ascension. The crowned man representing the first Emperor gracefully weaved across the dance floor as the other actors bowed submissively to him. Several performers climbed onto the backs of others, only to have another stand on theirs to form the Tower of Zuzumza complete with a dark, sparklingly cloth covering the top person to represent the Claw.

The audience held their breath expectantly for what was to come. The pretend Emperor climbed up the human tower and hid under the black cloth. In slow motion the tower collapsed as acrobats tumbled to the floor in a controlled fall. Only the black cloth and hidden ruler remained high in the air. The watching crowd knew the effect was done with thin rope, but in the dimly lit room, it appeared as if the glittery cloth floated magically twenty feet above the floor. The thorn shaped cloth rose higher into the air until level with the fourth floor balconies. The covering fell, exposing the Emperor actor hovering in the air. Suddenly, bright light flooded from the largest balcony, revealing the outline of an elaborated costumed actor representing Zuzumza, God of War. The crowned ruler danced expertly, flipping and twirling through the air, delighting the crowd. Finally with a triple somersault, he landed beside the god. Cheers filled the air as Zuzumza nodded in approval to the kneeling monarch.

All lights went out. A hush fell across the crowd. Usually this was the end of the annual performance—but not this night. Drums echoed through the vast room, sending chill bumps down people's arms. The flame bearers relit their twirling sticks, illumining the actors on the dance floor frozen in various positions. Through the costumed throng walked Phlegon, purposeful and bold. As he passed performers, each dramatically bowed. Reaching the edge of the dance floor, the Emperor continued through the crowd of nobles who followed the example of the actors. The monarch climbed the stairs leading to the embellished gold throne.

Turning to the hundreds gathered, he proclaimed in a booming voice, "Each year we remember the ascension of the first Emperor of Gog into the Third Firmament. Tonight we celebrate the ascension of the first Emperor of all Iona." A number of people cheered, but others remained silent, stunned by Phlegon's bold and unconventional proclamation. "Even as I speak, the mighty Gogian Navy and our undefeated Red Army move into key positions to strike the last of our adversaries from every side at once. I swear upon my life, the entire continent will belong to the Gogian Empire within three months." This time the entire chamber reverberated with deafening clapping.

The Emperor waited several moments until the crowd quieted. "Let the celebration continue!"

Candles and lanterns were relit. Musicians played upbeat tunes while couples danced across the great hall. Phlegon settled on the large throne, pleased with the ceremony.

Dressed in the brightest, lowest cut outfit at the ball, Lady Cassandra approached the throne and gave a deep bow. "I congratulate Your Majesty on your coming victory and ask for your first dance tonight."

The Emperor studied the gorgeous woman in front of him. Like his father, Phlegon let no tender feelings weaken his mind. Still, he needed to produce a strong heir to his throne and privately had promised Cassandra marriage after the war ended. Standing to accept her dance, he noticed two figures weaving through the dancers towards the throne. He immediately recognized Urbane, dressed in full military uniform. The second was a robed and hooded prisoner, hands tied. They stopped at the foot of the marble dais.

"General Herron, rumors circulate that you have been killed by the hands of our enemy. I am pleased you have proved the critics wrong yet again." Phlegon gave a rare, genuine smile. The somber and keen mind of Urbane stood out from the superficial aides whose only purpose was to heartily approve the Empire's plans. Urbane fought a holy war of vengeance—so did Phlegon, leading to a deep bond between the two men.

"You know me, Your Majesty. I never stop until my duty is complete. I bring one of the founders of the Tnias movement in Thorn."

"Again you are to be commended, General." Phlegon studied the hooded prisoner who kept her head bent downward. "Few have equaled your achievements in the entire history of Gog."

"You may not feel that way after you see who I have brought." Reaching over, Urbane removed the hood from the prisoner, revealing a woman of royal beauty.

Standing beside the Emperor, Cassandra gasped in frightened recognition, tightening her grip on Phlegon's arm. His face paled in shock as he recognized his dead sister. For a brief moment he was a scared bully cowering in front of a ghost demanding revenge for crimes long hidden. The moment passed. Pulling away from Cassandra, the monarch cocked his head slightly. "A joke? Herron, I did not think you had a sense of humor."

Nearby conversations stopped as nobles recognized the princess many had seen die years before. The bound woman took two steps up the dais. "I am what you see, brother."

"Is that right? A heretic about to be sentenced to death?" Amusement dripped from the ruler's voice like sticky honey waiting to trap irritating insects.

The woman raised her voice so all nearby could hear. "Yahweh has a message for Gog. 'Look, you scoffers, wonder and perish, for I am going to do something in your day that you would never believe even if someone told you.'"

With a bored expression, the Emperor turned to his right-hand man. "Enough of this show. General Herron, put this pretend soothsayer to death."

"I cannot, sir." Urbane squarely met the monarch's gaze. "I serve a higher power now."

The sharp words at first did not sink in, but when they did, even Phlegon's stone heart was slashed by them. The pain of deepest betrayal flashed across the handsome face of the Emperor, only to be replaced by murderous fury.

"Guards, kill these traitors!" he barked. Two Royal Guardsmen stationed on each side of the throne stepped forward with weapons drawn, but hesitated, confused by the sudden appearance of a dead princess and an order to kill their commanding officer.

Julie let the heavy robe drop from her shoulders as she shook off her bonds. Then she drew her sword. Immediately fire leaped along the blade's polished surface. Gasps escaped from bystanders. Someone screamed, cutting off the orchestra. The dancers stopped in the sudden quietness, and hundreds of eyes looked towards the unnatural sword held by a dead princess standing in front of the Emperor's throne.

"You will hear what I have to say, brother." Julie stepped forward boldly. "So speaks Yahweh, 'I am against you, O Gog. You are a fierce crocodile, but I have put a hook in your jaw. I will bring you from the far north and send you against my people. Get ready. Be prepared, you and all the hordes gathered about you. Take command of them. But you will never see the Mountains of Timbrel. I will strike the bow from your left hand and break the arrows in your right hand.'"

Phlegon laughed deeply. "Foolish woman, Zuzumza has given me this continent. Guards! To me now! Kill these heretics."

Soldiers pushed through the startled crowd, heading for the throne. Julie did not flinch. "Yahweh has selected a man after his own heart to take your place, brother."

As the guards reached the dais, both Julie and Urbane's bodies began to glow brighter than the fanciest lanterns. Silence reigned through the vast chamber as the huge crowd stared in bewildered astonishment. The guards froze, uncertain. Then one stepped closer. Suddenly he seemed to convulse by an unseen power then pass out. Terrified, the other soldiers refused to attack. Only Julie noticed the wink that the *unconscious* guard gave her. It was Tranton, a Tnias, who had let Manideck and the prisoners escape from the cage at Market Square.

Voice resounding against the high ceiling, Julie addressed the nobles, "Listen you who have ears. You will know Yahweh is the One True God by this sign—before two months pass, Emperor Phlegon will be smote down dishonorably in battle."

Enraged, knowing he had lost control of the situation, the young ruler screamed at his dead sister, "I will rip you shiny throat out with my bare hands. You will not say such sacrilegious things in my presence."

Wielding the Sword of Fire, Julie braced for his attack. It did not come. Though Phlegon boasted boldly, fear bound him as tightly as it did his useless soldiers. Turning, the radiate couple walked towards the double doors at the opposite end of the Great Hall of Kings. Nobles, servants, and soldiers cleared a path before them, too afraid to offer opposition. Nearing the exit, Julie's eyes met Thasbow. The younger sibling smiled proudly, unable to hide her delight. After the glowing couple disappeared into the night, silence hung thickly across the party. Slowly people turned to their neighbors, demanding to know if they had seen the same thing.

Phlegon growled to the nearest guard, "Gather my Cabinet. We will meet in the Chamber of Juxtaposition, immediately."

Lady Cassandra placed a hand on her fiancé shoulder, attempting to calm him. "General Herron would never betray you. He must have been killed in battle, and his soul captured by our enemy."

The Emperor looked at her coldly. "I have work to do."

He marched out of the ballroom, leaving the beautiful woman standing alone. The orchestra began playing again, but only a few couples returned to dancing. The crowd began to disperse, with gossiping groups forming about the great hall.

Lady Mahan caught up to Thasbow in a hallway. "Who was that?"

"You do not recognize my sister?"

"But she's dead. We all know that."

"Yes, she is." The princess turned to walk away, wanting to quickly head to the Haven and tell Manideck all she had witnessed.

Lady Mahan grabbed her arm. "You know something. I saw her smile at you. Please, I need to know. What has become of General Herron? Is he under a spell like they say?"

"Do not ask me this, Mahan. I value my life as much as you do."

"I am your friend and would never betray you. I have suspected for some time that you're one of them. Please, Thasbow, I must understand what is going on."

The teenager wavered, uncertain. When it came to politics and religion, even the closest friends would stab their comrades in the back if it meant security for themselves. "Can you face doubting everything you believe in? Discovering your world is only an illusion?"

"I already know it is. We aristocrats spend our whole lives pretending to be more than what we are. You know few of us care about which god we claim to worship. The deities are all the same."

"No, there is one that is completely different. If you are serious, I will tell you about him. If you accept him, your life will never be the same."

Nervously Lady Mahan glanced around. Despite the supernatural incident, the party still went on. Many drank, flirted, and danced as if life was an endless caper. Others soberly talked about the occurrence, wondering what it meant. She took a deep breath. "Let us go to the park where we can talk in private."

~~~~~~~~~

The Emperor paced around the huge oak table where his nervous advisors sat. His father had been known for his dangerous outbursts which often ended in someone's death while Phlegon was cold and calculating like a reptile—until tonight. He raged and yelled, pounding on the table, demanding answers no one had. The young monarch cursed himself for sending his smartest officials to battle where they would not publicly challenge his decisions. Now none left were capable of giving sensible advice in times of crisis.

The door opened to admit a courier. "Your Majesty, I have brought General Nereus as you asked."

"Bring him in." *This is truly my darkest hour,* thought Phlegon, *for I am seeking counsel from one of the men I despise the most.*

As the elderly soldier entered, leaning heavy on a cane, the Cabinet relaxed, believing the renowned war hero would soon put all to right. The general settled into an offered chair.

The Emperor reseated himself at the head of the huge table. "General Nereus, have you been briefed on what has happen?"

"I have been told the ghost of Princess Junia appeared with a glowing General Herron." The aged man spoke slowly, as if eternity itself rested on his shoulders.

"Not only did they have the impertinence to desecrate this holy night of celebration, but the witch claimed I will die within two months in battle— dishonorably."

The general nodded, taking everything in. "It is obvious that she wants you to lead your armies into battle. If you happen to die, it makes her appear a prophet. I suggest safely staying in Thorn."

Phlegon was unsatisfied with that answer. "She has made me look like a fool in front of all the nobles. If I stay behind these walls, they will believe I am a weakling cowering before a false god."

"Then go, Your Majesty, but keep safely away from the front lines."

The Emperor nodded. "I accept your counsel." Turning to Captain Patrobas, he added, "While I am gone, do everything in your power to erase the sect. Bring me the heads of Junia and Herron, or your own head will decorate my wall when I come back."

The Reforcer captain bowed. "I consider it a personal disgrace what has been done to General Herron. I will destroy all who have blemished him."

Chapter Thirty-three

The Emperor left the next day to perform the role his former chief general should have been doing. He left behind a city in chaos. Less than a week ago a sixth of the population of Thorn had sat in the arena, watching a historic execution go awry. They saw gallant General Herron leading a charge across the sand, commanding and valiant in the face of danger. Now scandalous rumors rippled through the city, claiming the officer had appeared with his dead Tnias lover in the palace and placed a curse on the Emperor. The city waited in restless anticipation of what was to come.

The storm quickly blew into a hurricane. Captain Patrobas pounded Thorn with brutal persecution, upsetting even the nobles with endless new regulations and raids at the most unsuitable times. Businesses and homes where randomly invaded, for Patrobas suspected that the sect was being secretly supported by the upper classes. As the Reforcers strengthen, so did the Tnias rebellion. Curiosity caused many to seek the truth behind the stories, leading to new conversations. Over two thousand Tnias packed into the underground Great Hall to see Julie and Urbane married before the eyes of Yahweh. It was a day of great celebration.

Knowing it was losing control, the god Zuzumza frequently left its tower to fly over the city in broad daylight, striking fear in all who saw its monstrous form. Often it was seen perched on the top of its enormous temple, the worshipers inside dancing and spinning erotically. Those who once believed in no gods found faith by seeing, and the Mausoleum of Zuzumza became the most visited shrine in Thorn.

The war for souls grew fiercer.

~~~~~~~~~

A banging knock aroused Rufus from deep sleep. Beside him, Henna drowsily groaned. Groggily, he rose and cracked the door open. "It's the middle of the night. This better be important, Congter."

"Sir, there are several men downstairs demanding to see you. Two wear Reforcer uniforms."

Instantly Rufus was awake. "Henna, up now. You must take the kids and flee to the Haven with the servants."

The woman's lips trembled. "I will not leave you."

Kneeling, the thirty-year-old prince tenderly held her wife's hands. "We knew this day would come. You and the children must leave, now."

Crying Henna wrapped her arms around Rufus, kissing him passionately.

Reluctant to intrude on the private scene, Congter whispered from the doorway, "Sir, they're waiting."

Rufus broke away from his wife. "You must hurry. I will delay them as long as possible."

She nodded slowly, wiping away tears. Quickly she followed Congter to wake the children. Rufus took his time dressing, said a quick prayer for strength, and luxuriously walked down the front staircase while scrutinizing the four men in his living room. Two were seated with their backs to him. He recognized Captain Patrobas standing beside a Reforcer lieutenant.

"Can I help you, gentlemen, this early morning?" Rufus put a slight irritation in his voice.

Captian Patrobas bowed politely. "We bring troubling news, Prince Rufus." He glanced towards one of the seated men expectantly.

"Forgive me for not standing. I am too old for these late night assembles," came the deep voice of General Nereus from the couch. "The Cabinet had an emergency meeting a few hours ago and invited me. It was imperative that we speak with you immediately."

Concerned, Rufus sat down, giving the aged general his full attention.

"Brace yourself, son. The Emperor, your brother, has died. We just received word."

Taking a deep breath, Rufus leaned back against the thick cushion. "How did this happen?"

Angrily Patrobas answered, "A night raid by a strike force thinking they were attacking our supplies tents. He was cut down without even a sword. He was found in his nightclothes, broken bow and arrows beside him, a knife in his back"

The general and prince exchanged a secret glance, remembering Julie's prophecy.

Calmly Nereus said, "You are the next in line, Rufus. We have come to take you to your palace."

The prince opened his mouth to speak but found no words. After taking a deep breath, he managed to say, "I have taken a vow to keep away from Gogian politics."

"Because of its corruption," said Henna from the doorway, body taut. She had sent her children away with the servants but refused to leave without her husband.

Rufus stood, pleased to see his wife. She hugged him and quietly whispered, "Yahweh is giving you this opportunity to serve him. Don't turn it down."

He looked into her eyes, seeing her deep resolve. The hardest sacrifices would be on her, a simple peasant, thrown into a world of snobbish intellects and inflated egos. How would he raise his children with strong values growing up among endless wealth? Being Emperor meant dealing with arrogant aristocrats who cared nothing about the people below them. He would spend a lifetime attempting to change an entire society's attitudes, facing outright enemies, false friends seeking favors, and heated opposition. It was not a life he wished for his wife and children.

As Rufus turned to face the men, he already knew what his answer would be. Yahweh had foreseen this moment and already chosen the new ruler of the Gog Empire.

~~~~~~~~~

The sun rose, casting its dazzling light upon Thorn. Merchants and peddlers made their way through gates into the city to sell wares. Streets began to bustle with activity as people headed to work, shopped, or sought entertainment. Horses trotted along cobbled streets pulling carriages or cargo. Early morning pedestrians strolled along paths of the city parks. The day started as every day had for the past few millenniums—but today marked a historic change that would forever alter their destiny.

A small ripple of excitement darted through the air when early morning worshipers to the Mausoleum of Zuzumza found the priests mourning, claiming that Emperor was dead. Phlegon, like his father before him, was not liked by the masses who suffered under heavy taxation, military drafts, and strict regulations. The people idolized legendary rulers like Achoziez, renowned for caring for his citizens. The news spread like wildfire as worshipers told friends who in turn told others. Long before official word was released, the park and streets near Blackwall Palace filled with people celebrating. They knew who was next in line for emperorship—a man who had lived among them, even married one of their own. Zealous citizens, ignoring the dozen guards barking that the area was off limits, soon overrun the Royal Garden.

~~~~~~~~~

Tranton, in full uniform, appeared in the Haven with six guards, claiming the Emperor wished to meet with the four Salts and General Herron. Roshell laughed in his face then drew her sword. Matthan was not so quick to dismiss the summon, for Tranton had repeatedly saved lives of Tnias. As curious people gathered, Tranton informed them Phlegon was dead. Bystanders stared at him in silent disbelief.

The soldier placed a hand over his heart. "I swear by Yahweh's holy name, that Prince Rufus was crowned not two hours ago. His first decree as Emperor ended all religious persecution. His second declaration called for a ceasefire with the Triad."

A shockwave thundered through the Haven. Shouts and yells followed. Many Tnias dropped to their knees, crying in relief or praying thanks. Some simply stared into space, quietly thinking of dead love ones.

Soon Roshell found herself and her friends openly strolling down Main Street escorted by Royal Guards. The soldiers formed a tight circle around their charges, pushing through excited throngs. The streets were overrun with people too ecstatic to work. Factories and stores closed across the city.

Glancing at the armed soldiers, the southerner muttered, "How ironic can life get? We're being protected by the same guards who tried to kill us a short time ago."

"And you ate breakfast with one too," Urbane said playfully.

Beaming, Julie hugged her husband then spread out her arms, yelling, "Yahweh is awesome!" Several passersby stared, shocked at the bold words, thinking she must be a heretic walking to her execution.

A baker, placing a closed sign on his door, shouted back, "He is the One True God!" Several Royal Guards glanced uneasily at the man but kept walking.

Matthan raised his voice so all nearby could hear. "Yahweh reigns supreme!" His words were echoed back by several happy Gogians.

Danielle started humming a hymn, and the other Salts joined in. Several people fell in step behind the soldiers, singing loudly. Watchers yelled out both curses and praises.

A young woman pushed her way through the soldiers and dropped to her knees in front of Julie. "I must know, are you Princess Junia?"

Julie looked into the youth's hopeful eyes. "Yes, I am."

The woman exhaled sharply, "By the gods, I've tried to follow your example. I've even made it to corporal in the Red Army, but when I became pregnant, I was sent home."

The princess gently pulled the maiden up. "Then by Yahweh, be the best mother you can be. Lovingly raising one child is far more worthy than slaughtering a thousand foes."

"I will raise my child the best I can—by Yahweh."

The guards quickly hurried their charges onward. Despite being dressed as a commoner, Urbane was easily recognized by several teenagers leaning out of second-story windows. Waving excitedly, they called out his name, attracting attention of curious pedestrians who crowded close to glimpse the famous general. Seven Royal Guards were not enough to keep back the thrilled mass.

Spotting several Reforcers disdainfully glaring at the singing Tnias, Tranton called out, "To me, soldiers. Keep back this crowd."

One answered scornfully, "We kill heretics, not protect them."

Tranton barked back, "I will report your traitorous words to the Emperor when I get to the palace, unless," he paused dramatically, "you give me a reason to change my mind."

The Reforcers joined the Royal Guardsmen, keeping the spectators at bay. What should have been an hour's stroll turned into a three-hour parade. When the Salts finally reached the castle gate, several hundred Tnias marched rapturously behind the guards, singing and dancing. Their sounds mixed with the ecstatic chants of thousands of citizens gathered in the nearby parks. The deep clank of the closing portcullis, separating the travelers from the city, brought deep relief to the tired soldiers. Tranton led the soldiers and Salts to the Great Hall of Kings.

Entering, Julie paused, sharp memories resurfacing of the last time she had been there with both Rufus and Urbane. Sensing her thoughts, Urbane squeezed her hand.

The new Emperor sat on the broad gold throne at the opposite end of the room with Empress Henna in a wooden chair beside him. Breaking centuries of tradition, Rufus had given his wife equal status. Workmen scattered back and forth, taking measurements, for Rufus had ordered the pompous throne to be replaced with two smaller ones. Aides whispered nearby while servants dashed to tend the needs of the growing crowd of nobles biding congratulations to their new Emperor.

"Welcome!" echoed Rufus's voice throughout the colonnade chamber.

Every person focused on the newcomers, many showing surprise, others hostility. Princess Thasbow winked as her sister passed, Lady Mahan smiled sweetly, and General Nereus gave a sober bow. Spectators contemptuously studied the dark-skin foreigner, alien couple, fallen general, and ghost princess. Many believed they were prisoners marching to their execution because over a dozen guards escorted them

Lady Richmon whispered to her husband, "What a brilliant way for the Emperor to start his reign, capturing those who shamed his brother."

Reaching the front, all five Tnias kneeled. The great chamber went silent as all watched.

Head touching floor, Urbane held his sword high up. "My life I place in your hands, Great Emperor. Do with it as you must."

Somberly, the monarch took Urbane's weapon. "Arise, General Herron. Your betrayal against my brother is pardoned. I give back your life in return for your service to the throne of Gog." He passed the weapon back, handle first as a sign of trust. "The four known as Salts are also pardon of all crimes standing against them, and I appoint them to my new Cabinet."

Startled gasps escaped from haughtily aristocrats while cheers burst from friends and admirers. Leaving the upset nobles to strew in their own anger, Rufus met with his friends in a private room. Henna settled by her husband on a velvet cushion.

"I cannot believe it," grinned Julie, "You, an Emperor!"

"Yahweh works in mysterious ways," said her brother.

"What I liked best," said Roshell, "was the look on their faces when you appointed us advisors. I can die happy now."

Laughing, Henna added, "You should have been here this morning when he declared an end to war and religious persecution. Phlegon's cabinet almost caused a riot—so Rufus reappointed many of them to oversee the street, agricultural, and sewage departments."

"Wait until they discover that is where we have been this whole time," giggled Danielle.

Rufus waited until the laughter died down to attack the subject pressing on his mind. "I can change peoples' jobs, but not their hearts. That comes with living every day showing the genuine love Yahweh has given us."

Knowing the timing was right, Roshell suggested, "Fund shelters for street kids, prostitutes, and the homeless. I can organize them not only in Thorn but throughout the Empire."

"I will implement the plan in the first Cabinet meeting," answer Rufus. "But Gog is still enslaved."

"Zuzumza," said Urbane.

The Emperor nodded. "Until the God of War is banished, the land cannot heal. The quicker we face this demon, the better, before it causes more problems."

Chapter Thirty-four

Five solemn warriors climbed the seemingly endless stairs inside the tower leading up to the Claw. There were no windows, no source of light except the lanterns they carried. As they progressed higher, the dense, lifeless air became an invisible weight pressing heavily upon their bodies. Unreasonable terror screamed through their minds. Each step was a psychological battle, pushing against their sanity.

Mentally exhausted, Urbane stopped on a landing. "We cannot go on like this."

"Then we pray," said Matthan.

The five soldiers kneeled on the cold stone, talking fervently to their deity. The atmosphere lightened and fears vanished. They rose, revitalized, and continued the climb. Reaching the top of the immense structure, a locked ornate gold door awaited them.

"Do you have a key?" Julie asked Rufus.

"There is only one key and our father gave it to Phlegon. I do not know if he carried it with him into battle or kept it hidden inside the castle."

"That's no problem." Roshell pulled out a thin metal rod from a pocket and inserted it into the lock. After a few minutes the heavy door swung open. "You learn much growing up on the streets."

Cautiously they walked into the colossal, symmetrical chamber where only emperors had trodden before. All was darkness except for a distance light coming from an open balcony doorway. Slowly they moved further into the vast room, their footsteps echoing against the smooth stone walls. A central dais could dimly be made out, rising ten feet above the marble floor. Suddenly the room flooded in light as dozens of torches along the walls self-ignited. Startled, the Tnias jumped then pulled out their weapons.

"This is an unholy place," mumbled Roshell.

Rufus walked towards the dais. "Show yourself, Zuzumza! In Yahweh's name, we have come to end your reign."

A cold, hideous laugh resounded through the chamber—and their souls. "A mortal daring to order me, God of War? I created Gog. I empowered Achoziez's line. You would never have been born except I granted it. I designed you for emperorship. Now kneel before your Master!"

The ceremonial gold lamps on the dais dimmed. The flames still burn, but light was not given off. A dark mist formed in the middle of the platform, becoming denser, larger. As it solidified, light was absorbed instead of reflected. The huge black cloud formed leathery wings, clawed limbs, spiked tail, gaping maw, and red eyes of pure hate.

The Emperor commanded, "It is you who will bow before Yahweh, your creator."

The god hissed. "Human, you are in my lair."

A hideous presence touched Rufus's mind, awaking the man's darkest deeds, his blackest thoughts.

"You led my armies, killed my enemies, and wore my medal. Now you stand before me, accusingly? How typical of Tnias."

Rufus shook his head, unable to clear his mind. Julie placed a firm hand on her brother's shoulder then faced the apparition.

"We are all forgiven by Yahweh. Our crimes are erased in his eyes. It is Yahweh that judges you and has found you guilty."

The fiend opened his mouth in a sinister grin. "Yahweh is powerless beyond his mountains, so he sends mortals to do his bidding. Does he really care for you, Junia?" The creature bent its long neck downward, coming within a yard of the woman. A malevolent presence pounded through her mind, bending and reshaping her thoughts. "You are a daughter after my own heart. When all deserted you including your own father, I heard your prayers, giving you the life of the Galand king. I protected you with the gift of invincibility in battle. It was I who gave you the desires of your heart. Come to me, child, and we will be one."

Red eyes filled the princess's sight. Waves of power and passion flowed around her. Julie faded before the onslaught, six years of memories stripped away, leaving Princess Junia craving the sensations, relishing hatred and domination. Her breath quickened as she began climbing the dais steps. Rufus reached for her arm, but Zuzumza'a long tail whipped out, sending the unprepared man sprawling to the floor. Urbane, Roshell, and Matthan dashed forward. The general reached Julie first.

Gripping shoulders, he roughly shook her. "Snap out of it, Junia!"

She smiled at him. "This is what we both wanted—the power. Gog can be ours."

"No! It is not you talking. Remember Yahweh!"

The princess wavered as a nagging feeling swam through her subconscious, telling her there was something special about that name. Zuzumza's power assaulted her brain, whipping away the memory before it could be recalled. She took another step towards the waiting god. Urbane wrapped his strong arms around her slender body, pulling her to him. Firmly he kissed her, refusing to let go as she attempted to push away. She relaxed, her arms curving around him, kissing him back.

Finally Julie spoke, "I am okay now, husband."

Feet spread apart, sword raised, Roshell planted herself higher up the steps. "Enough of this, demon! Before you claw your way through my brain, know that Yahweh beat you to it. The difference is, he changes hearts. You only twist minds." Matthan stood beside her, equally ready for battle.

The fiend fixed its red eyes on the two warriors, searching their minds for weaknesses. Memories of dead families and friends filled them, carried upon a wave of anger against the murderers. Matthan again felt the guilt of not being there to protect his family and rage against Yahweh for letting it happen. Roshell's smoldered in hatred against the Red Army and all its members for mercilessly taking country after country, raping the land and killing those she cared about. So much unpunished atrocities had been committed.

"Greater is he that is in me than he that is in the world." Matthan whispered the words, clinging to them like a drowning man to driftwood. He repeated the phrase louder, more confident.

Roshell joined in. "Greater is he that is in me than he that is in the world."

Angrily the god hissed, increasing his mental attack. Weapon raised, Rufus joined the two Salts in the chant. Julie and Urbane added their voices.

Five voices echoed through the ornamental chamber, "Greater is he that is in me than he that is in the world!"

Quicker than a striking cobra, enraged Zuzumza whipped his massive tail across the steps. Prepared, Rufus and Matthan jumped over it, but Roshell fell, tumbling backwards into the princess and general. Zuzumza circled around the two standing soldiers to attack the three untangling themselves on the marble floor. Both Rufus and Matthan charged the deity's back, their swords bouncing harmlessly off its thick scales. The god swished its tail like a cow shooing away flies then snapped its jaws down upon the raising threesome, its jagged teeth piercing Roshell's leather armor. The southerner screamed in pain.

Urbane slashed with all his might, but his blade slid across Zuzumza's snout, unable to pierce the creature's scaly skin. The god raised its nightmarish head, dangling Roshell fifteen feet above the floor. It tossed her effortlessly up in the air, catching her around the middle for better chewing.

"Drop her!" screamed Julie, stabbing at a muscular limb.

Her fiery blade sliced through scales and flesh. Zuzumza roared in pain, dropping his snack. Urbane caught Roshell, both crashing to the floor in a heap. The general quickly regained his footing, but the southerner lay semi-conscious from pain. Rufus and Matthan continued to assault the back of the fiend, attempting to dodge spiked tail and hind claws as they sought a venerable spot.

"Junia," barked Urbane, "your weapon is the only one which can hurt it. Try to reach its heart!"

It was easier said than done. The men taunted the fiend, darted between swift moving claws and tail, vainly assaulting thickly scaled limbs, themselves taking multiple wounds. Julie circled the fighters, looking for an opportunity to roll under the beast and stab its underside. A fast moving forepaw threw Matthan through the air, slamming him against a wall. Its whipping tail sent Urbane sliding across the smooth floor, his sword flying in the opposite direction. Yelling, Rufus ran towards Zuzumza's head, slashing at the beast's ugly snout.

Seeing the god detracted, Julie stabbed at its ribcage, burying her entire blade into its flesh. Zuzumza screamed in pain, rapidly twisting around. Julie was knocked to the ground, her sword still embedded in the monster's body. Enraged the god pinned Julie to the floor with a huge, clawed foot. Stretching its long neck, it pulled the holy sword from its body, dropping the weapon with a clang to the cold floor.

"Did you really think you could kill me? Fool, I am immortal, but you are not." Zuzumza pressed down with its forepaw, pushing the air out of Julie's lungs. She gasped for breath but could not inhale.

Determine to save his sister, Rufus hacked at the underside of the god, putting all his strength behind each blow. He was effective as an angry child pounding against a stone wall. Zuzumza quickly pivoted while keeping Julie pinned down. Rufus suddenly found himself beside a massive hind leg. The god kicked out, sending the new Emperor flying through the air. During the diversion, Julie took several desperate breaths, but Zuzumza now turned his attention back to her. Slowly he pressed against her chest, enjoying her helpless struggle. Furiously she pounded and kicked against the massive forepaw trapping her. Her mouth gapped open, but no air could enter her oppressed lungs. Her skin began to take on a bluish hue.

"How about picking on someone with a weapon, God of Bullies." Roshell shouted from across the chamber. She half sat, half stood on the steps of the dais with one hand holding a sword, the other pressed against her bleeding side.

"You will be next, dark child." Zuzumza's voice boomed across the room.

The southerner laughed. "I don't fear he who destroys the body but cannot touch the soul. You're nothing but a puppet for a weak demon that can't escape from the bowls of the abyss it rots in."

The fiend hissed in fury. "Know the power of my wrath!"

A wave of pure hate pounded Roshell, washing around her like a rock on a beach grounded by surf at high tide. Memories of hideous deeds and dead friends flashed pass. Old anger swelled inside the southerner. She winced when the image of her dead parents visualized in front of her. Curses spoken in the past by her own mouth echoed in her ears.

"Do you think the God of Love could ever accept you?" The fiend smiled sinisterly. "You are a child after my own black heart. Your hatred is blood pumping through my veins."

Struggled to keep her sanity, Roshell forced her eyes towards Zuzumza, "Do you really think you can win this battle? I'm honored to fight today beside three comrades who once served in your army. I believe that's proof enough that I've come a long way with dealing with my anger."

Though she pretended to be looking directly at the demon, her eyes were focused on Urbane who had quietly crept across the room and now stood behind Zuzumza. The general glanced at Julie's unconscious form trapped under a massive claw. Silently he picked up his wife's fallen sword. Immediately flames leaped along its surface. Shocked, he almost dropped the weapon again. Spotting the supernatural flames, Roshell stuttered over her words midsentence. Sensing something wrong, Zuzumza began to turn his head.

Reacting quickly, Roshell forced her injured body to take several steps forward while yelling at the archdemon. "Don't you have anything else up your sleeves? A roadside con artist can perform more tricks than you while providing better entertainment."

Zuzumza answered her challenge in a deep, threatening voice. "Enjoy this entertainment."

The God of War bent its hideous head down to finish off Julie, closing its mouth around her lifeless head. Standing unnoticed under the monster, Urbane stabbed upward with all his might. Zuzumza reared back in pain, its great wings beating the air furiously. The general kept a tight hold on the sword's handle, and it pulled free from Zuzumza's body. Vile, green blood poured from the wound. The enraged creature bit downward. Urbane waited to the last instance, then sidestep, swinging his sword where he had stood only a moment before. Zuzumza jerked its head up, green ooze flowing down a deep gash where head met neck. Warily of its dangerous tail, Urbane backed up, protectively standing over Julie's body.

"Zuzumza, your rule is over," came Rufus's commanding voice. Limping, he and Matthan marched boldly towards the bleeding fiend. The green pool of blood under the god widened quickly.

"I am immortal," wheezed the God of War. "No weapon formed by man can slay me."

"Then look upon your doom," boasted Urbane, holding the blade aloft, bright flames dancing across its polished surface. "This is your bane, forged by Yahweh himself."

For the first time in its existence, Zuzumza knew fear. It backed away towards the balcony as the three men approached. Determined to keep the creature from escaping, Rufus circled behind, positioning himself in front of the exit. Matthan and Urbane closed in, tightening the circle. Across the chamber, Roshell stumbled to Julie's side. The princess gulped in deep breaths of air.

Though afraid, panic did not consume Zuzumza's keen mind. With lightening reflexes, it snatched Rufus around the middle with a foreclaw, ignoring the slashes of the Emperor's blade. "As Achoziez's line was created by me, so will I end it." Zuzumza spread his vast leathery wings, raising himself into the air.

Matthan rushed forward and jumped onto the claw, jabbing frantically with his blade but unable to pierce its thick skin. Urbane attempted to help, but Zuzumza rose out of his reach, each beat of its wings creating a windstorm of turbulent drifts. It soared through the vast chamber towards the wide balcony.

"No!" screamed Roshell, horrified, knowing both Rufus and Matthan would be thrown to their deaths on the ground far below.

Urbane chased after the fiend, desperate to find a way to stop its flight. Above the broad balcony, Zuzumza beat its powerful wings, rising straight upward towards open sky. Acting on instinct, Urbane threw the blade of fire, praying his aim was true. The weapon sliced through a thin leather wing, cutting veins then continued on its protraction. Falling, Zuzumza roared in frustration, his right wing useless. A hindclaw grabbed the balcony railing, leaving Zuzumza dangling high above the palace's smaller towers.

In hatred, it opened a forepaw to drop the Emperor to his death, but Matthan was ready. Body precariously balanced on top of the clawed foot, Matthan grabbed Rufus's hands tightly while both their swords tumbling through the air, striking a roof, bouncing, then continuing their downward plunge. Rufus clasped a dangling claw and hauled himself, with Matthan's aid, to the top of the foot. Bleeding profusely, Zuzumza attempted to climb upward. Its second hindclaw could not get a safe hold, so the fiend twisted its long neck, biting the railing with its sharp teeth for balance.

Weaponless, Urbane tried to close in, but the lashing spiked tail kept him at bay. Roshell hurried across the enormous chamber as fast as her ailing body would allow, praying fervently for a miracle. Seeing a lifeless wing sagging a yard away, Matthan grabbed it and started climbing up the bulging veins and thin bones that stood out from their thin skin covering. Rufus followed after.

The balcony railing, not designed to hold the heavy weight of a dangling god, began to crumble. The weakening fiend switched foot and mouth holds, attempting to gain balance by flapping its uninjured left wing. Then Zuzumza realized its useless right wing was being used as a ladder for its enemies. With a bellow of rage, the God of War let go of the balcony, willing to end its own existence to kill its hated enemies. Zuzumza's bulky body fell heavily, striking a small tower that collapsed. Flesh and rubble tumbled downward, hitting a large roof. The fiend's body bounced, slid slowly, and fell off the edge of the high roof. The lifeless mass plunged through the air, crashing into a courtyard with a sickening thud. Terrified horses and grooms ran into the nearest stable. Thousands in the celebrating crowds filling nearby parks and streets watched the sudden fall of the Gogian god.

"Emperor!" screamed Urbane, dashing to the edge of the ruined balcony. He saw the smashed body of Zuzumza far below. Gut-wrenching fear caused his body to tremble. He had failed in his charge to protect his sovereign. Shame hammered through him far greater than when he had betrayed Phlegon.

Painfully Roshell limped up behind Urbane, her face pale with fear for Rufus and Matthan. "They can't be dead," she sputtered, "not after all we've been through."

Julie, finally on her feet, ran towards the others only to be brought to a stop by her aching sides. She finally reached the balcony and peered over the remains of the railing, eyes searching, along with her friends. After a long moment, she excitedly pointed, "There they are! Look at the ruin tower!"

Sure enough, Matthan cling to a window ledge located mid-way up the small tower. Rufus was already inside, hauling the dangling Salt up. Nearby people on the ground cheered as their heroic Emperor was recognized. Royal Guards poured out of the palace and surrounded the body of Zuzumza, poking it with swords and pikes to make sure the demon was really dead. Others soldiers climbed up the tower steps to help the Emperor.

The five exhausted warriors met in the clinic. All suffered from bruises and abrasions, a few with broken bones. Henna warmly embraced her aching husband while Danielle personally saw to the setting of Matthan's broken arm. Urbane and Julie sat close, content to be alive, waiting while the more seriously injured were tended to. A doctor and his aid worked on grumbling Roshell, stitching several deep gashes along her side—teeth marks from Zuzumza.

Seeing the Emperor being treated on a nearby table, Roshell complained, "Your Majesty, don't take this the wrong way, but the next time you decide to take on an archdemon, don't forget to bring a regiment or three. It fact a whole army will work quite nicely."

Rufus exhaustingly smiled. "I don't plan to battle anything but politicians the rest of my life. And that can be almost as dangerous."

"There are more demons out there," said Julie. "Most are small, invisible, and can be found near any temple or household shrine."

"I'm not spending the rest of my life chasing invisible spirits," protested Roshell. "Ouch! Watch that needle."

"No, you won't," answered Julie. "You will be too busy changing the social institutions of an entire nation."

Roshell cocked an eyebrow. "Is that prophecy or your own opinion?"

"Wait and find out."

~~~~~~~~~~

The Hall of Kings was jammed with nobles, ordinary citizens, and almost every servant in the entire palace, all anxiously waiting to hear the new Emperor's address to the people. Yesterday thousands of citizens had seen the God of War fall to its doom. Awe filled the city as even Rufus's most vicious critics were silenced by fear. The new ruler had begun his reign by destroying the nation's chief god. Who could stand against him when the Firmaments blessed him? Commoners adored him, nobles feared him, and priests hated him. When the battle was retold over the years, Rufus would always gave equal credit to the others for destroying Zuzumza, but the history books labeled the first Tnias Emperor of Gog as a slayer of gods.

In a connecting room, servants donned a ceremonial robe over Rufus's stately clothing, careful not to re-injure his sprained arm hanging in a sling. Henna was also lavishly dressed. Urbane conversed with his Emperor while Thasbow and Julie entertained the royal couple's two children.

Newly promoted Tranton entered and bowed before the Emperor and his general. "Your Highness, we have looked everywhere for the missing sword. I've had men lowered on ropes to investigate the hardest to reach roofs of the palace. Every nook and cranny has been searched thrice, but all that can be found are these." He held out two swords, one twisted and bent. The other contained tiny chips here and there.

Rufus took the twisted sword. "This is mine, and from its looks, it will never be used again."

Urbane examined the other. "I will give this back to Matthan. The swords of Shalom are well made." Concern, he glanced at Julie playing with young Nadine. The Salt glanced up, having heard the conversation.

She walked over and gently placed a hand on her husband's shoulder. "It is alright. I have come to realize that the Sword of Fire was never created for normal warfare. Yahweh intended it as a weapon against archdemons. It has served its purpose. I am guessing Yahweh has summoned it back to him."

Urbane nodded. "Never have I beheld such a blade. Nor do I understand why it flared when I held it that last time. Even in Matthan and Roshell's hands it appeared ordinary."

"There is much we mortals cannot understand. Let it rest at that," answered Julie.

"It's time, Your Majesty" announced an aide. "As you ordered, all were allowed entry, including commoners until we could hold no more. Never has the hall been so packed."

The royal family entered the Hall of Kings. The energized crowd immediately hushed, closely watching the dignified Emperor strolling beside the gorgeous Empress who had once been called plain. Thasbow followed, smiling broadly, holding the hands of her curious niece and nephew. Urbane and Julie came last, arms linked. While the rest of the family settled in chairs reserved near the front, Rufus and Henna climbed the steps of the dais. The enormous gold throne was missing, for the metal smith had taken it to melt into two smaller, more elegant thrones. Any other time the situation would have been laughable—the Emperor, with arm in a sling, sitting beside his wife, both in simple wooden chairs. Today no one laughed or snubbed their noses.

Rufus spoke in a voice that echoed through the vast chamber. "Gog has bowed for centuries to the God of War. Zuzumza's reign is over. I hear your whispered fears. What is to come? Who do we worship now? Contrary to recent popular thought, I am a man—not a deity. No temples will be erected in my name. My entire family and I owe our allegiance to a god many of you have cursed. This scares many of you."

The monarch stood up. "What I have to say will terrify those people even more. I place all of the Empire of Gog into the hands of Yahweh. This kingdom is his. I proclaim this boldly with all my heart." Tense people whispered to neighbors while others strained to hear more.

The Emperor glanced to a balcony where the powerful priests of Zuzumza had gathered. "This kingdom can be divided by hatred or united by love. My father and brother chose the former, destroying all who opposed them, torturing the innocent, killing for the sport of it. I choose the latter. I offer to you, my people, understanding and love. This invitation does not come from me, but from Yahweh. Put hate behind you and accept your neighbors as beloved brothers and sisters."

316

Cheers and hoots filled the room. Several ecstatic Tnias clasped the hands of people around them, giving hearty shakes. Laughter broke the tension. Soon hundreds of cheerful citizens where greeting strangers, but the Emperor observed the cold faces of many nobles and priests who hurried away, quickly vanishing from the chamber.

Yahweh, Rufus silently prayed, *this will be difficult. Many are still bound by darkness.*

As the people milled joyfully around the room, even climbing up the dais to meet the royal couple, a quiet voice answered the Emperor. *I am with you always, even to the very end.*

Grinning, with arms spread, Empress Henna called to her people, "Come, a bounteous feast has been prepared. All are welcome."

317

Epilogue

Five years later

The late winter sun bathed playful ice skaters in a kiss of light. From a high window in the palace, Emperor Rufus studied the carefree frolickers, momentary wishing he could join them. Behind him the Cabinet meeting droned on with General Patrobas, the former captain of the Reforcers, addressing military concerns.

"The northern island providence of Getrodger has declared its secession from the Empire." A surprised mummer filled the Chamber of Juxtaposition. "I suggest immediate military action. We can easily overrun their few defenses. Within two weeks, the island will be back under Gogian control."

Heads nodded in agreement while others angrily muttered against the outrageous actions of Getrodger. Rufus held his hand up for silence. All looked his way expectantly. "We will not invade but recognize Getrodger's independence."

"What!" General Patrobas was taken back. Others were equally shocked. "If you let one revolt, others will upraise. Your Majesty, I highly request you to rethink this decision."

"I agree," said retired General Nereus, an honorary member of the Cabinet who came when his heath and interests matched. "If you do not use the firm hand of discipline, children become wild and uncontrollable. And so do nations."

Rufus searched the faces of the large Cabinet, noting several missing for various reasons. His eyes came to rest on Urbane. Over the years the two had developed a close friendship. The Chief General gave a brief nod, supporting his friend and lord, both vividly remembering the Second War of Galand. Opponents of Rufus's new reign had secretly organized a strong army in the mountainous providence, including several of his half-brothers. Entire regiments betrayed their Emperor by unwitting following their bribed supervisors, not realizing until it was too late that they were to battle their own kinsmen. Urbane had led the Red Army against the soldiers of the rebellious nobles. What followed was the bloodiest civil war ever fought on Gogian soil as comrades slaughtered each other for the sake of aristocratic power. Overlooking the final gruesome battlefield of thousands of mingled bodies, Rufus swore to Yahweh he would never again order others to die for his supremacy. Only Henna, Urbane, and Julie knew of his vow that had not been tested until this day.

"Scribe, ready you quill," the monarch commanded then waited as the elderly man dipped his feather into ink. "On this day of the fifth year of the reign of Emperor Rufus, Gog recognizes the independence of Getrodger."

"Sir, you cannot do this," protested Patrobas. The officer glanced towards Urbane, hoping for support. If anyone understood the danger of secession, it was the renowned Chief General who had promoted Patrobas into his position.

Urbane said, "The Emperor's judgment is sound."

Rufus ignored the interruption. "As a separate state, you will no longer receive military support in case of barbarian or pirate raids. A trading ban will be placed on all goods from Getrodger. No Gogian port or city will buy or sell your products. Any ship flying your flags will be confiscated on sight."

"A harsh command, Your Majesty," added Matthan. "They will quickly change their minds."

Patrobas settled back into his seat in defeat, a silver Tree of Life jiggling on its chain around his neck. "Or become sick of eating fish twelve months a year."

The door swung open to admit the confident figure of Roshell, her well-made clothes dusty from several days travel.

Rufus greeted her. "Welcome back. Our Cabinet debates have been dull without you to liven them up."

"Anything to serve Gog," smiled a tired Roshell looking for an empty chair in the packed room. Matthan stood up, indicating for the woman to take his seat. "It would be a relief, Your Majesty, when your new meeting chamber is complete."

An entire new wing to the palace was being added, designed in amphitheater style, which would hold several hundred representatives from across the Empire— causing more than one person to wonder if Rufus had finally cracked under the strain of leadership. Knowing that power corrupts, Rufus had decided to take steps to prevent ultimate supremacy from belonging to only one person again. During the spring, the monarch had suddenly declared that three ambassadors from each province would be chosen to have a voice on a large council that would have equal power in governing Gog. The nation was still in shock from that unprecedented announcement. Few fully understood how it would work, but many supported the idea.

"We wait your full report of how our southern provinces bear," the Emperor continued.

"I will keep this quick for I have promised to visit the children tonight," spoke the weary Salt. "Overall things went well. The newly opened public schools in Ametic are popular. The network of children's homes is growing fast. Matthan, tell

Danielle that the heath policy she was pushing in Telumza has passed with flying colors."

General Patrobas interrupted, "What about rumors of rebellion in Lasko?"

Roshell frowned at the disruption. "The economy in Lasko and Ametic is booming with the open trade with Ulmjo and the Triad." She glanced sharply towards several gruff Cabinet members. "The Emperor's decision to hand Ulmjo over to the Triad as a peace offering has done wonders for all. The leaders I've spoken with will support the Emperor as long as he keeps his promise that each province has the right to make its own laws in interest of its people."

Rufus nodded. "Next spring will bring great contentment when they will have a voice in our national laws. Much, gentlemen, has yet to be changed." Some nodded in agreement while others worried about unforeseen problems. "I call this meeting adjourned, for I have an important meeting to keep."

As the occupants stood in honor of the departing monarch, Roshell whispered to Matthan. "Why do I happen to be the only woman present today?"

"Because we men were not quick enough to find legit excuses for not attending," the Telumzan smiled back. "Today Danielle is one of the volunteers taking the city orphans skating. Julie prefers instructing students in the art of painting than battling politics. She claims Urbane keeps her up-to-date on what's important and only comes when issues are controversial."

"With me around, that's every day," laughed Roshell. "I must head to the park, myself, to meet my children."

The two Salts quickly made their way through the palace to the enormous adjoining park. Across the vast frozen lake skated hundreds of energetic people. Recognizing Roshell, children from the city orphanage crowded close, all eager to hug the Salt they viewed as a boundless mother of love.

Danielle, with two of her own offspring in tow, attempted to rescue her close friend. "Go skate, children. Time is short."

"You will all have time to see her later," promised Minira, the headmistress. "It is good to see you, Roshell. The children and I have missed you greatly."

"I'm done with traveling, at least till the spring thaw. Snows will be too thick for southerners like me to handle." A new group approaching the lake drew Roshell's attention. "I see the Emperor has kept his pressing meeting."

Guards surrounded the royal family and Urbane as they put on skates. Empress Henna firmly tied skates for her youngest child, a two-year-old, while Nadine and Juke quickly took to the ice. Rufus scooped up his youngest son and flew across the ice with the giggling toddler on his shoulders. Sentinels stationed themselves around the edge of the lake or on the ice, keeping a keen lookout.

Speeding across the icy surface, a four year old attempted to follow her mother's twist and turns. When the mother performed a double axis, the child jumped also, only to fall onto hard ice. Julie helped her daughter up.

"Good try, Ruby. It will not be long before you are outjumping me."

Urbane skidded to a stop beside his wife and daughter. Bending down, he brushed ice chips off Ruby's thick coat. "It looks as if someone has been playing with paint again."

The child beamed proudly, caring little about the smudges of green and red on her face. "Mommy let me paint my first picture on canvas today! Look, my cousins are here!" Excitedly Ruby skated over to Naden and Juke.

Standing close to Julie, Urbane asked, "Think she will be a master artist like her mother?"

"Perhaps. She shows great promise but must choose her own path. How about a spin?"

In perfect union, the couple glided across the frozen lake, jumping and twirling. Others stopped to admire the general and princess.

"Showoffs!" yelled Roshell.

Recognizing the voice, Julie hurried to the lake edge to embrace her dear friend. "Welcome back. I must hear every detail of your trip."

"There is the rest of the winter to talk about such things. Now is the time for recreation."

"Then you will finally join me on the ice?"

Mock horror crossed Roshell's face. "If Yahweh had wanted us to skate…"

"We would have been born with skates instead of feet. I know that line far too well."

For a brief moment seriousness filled the southerner's brown eyes. "You know me too well, princess of the brushes."

"The feeling is mutual, orphan who bears hope," Julie spoke tenderly.

"Junia. Roshell," called out a cheerful voice. "You will never guess!" Thasbow bounded up, a beaming Manideck by her side.

The young husband finished for her, "We're having a baby!"

Overhearing the conversation, Urbane skated up to the group with Ruby. He whispered to his daughter, "Looks like another cousin for you."

"Hurrah," piped up the child named after her grandmother. "More playmates! More playmates!"

The evening sped along too quickly. As the sun sent its last fiery rays across the frozen landscape, skaters headed home. Roshell rounded up stragglers from Thorn Children's Home. Beside a highly trafficked sidewalk, she spotted an eight year old struggling to read the words carved in a base of a statue. Roshell glanced at the lifelike image of Yahweh chiseled by the former prostitute Violet. Basing the deity's facial features on Julie's famous mural, Violet's work presented a friendly man looking over the park, arms raised in welcome.

Frustrated, young Jonu asked, "What does it say? I don't know all the words."

Bending down eyelevel with the child, Roshell explained. "It's an ancient song written about the One True God. It says:

Praise Yahweh,
O servants of Yahweh.
Let the name of Yahweh be praised both now and forevermore.
From the rising of the sun to the place where it sets,
The name of Yahweh is to be praised.

Yahweh is exalted over all the nations,
His glory above the highest Firmament.
Who is like Yahweh our God,
The One who sits enthroned on high?

He raises the poor from the dust
And lifts the needy from the ash heap;
He seats them with princes of their people.
He settles the barren woman in her home
As a happy mother of children.
Praise Yahweh."

The child looked confused. "I don't understand it—accept the part about praising Yahweh. It's used a lot."

"It means," smiled Roshell, "that nothing is greater than Yahweh, and he is looking out for..." she tweaked the child's nose, "...you and me."

"What's a barren woman? Someone old and wrinkled?"

Pushing back a stay braid of her thick hair, Roshell laughed. "It's someone like me who has never given birth to her own children."

"And now you're a happy mother," concluded Jonu. For a moment soberness replaced childish mirth. "When I grow up, I want to be just like you."

Roshell took the child seriously. "It is a tough road, Jonu, full of sacrifice and hardship."

The eight year old placed small hands on hips. "I'm ready. I was born on the streets just like you. It was hard, but Yahweh protected me and my brother. I'm ready to follow him anywhere."

Standing up, the Salt took Jonu's hand. "Then come, child. Yahweh has much waiting for you to accomplish."

Author's Message

Books have fascinated me since I was a small child sitting beside my mother, listening to her read books I had selected from the library. Soon I was reading on my own, and I never stopped. Over the years my interests have varied wildly from stories about animals to the classics to science fiction, and much in between.

In sixth grade my English teacher assigned us to write a short story. I got a tad carried away, writing a VERY long story about the adventures of a cat. Part of the way through the writing process, I realized this is what I wanted to do the rest of my life.

So I began writing short stories and eventually novels. I also became an English teacher because I wanted to share my love of literature with others. I later branched into teaching technology, another one of my passions.

The results you hold in your hands is from years of exploring my imagination and the intensive but exciting labor of writing.

I would appreciate, if you have a moment, giving my book a rating at Amazon, Goodreads, and other sites that interest you. In the limited free time I now have, the books I choose to read are usually recommended to me by friends, so I know the power of word-of-mouth.

I hope you enjoyed reading this book as much as I enjoyed writing it.

Sincerely,

Vista Townsend

Updates for new projects can be found at:
Website: vistatownsend.net
Facebook: Vista.townsend
Twitter: Vista_Townsend

www.ingramcontent.com/pod-product-compliance
Lightning Source LLC
Chambersburg PA
CBHW071055250626
47159CB00002B/475